The Rise of the Roman Empire

The Rise of the Roman Empire

An Alternative History, AD 375–641

Timothy Venning

Pen & Sword
MILITARY

First published in Great Britain in 2025 by
Pen & Sword Military
An imprint of Pen & Sword Books Limited
Yorkshire – Philadelphia

Copyright © Timothy Venning 2025

ISBN 978 1 39903 439 5

The right of Timothy Venning to be identified as
Author of this Work has been asserted by him in accordance
with the Copyright, Designs and Patents Act 1988.

A CIP catalogue record for this book is
available from the British Library.

All rights reserved. No part of this book may be reproduced,
transmitted, downloaded, decompiled or reverse engineered in
any form or by any means, electronic or mechanical including
photocopying, recording or by any information storage and retrieval
system, without permission from the Publisher in writing. No part of
this book may be used or reproduced in any manner for the purpose
of training artificial intelligence technologies or systems.

Typeset by Mac Style
Printed in the UK by CPI Group (UK) Ltd, Croydon, CR0 4YY.

The Publisher's authorised representative in the EU for product
safety is Authorised Rep Compliance Ltd., Ground Floor,
71 Lower Baggot Street, Dublin D02 P593, Ireland.
www.arccompliance.com

For a complete list of Pen & Sword titles please contact

PEN & SWORD BOOKS LIMITED
47 Church Street, Barnsley, South Yorkshire, S70 2AS, England
E-mail: enquiries@pen-and-sword.co.uk
Website: www.pen-and-sword.co.uk
or
PEN AND SWORD BOOKS
1950 Lawrence Road, Havertown, PA 19083, USA
E-mail: uspen-and-sword@casematepublishers.com
Website: www.penandswordbooks.com

Contents

Introduction		vii

Part I: Restoration. Showdown with the Goths. Julian, the Pagan, Succeeded by Valentinian and Theodosius, the Christians. 375 to 407 1

Chapter 1	The House of Valentinian	7
Chapter 2	The House of Theodosius – and the Children of Valentinian	15
Chapter 3	Challenges to Theodosius in the West: Magnus Maximus and the Deaths of Gratian and Valentinian II	23
Chapter 4	Reunification	33

Part II: Division, 407 to 491 47

Chapter 5	Crisis: The Barbarians at Large Inside the Empire, and the Fall of Stilicho	49
Chapter 6	A Return to Stability? Pulcheria Rules the East, and Constantius III and Aetius Rule the West	64
Chapter 7	Battle for the Empire: Aetius vs Attila, Monophysites vs Catholics	80
Chapter 8	Aetius (and his Son Gaudentius as Western Emperor 455–469), Majorian, and the Rise of the Anthemii in the West	95

Part III: Reunification. 491 to 542 121

Chapter 9	The Road to Union: Titus II in the West, Anastasius in the East, to 516	123
Chapter 10	After Reunion in 516: The Dynasty Of Titus II	136

Part IV: Expansion, 542 to 641. The Conquest of Eastern Persia and Bactria: To the Indus   157

Chapter 11	Heraclius I 542–559: The Scholar	159
Chapter 12	Anastasius II 551–559: The Maverick	167
Chapter 13	Nerva II 559–570: The Man of Justice	176
Chapter 14	Gallus 570–582: The Warlord	186
Chapter 15	Rillanus 582–590: The Idealist	193
Chapter 16	Carus I 590–615: The Bureaucrat	199
Chapter 17	Claudius III 615–630: The Conqueror	215
Chapter 18	Carus II 630–641: The Orientophile	229

Conclusion   239
Glossary   243
Bibliography   261

Introduction

Having been a fan of Classical History since I first read the Ancient Greek myths at the age of nine or so and also taken at an early age to reading and writing historical fiction, I have often wondered what would happen if specific events had turned out differently. How 'inevitable' is the course of events, what could have changed things in the short and the long term, and what would have happened then? This was way back before the invention of the internet enabled easier interaction with other writers and picking up their own ideas, although already literary as well as televisual 'sci-fi' existed to stimulate the imagination. Thus my own creation of 'counter-factual' historical narrative as a form of fiction utilizing my own interests was born, when I was about ten – and it was centred on the world of Greece and Rome, where questions were easy to pose about such sudden shifts of fortune as Alexander the Great overthrowing the mighty Achaemenid Persian Empire to create a new Greek empire in the Middle East and then dying in mid-career at the age of 32.

As explained in my introduction to my first Pen and Sword 'What If?' book , 'If Rome Hadn't Fallen' (2011), my concentration as a teenager on the question of the Roman Empire not breaking up but surviving into the modern era was stimulated by the long-running sci-fi serial in the children's educational magazine *Look and Learn* in the late 1960s and the 1970s .

'The Rise and Fall of the Trigan Empire', where a Roman-like civilization existed on a distant planet with the trappings of space-age technology combined with elements of real Roman and Greek cultures (and even dinosaurs). I began to work out how the Roman world could have survived for two millennia or so to create that kind of civilization itself, and to ponder the questions of what would have resulted if assorted battles and military campaigns had been won not lost (by better generals, more resources, or sheer luck), if the usually ethnically 'inclusive' Empire which had absorbed most of the Mediterranean world had managed to absorb the restive German tribes to its north and the civilized and autocratic Sassanid Persian empire to its east, and what would have happened had certain divisive and resource-sapping civil wars been avoided at crucial points. Come to that, what if a number of talented and successful Emperors had not died comparatively young (naturally or by death in battle or murder) and had been as long-lasting and 'stabilising' rulers as the greatest early Emperors of the first and second centuries AD – or had been able to set up long-lasting dynasties? If the Empire's nearest civilizational equivalent, China, had managed to pull itself back together after assorted disasters and temporary break-ups, what if Rome had managed to do that too? As I acquired more knowledge of the historical process I 'fleshed out' my sketchy initial picture of events, which had owed much to instinct and guesswork rather than knowledge, and I did a substantial overhaul of my reasoning and my timelines after I had completed a History degree at the University of London in the late 1970s and had been taught by some of the leading UK Roman and Byzantine historians of the time. My parallel interest in 'Byzantium' (the surviving eastern half of the Empire from the fifth to the fifteenth centuries) provided me with detail and ideas for a more successful Mediterranean=wide Roman Empire in the medieval period. I had read a few essays on 'Counter-Factual History' by scholars such as Arnold Toynbee (on Philip II of Macedon and Alexander surviving longer) but had no idea to what extent CF was a viable or widely imitated genre, and this was before any internet cross-fertilisation of ideas.

I had no dealings with the latter until recent years, long after my last main updating of my long-running 'The Roman Empire Survives' storyline in the late 1980s, and although I have written on my reasoning and basic ideas concerning how a surviving Rome could easily have turned out for Pen and Sword in my 2011 book (before moving on to my Alternative History of Britain series in 2012–15, another hobby of mine) I did not tackle my Roman fictional timeline saga itself until I had an unexpected chance to do this in the first UK coronavirus lockdown in 2020. My pile of Roman CF history exercise-books had never been written up on a computer, and this was now remedied –commencing with my speculation about the results of the last of the 'Five Good Emperors' of the Antonine era in the C2nd, Marcus Aurelius, not dying during his German campaign in 180 but surviving to permanently annex the lands of what became the Czech Republic and Slovakia, North of the upper Danube. This would have put the problematic northern frontier of the Empire at the Carpathian Mountains, not the Danube, and brought many tribes that were to be hostile foes of the Empire in later centuries into its orbit as Roman citizens, governed by Roman bureaucracy not their own war-leaders, and providing their restive and glory-hunting menfolk as warriors to the Roman army. (Since the conquest of Dacia, i.e. modern Transylvania, by Trajan in the 100s the eastern Roman frontier in northern Europe had stood at the Carpathians in modern Rumania, so the empire already had a mountain not river frontier in this region; the conquest of the Czech lands as 'Marcomannia' would have completed the Roman advance northwards.)

As with similar abortive Roman moves to annex – or at least to indirectly control – the lands east of the lower and middle Rhine in the early first century, which were halted abruptly by a major defeat by German tribes in AD 9, the question arose of whether annexation (with a 'light touch' or with full 'Romanization', as had occurred to the long troublesome Gaul under Julius Caesar in the 50s BC) would have prevented (or just lessened?) the disastrous Germanic attacks on the Empire after the early third century. The Empire could well have still suffered from domestic instability given its unstable political situation and lack of a long-term and politically acceptable mechanism for determining the Imperial succession (as well as revenue- and manpower-sapping plagues, e.g. in the early 250s). But would 'neutralising' either the Rhine or the upper Danube 'Germanic threats' – or both – have given the Empire a crucial 'edge' against its potential enemies? It would have enrolled large numbers of their tribal warriors into its armies meaning that when the Empire faced a long-term threat from the revived Persian state from the 220s it did not have other simultaneous long-term threats in Europe so it could tackle its foes easier? Logically the combination of three military threats at the same time (the Rhine, the Danube, and Persia) around 260, along with the aftermath of a major plague and the long-running crop of military coups and provincial military rebellions that had followed the end of the Severan dynasty in 235, was the prime instance of a nearly fatal multi-faceted disaster for the Empire which could have been avoided by there being one or more less challenge at this point. This was one serious threat to the Empire's survival that I could 'tweak' out of existence – or rather, reduce in its scope and seriousness – by giving the 'old', pre-crisis Empire better odds of survival. Accordingly, I made Marcus Aurelius (fifty-eight at his death in real-life 180 and in weak health already) survive some years longer, complete his work on the northern frontier, and not be succeeded by his controversial, weak-willed, and somewhat megalomaniac son Commodus – a mercurial ruler still in his teens who may have been under-rated and who faced serious problems but was at best a poor judge of men, increasingly vengeful and violent towards a hostile political elite, and was short of a sense of duty like his father's.

In real life, the unstable 'tyrant' Commodus ended up murdered by his fearful intimates in 192, a stern and virtuous but unpopularly draconian general called Pertinax who might have been able to restore the situation took over but was soon killed by the privileged and 'spoilt' Praetorian Guards who he had unwisely infuriated; a vicious civil war followed before the emergence of the victor, Septimius Severus (ruled 193 to 211), as Emperor. Septimius was more capable and successful than his two predecessors but arguably gave the army too much power and set a bad example of ruling by autocratic 'fiat' rather than in the more 'inclusive' and consultational civilian-style manner of the 'Antonines';

his quarrelling sons then took to fratricide, their successors were inadequate, and the end of the dynasty by a military coup in 235 was followed by escalating instability. No ruler was now seen as legitimate or unchallengeable – and indeed, as in other militarily powerful but unstable states in the modern era, one successful coup or rebellion tended to spark off others by ambitious men. Avoiding this run of disasters from 180 to 260 would have reduced the scope of the crises that hit the Empire in the 250s and 260s, though realistically the chances of avoiding any disputed successions, incompetent or 'tyrant' emperors, and civil wars in this era – a replay of the 'luckier' Rome of the early-mid-second century – was not that realistic. So in my version of events I have Marcus Aurelius surviving his son Commodus (who indulged in dangerous sports so a fatal accident to him was not that unlikely) and being succeeded briefly by a young grandson with Pertinax as regent in 190, then Pertinax ruling for longer than in real life and being succeeded by Septimius Severus. The latter is then succeeded by his younger and less vicious son, Geta, not the elder, the mercurial and brutal Caracalla. The run of 'good emperors plus no civil wars' from the second century thus continues well into the third century, and the outbreak of coups plus German and Persian wars plus plagues then is less extensive. The empire does break up after 260, but only for a shorter period and it is reunited quicker by the real-life (and often overlooked) great emperor Aurelian – who is not assassinated in 275 as in real life, so he maintains stability then for longer. I mix up some extra luck and good governance for the Empire with some of the real-life disasters still occurring, so this is not an unbroken and unrealistic picture.

But the lesser run of disasters means that though (as in real life) there is still a powerful attraction for the notion of 'strong man' and bureaucratic stability, as exploited by the institutional reformer Diocletian in the 280s, and as the cults of the 'Twelve Olympian' gods duly becomes less attractive than the appeal of one 'Saviour God' (initially the sun-god, later the Christian God) there is a less drastic or fast evolution in this major cultural shift. Less successful Germanic invasions (e.g. of the Balkans, Greece, and Asia Minor) means less economic disruption and less psychologically damaging events such as the sack of Athens, plus more prosperous citizens to shoulder the far larger tax-burden of the Late Empire – so my Empire of the fourth century and fifth century has been through less trauma than the real-life Empire did and it is better able to deal with new challenges (and closer in 'tone' to the 'Classical' Empire). From this basis, the Empire surviving its challenges of the fifth century too without breaking up is a more viable option – and I make the (in real life unsuccessful) invasion of Rome's Middle Eastern rival Persia by Julian in 363 better able to succeed by having two previous Persian wars that were aborted by the deaths of their Roman planners, Aurelian in 275 and Constantine 'the Great' in 337, take place as these men survive for longer. Sassanian Persian power has thus already been weakened by Roman attacks on Mesopotamia (modern Iraq) in the mid-270s and late 330s, so my story of Julian's conquest of western and break-up of eastern Persia in the mid-360s is more logical and plausible.

The stabilization of the political and socio-economic situations by the pragmatic and ruthless bureaucratic reformer Diocletian (and his colleague Maximian) in the period 284305 after emperor Aurelian (ruling in 270–275 in real life, in 270–280 in my version) had ended the run of invasions and civil wars was counter-acted by Diocletian's unnecessary and divisive ideological-led 'purge' of the Christian community as an 'unpatriotic threat'. After his abdication his careful but unworkable scheme for a regular system of non-dynastic succession to the Empire collapsed into civil wars. Both these crises were avoidable to some degree, the 'Great Persecution' more so given that Diocletian had no male kin to succeed him and his political heirs were violently at odds with one other in an era of large and war-ready armies that could assist their ambitions. The situation was then stabilized and the Christian religion not only legalized but 'empowered' as an essential ally of the Emperor by the newly Christian reunifier Constantine 'the Great' (ruled 306/ 312/ 324 to 337 in real life, but I have him surviving to 340). But despite his many successes he left a feuding family of sons and nephews behind him and the question of what doctrinal form of Christianity was to dominate the Empire was unresolved too. Was there to be one doctrine for one Empire, what was to be done with the still large and culturally powerful traditionalist 'pagan' religious communities, and was the 'top-down' civilian and military bureaucracy of the Empire to help the aggressively conformist Christian clergy to promote 'one empire, one faith' and persecute all other sects and faiths? All of these problems then came to a head in the mid-late fourth century, just as the arrival of incoming land-seeking Central Asian steppe nomads, the Huns, in the steppes north-east of the Danube touched off a (disputed in size) 'wandering' movement of refugee Germans towards the Roman borders. Disaster from the clash of a horde of culturally alien 'asylum-seekers' and the Mediterranean Roman world followed at the battle of Adrianople near the modern Greek/ Turkish/ Bulgarian border in 378, with the first major Roman defeat for many years and a permanent incursion of uncontrollable settlers inside the Empire.

This is the real, OTL ('Our Time-Line') world of the 'fall' of the Roman Empire – or more accurately the fragmentation of the Western Empire into a still socio-culturally partly Roman world dominated by new German-led 'tribal' states and the survival of a weaker but resilient Eastern Empire which still dominated the eastern Mediterranean and was to attempt to reconquer the West in the sixth century. My alterations of history in this period see some major and some more minor 'tweaks' – most of the OTL Roman Emperors (and Empresses) and other important figures appear, some more or less as in real life but others with significantly altered careers. Some rulers and their generals and ministers survive longer and have more success, others the reverse; the Empire has notably less coups and revolts in the mid-third century so it is able to survive with less strain and socio-economic losses (and with more resources so tax-revenues to pay for the army and government are larger and the tax-payers are less burdened). Crucially, the victory of Christianity over its 'pagan' rivals in the course of the fourth century is less complete and less easily secured due to the longer survival of the last pagan emperor, Julian (killed in a skirmish while invading Persia in 363 in OTL), and he is able to permanently neuter the military threat posed by Persia and reduce it to a divided set of Roman vassal-states. There are less civil wars in the mid-later fourth century or the fifth century, while the aggressively Christianizing emperor Theodosius 'the Great' (ruled 379/ 388 – 395) is more militarily but less religiously successful and though the Empire does then split up (as in reality) it has better and more coherent leadership through the fifth century. As argued to be a plausible possibility in my 2011 book *If Rome Had Not Fallen*, the Western Empire has a coherent chain of successful military leaders through from the 390s to the 470s (Theodosius, Stilicho, Constantius III, Aetius, and Majorian) and is able to absorb the German tribes who are in flight west from Attila the Hun – and it is the West which is left as the stronger Roman state and is then able to reunify the Empire. In my version of events, Theodosius is not able to overwhelm the 'pagan' aristocracy of the western capital, Rome, and impose one sole legal religion – Catholic Christianity – as in real life, as the OTL Western rebellion against him in 392 which he then suppressed does not take place and in addition the position of the pagan senatorial elite in the government of the West has been cemented in the 360s and 370s by a longer-ruling Julian. Theodosius in 394, when he suppressed paganism in real life, is not the war-winning autocrat who can do what he likes in my version of events – he has distractions such as Persia's eastern frontier with the Central Asian nomads and needs to keep the Western aristocracy 'on side' to fend off more revolts.

He survives to 407 not the OTL 395, which is not unreasonable as he was only forty-seven in the latter year; but though he can use his legislative and patronage powers to advance Catholicism this is less complete than in reality. (Tolerating other religions so long as their adherents were politically loyal to the State was the traditional Roman manner of governance in the first century and second century anyway; 'one state one religion' plus persecutions of 'dissidents' was an innovation of the crisis-hit later third century.) After Theodosius, his weak son Honorius' half-German general and regent Stilicho and the latter's military heirs, emperor Constantius III (died in 421 in real life) and general Aetius (assassinated in 454 in real life) survive for longer and keep the Western Roman armies powerful in my altered history – though not all disasters are avoided and I still have Stilicho being murdered in a courtier plot. The West leads the Germans to defeat Attila the Hun in 451 as in real life – but it then goes on under Aetius to set up a form of military 'protectorate' in central Europe whereby Rome leads a coalition of Germanic kingdoms and can call on them to aid its army. In real life the Romano-German politico-military alliance collapsed repeatedly into conflict and in the end the Germans overwhelmed the under-resourced and often poorly led Empire; in my version the Empire triumphs due to a mixture of luck, skill, and better understanding of the Germans' potential as allies.

My 'reunifying dynasty' which then takes over the civil-war-hit East in 516/18 is invented, though its dynastic progenitors and the then Eastern civil war are not; and the Empire then goes on to further success in the sixth century and early seventh century. I have included at the start of the text a list of the main changes that I have made from real history, which will explain the setting and show the basics of what happened. None of it is, I hope, too implausible – and if the Empire is indeed 'lucky' in a number of outcomes it was surely unlucky in them in real life.

Changes to the timeline from OTL include:

- Marcus Aurelius does not die in 180 but incorporates the lands of Bohemia and Moravia and their Germanic tribes in the Empire; Commodus does not succeed him so there is no tyranny in 180–92.
- Pertinax succeeds by arrangement with Marcus in 190, not by a coup; he is not overthrown either and is another of the 'Good Emperors'.
- Septimius Severus succeeds Pertinax by adoption in 197 not by civil war, though there is a civil war with Albinus in 197; he is less of an autocrat as less insecure but still harsh.
- Severus dies in 218 not 211, and Caracalla predeceases him so no tyranny then; weaker younger son Geta succeeds Severus.
- No controversial emperor Elagabalus, but straight transfer of power from Geta to Alexander Severus in 228; and no coup in 235 or civil war in 238, as straight transfer of power to the Gordians after death of Alexander in 242.
- Lesser mid-C3rd crisis, though still plague and Germanic invasions plus a division of Empire in 260–73; the Empire holds the Carpathian and Rhine frontiers so crises of invasion centred on Balkans, and no invasions of Greece

or Asia Minor; no sack of Athens. Less civic and agricultural damage so the later Empire can bear its increased tax-burden better and towns decline less.
- Aurelian the reunifier not assassinated in 275 but rules into 280s, and fewer shortterm rulers then.
- The new bureaucratic centralized autocracy of Diocletian (to 305) and Constantine 'the Great' (to 340), the first of them a militant and persecuting pagan and the second the creator of a Christian-led Empire, is much as in OTL, but they are ruling a less ravaged and insecure Empire. The persecution of the Christians by Diocletian and company. is less harsh and traumatic across the Empire than in OTL due to the earlier downfall of the leading persecutor, Galerius.
- Constantine dies later, 340 not 337, and there is less turbulence and civil war under his sons in the 340s and 350s: but still a civil war in 350–3. As in OTL, the paranoid survivor of Constantine's sons, Constantius II, tries to promote the 'heretic' Arian doctrine and gives power to its bishops and divides the quarrelling Christian sects further; he is then overthrown by his young cousin Julian, an idealistic pagan and would-be restorer of the traditional Classical empire and pagan religion. In this version, Julian has fourteen not two years to use his resources and supporters to redress the balance of government in favour of the pagans and hinder Christianity, and he also has the prestige of defeating Persia and annexing Mesopotamia – but he has no heir.
- Julian defeats Persia in 363–4 (more luck and more resources), annexes Mesopotamia with its trade-routes and riches, breaks up Persia into a network of vassal-states supplying him with troops and money, and lasts to 377. Paganism is revived and has a more 'level playing-field' to contest with Christianity on. He revives the cultural and educational aspects of paganism and its leading priesthoods' wealthy aristocratic social 'input' to keep a substantial section of society committed to it, and does his best to paint Christianity as unpatriotic, illogical in its divisive theology, and prone to feuding. He also brings supporters of his beliefs into the mainstream of government. His work is cut off short but not as soon as in real life – and his military success helps to add to his elite (including military) support and to warn his Christian successors off drastic measures against the pagans. The continued conversions to Christianity are slower in the later C4th and the great pagan cults last longer. Their aristocratic personnel are less hostile to and divorced from work for the State than in OTL, so the Empire has a broader 'base' of expert officials and slightly better (and less corrupt as not needing to make cash quickly) ministers – a 'tweak' in favour of more competent rule. There is less of a divergence between the elites in Rome itself and at the Western Court in Mediolanum/Milan than in OTL – and the importance

of the 'Julianic' elite to the govt in the 370s means that this 'bloc' has to be courted by Julian's Christian successors, Valentinian and Theodosius, more than in OTL. This means less aggressive 'Christianizing' legislation – and no mass-closures of temples and cults (or the Olympic Games). Fearing plots, the aggressively Catholic Theodosius has to be more cautious than in real life.

- Also, the eclectic Julian does not promote Christianity when he overruns Mesopotamia and western Persia and he allows local Zoroastrianism to continue and co-opts the elites into his army and civil service, so the landed aristocracy and priests are not as anti-Rome as they would be under a Christian empire – though now the Empire has to help its vassal-kings in upland Persia/Media (modern Iran) keep back the raiding Turkic nomads from Central Asia so it has an added security problem. This will distract even the capable and alert Julian from tackling the hordes of Gothic refugees from the Huns in 376–7 so he is not much better than the real-life sluggish Emperor Valens in averting disaster.

(This is where the text of this book commences, in the run-up to the 378 crisis as the Goths flee West from the Ukraine steppes from the Huns and threaten to cross the Danube by force.)

- The capable and Christian Valentinian succeeds Julian in 377 (emperor in 364–75 in OTL) and fights the invading Goths in 378, not his less competent brother Valens as in OTL; he was ruler of just the West and died in 375 in OTL. He wins the equivalent to the battle of Adrianople (but is killed there) so the Goths cannot settle as a semi-autonomous kingdom within Empire as they did in OTL .
- Theodosius then succeeds to the East in 379 as the choice of Valentinian's inexperienced elder son Gratian, ruler of the West, as in OTL, and is a militant Catholic as in OTL, but is too weak to ban paganism as in OTL as Julian has given it stronger hold within the elite and resources and he is too scared of causing a rebellion by its backers; he does defeat the Western emperors Maximus tian's overthrower) in 383–8 as in OTL.
- There is no 392 rebellion in the West, so Theodosius has no excuse to shut down pagan worship after this: in OTL the pagan elite of Rome aided the rebels so he repressed them and their religion after his victory in 394.
- Theodosius does not die in 395, aged forty-seven, as in OTL so the Empire is not broken up into separate states ruled by his young sons Arcadius (East) and Honorius (West) then, and there is no Gothic attack on Greece either as the Goths are Roman vassal allies north of the lower Danube after losing the 378 confrontation.

- Theodosius does not lose Italy to a pagan-led revolt in 392 so he does not purge the pagans, though he restricts their cults and cuts State funding to them; he dies in 407 not 395 and has secured the Rhine frontier plus an allied German protectorate from the Rhine to the Elbe so the great 'barbarian' crossing of the frontier in 408 (OTL406) is of the Elbe not the Rhine.

The crossing is impelled both by the Huns' advance and by German land-hunger, as in OTL, and advantage is taken of Theodosius' recent death in my version but of a weak Western regency's govt over past decade in OTL. In my version the West is stronger as it has had no 392–4 civil war and Theodosius (and his predecessors) retained Roman rule of Dacia and Marcomannia / Bohemia so the 'central region' Roman frontier is the Carpathian chain, not crossable rivers all the way from the Channel to the Danube. The German invasions are on a narrower front, and there are no Goths already within the East (Thrace) to weaken it as in OTL.

As a result there is an invasion across the Elbe and then the Rhine which is pushed back by Rome, which it did not do in OTL – though the internal tensions in the Empire then destroy war-winner, Western commander in chief/ regent Stilicho (but not his officer-corps as in OTL so the West has a stronger army after this). The uncontrolled German tribal wanderings and disruption within the weakened Western Empire in the 410s to the early 450s are in Germany east of the Rhine, a lightly Romanised 'allied German kingdoms' area, not in the more crucial Rhineland and Gaul to the West – so the effect on the Empire and its revenues is much less.

- As a result, the 'arc' of crisis and disruption in the period after Theodosius' death in the West is less, Italy is not touched, there is a stronger Western military leadership able to keep the Germans as semi-subject allies, the coalition that fights Attila the Hun is more heavily weighted in Rome's favour – and the West can recover after the defeat of Attila in 451, which in OTL it does not.
- The invasion crises of the late 400s do not involve Alaric the Goth attacking the Empire and ravaging Italy as he is by now a Roman general; he fights for power within the Roman military power-structure, as a semi-autonomous general, gets involved with a revolt by Roman generals on the Rhine to help the regency government out in return for land, and loses. The half-German general Stilicho is regent of the West for his son-in-law Honorius only in 407–12, once Theodosius dies, not in 395–408 as in OTL, and ends up killed in a purge in 412 (not 408 as in OTL) in different circumstances. There is a civil war and a German invasion around 408–12 as in OTL but it has a different trajectory, and the Western Empire holds the Rhine frontier (shakily)

and keeps Britain. The civil war is less dangerous as the army in Britain does not get involved, and less of Gaul (and none of Spain) is overrun – so the Vandals do not get into a position ready to invade North Africa and cut off the West's grain-supplies later in the 420s.
- After 412 the strongman of the West is Constantius III, the general married to weak emperor Honorius' sister Galla Placidia, as after 410/11 in OTL, but he does not die in 421 but lives until 439 so there is no lapse in central leadership and civil war in the 420s; the Vandals etc are contained east of the Rhine and do not penetrate to Spain and North Africa as in OTL. The Constantinian regime is stronger than in OTL as well as lasting longer, and integrates more German officers and soldiers into the Roman military 'machine' to help it keep the anti-Roman tribes beyond the Elbe and the Husn behind them at bay. As there are no German tribal states within the old Roman frontier, the Empire keeps its full 390slevel tax-revenues and can fund a large army – and the lack of real-life ravaging means more agricultural prosperity and more govt income.
- Constantius III passes on a unified and strong Western Roman army and government to Aetius as chief minister in 439, and the Vandals under Gaiseric are kept back east of the Rhine while Attila the Hun is kept out of Dacia and Hungary by the Roman control of the Carpathians; the Huns can only attack the east, via the Lower Danube.
- Attila the Hun is less of a threat to the East or West in the 440s as the Empire holds the Carpathian frontier, but still takes over the lower Danube region; he then heads W via Poland to destroy the Vandal kingdom in the Elbe region and invades the Rhineland in 451. Aetius with a stronger Romano-German force defeats him there, east of the Rhine, and after his death creates a Roman protectorate of his revolted ex-vassals in Poland/ W Ukraine. The West is thus militarily stronger than the East, but the latter has been reinforced in the 430s-40s by refugees from Attila so it has a larger army and more tax-revenues. The East is not so dependant on Aspar and other German generals, and the West is dominated militarily by a mixed Romano-German 'high command' under Constantius III and then Aetius (Aetius strongman and commander in chief to Constantius' and Galla Placidia's weak and immature son Valentinian III. Britain remains Roman, the Saxons are less of a threat, and Ireland is converted by St Patrick as in OTL but as a Roman ploy to Christianise and 'de-fang' the raiding Irish kingdoms and so save on expense on an Irish Sea anti-piracy fleet.
- Valentinian III is betrayed as he tries to have Aetius murdered in 454, instead of killing him as in OTL; instead Aetius has the emperor killed in 455 and puts his son Gaudentius on the Western throne as his puppet, married to

Valentinian's daughter Placidia. The West is run by a military 'junta' of Aetius and his officers, and after Aetius dies in 469 Gaudentius is murdered for trying to stage a comeback and replaced by the dynamic military commander Majorian (OTL emperor in 457–62). The Romano-German officer corps dominates the Empire and forces the landed aristocracy to pay enough taxes to fund an impressively large army, with the German lands NE of the Rhine as Roman allied vassal-states and the surviving Huns back in the Ukraine as a second-rate raiding threat to the East. In the East, Leo I disposes of his military 'strongman' Aspar easier than in OTL.

- Majorian has no children and is succeeded by the OTL Western Emperor of 467–72 who is slightly altered in name and ability, 'Tiberius II Anthemius', in 488. By this point, due to the Eastern rebellion of 484 and the contentious nature of Zeno's emperorship there in 474–91, the West is the more stable state and is stronger militarily.
- In this version of events the Rome-allied German states between Rhine and Elbe after Attila's downfall include the refugee Franks and Ostrogoths, and their rulers include the OTL kings Clovis and Theodoric; and their pressure on land in the Lower Saxony region drives some local Saxons as refugees to Britain as 'boat people' in the late fifth century to settle on the 'Saxon Shore' in the south-east. They include the OTL South Saxon King Aelle; and the Roman 'Counts of Britain' who have to deal with the Saxons include Ambrosius Aurelianus (OTL British leader) and Artorius (OTL 'King Arthur').
- As Western Emperor from 496, Tiberius' son Titus II (my creation) proceeds to expand the West's trade and military power and incorporates incoming German settlers and soldiers into the Empire, once Romanised, to add to agricultural and military manpower. Some of the OTL late fifth-and sixth centuries. Germanic kings are among them, with the dynasty of Frankish king Clovis and some of the OTL settlers in Britain, where a part of the Angles from Denmark move after their lands are attacked by the Ostrogothic king Theodoric (in this version settled in N Germany); there is thus an 'Anglian' settlement in East Anglia and Lincolnshire in Britain. The Roman trading allies in the Baltic include the Geatish king Beowulf (appears in OTL legends). To the south, Roman trade extends over the Sahara to Lake Chad and by sea from Gades (Cadiz) to explore the West African coast and find the Canary Islands, using past Carthaginian exploration records – and there are rumours of America (ignored).
- The orthodox/ Catholic revolt against Eastern Emperor Anastasius' attempt to enforce a religious compromise with the Monophysites, led by rebel Catholic general Vitalian as in OTL, is used by Emperor Titus of the West to invade and help the Catholic cause, backing up the Pope. Anastasius has to accept

a fully Orthodox Church, as in OTL, but in this version Titus makes him agree to himself as co-ruler too; when Anastasius dies in 518 Titus reunifies the Empire. Thus there is no Emperor Justin in the East in 518–27 as in OTL, and his nephew and heir 'Justinian' (born Petrus Sabbatius) appears in this story as a civilian chief minister (Praefect of Constantinople) of the main part of the East to Titus II but not as Emperor. With no Justinian in charge, there is no harsh persecution of non-orthodox Christians or pagans, and there is no 'thought control' of the intellectual atmosphere to marginalise pagan philosophy and drive the pagans out of the University of Athens. There is bureaucratic centralization as in OTL, but under a ruler more sympathetic to paganism and the Classical inheritance and to non-orthodox thinkers – and with no costly wars to reconquer the West and Persia a quiescent vassal state the Empire is less exhausted by oppressive taxation.

- In this version of events, Titus (d 542) and his dynasty then rule all of the Empire, usually from Rome; the eastern border is now at the River Oxus and along the approx. modern Iran/Afghanistan border, with the broken-up sub-states of the former Sassanid empire (atomized by Julian in 363–4) under Rome-allied Sassanid princes in Persis, Hycrania and Media – and by this point Rome has taken over Bactria too. Following an Epthalite Hun attempt to install a vassal-state in Sogdiana (N of River Oxus, i.e. approx. Uzbekistan) in the 520s, Rome takes it over to stop attacks on Bactria. The Roman victor is Belisarius, the OTL reconqueror of the West; in this version he is the hero who finishes off the Sassanid state of Sogdiana as a threat to Rome and stabilizes the Eastern frontier.

- No 'Plague of Justinian' in this version; a larger population and a more prosperous and confident Empire. With Persia conquered and its resources in Roman hands, there is no massive 'Persia vs Rome' war after 602 as in OTL, and thus no mutual exhaustion of the two Empires as the Arabs unite. In fact the Roman Empire has already used the (real life) war between the Yemeni Arab state in south-west Arabia and Christian Abyssinia/ Ethiopia in the 520s to destroy the former and set up a Roman province in Yemen, controlling the trade-route from Egypt via the Red Sea to India. In OTL the Eastern Roman Empire just used Abyssinia to conquer Yemen and keep Christian control of the Red Sea trade route; in this version a stronger Rome has restored the Pharoanic canal from Nile to Red Sea and controls the Red Sea and the port of Aden with a Roman fleet. Rome thence rules south-west Arabia and dominates the local tribes – the war is led by the OTL East Roman General Belisarius instead of him being the 530s Eastern reconqueror of North Africa and Italy. As a result there is no unification of Arabia by Mohammed and Islam after the 610s, though the Prophet does rule the Mecca/ Medina area, the latter is a trading- led ally of the Roman Empire which supplies regular troops to the Empire, and there is no Islamic conquest of the Middle East. Nor is there an Avar tribal conquest of the Balkans, though the Avars do inherit the Huns' role ruling the steppes of the Ukraine.

List of Emperors (and One Empress)

Marcus Aurelius 161–190
Pertinax 190–197 (and co-ruler, titular, Titus Aurelius 190–2)
Septimius Severus 197–218
(Caracalla, co-ruler 198–217)
Geta Severus, 218–228
Alexander Severus, 228–242
Gordianus I, 242–243.
Gordianus II, 243–251.
Gordianus III, 243–252.
Trebonius Gallus, 252–253.
Aemilius Aemilianus, 253.
Lucius Valerian(us), 253 -260.
Gallienus, 253–268.
Claudius II, 268–270.
(Gallic breakaway Empire: Postumus 264- 269, Victorinus 269–70, Tetricus 270–274.)
Aurelianus Restitutor Orbis', 270–280.
Probus, 280–284.
Diocletian, 284–305.
Maximian, 286–305, 307–310.
(British breakaway empire: Carausius 287–293, Allectus 293–296.)
Constantius I 'Chlorus: 'Caesar' (West) 293–305; 'Augustus' (West) 305–306.
Galerius: 'Caesar' (East) 293–304
Constantine I 'the Great': Far West 306–340
  : Centre West 312–340
  : East 324–340.
Maxentius: Centre West 306–312
Severus: Centre West 306–307.
Licinius: 'Caesar': East 304–305
'Augustus: East 305–324
Maximin(us): East 311–313.
Constantine II; Far West 340–344.
Constans: Centre West 340–350, Far West 344–350.

(Magnentius, usurper, Far West/Centre West 350–353)
Constantius II: East 340–361.
   : Centre West 352–361, Far West 353–361.
Julian: Far West 360–377
   : Centre West/ East 361–377.
Valentinian I 377–378
Gratian: Far West 377–383
Valentinian II: Centre West 378–387
   : Far West 389–392
Magnus Maximus: Far West 383–388
   : Centre West 387–388
Theodosius I 'the Great: East 379–407
   : Centre West 388–392, 394–407
   : Far West 394–407
Arcadius: East 393–412
Honorius: West 392/ 407–423
Theodosius II: East 412–450
Pulcheria, 'Augusta': East 414–458
Constantius III: West 421–439
Valentinian III: West 423–455
Marcian: East 450–459
Gaudentius: West 455–469
Leo I: East 459–474
Majorian: West 469–488.
Leo II: East 474
Zeno: East 474–475, 476–491
Basiliscus: East 475–476
Tiberius II Anthemius: West 488–496.
Anastasius I: East 491–518
Titus II 'the Reunifier': West 496–542
   : East 515–542.
Heraclius (brother) 542–551.
Anastasius II (son) 551–559.
Nerva II (brother) 559–570.
Gallus (son) 570–582
Rillanus (eldest son) 582–590
Carus I (second son) 590–615
Claudius III (third son) 615–630
Carus II (son of Carus I) 630–641: end of dynasty.

Part I

Restoration. Showdown with the Goths. Julian, the Pagan, Succeeded by Valentinian and Theodosius, the Christians. 375 to 407

The End of Julian; A Christian (and less competent) Successor at a Time of Crisis, Valentinian. Battle With the Asylum-Seeking Goths. 375 to 378

The controversial pagan Emperor Julian's cousin, contemporary, and ideological supporter Procopius had long been his presumed heir, as the only adult male left of the Imperial kin of Constantine 'the Great'. He was not a direct descendant of Constantine, which meant that legitimists (including some important senatorial pagan leaders in Rome who were among Julian's closest civilian allies) did not regard him as a suitable successor. But he was both a committed pagan and a capable if not that inspiring general, so as the Emperor did not have any children he was seen by many of the Emperor's closest allies, ministers and military officers alike, as a man who would be loyal to Julian's legacy and could be trusted with the throne. Similarly, the remaining Christian ministers and senior officers distrusted him on this account – though he was a cautious character lacking strong opinions who might be amenable as Emperor to widening the basis of his backing by reversing much of Julian's pro-pagan legislation and readmitting the less aggressive Catholic bishops to Imperial favour. Julian's own intentions were as ambiguous in the mid-370s as they had been a decade earlier. But Procopius died suddenly shortly after his arrival in Alexandria to be Praefect there at the end of his service as Praefect in Constantinople in summer 375.

With no heir handy if he should die on campaign – he had refused numerous requests to divorce his childless but loyal and wise wife Helena – Julian gave up his planning at Antioch, his main Eastern base, for another war in eastern Persia as he had to consider the looming threat of the Goths, who were moving into 'Sarmatia' (OTL southern Rumania, i.e. Wallachia, North of the lower Danube) in flight from the attacking Huns. The major defeat that the Gothic tribal 'empire' on the steppes of Ukraine had suffered at the hands of the fierce incoming Hunnic nomad cavalry earlier in 375, with its king Ermaneric killed, had left their lands – with no geographical barriers to swift horse-borne raiders – open to attack, and the Huns had duly started to sack and pillage their settlements along the Don and lower Dnieper valleys and drive the survivors into fleeing. The Gothic forces were demoralised by the deaths of their king and many of his senior commanders, and large numbers of them were now heading for the Danube and driving out the existing, smaller and weaker local tribes north of the river. Some of the Goths' fractured and panicking leadership, believing the Huns to be invincible, had indeed now contacted the Roman authorities along the Danube demanding either military help or, as Rome's tributary allies since the days of Julian's predecessor Constantius II, the right to enter and settle safely in the Empire. The Roman 'duces' (provincial military commanders) had been wary of that, given the rumours of a huge flood of tens of thousands of Goths moving across Sarmatia (i.e. Wallachia) and more behind them. If they allowed one body of 'refugees' in, would they be followed by others and would all of them insist on keeping their own weapons and leaders not (as usual for Germanic incomers to the Roman Empire and army) being broken up into manageable groups under close Roman command? Would they not wait patiently to be allocated farms – assuming that there were enough of the latter to satisfy such hordes of incomers – but start seizing land and defying the Roman authorities?

Some of the Roman 'high command' of the Eastern central army ('comitatus') in Constantinople and the command in conquered Mesopotamia were less inclined to panic about Gothic numbers and wanted to use this chance to hire large numbers of them as soldiers to add to the Roman army. They were fierce and hard-bitten, if undisciplined, soldiers and had been used successfully in large numbers by Constantine 'the Great' and his son Constantius II. Both these arguments were now put to Julian by his advisers, as he headed to Italy by sea from his current stay in Syria to consider his future and whether to intervene on the lower Danube in person. He duly decided to solve the problem of the probable extinction of the House of Constantine in the male line by selecting an heir from among his most suitable and competent senior generals and civilian officials with formal advice from the Senate and to make sure that the choice was a committed as well as nominal pagan. The successful candidate was to be required to marry his only surviving relative in the younger generation, Constantius II's daughter, Constantia (born 360), or if the age-gap was too great to marry off his son and heir to her. The Emperor was, however, in no hurry to name an heir and he proceeded to consult widely during his winter in Italy in winter 375–6, based in Rome and Baiae. He had the dilemma that though his own preferences were for a man who could be relied on to keep to his anti-Christian legislation and promotion of pagans in senior civilian and military office several of his best pagan generals, older figures in their sixties who had been in their teens before Constantine 'the Great' and his equally zealous Christian sons had increasingly restricted promotion to known (and usually baptized) Christians from the late 320s, had died in recent years. He had been promoting pagans in the army since he achieved full power in late 361, but most of the older and more experienced officers had been recruited and trained before then so they were Christians. He had chosen, as a sensible commander in need of reliable and well-trained generals in his 360s Persian wars, to keep them in their commands and (where they had proved a success) promoting them. The needs of Rome had come first, and so there was still a substantial body of first-class – and popular – Christian generals in his 'high command' and in charge of provincial and frontier armies. Setting all of them aside to nominate a pagan heir from more junior ranks – and Rome needed a military ruler at this crisis of expected Gothic attack – would invite a coup or civil war and Julian could not risk that. Instead he concentrated on the Gothic crisis, and as more and more refugee Goths poured into Sarmatia as spring came in 376 – rumoured to be in the tens of thousands – he came to the conclusion that admitting large numbers of them to Roman lands would risk overwhelming the frontier armies and having unruly hordes of armed settlers seizing farms or food-supplies.

There had not been large numbers of Roman troops stationed on the peaceful lower Danube since he took about a third of the military forces there off to invade Persia in 363, and it was too dangerous to recall any of his large armies in the East to deal with the Goths – that could lead to revolt in Persia. Bringing in troops from the Rhine would risk rebellion by the Empire's German foes there who he had defeated and reduced to vassalage in the mid-350s; so he resorted for the moment to a cautious policy of bringing in smaller numbers of troops from Britain, the Rhine, and North Africa to the Danube, in numbers that should not risk attack by frontier raiders in those areas. In the meantime more troops were levied and trained from the civilian population across the Empire, with Julian reversing his predecessors' policy of relying on existing soldiers' sons for new recruits to accept any volunteers (though landowners complained that their tenants ran away to join up). Traditionalist Julian hoped to revive the republican practice of widespread military service. A 'crack force' of Guards and other troops from the central Western army ('comitatus') in northern Italy were sent to the lower Danube to man the river-crossings and forts and forbid any Goths to cross. The Balkan provinces' officials were to collect levies of food, mainly grain and cattle, and bring them to the Danube for shipping across the river and distribution to the Goths in Sarmatia – who had had to flee their own farms on the steppes and only had such food as they were managing to take from the local tribes, plus their own herds of cattle and sheep (where they had managed to bring these from the steppes and the Huns had not taken them).

Thousands more Goths fled south-west towards Roman territory seeking sanctuary as the Huns continued to pour across the steppes and raided West of the lower Dnieper, and in summer 376 up to 20,0000 of the Tervingi grouping (aka the 'Visigoths', West Goths) arrived at the lower Danube in Sarmatia. Others under their war-leader/ 'king'; Athanaric threatened to invade Dacia (W Rumania) via the Ostrava Gap if they were not admitted, but were blocked for the moment by Roman garrisons on the fortified 'limes' frontier and in the Beskid hills. The Emperor's most senior and trusted military commander Dagalaiphus arrived in the lower-middle Danube region around Sirmium (OTL: Belgrade area)with the first detachments from the Western 'comitatus' army in July and received envoys from the Goths seeking peace but a large grant of farmlands on the Southern bank of the river – within the Empire so 'safe' from the Huns. The Goths however refused to divide up their (mixed) groups of civilian noncombatants and warriors, most of the latter having travelled with their families, and to form smaller and manageable groups, hand over their weapons, and move to fixed (and widely distanced apart) towns and forts in Lower and Upper Moesia (Bulgaria) where food and Roman officers would be positioned for them. They insisted on staying in larger bodies and keeping their arms and their own commanders, though the Gothic leadership was willing to transmit such orders that the Emperor and his generals sent to them on to their people, and some bolder 'barbarians' told the Roman delegates that they were aware that their numbers were greater than that of the Roman frontier command so if necessary they would cross the Danube by force uninvited and settle where they wanted.

The Gothic leaders insisted that their people faced annihilation by the Huns so they had to do what was necessary to save them and that meant crossing the Danube and they meant no disrespect to the Emperor. But though the realist (partly German himself) Dagalaiphus understood this and sent Julian reassurance that the Goths were desperate and would not turn violent or rebellious if handled properly most of the Roman officers were angry at the 'insolence of the barbarians' and they sent dire warnings to Julian of the need to face down and overawe them, barring them from crossing. The Emperor, perhaps fearing that the Goths were exaggerating the Hunnic threat and were intent on seizing land like the invading Alemanni had been on the Rhine when he had faced them in the mid-350s, backed the 'hard-liners' and refused to let the Goths cross except in small, manageable numbers while he recalled more troops from the East. But at this juncture Dagalaiphus died of a fever caught while inspecting marshy Danube crossing-points, and while the Roman 'field army' was immobile, awaiting his replacement's arrival, large groups of Goths crossed the river unmolested and set up fortified camps in case of Roman attack.

Julian, the Pagan, Succeeded by Valentinian and Theodosius 5

The departure of some 20,000 troops from Mesopotamia and Media for the Danube inspired local foes of Rome as Julian had feared. The Bactrian kingdom of the late Persian 'Great King' Shapur (evicted by Julian in 363–4)'s heir Ardashir was threatening to take over the pro-Roman principality of Hyrcania (the south shore of the Caspian) with a horde of Turkic mercenaries and had killed king Arsaces in summer – autumn 376, and Julian now had the idea of sending a large force of refugee Gothic warriors off to Persia in small, manageable regiments under Roman officers to stiffen his army there without his having to use valuable Rhine and Dacian/ Marcomannian troops (and too much money). He arrived on the middle Danube with his household and most of the 'comitatus' from Italy in October 376 and set up his base at Carnuntum for negotiations with both those Goths already on the south bank of the Danube – which number had more than trebled as he was travelling with his slow artillery-train and Court from Mediolanum – and those still on the northern bank. These talks took many months as he had to allocate empty farms in his Danube terrotories for non-combatant Goths and their womenfolk and children and see that the refugees were given adequate food and shelter. Alternatively, if the talks failed it would have to be war – and while he was worrying about which troops to bring in from his outer frontiers in spring 377 without risking local frontier attacks, assessing potential commanders, and training his army around Carnuntum as much as the winter weather would allow his officials in the Balkans were having difficulties in collecting enough supplies to feed the huge Gothic camps. It had been a poor harvest in 376 and the local Roman farmers, short of food, and the civic councils in the towns did not want to hand any of their grain over – and requisitioning it would lead to riots so nervous officials took what they could get and pretended that they had enough food to meet Julian's estimated requirements. Haughty, Goth-detesting senior officials were not interested in feeding a raggle-taggle 'horde' of indigent 'barbarians' either, not least as they might well be exaggerating the Hunnic threat and planning to steal or extort land from the Romans, so they covered up the lack of supplies. The Goths starved, complained to the local Romans to no avail, and started to send out armed parties to steal food and cattle – which was duly reported to the preoccupied Emperor as evidence of their malicious intentions.

Julian was more inclined to listen to alarmist generals urging war after that problem erupted, and as troops began to arrive on the middle Danube from across the Empire as the roads and seas became navigable in spring 377 war seemed probable. But disaster now struck, as on 15 April 377, aged forty-five, Julian was killed in a freak hunting accident near Carnuntum while out chasing boar with a group of his senior courtiers and officers. The most remarkable of the dynasty of Constantine 'the Great' and more like his uncle in his stubborn idealism and desire to wrest the course of destiny his way than he would have admitted, Julian had endeavoured to turn the course of events away from what most of the Roman elite in his era – the Christians in particular – had expected. He had stood in the way of their seemingly 'inevitable' march to dominating the Empire's future for seventeen years and was accordingly hated by them for it with a vigour and a long-term resentment that only the arch-persecutors Diocletian, Galerius, and Maximin also attracted, with his devotion to justice and to the traditional Greco-Roman cultural 'norms' ignored – though his one-time fellow-student St Basil of Caesarea did pay tribute to these qualities in his first sermon after he heard the news of the death of the supposed 'Antichrist'.

Conversely, he attracted a passionate following among the substantial Neoplatonist intellectual community and the traditionalist aristocratic (and imitation aristocratic) believers in the ancient Greco-Roman cultural world of the 'Twelve Olympians', long-established pagan rites and festivals, and a literary and artistic culture free from Christian influence and morals – and prohibitions, e.g. on nudity. The Neoplatonists, a philosophical school centred on the C3rd AD adaptation by Plotinus of the more mystical/ spiritual works of Plato 600 years before, indeed believed in one 'Supreme Being' (or spiritual force) directing the universe, so there was a degree of similarity to Christian theology – and some 'crossover' of personnel (including Julian himself). Where the cold and efficient bureaucrat Diocletian had attracted few admirers before let alone after his death Julian was eulogized and was made the subject of laudatory writings from a body of devoted followers for many centuries after his time, both before and during the 'Classical Restoration' from the fifteenth century and was seen as being the most attractive of the emperors of the period between Marcus Aurelius (another candidate to be Plato's 'Philosopher Ruler' in action) and Titus II 'the Restorer'. As a man of culture and a Hellenophile he was seen as second only to Hadrian among the emperors of Rome's first centuries, and in addition his conquest of (most of) Persia brought him into a legendary role in Middle Eastern culture second only to 'Iskander the Two-Horned', his great predecessor and model Alexander. Arguably, he also stood in the way of a Christian cultural and politico-social 'takeover' of the Roman world long enough to blunt the impact of this and to ensure that his successors, facing a stronger and more confident pagan faction among the Roman elites, had to be more cautious and conciliatory than they would otherwise have been. If he had reigned longer he would have made even more of an impact – and the luck (or Divine plan, said Christian commentators) of his dying suddenly in his mid-forties without an heir as the last of his dynasty passed the throne back to a Christian.

Chapter 1

The House of Valentinian

(In OTL, Julian has been dead since 363 and Valentinian is already emperor as of 364; he rules the West with the nominal co-emperorship of his son Gratian and he has passed the East over to his incompetent younger brother Valens, who will lose the battle of Adrianople to the invading Goths and get killed in 378. The 'fall' of the Empire then commences as the Goths are at large within the Empire thereafter and it has lost control of part of its territory, though its new Eastern Emperor Theodosius will force the Goths into semi-dependant vassalage in 381. In this version, the united Empire is still led until 377 by the capable general Julian, who has now secured the Eastern frontier by the conquest of Persia and acquired extra, Persian revenues and troops.)

The Emperor's sudden demise after a reign of seventeen years in the West and fifteen in the East, without any named heir, was a major shock to his elite and to the Empire, though many Christians rejoiced and there were rumours for years that some secretly Christian officers had arranged the 'accident' with clerical support to be rid of the 'Antichrist'. The senior aristocratic general Sallust, a pagan but sympathetic to the Catholic cause and their theology provided that there was no persecution of Arians, was offered the throne but refused; Equitius, veteran commander of the leading regiment of the 'Scutarii' guards, was rejected as too uncouth and the hugely popular and capable Januarius, former 'dux' of Lower Germany in the late 360s and a confidante of Julian, was rejected as he was serving too far away (as 'dux' of Illyricum) to be able to take over quickly. Several civilian ministers were rejected as not having the confidence of the generals that they would keep up Julian's expensive military plans, and senior Italian pagan nobles currently serving in the administration at Mediolanum and the City Praefect were rejected as being too hostile to the increasing numbers of Germans in senior military ranks and so likely to purge them and stir up resentment from their colleagues. Eventually the 369–74 military commander of Pannonia, Count Valentinian, son of Count Gratian and recently made commander of the second regiment of 'Scutarii' (Shield-Bearers), was elected (aged fifty-six) as a compromise despite his being a Christian and was summoned from his post with his guards-regiment at the nearby city. He was known as a capable commander, a hard worker, and a man of humility and honesty who would not have his head turned by the lifestyle of an Emperor, as he had lived as much like an ordinary soldier as possible since he became a general and harked back enthusiastically to his upbringing on a small farm in the Cilician hills of south-eastern Anatolia. More importantly, though he was a Catholic who had not joined the rush of ambitious rising officers to take part in pagan ceremonies in the army and so impress the Emperor he was uninterested in matters of doctrine and was very unlikely to return to Constantius II's obsessive interest in securing fellow religionists in all senior Church sees and driving 'heretics' out of the elite. As such, pagans and supporters of rival sects of Christians alike were not wary of him as they were of those senior officers and nobles who had more pronounced religious opinions.

Valentinian arrived next day to accept the offer and to assume the throne, was hailed as Emperor on the parade-ground, and asked his officers' opinion about appointing a co-ruler to be told by Julian's most senior general Arbetio that if he loved his family he would appoint his brother Valens, a competent but unimaginative guards-officer on the Imperial staff a few years his junior, but if he loved the State he would look more carefully. (OTL event, but in 364 when Valentinian was elected.) He decided on doing the latter, and ended up choosing his 18-year-old elder son Gratian as his nominal co-ruler and marrying him off to Julian's young cousin Constantia, daughter of Constantius II by his second wife, to add to his legitimacy by a link to the House of Constantine. Valentinian had remarried in 370 to the late rebel Magnentius' widow Justina so the latter now had a second term as Empress which was unprecedented; her son by Valentinian, the younger Valentinian (II), was aged only six so he was too young to be even nominal co-emperor but was promised the rule of Italy when he was adult.

> (In OTL he ignored this advice when he assumed the throne in 364 and appointed Valens, the man who was to lose the battle of Adrianople to the Goths in 378, as his co-emperor.)

A cautious man and lacking any confidence in upsetting either pagan or Christian factions (Catholic/ orthodox or Arian) by moving too quickly to support either of them, for the moment Valentinain declared his general adherence to the policies of the House of Constantine. He dispatched his son Gratian to Trier to rule Gaul, Britain and the Rhineland with a large entourage including his new tutor in classical literature and philosophy, the learned Aquitaine aristocrat Gessius Ausonius from Burdigala who acted as the new north-west Roman regime's poetic 'cheerleader'. Most of Julian's ministers were kept on and the senior general Severus was made 'Magister Peditum' (supreme infantry commander) in the West and Julian's pagan south-east Balkans protege Trajan was made 'Magister Peditum' in the East. But Valentinian notably retired a number of Julian's closest military advisers despite their expertise being useful with a major Gothic tribal movement apparently imminent. Jovinus, Jovius, Arbetio, and Arintheus, all in their fifties or sixties, were retired and the expert Count Theodosius, the man who had driven off a major Pictish and Irish attack on northern Britain in 369–70, was packed off to Mauretania. Probably the most dynamic and strategically flexible of Julian's commanders and a man capable of outwitting the huge Gothic army by skill and imagination, he would have been ideal to assist the more dogmatic and 'rule-bound' Valentinian in the forthcoming war on the Danube but was now sidelined by his jealous foes and his suspicious new Emperor. (Similarly, as he was a committed Catholic Julian had never considered him as his successor despite his strategic skills and his popularity with the troops.)

Berber raiders had been attacking traders in the Atlas Mountains and plundering local Romano-Mauretanian farms and towns in the lowlands towards the coast, and Count Theodosius was sent off on an 'important' but 'out of the way' campaign to set up new Roman forts in crucial passes, hunt down raiders, and fortify towns and estate villas. In the event this was to lead to more success long-term for Rome than Valentinian had planned, as the initiative-seizing Count realized the potential of Sahara trade across the deserts by camel-caravan to the line of oases as far as the distant River Niger and despatched a small but well-equipped Roman force along this route with local scouts to set up garrisons and lavish gifts on tribal chiefs in 378. This and the resultant Roman commercial alliance with the local Tuareg duly secured a useful and lucrative trade-route to the Niger and its emerging towns and cities, and the dilemma posed by Rome's top geographers at the Library and university of Alexandria since second century AD geographer Ptolemy's time that it would be too costly and time-consuming to send trading ships along the difficult West African coast to trade with the tribal kingdoms of the Malinke and Wolof peoples of the savannah up the Niger were solved by merchants and officers from Rome running a new and shorter desert trade-route.

(This is not as in OTL, but Theodosius did pursue a successful similar cross-border policy in northern Britain c. 370 in OTL.)

For the immediate future it meant that Theodosius was out of the running for a major post, and so was his eponymous son the younger Theodosius – who took over the Mauretanian project and welcomed new entrepreneurs from Rome and Carthage to come South and try out the Saharan oases trade-route later in 378 when his father fell ill and died. (Some said that Valentinian had had him poisoned out of jealousy.) Valentinian postponed any showdown with the Goths while he secured his position, taking most of his troops off for intensive training in lower Pannonia while a 'holding force' kept an eye on the Goths in Lower Moesia – and the delay enabled more troops to be levied and trained for the war in the western provinces but left the commanders who were facing more and more armed refugees crossing the lower Danube, too well-armed to be tackled, nervous and demoralised. Valentinian, now holding Court at the city of Poetovio in Pannonia while retired Julianic general Arintheus took over as Praefect in Rome to transmit his orders to the capital, launched an initial reconciliatory 'raft' of cancellations of Julian's banishment of assorted clerics from their sees, confiscations of Church property, and banning of Christians from teaching posts by reversing the oppressive tax-'hikes' on their clergy. This duly made him popular among all Christian sects, while his reduction of State grants to pagan priesthoods and temples was not so steep as to arouse alarm that he was irrevocably committed to resuming the Constantinian 'drive' for conversions and he cleverly blamed it all on the cost of the Gothic crisis. But his wife Justina was funding Arian clerics and churches out of her own fortune and encouraging him to invite Arian as well as orthodox clerics to his court, and in 377–8 tension began to rise at the Court as assorted pagan ministers and courtiers were removed and Valentinian invited the current leading Catholic theologian Basil of Caesarea, Julian's old intellectual sparring partner from Athens 'university', to court to hold talks with other clerics about a new Church Council and statement of doctrine that would comprehend the Arians in the Church. The militant leader Athanasius of Alexandria had died in 377 shortly before Julian so there was no need to put him back in his see and it could be given to a moderate pro-government cleric from Syria, Palladius, who was used to obeying orders and avoided stirring up his excitable and anti-Arian congregation. But in Mediolanum, the usual Imperial residence in the West where the Empress Justina and her Household arrived in early autumn 377 from the Danube, the learned and well-liked Christian 'moderate' ex-'corrector' (regional sub-governor) Aurelius Ambrosius, who had become Bishop in late 376 by popular demand though not even a deacon, was soon warning his congregation about Arians (OTL: St. Ambrose). He and Arian ally Justina became bitter enemies.

The incoming horde of Huns had destroyed the Ostrogothic kingdom on the South Russian steppes in 375 and were now moving as far as the Dniester, burning Gothic settlements and taking the land for their huge flocks of sheep to graze on. Thousands of Gothic farmers and their families were fleeing ahead of them towards the Danube, with those Gothic warlords who tried to fight (on foot) being overwhelmed by fast-moving Hunnic cavalry archers. As a result the demoralized Goths were able to pass on news of what had happened to the Roman frontier commanders when they arrived at the river and sought sanctuary and/or food. Those Goths (in small numbers) who were taken on as recruits by the increasingly nervous Romans could alert the latter to the need to improve cavalry and defence against archers if the Romans were to face the Huns themselves later. The recent potential Imperial candidate Januarius was not given any role in negotiating with the Goths as he asked to do (as he had commanded some of their countrymen under Julian), and was ignored as he proposed a generous mass-grant of lands across Moesia and better control of the inadequate food-supplies which were being delivered to 'loyal' Gothic camps which obeyed Roman orders. He was soon sacked from Court by the increasingly suspicious Valentinian – probably out of fear of a success in averting war making Januarius too popular and him seizing the throne. Valentinian soon appointed his authoritarian new 'Pro-Praefect' (i.e. deputy chief official) of Rome, his fellow-Cilician and trusted ally Maximin, with the Praetorian Praefecture (i.e. over-governorship) of Italy and Africa instead of sacking him after reports of his arbitrary arrests and exiles of 'plotters' later in 377, so signs of his paranoia were becoming apparent. Now Alavivus and Fritigern, commanders of the West Goths (Visigoths) on the North bank of the lower Danube, sent an embassy to Valentinian at Sirmium, his winter 377–8 headquarters, requesting permission to settle in the Empire with their people. It was granted within a supposed limit of 20,000 males and their women and children as the Emperor had now received reports from Lower Moesia indicating where there were enough vacant farms to be occupied. The Goths crossed the Danube in April 378 on schedule, but as might be expected far more than were legally permitted crossed the river – probably due to panic over recent Hunnic raids into Sarmatia heading in their direction – and the Emperor did not bother to visit the region to oversee the arrival. He ordered his generals on the lower Danube to collect the required levy of Gothic menfolk of military age for the Persian 'front', as per Julian's original plan to send a large body of them to the East, and send them to Constantinople ready to leave for Antioch in July 378. The Gothic civilians left behind would then be submissive to Roman military requirements, and those bands of refugees still roaming around the riverside stealing food and clashing with locals could be suppressed by the large assembled Western Roman 'comitatus'.

Disastrously, the incoming Goths were cheated over food-supplies by the corrupt and inefficient local governor Lupicinus (a man who Valentinian had promoted when Julian had refused to do this, as he was no threat and did what he was told) and his officials. They were presented with useless and stale food to eat and inadequate shelter, and .when they objected told to shut up or they would be flogged for mutiny under Roman military law, and a Gothic revolt inevitably followed – this time by a far larger and more coherent body of experienced warriors than with the problems in 376. The Goths started ravaging lower Moesia and stealing food from towns which they burnt while the local garrisons hid in their forts, but when Roman reinforcements arrived from Sirmium and Dacia the Goths were blockaded by generals Trajan and Profutus in the Dobrudja at the mouth of the Danube. Thinking this a minor mutiny, Valentinian did not bother to send in his main army from the Eastern capital but ordered his local commanders to punish the rioters' leaders and send the rounded-up levies on to him as he cleared smaller bodies of Goths out of Upper Moesia and then proceeded into Dacia to deal with a reported large Gothic crossing of the passes near Alba Iulia ahead of the winter snows. But the Moesian Gothic revolt was worse than he had thought, and it is probable that he ignored Trajan's warnings about it as he feared the latter was trying to play it up in order to get popularity for suppressing it and then launch a coup.

Gothic reinforcements from across the Danube now forced Trajan and Profutus to withdraw, and in early spring 378 the Goths moved south into Thrace to head for Anchialus on the coast and take the Roman garrisons in the Balkan range passes, including the well-fortified and defended Shipka Pass, by surprise by avoiding them rather than fighting. The situation was getting out of control, and in May Valentinian had to admit that his Eastern campaign would have to wait and moved back to Sirmium to await the arrival of reinforcements from Constantinople. He arranged a truce with the rebel Bactrian Persians and accepted their occupation of Hyrcania to concentrate on the Goths, though this infuriated his generals at Ctesiphon who were on the point of invading Hyrcania from Media (OTL: Hamadan area, to South) and felt abandoned so had he lasted as Emperor a rebellion might have followed. Another advance west by the Huns in April-May 378 across the Dniester sent a new wave of Goths fleeing into Sarmatia/Wallachia. Their warlords Alatheus and Saphrax led the "Gaethungi" tribal grouping over the lower Danube to reinforce Fritigern, and the Imperial generals in Moesia, halted at Silistria, left adequate garrisons there and in other riverine fortresses. They moved south towards the Hebrus (OTL: Maritza) valley to await the Emperor's arrival (heading south-east) via Naissus from Sirmium and the arrival of 40,000 veteran troops from the Rhine sent by the Emperor's son Gratian.

Count Sebastian, the new 'Magister Peditum' (infantry commander), led the Imperial vanguard North to catch the main force of Goths camped outside Anchialus and blockade their camp. The arriving Western forces under Count Richomer arrived via Illyria in the Hebrus (Maritza) river valley and headed

East to join them but were a couple of weeks behind schedule; a contingent from the 'comitatus' at Mediolanum had however arrived (by sea to Thessalonica then marching north-east) to join Valentinian himself. Also arrived in July were a contingent from North Africa under the deceased Count Theodosius' son Theodosius, who won a high reputation by calmly fighting off an ambush by a large roving raiding-party of Goths on his troops in the hills south-east of the Sredna Gore range as he marched to join the Marcomannian/ Danube troops near Anchialus. Emboldened by Sebastian's blockade of the main Gothic force in Anchialus, Valentinian refused to wait for the remaining Western force under Richomer to join him or to listen to Fritigern's peace-envoys; he advanced on the Gothic fortified camp near the city and on 9 August 378 attacked with an army which he confidently assumed was much larger and better-armed. As a result the battle of Anchialus was a more 'close-run thing' than he expected and his arrogance was criticized by both the exasperated Trajan and by other former generals of Julian who had been used to that ruler's methodical planning. The superior and better-armoured Roman cavalry reached the Gothic baggage-train and started to pillage it but was cut off by a surprise arrival of more Goths from the Northern side of the camp whose presence had eluded Trajan's scouts so he had not told Valentinian to beware of reinforcements. Discipline held and the Romans rode back to safety with the main army, but the infantry had to hurry into defensive positions sooner than expected and drive back the imminent Gothic assault and if it had not been for their archers they would have been overwhelmed as the enemy vanguard was twice the size anticipated. Valentinian tried to launch a diversion round one wing to tackle the enemy from a new angle, but was cut off and as Trajan and the Imperial army's deputy commander Count Victor vainly tried to find the Batavian regiment to rescue him he disappeared in the melee. He either fell in the melee or collapsed with a seizure and was carried out of the fighting to a nearby farmhouse which the Goths surrounded and burnt down not knowing who was inside, but he was definitely killed, aged fifty-seven.

It was a Roman victory and the surviving Goths broke out of their blockade and fled back to the lower Danube, but with the Emperor missing and soon assumed to be dead the leading generals, who had lost perhaps a third of their army, were too dazed – and too scared of more Goths turning up and attacking them – to pursue them. The battle was declared as a 'victory' and fortunately the enemy leader Fritigern, a former Roman hostage in the 360s and not ill-disposed to the Empire but just angry with its arrogant and crooked officials, had lost at least half his army and also had a train of escaping and starving women and children from the wrecked camp to protect. Fearing a Roman cavalry attack, he quickly sent envoys to the Romans asking for peace and a safe passage back to the Danube to settle his people temporarily on the river-bank below Silistria and Trajan and Victor agreed and pretended that the Emperor was just wounded. They had to accept that the Empire had had a 'near miss' for a repeat of the disaster of 251 when Emperor Gordian and his top commander Decius had been killed by the Goths at Abrittus in the Dobrudja, and with Valentinian dead the latter could be blamed for poor 'command decisions' and sidelining competent generals out of jealousy. His son Gratian, aged nineteen and currently marching from the upper Rhine to join his father, was blameless and had the Western army behind him so when he arrived at the main camp a fortnight after the battle he was accepted and hailed as Emperor of the East and West. But his position was precarious and if any of the House of Constantine had been alive they would probably have been raised to the throne as co-emperor as the generals and troops alike were abusing Valentinian's memory and the late Emperor was not hailed as a hero as the equally brave but unfortunate Gordian III had been after being killed at Abrittus in 251. It was let out that he had been taken ill during the battle and had been trampled underfoot (which was one of the theories about what had actually happened). Needing to avoid a mutiny, Gratian had to accept this.

On 19 January 379 at Constantinople, Gratian raised the younger Theodosius (aged thirty-one), son of the late Count Theodosius and hugely popular with the troops but less of a threat to him than senior generals like Trajan, Victor, or even his own backer Richomer, to the Emperorship of the East.' Praetorian Praefect of Illyricum' Olybrius took charge of the transfer of generals and men from the West to reinforce the Eastern army, and a few weeks later Gratian returned to the Rhine. He was probably looking to a number of former senior civil officials of his father's regime who were close to Theodosius to cement their relationships and keep the latter tied to him as his client – e.g. Valentinian I's former 'quaestor' (chief legal official) in 377–8, Claudius Antonius, a Catholic Spanish cousin of the new Emperor who now moved to the East with him, and Theodosius' maternal uncle Flavius Eucherius, Valentinian's 'Count of the Sacred Largesses' (finance minister) in 377–8, who also moved East to become a senior courtier in 380 and was consul in 381.

Chapter 2

The House of Theodosius – and the Children of Valentinian

The surviving Goths, still over 40,000 strong in scattered groupings across Lower and Upper Moesia along with their non-combatants, needed to be defeated – and as the Roman army had lost considerable numbers of men in the battle the Romans needed to look at recruiting from those Gothic warriors who could be trusted to fight for the Empire long-term if they were paid enough and were given farms on retirement. This campaign to break up the retreating Goths into manageable groupings and force their commanders to surrender took the capable but locally inexperienced Theodosius most of 379. Luckily their main leader Fritigern, a Christian if disliked by the conventionally Catholic emperor as an Arian 'heretic', was both alarmed at rival 'kings' and bandit-leaders escaping his authority by waging war on the Empire successfully and the possibility of the Romans driving his people back into 'Sarmatia' north of the Danube to face massacre by the Huns so he soon opened talks and offered to become a Roman client in return for staying in the Empire.

Theodosius would not concede the latter to any sort of Gothic kingdom, but he did offer to let non-combatants stay on as farmers and to enrol repentant warriors in the Danube and Rhine armies as farmer-soldier 'limitanei' and to take on small groups of expert Gothic warriors as officers in the Guards. The Goths would have to be broken up as a coherent force and integrated into the Roman army, across the Empire. As he proceeded to round up or kill roaming groups of raiders across Moesia in 379 the bargaining-position of Fritigern weakened and some of his rivals entered the Roman army as officers in return for surrendering and swearing allegiance to the Emperor. Late in 379 Fritigern finally gave up and agreed a treaty whereby he would move back North of the Danube and rule his people on the river's far bank as a Roman client-king but Rome would loan him elite cavalry, archers, and artillery if he needed them to keep the Huns back and send troops East from the Carpathian passes to take the Huns in the rear. This ended the war that November, and was duly celebrated by a Triumph in Constantinople and flattering odes to the 'victor' by his Antiochene – and orthodox Christian – orator protégé, the senator Themistius. But in reality several score thousand Goths and their women and children now settled in the lower and middle Danube provinces along with those who had been admitted from the North of Dacia earlier. As the demographic make-up of the region became more German – many of the local rural settlers had fled from the Gothic war and settled in the southern Balkans as it was safer – the Empire had to tread carefully to ensure that the peace was kept with the locals and the Gothic soldiers and officers obeyed their Roman superiors.

Several thousand 'Romano-Gothic' officers now entered the Roman army in the 380s and 390s, especially in the East, and mostly did well and some entered the Guards regiments in the Palace in Constantinople or even civilian office. But they and other 'new men' Germans were looked down on by great nobles of Greek or Italian origin, though they had the support of Theodosius (provided that they were not only Christian but, if Arian, converted to Catholicism as his bishops insisted that he did this as his 'duty to God'). Theodosius, like Julian, believed that the crisis facing the Empire from the enemies massing to its north-east required him to take in capable soldiers from whatever source was available – but unlike Julian he believed in enforcing a religious 'test' to make sure that his own chosen religious grouping was not sidelined in future by a ruler or chief minister coming from another sect/ religion. The most notable of these Germans to progress fast and far in Imperial service (at a time when many snobbish young Italian nobles of ancient family looked down on the army as an 'uncouth' and uncivilized career and refused to join it, except occasionally the Guards regiments in the capitals) were to be Theodosius' half-Vandal general Stilicho and half- Gothic general Argobast. They were supposed to be the latest, 'alien' – and often Arian – equivalent of Julian's pagan 'new men', personal proteges of the Emperor and servants of his autocratic tendencies instead of the 'old order' of Senatorial power, by suspicious and resentful Constantinopolitan nobles. For that matter, the 'in' set of senior noble families and court 'service nobility' at Constantinople, centred on the Senate, looked down on the 'provincial Spaniard' Theodosius as the son of a creation of the pagan Julian, almost as bad as his German officers, and sneered at his trusted Spanish advisers – especially the religious fanatics among them like the ultra-Catholic Maternus Cynegius, his usual choice for investigating and closing pagan cults in the 380s. The latter was done on the grounds of 'immoral behaviour', eg drunken feasting and sexual excess, not on religious grounds to reassure pagan nobles at court – though the Emperor's real motives were doubted. All the elite in Constantinople were still treated with hostility as transplanted Westerners, brought into a Greek city by Constantine 'the Great', by many long-established noble families in the Greek and Greco-Aramaic Levantine provinces, and this probably added to the watchful and canny Theodosius' suspicious and autocratic approach to them.

Their literary men may also have exaggerated the officious and interfering habits of this 'autocrat' and his low-born officials out of snobbery, and their nobles were more than ready to use strategies to dodge paying their fair share of taxes even during military crises. Theodosius was keen to stamp this out and regularly had his legal rulings updated to abolish 'loopholes' and sent legal commissioners round the East to sniff out tax-dodges and prosecute offenders, to the latter's fury. Even the undoubtably corrupt and greedy early 390s 'strongman' Rufinus, another Spanish protege of the Emperor, had started off as a tax-dodge-investigating finance department lawyer and was loathed by the nobility and their literary allies on that count. Those ministers who were both tough on law-evasion and regarded well by the era's writers and poets, e.g. Tatian and his son Proculus, were rare, and when Theodosius tried to lure – Christian – scholars, poets and orators to his court from Syria and Egypt in the 380s to show that he was a learned man of culture like Julian few responded. Themistius the Antiochene poet, who provided the elegant and learned quotation-littered orations for the annual religious and secular ceremonies at Court, was a rarity at the new Court; most literary men sneered at the cultural milieu of Constantinople as full of imported Italian 'yes-men' courtiers who did not even speak good Greek. Nor did the young emperor Gratian in the West (ruled 378 – 383) escape criticism from the nobility despite his more amiable character and his court's reliance on local Gallic and Cisalpine Gallic nobles to staff many senior jobs and his elegant, well-connected aristocratic Aquitaine tutor Ausonius of Burdigala, given his fondness for hunting and carousing with a clique of younger officers including some Germans and Alans (360s veterans of Julian's army or their sons). He initially had a Constantinian link via his wife Constantia, daughter of Constantius II by his second wife, but she died young in 381 and he remarried to a rich heiress of Christian senatorial connections in Rome, Laeta, to cement his intended alliance with the minority of Catholic senators and to Pope Damasus against the pagan families who had backed Julian and who he now feared as potential plotters.

Religious policy was also a problem, with the new Emperor having strong ideals of his own – and despite his respect for traditional culture he had a distinct anti-pagan Catholic stance and was equally dubious of his predecessor's widow, Justina, still an important 'power-broker' in the West, as an Arian sympathiser. Theodosius had initially conciliated Julian's pagan advisers about policy changes, but in February 380 he showed his personal religious belief by issuing an edict restoring Nicene (i.e. 325 Church Council of Nicaea) doctrinal orthodoxy in the East at a Church Council in Constantinople. He declared it to be the sole legitimate Christian faith, as practiced by Pope Damasus and Bishop Peter of Alexandria. Patriarch Demophilus of Constantinople, who Julian had allowed to take the see in 364 to annoy the orthodox, was deposed as an Arian, and Theodosius summoned and installed the respected Cappadocian orthodox theologian Gregory of Nazianzus (an ally of the late monastic founder St.Basil of Caesarea, Julian's ex-fellow-student from Athens university) as his successor. Gregory's inauguration was booed by Arian crowds, so Theodosius expelled the Arian clergy from their churches in Constantinople and turned it into an orthodox stronghold. He had recently been baptized during an illness at Thessalonica by orthodox Bishop Acholius as he dealt with roaming bands of Gothic brigands up the Nestus valley, and he now condemned all Arians to banishment from the Eastern capital. Clearing them out of their churches in Asia Minor followed, and from 381 the Emperor made a cautious start to cutting subsidies to all pagan shrines and priesthoods across the East – on the excuse of financial retrenchment but clearly as a gesture of support to the Christians as he continued to fund new orthodox churches and monasteries.

There was also trouble in the Western Church in Spain in 380–1 over the ascetic and Gnostic 'Priscillianist' heresy, established by the layman Priscillian with some support in the local Church. Spain was an area of growing, enthusiastic, and multi-dimensional Christianity among all classes (as was neighbouring Gaul, despite Julian's attempt to make paganism more financially rewarding and career-aiding for the 'office-holding' classes and to revive the public's participation in the round of local pagan festivals) – as testified to by the notable 'gentlemanly' landed Christian poet, Aurelius Prudentius Clemens. Spain was featuring a growing number of local cults at their shrines of famous 'martyrs' of the Diocletianic persecutions. The nobility were by now mostly Christian by religion and genuine idealism, while remaining culturally 'gentlemen (and ladies) of leisure' in the tradition of the Augustan era – which they did not see as a paradox, unlike the puzzled and infuriated Julian had done. They were leading the way in paying for and commissioning new shrines, which were taking over as centres of local festivities through the year as the saints were taking over as 'protectors' of their local towns in the place of the old pre-Roman, imperfectly Romanised tribal 'Celtic' deities.

The evangelization of the Spanish locals was being co-ordinated on a regular basis by a series of enthusiastic, hard-working, and popular 'community leader' bishops, who were mostly of landed aristocratic or wealthy urban business family origins and so were used to command and had substantial resources plus private staffs. Almost without exception these bishops were known men of integrity and were not interested in obedience to the changing doctrinal whims of the State, as they did not seek secular office or approval. The (Catholic) bishops had been appreciated for this integrity by the public since the time of their opposition to the 'heretic' new emperor Constantius II in the 350s – a man who had purged his Catholic predecessor's supporters. The same dynamic, popular episcopate arose in Gaul, with the setting-up of regional shrines and conversion of the locals by such principled leaders as Bishops Martinus of Turones/ Martin of Tours, in the 360s to 380s; such towns became major Christian shrines and centres of local cults and festivals. Prominent local pre-Roman rural 'cultic' religious centres were also transformed into Christian churches, or were pulled down totally (as with the shrine of the 'Dea Sequana' at the source of the River Senona (OTL: Seine) – with no sign of local resistance despite Julian's enthusiasm for and gifts to these places only a decade or so before. Gaul and Spain became Catholic cultural strongpoints.

The great 'master of letters' and exemplars of leisured rural landed culture, Garonne valley poet Decimius Magnus Ausonius, was one of a number of Gallic aristocratic supporters of the 'Christian but 'anti-persecution' new emperor Valentinian who was invited to Court in 378 by the Emperor's orders sent to his wife Justina. He delivered an elegant oration of thanks for the accession of a Catholic ruler instead of a pagan, while praising Julian's patriotism and defeat of the ancient enemy Persia. He was appointed the emperor's heir/ co-ruler Gratian's tutor – and was nominal Praetorian Praefect of the Gallic provinces for a year in 378–9, though he left most of the work to his more administratively-minded son. Ausonius saw nothing 'unpatriotic' in being a committed Catholic despite the complaints of assorted sidelined pagan poet protégés of Julian who were now told to leave Rome, venerating the 'Fathers' of the Church and the principled heroism of the martyrs as he similarly venerated Horace and Vergil and the Emperor Augustus' establishment of peace. (This is all as in OTL.) Indeed, both Theodosius and a group of his leading advisers came from this landed but now Christian Western provincial milieu and brought its values as 'both patriotic Roman and doctrinally Catholic' to the courts and administration of Constantinople and later of Rome. Ausonius himself was more sceptical about the unpleasant compromises and betrayals of friendship that could come from too narrow a devotion to one's career, and was glad to retire from the Western court to his huge estates and vineyards on the Garonne after a few years of promoting his educational ideals to the young emperor Gratian in 382. Some of the most committed Catholic enthusiasts now occasionally joined the monastic movement, either providing recruits to local monasteries in Spain and Gaul (few and far between in the 380s, with St Martinus' near Turones the most famous) or journeying to Italy and even Palestine. One of the most notable of these was Ausonius landed friend (St) Paulinus, from Aquitaine but known as 'of Nola' (Campania) as he had been very impressed with the new cult of St Felix there while serving as under-governor of Campania and he later emigrated to Nola to found a long-lasting monastery.

Christian idealism among elites across the Western provinces could also lead to doctrinal 'questioning' and unorthodox conclusions by those who did not heed warnings by their bishops, and this was now the case with the 'Priscillianists' in Spain. Their prosecution became a 'warning shot' from the Church that it was not cowed into accepting a 'big tent' of varying religious views inside its establishment or even allowing such 'heretics' to worship in peace, despite the decade and a half of teasing and pointed remarks (and writings) against its 'betrayal of the principles of its founder' by Julian and his pagan allies. Nor did Gratian or his ministers intervene to help the accused. A local Church Council at Caesaragusta/ Saragossa excommunicated Priscillian, the dissident thinker and self-proclaimed 'bishop' of his 'flock', and his State Church episcopal supporters Instantius and Salvian in 380, but the latter retaliated by making Priscillian Bishop of Avila in his own diocese. This gave a non-Catholic proselytizer and writer a foothold in the Church, and was seized upon by the new 'bishop's enemies. The Spanish Catholic hierarchy, backed by Ausonius' friend Bishop Delphinius of Burdigala appealed to Gratian who ordered the 'heretic' and a list of his allies to keep out of churches and towns and denied their bishops any sees, requiring all who were reported to him for 'heresy' to sign decrees of orthodoxy backing up Theodosius' new Eastern doctrine as the 'only True Faith' or be sacked. A party of exiled clerics and their leader Priscillian, who had defiantly been holding 'illegal' services and tutorials in his doctrines, journeyed to Rome in 381 in a vain effort to secure the new Pope Siricius' support. (As in OTL.) The Emperor had passed on the rule of Italy, the central Danube region and North Africa in May 381 to the regency regime for his 10-year-old half-brother Valentinian II, led by the latter's mother Dowager Empress Justina – and as she was an Arian and was doing her best to set up new Arian churches and communities in Italy to keep her co-religionists 'in the running' as a coherent religious community the Spanish sect hoped for her support. Later at Mediolanum, where she had her court, 'Master of Offices' (chief of the civil administration) Macedonius recognised the Priscillianist bishops as fully legal in a snub to Gratian and Siricius, but at Siricius' request Gratian refused to let them have their sees back and he then ordered all lay Priscillianists to attend Catholic churches. (This was largely evaded).

In May 381 a new "Oecumenical/World Council" (i.e. of all the Empire, and meant to represent the West as well as the East) opened at Constantinople under the presidency of the orthodox Patriarch Miletius of Antioch, but no Roman Church representative turned up as Miletius would not defer to Siricius and let him preside as representative of the senior Apostle as was demanded. Miletius was backed up by Theodosius and the Roman Church ordered all its junior bishops not to attend which was duly obeyed, but soon after the Council opened

Miletius died. Patriarch Gregory of Constantinople proposed the restoration to Antioch of his rival Paulinus so that the latter, a friend of the Roman Church, would be acceptable as president of the Council to Siricius and he would let his Western bishops attend, but he was then verbally attacked too. He offered his resignation sooner than see a Church split as his enemies started to boycott the Council, and Theodosius accepted it. Miletius' ally Flavius was sent to Antioch and was duly accepted by the Pope as legal; Nectarius (not even baptized but an Imperial favourite and a leading bureaucratic advocate of restoring the Church's legal privileges in 378 so liked by orthodox bishops) was appointed at Constantinople. Gregory retired to Cappadocia and concentrated on writing and founding monasteries. Once the bishops were all assembled in the autumn the Council recommenced, and 'Nicene' Orthodoxy (i.e. the Catholic doctrine approved at the Council of Nicaea in 325) was re-defined and reasserted as the only correct religious doctrine. Constantinople was declared second in rank to Rome in the list of senior Patriarchates as the Imperial capital – not accepted by Siricius as the city's bishopric had only been created in the 350s. After this, all Arian clergy were expelled from all their churches in East, and a list was announced of all acceptable, orthodox bishops – i.e. those who had signed up to the decretals of this Council .

Gratian was determined to show that he was as orthodox as Theodosius, possibly at the instigation of Catholic advisers who had their own agenda in turning him against his stepmother Justina and under-age half-brother Valentinian II in the hope that he would evict them from the rule of Italy. He now ordered the removal of the iconic "Altar of Victory" in the Senate House at Rome in spring 382 on the grounds that it was a pagan cult-object and so was an insult to the Christian religion and was embarrassing Christian senators who resented the way that 'godless' senators sacrificed incense to it as to an 'idol'. This snub by him to the pro-pagan/ antiquarian measures of Julian, designed to win Church and Italian lay Catholic favour, led to a famous delegation to Gratian's court, which was at Mediolanum with his half-brother's that spring ahead of military manoeuvres on the upper Danube, by leading senators to seek a review and retraction of this. The pagan senators argued that it was an integral part of the apparatus of annual worship in Rome and had helped to bring luck and divine backing to the state for over 800 years and the moderate Christians argued that it was not an object of worship but a memorial of the 'Victory' (not a goddess but a concept) that Rome had had for many centuries and honouring it did no harm. The delegation was led by 381–2 Praefect of Rome Aurelius Symmachus, a leading pagan member of the old dynastic elite and upholder of Roman tradition who had kept up the lifestyle, pagan rituals, and cultural exclusivism of the later Republican nobility for most of his nearly fifty years and who was seen as the living embodiment of the virtues of people like Cicero and Horace. The centre of a huge network of family connections and descended from several lines of consuls, learned and idealistic Symmachus had been favoured by Julian and given honorary offices under him and had been honoured too as a reliable loyalist and a 'bridge' to the old Roman families by Valentinian I, but he had avoided taking on any senior governorships (despite offers by Julian). The ideal of cultured leisure and literary posings at dinner-parties, 'otium', had not been looked on favourably by either Constantine I or Valentinian though Julian had been more tolerant, and Symacchus' devotion to this lifestyle in principle and in practice probably helped the hard-line Catholics at Gratian's court, now joined by Bishop Ambrosius (Ambrose, later 'St') of Mediolanum, to get the senatorial appeal to keep the 'Altar of Victory' turned down. It was duly taken down in autumn 382 and Gratian declared as he headed back to Gaul that in future Rome would rely on Christ and His saints to grant victory not a 'lump of silver' to which people 'blasphemously' sacrificed. But his stepmother Justina, furious at his shutting down her proteges' Arian churches in

Italy and ordering her regency to obey his and the 381 Church Council's orders, was to make no move to help him as he faced rebellion in 383. This would help to bring the new dynasty down.

Chapter 3

Challenges to Theodosius in the West: Magnus Maximus and the Deaths of Gratian and Valentinian II

Gratian however had his own 'weak spot' – his lack of any military experience or reputation, which contrasted with that of Theodosius. In April 383 Magnus Maximus, the Spanish 'Count of Britain', i.e. supreme army commander in the island, and former subordinate to Theodosius' father in Britain in 369, revolted with the support of the local troops on Hadrian's Wall after the non-arrival of promised arrears of pay caused military dissent. There were rumours that Gratian, who had cancelled a planned visit to the island and was hunting in central Gaul, could not be bothered with the north-west of his empire and was planning to call away half its army to aid a grandiose expedition in Germany to annex the Rhine-Elbe region. The troops had little loyalty to him anyway as a remote and inexperienced young ruler; Maximus was over twenty years older, in his late forties, and had been a charismatic and capable commander in Britain. Maximus proclaimed himself Emperor, and seized Britain with little opposition as the fleet on the south coast 'Saxon Shore', based at Dubris (Dover) and Rutupiae (Richborough) defected – the latter were possibly not relishing the idea of a dangerous North Sea naval campaign to land troops on the Frisian islands and at the mouth of the Elbe which officers sent from Gratian's HQ at Trier were drawing up. Maximus crossed to the mouth of the Rhine and won over their garrisons and commanders, being seen as a far more experienced and reliable ruler than the vain, inexperienced young Emperor. He seized Trier as his capital. In June Gratian abandoned his planned 383 Alemannic campaign and set out from Moguntiacum (Mainz) for Gaul; he confronted Maximus near Lutetia (Paris) but the latter won over his cavalry after skirmishes and the Upper Rhine army demanded a move back to protect their own territory from a Maximan advance to Colonia Agrippinensis (Cologne).

Gratian refused so they deserted en masse and killed those officers who resisted. Gratian fled South with 200 cavalry, was caught up at Lugdunum by Maximus' general Andragaithus, and surrendered to be promised his life. But on 25 August 383 he was stabbed at a banquet by his captor, aged twenty-four, for an alleged plan to escape which was probably an excuse to be rid of him. Gratian's half-brother Valentinian II, aged twelve, and his mother and regent Justina resisted Maximus at Mediolanum and blocked the Alpine passes, and luckily for them Marcomannia and Rhaetia remained loyal. Theodosius did not reply to Maximus' envoys offering alliance or war. The end of Gratian did not elicit many regrets and he was written off both at the time and later as a minor and unimportant ruler, but he had managed the aftermath of the battle of Adrianople well and chosen a capable and strong colleague rather than just a 'safe' dependant as his co-ruler and arguably the successes of Theodosius in 'holding the line' against the German tribes in 379–405 were partly due to him. He was unlucky to face a more capable and charismatic challenger in Magnus Maximus in 383.

Maximus requested that Valentinian II join him at the Western administrative headquarters, Trier, 'like a son', and Justina sent her most respected though not personally compatible cleric Bishop Ambrose (a Catholic enemy of her own Arian 'heretic' proteges) to Trier in October to refuse. Justina's army blocked the Alpine passes before winter and Maximus accepted the continuance of a separate regime under Justina at Mediolanum as Theodosius made it clear that he would support the latter if necessary. Gratian's ex-tutor, the aristocratic Gallic poet and rhetorician Ausonius, retired from court at Trier to his estate in the Garonne valley as part of a general disdain by the Gallic nobility for the 'uncouth' and 'uneducated' military man Maximus, who was seen as relying too much on soldiers. Maximus brought more of his own British troops – led by the North Wales troops loyal to his wife Helena's local brother Conan, one of his senior officers – to settle in Armorica (OTL: Brittany) and man naval and 'watch'tower' positions against Channel German pirates but also to keep an eye on the Gallic elites for subversion. Maximus now announced his support for the orthodox Catholic Church in attacking the 'heretic' and non-Christian sect of Manichaeans – 'dualists' who believed in two supreme deities, one good and one evil – and established the principle that heresy was a civil crime too and must be prosecuted by the State. This was probably aimed as a criticism of Justina's pro-Arian policies in Italy and as a bid for official Church support. His devoutly Catholic British wife Helena, from a landed dynasty in a hilly area of southern Ordovicia (Powys, Wales), was useful to him in religious terms to reassure the network of Catholic bishops across the West as well as in adding to his local support in Britain, where had served as a successful anti-Irish piracy commander at Segontium (Caernarfon) in the 370s. The pioneering monastic leader in Gaul, the Pannonian Bishop (St) Martin of Turones (Tours), persuaded Maximus' henchman Count Avitianus to release assorted suspects rounded up as partisans of Gratian and loudly backed the new Emperor as a defender of orthodoxy; later Martin visited Maximus at his court at Trier to secure a promise of clemency for assorted arrested pro-Gratian officials and encourage him to support the orthodox Church against heretics. Martin allegedly received support from Maximus' wife Helena too. In 384 the Gallic Church Council of Burdigala (Bordeaux) condemned the Spanish 'heretic' Priscillianists and dismissed their bishop Instantius from a local see which he had acquired since Gratian's death; the Priscillianists appealed to Maximus who ordered a judicial investigation at Trier. This confirmed the deposition and ruled that none of their sect were fit to hold Church office as they violated the 381 Church Council decrees by not accepting the Christian doctrines which it had approved for all clergy to have to support. The Priscillianist leaders were forced to face a formal enquiry into their orthodoxy by a panel of State-backed clergy and lay (Christian) judges at Trier, and their enemies under the Lusitanian (SW Spain) Bishop Ithacius demanded their execution. Martin of Turones merely wanted them expelled from their churches and congregations so they had to worship in private as 'outcasts' and no killings, but despite Maximus' initial promise to that effect the ultra-orthodox zealots' demands for executions won. This was a blow to the Catholics' reputation across the Empire – for the first time Christians had resorted to killing 'unbelievers' like the pagan Diocletian had done. Admirers of Julian duly took note.

The trial proceeded with the new Western Emperor abandoning the 'heretics' to the Catholics to keep the latter loyal. Bishop Ithacius and his zealots accused Priscillian of encouraging an entourage of loose women, praying naked, and other moral crimes, and encouraged Maximus to order a round-up of all suspects in Spain who could be identified. The Emperor, who approved of moral holy men like Martin and other monastic leaders wearing sackcloth and fasting but disliked sexual laxity, agreed. Martin was reluctantly persuaded to accept communion with the triumphant persecuting orthodox clerics; the trial in Trier ended with the death-sentence for Priscillian, the poet Latronian, the Gallic hostess Euchrotia (daughter of a leading professor of rhetoric and head teacher of a school at Burdigala), and clerks Armenius and Felicissimus; Bishop Instantius was exiled to the Scilly Isles off the south-west coast of Britain, followed by the writer Tiberian. (As in OTL.) The trial caused disquiet in Roman noble circles as showing Maximus as no better than Gratian and as harshly devout so he would not return the 'Altar of Victory' if he deposed Valentinian II, but Theodosius was no better and in 385–6 the revival of Arian churches in Italy by Justina's orders while Theodosius was busy with an Eastern war (to reannex Hyrcania) led to anger from the Catholic community there.

Bishop Ambrose rallied the Catholic 'faithful' in a stand to back his refusal to hand over one of his Mediolanum/ Milan churches, the Basilica Portiana, to the local Arians for them to carry out their services. Reluctant Imperial Guards were forced by Justina to defend Arian churches in Mediolanum from angry mobs of rioting Catholics after she tried to have the Guards seize the disputed church from Ambrose and he and his congregation shut themselves inside, but her agreement to let the protesters stay in possession of the church was only temporary. She soon sent the rioters' alleged inspiration Bishop Ambrose into exile for stirring up the disturbances and had assorted rioters tried and sent to the slave-mines in Marcomania, and sought the backing of the most prominent but moderate Catholic – or even pagan – nobles in the Senate by a judicious redistribution of top posts in the Italian administrative hierarchy after the flight to Theodosius' court of leading multimillionaire Senate 'bigwig' and Praetorian Praefect of Italy Petronius Probus. But in autumn 386 she had to pardon all the rioters and recall Ambrose after Theodosius, who had spent much of the year in Syria closing down prominent pagan shrines on various legal excuses and had appointed a vigorously anti-pagan new Patriarch of Alexandria (Theophilus), arrived back in his capital and made it clear that any aid from him if Maximus invaded Italy would be dependant on full support for the Catholic Church there.

The triumphant Ambrose, treated as a hero by his congregation for defying Justina and determined to press his advantage, now used the completion of the building of a huge new cathedral for his see in Mediolanum, soon known as the 'Basilica Ambrosiana' in his honour and the site of his own shrine after he died in 397, to install the just-discovered relics of the local martyrs of the Diocletianic persecution, Ss. Gervasius and Protasius, at the cathedral with a massive public procession which passed the Palace. The cult soon acquired crowds of pilgrims to boost the Bishop's and the city's income, while he built up ties of mutual friendship and patronage with leading senators in Rome – including the great pagan 'man of culture' and multimillionaire Symmachus, self-promoting leader of the most important group of Italian landed nobles. Indeed the versatile Ambrose made a point of showing to Classically-educated and learned courtiers that he understood, could quote from, and was not hostile to the works of assorted Neoplatonist philosophers (whose works Julian had promoted) and that in his opinion they had shed valuable light on the mysteries of the nature of the Universe, with Plato as a 'pointer to the Truth' of Christianity. His hostility was more noted to the 'heretic' Arians than to useful pagan courtiers as long as the latter did not attack Christianity, though he encouraged those who were more flexible to convert. His friends at Court were to serve Ambrose well when in 388 the Catholic Theodosius took over power in Italy – and among the young and intellectually 'questing' overseas recruits to the learned courtier circles in Mediolanum in this period was the future Catholic leader (St) Augustine of

Hippo in Numidia, who arrived there in 384 as a junior teacher of rhetoric recommended to the court by his then patron Symmachus in Rome. (As in OTL.)

In August 387 Maximus suddenly invaded Italy by surprise over the poorly-defended Alpine passes into the Augusta Taurinorum (Turin) region and led a cavalry assault to take Mediolanum as the Imperial court there had to flee at a few hours' notice to escape him. Valentinian II and Justina fled via ship from Aquileia to the East and met Theodosius at Thessalonica to request aid; Theodosius agreed and as his wife Aelia Flacilla, another Spaniard, had died a few months earlier (leaving two sons, Arcadius, now ten, and Honorius, now three) married Justina's daughter Galla who was aged fourteen to his forty. The senior senator Symmachus took the Senate's greetings to Maximus at Mediolanum as the usurper assumed the consulship there (not recognized by Theodosius) and duly had some explaining to do to him later, Petronius Probus, head of the Anicii dynasty, and a more representative sample of the Senate leadership joined Theodosius in the Balkans and denounced Maximus to him. Theodosius gathered his army at Thessalonica in winter 387–8; Theodosius' elder son Arcadius, was left in nominal command at the capital but was 'run' by a small group of senior officials, led by a group of expatriate Spanish proteges of the Theodosian dynasty some of whom had once served on the elder Theodosius' staff in Britain and Mauretania.

In spring 388 Theodosius was on the march west, and he proceeded on to Sirmium and across Illyria to the Adriatic while some detachments took over Marcomannia in the name of Valentinian II as the region's new Maximan commanders, lacking local support, had to flee. Promotus commanded the cavalry, Timasius the infantry, and the veteran General Richomer the 'barbarians' (mostly Germans) as Theodosius advanced via Illyria, where Maximus' brother Marcellinus was defeated at Poetovio and pro-Valentinian Aemona (Ljubljana) was relieved from a siege, into the Julian Alps. In August Theodosius outmanoeuvred Maximus to cross a crucial river near Aquileia and cut off his retreat south-west to Mediolanum. Maximus retreated into Aquileia and was besieged, but his messengers sent west to summon troops from Gaul were intercepted and paraded in front of the walls by Theodosius to show that there would be no rescue. A week later, as the city surrendered he gave himself up and was taken to Theodosius' camp and executed, aged probably around fifty. His fleet was defeated off Sicily as it tried to intercept the Theodosian fleet bringing Valentinian II back to Italy, and the naval commander Andragaithus threw himself overboard as his ship surrendered to the Theodosian flagship; the Eastern troops then landed at Naples and marched on Rome as a second Theodosian naval contingent landed on the East coast at Ancona. The Eastern (German) General Argobast was sent to Trier to arrest and execute Maximus' eldest son Victor, a teenager, but Theodosius spared Maximus' other relatives who included his son (Constantine) and daughter (Severa) by his wife Helena. In early October 388 Theodosius entered Mediolanum; he resided at Mediolanum for the winter and encountered Bishop Ambrose and his staunchly Catholic supporters, whose firm Catholicism was congenial to him – and he agreed that the Arians in Italy must be given no second chance so he would take on the role of Emperor in Italy and protector of Catholics. He moved Valentinian II and Justina to Gaul where there was only a negligible Arian community.

The new administration's tone was of reassurance to pagans and moderate orthodox/ Catholics alike, though the Priscillianists and other deported 'heretics' were not pardoned. But the influence of the moral and poor-favouring Bishop Ambrose on Theodosius was dubious in terms of support for reconciliation given his loathing of the Arians and he was also notably anti-Semitic. Julian had favoured the Jews – partly to annoy the Christians – and allowed them back into Judaea and Jerusalem from which Hadrian had banned them after the revolt in the 130s. But now when a riot by a fanatical orthodox faction of Christians at Callinicum on the upper Euphrates in autumn 388 led to them burning down the local synagogue and building a church on the site and the Jews appealed to the Emperor, Bishop Ambrose interfered. The Emperor ordered the local authorities to pull the illegal church down and rebuild the synagogue and to tax the local Christians so they would have to pay for it, but as the latter sent a delegation to Ambrose he told the Emperor that God would not forgive him or give him any more victories if he abandoned His people and helped those who had killed His son. To add to the message he ordered the gates of the city cathedral to be shut to the Emperor and the entire court ahead of the next Christian feast-day, and with the city's orthodox crowds defending the building noisily from guardsmen who attempted to break in the Emperor's chief military adviser Timasius told him that he must put the public good and the Empire-wide Law above the interests of a seditious group of extreme Christians and a rabble-rousing bishop. The Emperor should protect all his citizens, not one religion – as Julian had written in his edicts.

Theodosius was, however, afraid that Ambrose would undermine him as he had undermined Justina and gave in, apologizing in private to Ambrose who reputedly made him kneel in the Palace private chapel and pray for forgiveness for an hour before he would absolve him like an ordinary 'sinner'. The Jewish community of Callinicum were told off by an Imperial commission for threatening more riots if they had not had their synagogue rebuilt and as a compromise had to move to another Euphrates town and join the local Jews' synagogue there. The equally violent and threatening behaviour of the Christian community of Callinicum was ignored in a piece of blatant bias and their church's demolition was ruled as illegal under a suddenly-discovered law of Constantine I (aimed at demolitions in the 300s persecutions of Christians) but that of the synagogue was ignored; the Emperor put appeasing the Christian militants first in the interests of 'public order'. The Orthodox in Egypt took note, and as Patriarch Theophilus was not allowed to send his hammer-wielding militants to smash up the local pagan shrines – and the Praefects used troops to protect the latter – he made do with demolishing synagogues instead.

(In OTL the Emperor backed up the violence committed by Patriarch Theophilus against the Egyptian pagans; in this version he is more cautious and the 'rule of law' is upheld better.)

In spring 389 Theodosius sent Valentinian II, now aged eighteen, to rule the Western provinces (Gaul, Spain, Britain) from Trier, assisted by Frankish 'Magister Peditum' Argobast. From 13 June to 30 August Theodosius was on his first State visit to Rome; he received a ceremonial reception and a panegyric delivered in the Senate House but did not restore the 'Altar of Victory' despite eloquent appeals; the most he would do was to agree to the erection of a statue of the Roman Republic's greatest 'saviour' hero Camillus trampling the invading Gauls underfoot on the site and allow it to be known as the 'Victory Monument'. As part of his reconciliation with the leading aristocrats, he appointed the leading pagan Roman noble Nicomachus Flavianus as 'Quaestor of the Sacred Palace' (i.e. his main legal minister), and later as Praetorian Praefect of Italy in 390–2.

Theodosius' powerful adviser Rufinus, a ruthless and corrupt but efficient fellow-Spaniard who was not liked at court for his constant intrigues against his rivals, made the most of his own Catholic stance to drum up support from the official Church and imply that his ministerial rivals, e.g. Tatian and Timasius, were pagan sympathisers. His main ultra-Catholic rival at court, the energetic anti-pagan militant Cynegius who was a roving Imperial commissioner in Asia Minor to shut down pagan temples and seize their assets on dubious grounds (usually immorality or financial malfeasance) in the late 380s, was not let loose on Syria as he wanted (He was in OTL). The Emperor was scared of a purge there leading to pagan veterans of Julian's army in the current 'comitatus' at Antioch or provincial garrisons mutinying, especially devotees of the Persian god Mithras. Instead in 390–1 he was used to shut down the temples of the 'immoral' Eastern mother-goddess Cybele and her fertility symbol 'consort' for alleged gross sexual license, their assets being given to local churches and monasteries which were now expanding rapidly. The cult's drink-fuelled public celebrations were denounced as orgies. In 392 Cynegius returned to the capital with his eyes on the Praetorian Praefecture after Theodosius unexpectedly sacked

Tatian and sent him off to a minor but supposedly honorary and invaluable job running an irrigation commission in upper Egypt. It was Rufinus who secured the Praefecture instead and soon Cynegius ended up being investigated for embezzling money which he had seized from the closed temples, and his execution early in 393 confirmed Rufinus' rise to power at the Eastern court though his semi-exiled foe Tatian's son Proculus and the invaluable Timasius both stayed in office, as trusted by the Emperor. The closure of all Imperially-funded schools for pagan priests and their replacement by schools for orthodox clergy in 392 did not herald the threatened purge of all temples across the East as was widely expected (it did in OTL). But some senior cults in Greece, e.g. the oracles of Apollo at Delphi, Didyma, and Delos, were shut down as 'superstition' in 393, and their assets (land in particular) were given to the local Church or to important Christian aristocrats who the Emperor was luring into taking up sub-governorships (and later senior governorships) across the Balkans through the 390s to create a loyal local 'base'. The temple buildings remained intact as monuments, with the civil governors afraid of rural locals rioting about 'bad luck to the crops' if they were demolished – to bishops' annoyance.

The Emperor and his closest, almost all Catholic allies in the administration and the clergy were now using a mixture of the alleged needs for financial cuts to pay for the enlarged army (still facing a long-range Hunnic threat north of the lower Danube) and the winning of God's favour by combating vice and immorality to excuse shutting down the most easily targetable pagan cults. In the East all those involving ceremonial prostitution – including Julian's favourite cult at Daphne, Antioch – and castration were shut in 392–3. But so far the main temples and rounds of annual ritual at Rome itself and in Greece and Egypt survived due to major backing by the local nobles who the Emperor was scared of alienating. But on 15 May 392 the current equilibrium in the West ended suddenly, a couple of months after the death of the chief Arian backer, Justina, who had been removed from the Western court at Trier for alleged plotting against Argobast by the latter's insistence and sent off to a remote villa in the Cevennes. Valentinian II was found dead at his current residence at Vienne in the Rhone valley during a tour of the region, aged twenty-one; it was probably suicide but rumours blamed Argobast who had had a row before the politically neutered Emperor left Trier and was probably in fear of being sacked in favour of an ally of the family of Valentinian I. Indeed, it was reliably said that Argobast had recently refused with contempt to carry out a list of military office transfers given to him by his Emperor and told him that he took his military orders from Theodosius not him, and that Valentinian had attacked him with a sword and been disarmed; certainly the frustrated Emperor had written several times to Theodosius asking for help to rein in his overweening chief minister and had been ignored. Nor was the high-spending, racing-addicted Valentinian, who was slow to bother with official business, much respected by his ministers or bureaucrats though the public of Trier loved his extravagant spectacles. Argobast had the same high military reputation as Julian and the same impeccably Christian background as Valentinian and had many local military proteges who would back him. But as a German he would be unacceptable as Emperor to the nobility and his main backer at the Eastern imperial military HQ, the Frankish general Bauto, had recently died and assorted ethnically fully Roman generals disliked him as too brash and pushy for a 'barbarian'.

Argobast avoided seizing the throne though the dynasty of Valentinian I was now reduced to his daughter by Justina, Theodosius' teenage bride Galla. He offered to accept a new Western 'Augustus' named by Theodosius provided that he was kept on as commander-in-chief, though the contents of his envoys' offer to Theodosius at Constantinople in early July were never revealed. Keen to avoid war with a formidable general and the Rhine armies as although the main Eastern army had by now regained Hyrcania this had led to a war with raiding Turkish/ Hunnic tribal nomads from the distant Kara Kum deserts in Central Asia, Theodosius decided that his reputation would suffer and a revolt might follow if he ordered his army to invade Italy not save Julian's legacy of a secure frontier in the Caspian region. Argobast was not trusted, but he was told to announce that the Eastern Emperor's younger son Honorius (born 384) was the new nominal ruler of the West and on 18 October he did so, averting a dangerous 'East vs West' war.

(In OTL he was ignored by Theodosius and on 22 August 392 he proclaimed his chief secretary Eugenius as Emperor. Civil war followed and this led to a major battle between Theodosius and Argobast in the Istrian region of north-east Italy in late 394; Theodosius won and reunited the Empire. But the way that Argobast had gained pagan help in Rome by restoring the old pagan ceremonies there led to Theodosius having an excuse to shut down the pagan shrines and seizing their assets. This OTL crisis does not happen in this version of events.)

Theodosius waited until his armies in the East had regained full control of Hyrcania and driven the nomads out in 393–4, and then in summer 394 sent his best general Stilicho, married to his niece Serena, to Italy to escort the boy emperor Honorius to Mediolanum and meet Argobast. The latter was promised the continuing command as 'Master of Soldiers/ Magister Peditum', with Stilicho commanding the cavalry – but in the event Stilicho secretly delivered orders to the unaware Western commander's staff at a reception to accept himself as the full commander of both horse and foot in return for a large pay-rise and some promotions. The presence of a large army of veteran Eastern troops with Stilicho induced them to agree, and Argobast was arrested and executed for supposedly 'planning to murder Stilicho' (it is unclear if this was genuine or not) and was later accused of killing Valentinian II. The relieved Theodosius and his triumphant panegyrist Claudian, an earnest if somewhat sycophantic young Roman (Christian) noble poet who had accompanied a reassuring Roman Senatorial embassy to Constantinople in 393 and joined the Imperial court regarded the execution of Argobast as God's reply to the treacherous 'murder' of Valentinian II, but as the Senate stood by Theodosius he could hardly purge it of pagans or ban all pagan cults in Rome as Bishop Ambrose urged and the subsequent purge of winter 394–5 was centred at Trier instead and in the weakened Rhine army.

Chapter 4

Reunification

(In OTL Theodosius died in January 395 and the Empire split permanently between East and West, the two regimes often at odds – giving the Goths a chance to play one off against the other. Disaster followed.)

Stilicho, the Emperor's best commander and married to Theodosius' niece Serena, was now appointed "Master of Both Services" (infantry and cavalry) in the West as the first overall military supremo there, and in 395 he restructured the Rhine army and brought in a large number of Eastern soldiers. The Gothic regiments led by rising Visigothic military 'strongman' Alaric which had been recruited in 393 from the Gothic lands in Sarmatia/ Wallachia to help with Stilicho's march West (an easier option for the East than recalling larger numbers of regular troops from the rebuilding of coastal Hyrcania's anti-nomad 'limes'/ wall-and-ditch barrier) were split up into smaller groupings and dispersed around the Rhine armies. This annoyed Alaric who had been told that they were only needed for one campaign and would then be free to go home to the Danube, as he had been intending to use them to overthrow his superior, current king Altigern. He refused to accept an offer of a Countship in charge of part of the western Carpathian frontier, in a remote forested area of south-west Marcomannia (OTL: Bohemia), correctly judging that it was intended to 'dump' him in a far-flung corner of the Western Empire far from his tribal commander relatives and other allies back in Sarmatia. He returned home in disguise as a humble trader to stir up anti-Roman feeling, alleging that the Emperor had deliberately instructed Stilicho to send some of the most independent-minded Gothic officers to remote areas of the frontier to get rid of them and had let others be killed in recent skirmishes with pro-Argobast Rhine German frontier mutineers. The Emperor was too busy securing the West and remodelling its military command and high-ranking civilian office-holding to bother with the Sarmatian Goths who were mostly Arian anyway and he was annoyed with Altigern for refusing to convert to Catholicism. This inattention probably made it easier for Alaric to stir up trouble and in 397 to have the king assassinated and take his place. Rome was landed with a new threat – but this took time to mature as many top Gothic officers had been lured away from their post-378 tribal lands North of the lower Danube to pursue careers in the Roman army and Alaric had to build a new military 'machine' based on alliance with (and eventual assimilation of) other tribes living east of the Carpathians who had fled from the Huns' attacks on the Don and Dnieper steppes in the mid-370s.

(In OTL Theodosius' death in 395 and the division of the Empire under his two weak sons led to Alaric invading the East and ravaging Thrace and Greece, stirring up anger against Rome for deliberately exposing Gothic recruits to enemy attack as 'cannon fodder' in the 394 civil war.)

Theodosius and Bishop Ambrose celebrated the belated inauguration ceremony of Honorius as co-ruler of the West in April 395 with a service at Mediolanum's cathedral and all non-Catholic bishops appointed by Justina and Valentinian II were sacked as 'heretics'. Theodosius then proceeded to Rome to thank the Senate for backing him as lawful Emperor when Valentinian II died and admitting his new appointees as Praefect of Rome and Praetorian Praefect of Italy plus a detachment of Eastern guards-regiment troops in autumn 392. The ostentatiously pagan Nicomachus Flavianus, an admirer of Julian and too rich and well-connected to be sacked at once, was made Praefect of the ancient capital in 395–8 as a valuable ally and was not punished for his provocative holding of public celebrations of the pagan festivals of Cybele (loathed by the Church) during the hiatus in power in 392. But the sternly Catholic Emperor had not forgotten that, and once enough orthodox Eastern noble ministers had been put in the middle ranks of the administrations in Mediolanum and Rome to neutralize Flavianus' pagan allies the proud aristocrat was 'retired' and was sent off on an honorary but time-consuming Imperial commission to overhaul the creaky legal system in Gaul. Other leading pagans also found themselves 'invited' to work in important but distant provincial posts in the late 390s and the Emperor flooded the Senate with new, Catholic 'service nobility' bureaucrats from Mediolanum plus a sprinkling from Constantinople. The new Praetorian Praefect of Italy was one of his Spanish Catholic 'expatriate' allies who had been serving at his court through the 380s, Nummius Aemilianus Dexter, son of the late Bishop Pacianus of Barcelona. The intention was now for the Theodosian dynasty to rule all the Empire – and to promote Catholicism – with Arcadius as heir to the East, with Rufinus as chief minister there, and Honorius as deputy to his father in the West with Stilicho as his military supremo and the recalled Tatian as 'Master of Offices' from 396. Theodosius would reside at Mediolanum for as long as necessary to secure the war-weakened Western frontiers, and his Empress Galla would align the partisans of the House of Valentinian to him. Their daughter Galla Placidia (born 389) would duly be married off to some great Christian noble to enable the latter to support his brother-in-law Honorius, who it was clear by the late 390s was not too intelligent, lacked dynamism or initiative, and could not be trusted to rule alone. Galla was to inherit her grandfather Valentinian I's abilities; as with Arcadius' close kin, the dynasty's women were often more able.

Theodosius now concentrated on the frontiers of the West and in 396–7 led two major campaigns across the middle and lower Rhine to drive back the Franks and Alemanni, reduce them to the same state of vassalage as Julian had done in 357–9, and made them hand over both tribute and a levy of soldiers to the depleted Roman army there. The local Roman tree-felling and mining contractors east of the river had either fled or been killed in an upsurge of anti-Roman aggression in 392 so this part of 'Romanization' was now under threat and the Emperor had to offer large incentives and military protection to get anyone to venture East of the Rhine again for a decade. But behind the Franks and Alemanni, whose leaders were now forced to become Catholics in impressive mass-baptisms at the Imperial camps with the Emperor as their godfather, the restive and land-hungry Vandals and Suevi were lurking well away from the Roman frontier in Thuringia and the Frankish and Alemannic 'kings' were as wary of them as they were of Theodosius. When the local war was over in autumn 397 Theodosius set up a chain of Roman frontier forts on the Elbe, garrisoned by crack troops plus local mercenaries, and organized a system of regular supply to them from the Rhine along the Julianic regional roads plus naval support up the Elbe from the 'Classis Britannia' fleet in the Channel which was doubled in size. The Romans, Franks and Alemanni now co-operated to keep the Vandals and their allies back beyond the Elbe and more Eastern troops were moved into Marcomannia – which the Emperor then toured in 398 – to help launch raids on the hostile tribes to their north and force them to help Rome against the Vandals too.

There was also trouble with the Irish raiding western Britain again in the mid-late 390s due to local troops being sent off to the Rhine and in 398–9 Stilicho campaigned there to repel raiders, build new coastal forts, and even lead the Hibernian Sea fleet to raid Leinster in 399. New clashes with the Picts around the Cluta (Clyde) valley and in 'Gododdin' (the local name for the Rome-allied kingdom of the Votadini in Lothian) led to other Roman forces backing the regional vassal-states in repelling invaders in 398. After Stilicho followed up his summer 399 raids on Leinster with a naval descent on Argyll, the Irish-settled 'Coast of the Gael' north of the Cluta estuary, to help the local Brittonic/ Pictish tribes drive the incomers back and impose vassalage on them the poet Claudian boasted that Stilicho had led his fleet as far as 'Ultimate Thule' and bested the famous conqueror of the Caledonians in AD

79–85, Agricola. Certainly the campaigns restored a degree of peace to the north and west of Britain although 'hit and run' raids continued and famously in the early 400s the future, British evangeliser of the Irish, Patricius (St Patrick), was carried off from Siluria (Gwent) by raiders to be a slave in Leinster and spent a decade as a slave shepherd until he stowed away on a ship back to Britain.

(In OTL a more modified version of this British campaign was carried out for or by Stilicho as regent of the West.)

By 400 Theodosius had restored stability to the West's frontiers from the Hibernian Sea to Marcomannia and in that year he finally returned to Constantinople to join his son Arcadius. But by this date his elder as well as his younger son had shown himself to be a poor ruler and a worry for the future and in addition Rufinus, capable as a chief minister but greedy of power and money and hugely unpopular, had been brought down by his feuding with rivals at the Eastern court – which Arcadius, weak and easily suggestible, had failed to stop. The over-confident Rufinus assumed that with Arcadius too feeble to argue with him and Theodosius giving him his full confidence he was invulnerable and during 395–7 assorted ministerial rivals of his were dismissed on his reports to the senior Emperor about their alleged peculation or plots and some were arrested and tortured into confessions by his military police allies. But after he finally rid himself of Promotus by dint of getting some of his servants forced to confess to an alleged plot to kill him and Theodosius exiled that worthy minister to a Palestinian monastery as a forcibly tonsured monk other ministers got together. 'Count of the Sacred Largesses' Leo, afraid that Rufinus' Spanish ally the 'Count of the Privy Purse' Sabellius was after his job and its perks, employed old friends in the military from his time in the 'Protectores' to spread rumours of Rufinus embezzling money due to fallen officers' and soldiers' families and due to a new military hospital in the capital that was taking a long time to build.

At a parade held at Hebdoman military base west of Constantinople to celebrate the end of a successful campaign by the rising Gothic general Gainas, a self-made ex-farmer from Moesia turned officer and now 'dux' of Pontus, to defeat a Hunnic raid across the eastern Caucasus in November 397, Rufinus, turned up to take the salute and shower gold on the soldiers. He was booed and shouted at with questions about the missing money. For once the urbane master of intrigue and flattery lost his head and tried to argue with the rioters and then offer them money rather than withdrawing in a hurry and publishing the relevant accounts (which Leo had probably altered as the Emperor would have been merciless if Rufinus had really been cheating the soldiers). Rufinus ended up lynched with his head paraded around the base on a spear, and as his officers did not exactly hurry to try to rescue him they were probably in the plot. (In OTL Gainas and his allies did kill Rufinus in a similar manner, but back in 395 – probably at Stilicho's instigation. This was, however, in different circumstances, i.e. an invasion of the southern Balkans by the Goths who now went on to ravage Greece. This attack does not happen in my version of events.)

The ambitious Gainas, who had co-ordinated the killing and was rumoured to have cleared it with Stilicho beforehand so his old friend could talk the senior Emperor out of any retaliation, had to be promoted to a senior rank as he demanded. Theodosius was persuaded by Stilicho that Gainas was loyal and trustworthy and he feared to quibble lest this cause rebellion, but Stilicho's enemies duly claimed that the half-German general had assisted his fellow 'barbarian' in conning the Emperor out of a devious desire to surround Theodosius – and when the latter died, his sons – with greedy and power-hungry Germans. Gainas ended up as 'Magister Peditum' (Master of the Infantry) in 399 after he had defeated a Hunnic attack, this time south-east along the Euxine (Black Sea) coast into Pontus – an invasion that saw the Roman ally state of Iberia (OTL: Georgia) looted and wrecked so it had to be restored by Roman troops and a new client-king found. However, the promotion of yet another German officer, though resented by passed-over Roman officers and leading to Gainas' suspicious death in a street 'hit' in Constantinople in early 400 just after he had assumed the Eastern consulship did at least mean that Rufinus' allies at Court could be purged with the help of a ruthless and bribe-proof youngish 'man on the make'. An alliance between Gainas, the civilian supremo 'Master of Offices' from 397 Aurelian (consul in 399), and the latter's brother Caesarius (Praetorian Praefect of the East in 399–404 and consul in 400) kept the personal influence of the devious eunuch chamberlain Eutropius, a cunning and intrigue-loving Palace flunkey, in check until Theodosius returned to the East later in 400.

Eutropius, talented but crooked, was respected by the easily-influenced Arcadius and ran parties and private gambling-sessions for him to relax away from the round of church services, sermons, and attending to business which Theodosius had enforced on his unwilling son. He also acquired a stencil of the Imperial signature and 'helped' his master by signing documents for him, many of which involved grants of land and jewellery to himself. But at least Eutropius did not bother much with determining policy as long as he made money, though he also sponsored new churches to keep the court clerics backing him as a source of funds, so Aurelian and Caesarius effectively ran the Eastern Empire after early 397. Gainas, a prickly but brilliant German who was an 'outsider' to the palace circles and hated Eutropius, was the leading general in 397–400, and after he was assassinated (a crime that was never solved but may have been linked to anti-Stilicho courtiers) the new 'Magister Peditum', Timasius' protégé the Greek military engineer Callimachus of Miletus, took over. The early 400s saw the construction of a series of ditches and earthen banks on the lower Danube and in the marshy Dobrudja to hinder the threat of fast 'barbarian' raids on the region, and the building of new walls around the main river-bank towns – a 'double wall' for many of them, so preventing the fall of one wall to ladder-climbing infiltrators causing disaster, in a new architectural scheme drawn up by Callimachus which was later adapted for use in Constantinople after 404 to replace the single 'Constantinian' wall there.

The mixture of Roman defences in the passes and impenetrable forests and high mountains in the Carpathians kept the Huns out of Dacia and they had to cross Alaric the Goth's kingdom in 'Sarmatia' and defeat him to get to the Roman lower Danube, though they managed that successively in 398, 399 and 400. Following the latter year's attack Theodosius arrived on the lower Danube from Dacia to extend the river-bank fortifications and vainly chase a plunder-laden Hunnic cavalry force back across Sarmatia to the Dniester. He then went on to Constantinople for the winter of 400–01 and restored a degree of honesty to the financial proceedings of the extravagant Arcadian court there after having Eutropius arrested and deported to a Syrian monastery and his wealth confiscated. But despite his anger at Arcadius' incompetence and lack of judgment he did not deport him as well despite threats to move him to the West and choose a new deputy in the East, possibly due to Aurelian, Caesarius, and Arcadius' strong-willed Frankish wife Eudoxia (daughter of his late general Count Bauto) persuading him that they could manage Arcadius as their puppet. In June 401 Theodosius went on to Syria, and in line with his continuing religious obsession spent most of his efforts on closing down pagan shrines and redistributing their assets to local monasteries, founding more of the latter, interviewing and appointing new orthodox bishops, and rallying the people to the Church by staging public processions to the local saints and founding schools and hospitals staffed by churchmen. He also visited Armenia to crown the new and devoutly orthodox king Arsaces IV and ignored all military encouragement from the senior staff at Antioch to use the youth of the new Persian 'Great King' Yazdagerd, the latest ruler to be installed at Istakr, to annex his lands and extend Roman power as far as the Oxus. But he gave the orthodox Church in Mesopotamia a major boost in assets and energetic clergy and even despatched a missionary bishop with a trading-mission to the Gupta dynastic kingdom in northern India, rulers of the Ganges plains, with gifts in the hope of 'emulating St Thomas'.

A winter residing and building a new imperial Eastern palace and adjacent cathedral at the 'Blessed City of Edessa, where Christ had allegedly sent a letter to its C1st AD Hellenistic king, was followed by Theodosius' emotional pilgrimage to and showering of gifts on Jerusalem and Bethlehem. To him, as to his models Constantine 'the Great' and his mother (St) Helena, the 'Holy Places' were to be as central to the new Imperial religion as the great pagan shrines of Greece had been to the pagans – and like Julian he recognized the importance of creating a viable and enthusiastic 'tourist trade' at these places to provide revenue and encouraging the participants to regard the relevant religion as the centre of their lives. But his plans to go to Egypt and help Patriarch Theophilus to root out the pagan cults there had to be postponed due to an illness at Caesarea after his visit to the Holy City in June 402. In August, with his health precarious and Stilicho having had to fend off the largest German invasion since the early 390s that spring – a Vandal attack on Marcomannia combined with a major multiethnic raid on Rhaetia – he headed straight back to the West. Stilicho had allowed the Vandals – some of their nobles his own kin – to escape a blockade in the forests near the Vlatava river in N Marcomannia, and though his troops had been tired and demanding rest at the time and the invaders had had local guides to help evade him rumour had it that he had let them escape deliberately out of inter-German ethnic solidarity. (In OTL Stilicio was suspected in a similar manner of letting the blockaded Goths escape when he surrounded them in Epirus/ Albania in 397.) But Stilicho's subsequent crushing of the raiders in Rhaetia in a 'set-piece' clash near Augsburg had done something to restore his reputation amidst the anti-German nobility at court and in Rome, and the Emperor let him stage a very rare non-Imperial triumph and Games in Rome in September. Theodosius and Honorius, the latter married since 399 to Stilicho's daughter Maria, attended the Games and so saw a pacifist monk called Telemachus disrupt the gladiatorial combats of captured Germans and hired Roman slaves there (Julian had restored the gladiatorial matches banned by Constantine on special occasions in 366 as part of the Empire's heritage). Though the monk was stoned to death by the crowds for spoiling their fun they subsequently repented and joined the Church – now led since 401 in Rome by the holy Pope Innocent, son of his 397–401 predecessor Anastasius – in hailing him as a martyr. Theodosius duly abandoned gladiatorial combat for good as immoral and displeasing to God.

(The incident at the Games did probably happen – but in OTL it was during the celebrations for regent Stilicho's defeat of the invading Goths.)

In the East, 397 had seen the death of Patriarch Nectarius of Constantinople. Patriarch Theophilus of Alexandria put forward as his candidate Isidore, but Eutropius persuaded Theophilus to back off by threatening to tell the Emperor of his illegal dealings in hiring Alexandrian criminals and thugs as 'Church hospital attendants' on his payroll and sending them round to smash up pagan shrines in the city. (In OTL, Theophilus seems to have got away with this tactic for years.) Eutropius secured the election of a dynamic Antiochene priest, the zealous ascetic ex-hermit John "Chrysostom" (Golden Mouth), who was famous for his sermons against excessive wealth, greed, and corruption and had many followers there even among impressionable rich women who doted on him and gave him large sums of money for his charitable projects. He had the same effect on rich women in Constantinople and was soon making a lot of money for the city's charitable foundations by thundering about how the rich needed to save themselves by giving up their money before they were sent to Hell. But despite the support of the impressed Empress Eudoxia criticism soon grew of John, especially over his imperious attitude to women and demands that they gave up their expensive dresses, jewellery, and perfumes and dress simply, pray, and fast, which alienated several of Empress Eudoxia's closest friends. But on 10 April 401 the birth of Arcadius and Eudoxia's son Theodosius (II) cemented the security of the dynasty, and Theodosius I also attended the baptism at Hagia Sophia with grand ceremonial. He then went off to Syria after approving Patriarch John as holy and devoted to the poor, but his daughter-in-law began to tire of the Patriarch that summer as he would not let any of her German kin and friends who were Arian use any of his Church's facilities.

John soon left the capital on Church business so a showdown was postponed, and he then toured Western Anatolia where he dismissed thirteen bishops for irregularities in their finances or personal conduct – a degree of centralization that the locals were not used to and which led to resentment at this unprecedented interference from Constantinople. The victims added to the ranks of John's many critics within the 'lax' Church elite. The charismatic Patriarch however retained the support of the senior (but absent) Emperor Theodosius for his holiness and strictness and Arcadius was too scared to stand up to his father and sack John, so the latter's foes now concentrated on obtaining evidence of his being a 'heretic' to put Theodosius off him. They called in Patriarch Theophilus of Alexandria, who was angry that the senior Emperor had not come to Egypt as promised and blamed John for advising him. Shortly after Theodosius had left Palestine for Italy in 402 Theophilus held a synod to condemn the heretical views of the great third-century theologian Origen (d 264) and his local Egyptian admirers, particularly his speculations on the relationship between the parts of the Holy Trinity where he had considered the Holy Spirit to be the mediator between the Father (God) and the World and thus by implication a distinct 'being' – i.e. a 'heresy' foreshadowing Arianism? The many musings of Origen on the exact definition of various spiritual aspects of the Godhead and the relationship between the parts of the Trinity, influenced by his deep knowledge of Ancient Greek philosophy, and his extensive use of allegory in his Biblical studies (which by definition only the skilled could understand) had been accepted as orthodox by his own era's theologians and at the Council of Nicaea in 325. Strict and watchful (St) Athanasius of Alexandria, educated like Origen by Egyptian Biblical scholars in Alexandria, had not objected either. Origen had claimed that behind the 'surface' meaning of much of Scripture lay not only a 'moral' meaning, for the 'committed' and skilled devout Christian to discover, but an even deeper spiritual – mystic – meaning that extra skills or depth of spiritual knowledge were needed to decipher. This had appealed to monastic enthusiasts since the foundation of monasticism and 'desert' asceticism soon after 300, but it seemed to some to reek of creating a 'special' group of the spiritually privileged who were skilled in theology and spiritual exercises, not just devout believers – a form of Gnosticism. Ironically, the written work by Origen which was now arousing most questions was his own attack on the 'Gnostics' – 'On First Principles'.

The attack on Origen was spearheaded in the 390s by the zealous Bishop Epiphanius of Salamis in Cyprus. Crucially he was able to use some existing doubts about Origen's orthodoxy held by the era's most eminent learned Italian expatriate Biblical translator in Palestine, (St) Hieronymus/Jerome. This rigidly 'mainstream' Catholic thinker, from the mid-380s settled in a monastery in Bethlehem founded by his super-rich fellow-émigré the devout 'Lady' Paula, had been compiling inspiring biographies of Christian exemplars from the past three centuries, as well as starting his main work – a painstakingly accurate Latin translation of the Bible, later known as the 'Vulgate'. This was to be adopted as 'the' correct version of the Bible in Latin by the Western Church in the 420s-440s and was to make him a crucial figure in the Christian world for over a thousand years. But despite his many admirers in Western lay and ecclesiastical Christian circles – and the multiplication of copies of his works by teams of writers, partly paid for by the approving Emperor – his theological opinions on correct interpretation of the Bible were not yet seen as 'definitive'. His decision to tackle Origen and his admirers and to throw his weight behind Epiphanius was a major success for what had until that point (393) been seen as a 'minority' obsession by a few thinkers. He cast doubt on John's own theological competence and credibility.

While both sides sought support from the Pope in Rome – Jerome won – and assorted aristocratic and Court lay enthusiasts for Christianity, Jerome secured backing from Patriarch Theophilus of Alexandria who was all too pleased to be able to stand as the champion of orthodoxy and boost the prestige of the 'See of St. Mark' against that of Jerusalem, the original home of Christianity. In his assault on 'Origenist' enthusiasts in Egypt which also extended his see's close supervision of semi-autonomous desert and Upper Nile valley monasteries, Theophilus concentrated on the desert monks at Nitria oasis and their leaders the four "Tall Brothers". He evicted them from their collection of small but well-endowed monasteries at the oasis and installed his own orthodox monks there, and then when they settled in Palestine demanded their expulsion by the local bishops. Later in 402 Patriarch John at the Eastern capital received the 'Nitrian' leaders with honour in Constantinople after they were sent packing by a Palestinian synod at the behest of Theophilus, and lodged them at the Church of St Anastasia. Their piety impressed Eudoxia, who persuaded Arcadius to summon a synod to investigate their complaints against Theophilus for persecuting them; Theophilus was summoned to answer. In reply Bishop Epiphanius of Cyprus, Theophilus' close orthodox ally, held a synod to condemn Origen's writings, and Theophilus asked him to go to Constantinople on his behalf. In spring 403 Patriarch Theophilus excommunicated the 'Nitrian' leaders and censured John for supporting him, and sent written 'proof' of John supporting condemned heretics to Emperor Theodosius who was duly appalled and asked Pope Innocent for advice. Innocent backed Theophilus, and the Emperor duly stood aside from supporting John for once.

Epiphanius went to Constantinople at Theophilus' instigation, insisted that John censure the 'Nitrians' publicly or face an enquiry, and boycotted the cathedral of Hagia Sophia until they were evicted from the city. But John insisted that only a 'General Council' could rule on Origen's works being heretical or not; Epiphanius left after failing to persuade him to back Theophilus and died exhausted on the voyage home. Eudoxia, angry at this and at John's recent sermon against women for wearing 'decadent' apparel and make-up and wasting money on frivolity, supported Theophilus as he arrived in the capital in July 403 with his supporters. A synod of clerics called by Arcadius (at Eudoxia's instigation) to examine the charges against John met at 'The Oak', the late minister Rufinus' old palace near Chalcedon, and the Egyptian bishops and the accused Patriarch's archdeacon John led accusations against the Patriarch including gluttony, arrogance, abuse of power, intrigues, and corruption. He refused to attend or to accept verdict of any trial not carried out by a 'General Council', and was deposed in his absence; Arcadius announced his banishment.

The populace gathered at Hagia Sophia to protect John, who refused to leave and held out for three days, preaching a sermons calling Eudoxia 'Jezebel'. To avoid bloodshed he left at night and was deported to Praenetus in Bithynia. But a few days later, as the populace demanded John's return in large demonstrations, an earthquake terrified Eudoxia. She sent a plea to him to return and he did so.

Preparations for a 'General Council' of Eastern bishops were now made at John's request, but Theophilus had already returned home and he claimed that the

Council would not be a fair investigation as the crowds would terrify the bishops into backing John; he and the Egyptian Church would only accept it if it was moved out of the capital. The Church of Antioch backed John, but Jerusalem backed Theophilus and so did the Pope. In November 403 John miscalculated by making protests at the 'pagan' ceremonies, music, and dancing to inaugurate a new statue of Eudoxia in the Augusteum square during his service in the adjoining Hagia Sophia. Eudoxia took it as an affront, and he made matters worse by calling her "Herodias" demanding 'John's' head in a sermon – implying that he was like John 'the Baptist' and she was like the infamous pagan first-century Herodian princess Herodias. Emperor Theodosius backed her reaction.

The 'Council of the Church in the East' met early in 404. The meeting did agree to remove John on the grounds of his illegal political activity and encouraging law-breaking by his rioting followers. Arcadius deposed John, but on Good Friday, 15 April 404, forty bishops addressed Arcadius and Eudoxia urging John's temporary restoration for the Easter baptism of catechumens (new members of the Church) in case the disappointed crowds rioted. He relented, but insisted that John should not enter Hagia Sophia at Easter himself in case he stirred up disorder. At night soldiers evicted the huge crowds gathering at the Cathedral for the baptisms. On Easter Day, 17 April, the Easter service and baptisms were held in a field outside the city, watched by nervous troops. John now refused to leave his episcopal palace for exile as his deposition should be by God not the Emperor, but on 20 June after a long 'stand-off' the synod deposed John again and the late Patriarch Nectarius' brother Arsacius was made Patriarch. John reluctantly left Constantinople after Imperial orders were sent; a fire broke out that night (presumably arson) and the cathedral of Hagia Sophia was destroyed with the superstitious crowds watching the scene being encouraged by John's allies to think that the fire was Divine vengeance on John's persecutors. His supporters were blamed for the fire and punished, and he was deported to Cucusus in Armenia by Imperial troops and not allowed to appeal to Emperor Theodosius for his restoration as he wished to do. Pope Innocent condemned John's deposition and refused to accept Arsacius as Patriarch, but Theodosius accepted it and John was never restored, dying in exile in 407. The aftermath left Eudoxia unpopular with the Eastern capital's crowds but in political control with Aurelian and Caesarius, but on 6 October 404 she died of a miscarriage; the new Praetorian Praefect Anthemius headed the government from 404–8 in the name of the weak-minded Arcadius.

(The career and eviction of Patriarch John 'Chrysostom' are largely as in OTL, but with the surviving Theodosius I added to the complications.)

The advancing threat of the Huns now began to alarm Theodosius as a threat to both halves of the Empire and during his tour of Gaul and the upper Rhine in 405 he planned defensive measures with his military staff to hold them back. This included a massive new Hadrian's-Wall-style defensive stonework for the lower Danube and the Dobudja region to hold back mounted Hunnic cavalry raiders so that they would lose their main weapon of surprise and be held up for long enough for adequate Roman cavalry to arrive on the scene. New regiments of heavy cavalry, using Persian-style mail and learning steppe-style archery, were ordered for the Roman army on the Danube, many of the recruits being German tribesmen, and Theodosius and chief minister Anthemius of the East even hired some expert Armenian and Iberian cavalrymen from the Caucasus who had already had experience of fighting local Hunnic raiders of their mountains. The Gothic kingdom in Sarmatia was not strong or coherent enough to hold the Huns up and the Emperor would not back the distrusted king Alaric up as he was a 'heretic' as well as a 'deserter' from the Roman army. This enabled Alaric to argue to his warriors that the Romans were leaving their 'loyal allies' the Goths to face the Huns, and he urged them to use the Goths' extra new manpower of arriving Alan and Suevic refugees to invade the Eastern Empire and seize Moesia as a safe new home.

The question of what to do about the increasingly hostile Vandals as a threat to Transrhenus were unresolved when Theodosius fell ill with dropsy in autumn 406 as he returned to Mediolanum from a tour of the lower Rhine. On 17 January 407 the Emperor died aged fifty-nine after a twenty-eight-year reign in the East and a nineteen-year reign (since autumn 388) in the West. Frustrated in his poorly-concealed devotion to a hard-line form of Catholicism and desire for prosecution and marginalization of 'heretics', Theodosius was arguably over-rated as a ruler on account of his military success and was not a generous and 'inclusive' statesman in the manner of the great rulers of the first and second centuries AD – he was hardly a Vespasian or a Septimius Severus as a 'rebuilder' after civil war, let alone as much of a cultural enthusiast as Hadrian or as intellectual as Marcus Aurelius. His Catholic admirers, led by the incumbents of the Lateran (the Popes) and his grand-daughter Pulcheria in the East, saw to it that he was officially entitled 'the Great' and was hailed for his successes as a leader in war and in faith in the same way that Constantine 'the Great' had been – and like Constantine he backed away from too harsh an imposition of his own vision on the Empire and coaxed as well as bullied his subjects into adopting Catholic Christianity. He was not as interested in theology and in personally arguing with those who disagreed with him on that – and if necessary in changing official doctrine to try to accommodate them in the interests of unity – as was Constantine. In his view Catholicism was the 'correct' form of

Christianity, there was no need for any argument, and everyone should obey his orders and conform. He preferred religiously congenial but morally questionable thugs such as Cynegius and crooks such as Rufinus to loyal and honest but pagan ministers. His subservience to Bishop (St) Ambrose of Mediolanum was also criticised, with the Emperor choosing to submit to the moral guidance of a charismatic and fearless 'Man of God' like an ordinary lay 'sinner' which earned criticism then and later – though it showed that he was humble enough to accept that he could and did do wrong (often when in a temper).

He left a dynasty to honour his name for generations and was still seen as a model of a 'Restorer of Unity' by Titus II later in the century so he was luckier than Julian – but he was not devoid of talent and good qualities either. It was a tribute to his careful planning that the government continued barely changed in East and West after his death, with the trio of Aurelian (d 411), Caesarius (d 412), and Praefect Anthemius ruling the East in Arcadius' name and in the West 'Master of Both Services' Stilicho ruling in the name of his son-in-law Honorius, now nearly twenty-three but still a feeble nonentity and more interested in raising chickens in his palace gardens than in governing. As the Italian nobles, now led at court by the eponymous son of the forcibly retired Nicomachus Flavianus and the experienced Mediolanum aristocrat lawyer-minister Flavius Manlius Theodorus (consul 409), and the 'service nobility' at court were both hostile to a half-German as the real ruler and feared that Stilicho was promoting too many German officers of low social background the court of Honorius seethed with intrigue. As a result of the low-level plotting Stilicho had to abandon his plans (agreed with Theodosius in autumn 406) to go to the Rhine in 407 and negotiate an alliance with the Franks and the disintegrating warlord coalition that ran the Alemanni to launch a preventive attack on the Vandals.

The Vandals' new king Godegisl, an Arian, had been distrusted by both Stilicho and the late Emperor; the intention had been to force him to submit to Rome in 407 in return for a guarantee of a Rome-backed kingdom East of the Oder and then join the Roman army in Marcomannia in 408 to take the Huns in the rear from the West in an invasion across the Carpathians from Dacia. This would be backed up by a huge cavalry army from the East including 30,000 vassal Persian horsemen led by the Emperor's new ally Yazdagerd of Istakr to whom Theodosius had sent an embassy in 406 pointing out the Hunnic threat to his lands and inviting him to supply troops in return for some extra land in Media for his dynasty. But now Stilicho gave up his plan to lead that expedition and instead sent his top German protégé, 'self-made' junior officer turned senior cavalry general Sarus the Goth, to Lower Germany as 'dux' to plan a smaller expedition. The effective regent of the West also deputed his main Roman military protégé and loyalist Jovius to take part of the 'comitatus' north to Marcomannia in 407 and try to intimidate the Vandals into signing up to a war on the Huns without the need for an expedition. But instead Godegisl and his lords, backed up by a new influx of Suevi and Alans fleeing West from the Huns, spun out negotiations with Stilicho's delegates. As rumours were spread in the Lower Rhine army that Stilicho would hand valuable and under-farmed lands in the Rhine delta to his German mercenaries as settlers after the war and let their Arians worship in their own churches, a mixture of anti-German local soldiers and Catholic officers stirred up a mutiny. This seized control of some Rhine fortresses downstream from Colonia (OTL: Cologne) in autumn 407, and though it was suppressed by the new 'dux' of Lower Germany, the ambitious Jovinus, he had his own reasons for undermining Stilicho and blamed him for the rise in the number of military posts going to Germans. As a result the region's garrisons were distracted and busy with intrigue and talk of revolt as on 31 December 407 the Vandals and their allies crossed the frozen Elbe and invaded Transrhenus, and the local Franks and Alemanni were overwhelmed by a horde of up to 40,000 refugee Germans plus their non-combatants seeking new lands.

Part II

Division, 407 to 491

Chapter 5

Crisis: The Barbarians at Large Inside the Empire, and the Fall of Stilicho

Events in the faraway steppes where more Huns were arriving and pushing west to the Vistula had driven a new grouping of refugee Germans to flee west from them across the Vistula in 407, with the Huns sacking undefended farms in quick horse-borne attacks that the small, localized German tribal leaders could not stop. Any warband who intercepted the Huns was almost always small and was overwhelmed by their horse-borne archers, and the bolder Germans who fought on in this sort of situation ended up killed – leading to hordes of demoralized civilians fleeing their farms westwards in panic. The long columns of wagon-borne refugees (from many different tribes so with no clear leadership to be negotiated with) led by their armed menfolk had been a threat to the Vandal kingdom until the quick-thinking Godegisl had told their warriors that though he could not give them any Vandal farmland – there was none to spare in this largely forested region of small clearings for farming – there was much rich land available across the Elbe to the west. If they were prepared to accept his leadership the Vandals would help them take it, and the opportune death of the feared Emperor Theodosius reassured them that his feeble younger son Honorius was no match for their seasoned warriors. As some returned German traders from Italy with plenty of gossip from Mediolanum had reported to the Vandal king soon after the Emperor died, thanks to his fears of intrigue at Court the Empire's best general and commander in chief, Stilicho, would not dare to come to the Elbe in person with the best soldiers in the west for fear of being overthrown by a coup in his absence. The result was the large-scale crossing of the Elbe and a frantic appeal to Mediolanum for Roman troops by the local warlords of the Franks and Alemanni, loyal Roman vassals but outnumbered and soon preoccupied with evacuating their own civilians to safety in the forests and mountains as large columns of well-armed Vandals, Alans, Heruls, and Sueves approached their villages.

But Stilicho was unable or unwilling to march to save his allies from destruction and stayed at Mediolanum through spring and summer 408 as the German invaders pushed on. He was already controversial to many senior courtiers and Senators for encouraging Theodosius to recruit brave and battle-hardened

German warriors to the senior regiments of the Roman army, in the 'comitatus' at Mediolanum as well as to the frontiers commands. Since Theodosius died he had kept this policy up – leading to spiteful rumours that he wanted a German-dominated officer-corps that could keep him in power indefinitely. Instead, he sent several of the more loyal Italian or upper Danube/ Illyria region officers in the 'comitatus' with smallish armies to bolster the Roman forces on the middle and lower Rhine in 408–9, and gave orders for the fortifications along the river to be strengthened and bridges (only wood so they could be demolished quickly in a crisis) guarded heavily. He also allowed thousands of Frankish and Alemannic civilian refugees from the Vandals to cross and settle in the Mausella (OTL: Moselle) valley and the Argentorate (OTL: Strasbourg) region, with the civil government and the Church organizing food supplies better and more fairly than had been done for the Goths on the Danube in 378. Rome's 'disaster-relief' system was now better as Theodosius had overhauled it after Valentinian's mistakes, but the locals instead grumbled at 'barbarians' who had 'exaggerated' the threat of Vandal attacks moving into the Empire and taking money and food – and with rumours that the 'German' Stilicho would give them Roman farms next this proved the trigger for locally-based 'limitanei' (frontier troops) who owned farms to start grumbling about the Emperor and his senior commander in 409. This then fed into plots by alienated Rhine regional commanders such as the later rebel Jovinus, who had expected Stilicho to bring an army from Italy in 409 and regarded his small-scale dispatch of troops as inadequate – and they began to consider taking drastic action to 'save' the region from its 'neglect' by the government.

The Vandal-led coalition ravaged as far as the Rhine, with no indication to the dismayed local Rome-allied tribal inhabitants or Lower and Upper Germany west of the river that Stilicho was about to send more troops to deal with the attack. Those Vandals who reached the middle Rhine in summer-autumn 409 were held back by the Roman garrisons and their reinforcements and Godegisl and his senior warlords concentrated for the next year on settling their people on land in the Main valley seized from fleeing Alemanni and pushing north-west across Frankish lands (OTL: Westphalia). But this respite for Rome did not affect the continuing flight of the lost lands' German civilians to the banks of the Rhine and Stilicho's orders led to thousands of them being permitted to camp on the east bank in camps built originally for Roman soldiers in earlier wars, fed by the Roman authorities to avert famine. Stilicho's (mostly German-speaking) officers sent by him from Mediolanum to assess the situation reported back to him that autumn that the Vandals had halted but could be expected to attack West in 410, and to prevent this Stilicho had to prepare a counter-strike, but was unable to use the army in Marcomannia to attack the Vandals from

Crisis: The Barbarians at Large Inside the Empire, and the Fall of Stilicho

the south-east as he had hoped due to a new threat of invasion of that region by refugees from the Huns arriving at the Ostrava Gap. Thousands of refugees were massing there in winter 409–10 and demanding land and safety from the Hun raiders to their rear or they would invade, led by a self-made tribal strongman called Radagaisus (OTL: invader of Rhaetia in 405). Accordingly Stilicho ended up taking the long-delayed gamble of leaving Court in 410 not to save the Rhineland but to deal with the threat to Marcomannia – the economically more vital source of coinage and metals for swords and arrows from the local mines. In spring 410 Stilicho led the main Western 'comitatus' north over the upper Danube into Marcomannia as the German coalition led by Radagaisus breached the Roman 'limes' (fortified frontier) in the Ostrava gap, and joined up with the retreating and outnumbered local forces led by his lieutenant and local 'Count' Sarus the Goth. He had not lost his strategic flair and his ability to use the geography of a region to his advantage, and he was able to ambush the over-confident invaders – not used to fighting as a cohesive force, composed of five or six different tribal groups, and burdened by loot and civilians – in a forested bend of the upper River Vltava on 24 June 410. The Germans were showered with arrows, driven back from Roman 'squares' of infantry as they charged *en masse*, and then ridden down by the Roman cavalry and trapped against the river, and the muddled battle ended up with Radagaisus either dead or missing and his leaderless 'horde' in flight back down the river to the northern Carpathians. The cornered civilian Germanic womenfolk and children were taken prisoner and sold off as slaves, and those menfolk who were hunted down in flight in the coming weeks and surrendered were enrolled in the Roman army and separated into small and manageable groups which were marched off to serve in distant provinces.

The Carpathian frontier was safe for the moment and so were the Marcomannian mines – and Stilicho was able to return to Italy as a 'hero' and pose as the saviour of the Empire. A Triumph for him followed in Rome on a rare Imperial visit in spring 411, with the 'high command' lulled into a false sense that the crisis was abating as the Vandals were being held at the Rhine and the Germanic refugees who had crossed the river were being dispersed to unoccupied farmland or recruited into the army and trained quickly. But all of this had taken place in spring-summer 410 without solving the crisis in 'Transrhenus' east of the Rhine, the soldiers on the latter were in a restive mood fearing that they had been forgotten and that incomers were being given prime Roman farmland, and Stilicho would have been better employed marching quickly west with his army to the Rhine but preferred to keep close to the Court to stave off rumours of disaffection there. The nervous Honorius had been panicked by the Germanic invasion of Marcomannia into deciding that Mediolanum was at risk of a mass-migration by the invaders to Rhaetia if Stilicho was defeated and had temporarily moved to the safety of the marsh-bound Adriatic coastal city of Ravenna, to the scorn of some of his officers – and his confidence in Stilicho had been shaken though the latter had eventually defeated Radagaisus. To deal with the Vandals quickly Stilicho, putting off a plan to head personally to the Rhine in 412, now ended up signing an alliance with Alaric the Visigoth, who had his own reasons to move out of the way of the Huns as through 408 and 409 large numbers of their cavalry had been raiding into Sarmatia and defeating his own infantry. Alaric was hopelessly outnumbered by the Huns and had little cavalry and no heavy artillery and he knew it, so despite his dislike of the Empire once his personal foe Theodosius was dead he decided to try to manipulate Stilicho (who was half-German and no friend of 'hard-line' anti-German courtier aristocrats) and gain access to the rich lands south of the Danube. In spring 411 he offered to bring 8,000 of his warriors from north of the Danube to aid the Empire., and to organize a new force made up of those of his fellow-countrymen who were living in the middle Danube valley as 'limitanei' – provided that he was made their commander, as Count, with 'imperium' over the local 'duces' East of the Rhine so he could co-ordinate the war. In return he would be allowed to settle his civilians in Upper Moesia, south of the Danube, after the war and in the meantime he could evacuate those in direct fear of Hunnic attack to the area – in smaller numbers, unarmed, and under Roman supervision. Stilicho agreed and Alaric duly led his new army to the upper Rhine and in summer 411 into the Alemannic lands on the River Main to rally fleeing Alemanni. He then moved North, while a Roman force of troops sent from Britain and Belgica under Britain's 'Count' (supreme commander) Aulus Aquilius plus an allied force of Batavian tribesmen (mostly Frankish by ethnic origin) from the Rhine-mouth islands crossed the lower Rhine into Frisia to link up with the retreating main Frankish army in the lower Saxon lands (OTL: Hamburg area). They duly kept the local Vandal invaders, plus their Suevi allies, back from the mouth of the Rhine and drove them back across the boggy plains of Westphalia towards the safety of the forested Raurus (OTL: Ruhr)valley.

The use of an 'Arian barbarian' as a freelance and semi-autonomous general by Stilicho infuriated the Lower Rhine troops and a mutiny there was soon launched by Jovinus who alleged that Alaric was in league with the commander in chief to turn over the Rhineland to German settlement. He declared himself 'Count of the Rhine' and the loyal Catholic Roman general who would rescue Honorius from his 'evil genius' Stilicho and the unsavoury reliance that this 'alien' general had on the Goths. The Lower Rhine Roman garrison troops would not co-operate with Alaric, and some of the latter's Roman and Alemannic allies deserted his army to join Jovinus' nearest troops at Colonia. The war against the Vandals was held up; Alaric, short of men, had to move back West of the Rhine to Argentorate for winter 411–12 and took a large group of German refugees from the Vandals with him.

The Vandals crossed the frozen Rhine near Colonia Agrippinensis (Cologne) into the Roman province in January 412, taking the garrisons – denuded by Jovinus having taken half of them off on his own march on Argentorate – by surprise. Godegisl and his 'horde' now spread out over the region East of Trier. Spring saw the arrival of around 16,000 more Roman troops from Italy, sent by Stilicho from the 'Comitatus' and led by a loyal Theodosian confidante (and Catholic) officer called Marcus Equitius assisted by senior Palace Guards ('*Scholae*') commander Justinus Anullinus, in northern Gaul plus reinforcements from Mauretania and the Spanish garrisons. (The armies in Rhaetia and Marcomannia were tied down there in case of a Vandal attack south-east, and those in Dacia and Moesia were watching the Huns.) They secured Northern and Eastern Gaul and saved Trier from a Vandal attack, Godegisl was ambushed in the forests near Metz and lost so many men to Roman cavalry that he pulled back to the Rhine valley, and gradually the separate groups of Vandal and allied pillagers were rounded up or killed in a long season of campaigning. But the Roman armies could not tackle the elusive Alaric who hid in the Vosges and called in more German refugees from Transrhenus who were now roaming around the Argentorate region (OTL: Strasbourg) to help. Some of the Alemanni now pressed on South and South-West into eastern Gaul to loot countryside that had not seen invaders since Caesar's time while Stilicho's troops stayed inside the walled towns on the defensive and so undermined Stilicho's reputation, leading to rising discontent in Italy and to the troop-less authorities in Lugdunum (Lyons) calling on him for help in vain. With Alaric cleverly encouraging the plunderers to cause maximum chaos so that the main Western Empire 's forces would be distracted and he could name his price to defeat the invaders the Vandals completed their conquest of 'Transrhenus' in summer 412. Rebel Jovinus was left isolated in control of Lower Germany, aided by refugee Germans evicted from Transrhenus – mostly Franks – and Roman refugees from the fighting in the South. Stilicho sent Sarus the Goth with troops from Rhaetia to Lugdunum.

On 12 May 412 the increasingly alcoholic Arcadius died suddenly at Constantinople after a banquet, aged thirty-one. His son Theodosius II succeeded, aged eleven, under the regency of Praetorian Praefect Anthemius. This duly distracted Stilicho into considering that he had more right to be regent of the East as the man chosen by Theodosius I as the main prop of his family and government, and he started to make threats in his 'congratulatory' embassy to the new Emperor that if he was not named as regent he would invade the East. To do this safely, he was rumoured to be planning to leave dealing with Jovinus to his current armies in the Rhineland and Alaric, who he was secretly ordering to sign a truce and ally with each other. The Imperial chamberlain Olympius started a plot to remove Stilicho, but as he had control over the military police and spy service he chose to work on Honorius not on grumbling generals and he urged the Emperor to take up his duty as Theodosius II's uncle and go to Constantinople himself but send Stilicho off to Gaul to do his duty and fight Jovinus and the Vandals. Honorius announced to his court that he was intending to go to Constantinople and secure his nephew's regime and that Stilicho would go to Gaul and the general Jovius would take over as deputy commander of the army (in effect full commander in his senior's absence) at Mediolanum, but Stilicho resisted and delayed implementing his campaign plan or gathering his army. This infuriated his critics and caused several senior generals to desert his cause and ally with Olympius' plotters; Stilicho's enemies now decided to bring him down and stir up mutiny among troops alleging that Stilicho wanted his son Eucherius, in his late teens, to rule the East and if he arrived in Constantinople would depose Theodosius II. The Empress Maria, his daughter, had died a few months earlier so she could not reassure Honorius, who started to doubt Stilicho. During his Imperial visit to the expeditionary force gathering at Ticinum for the Gallic campaign, on 13 August 412 Olympius roused the troops to revolt against Stilicho as a traitor and revealed details of his 'treasonable' plot to put Eucherius on the Eastern throne and the likelihood that he would abandon Gaul to Jovinus in a secret' deal' to achieve this coup. The letters which he read out to the troops were probably fake, but were believed. Stilicho's principal supporters, including the ex-Praetorian Praefect Limenius and General Chariobaudes, were seized and executed in a riot and 'Master of Offices' Naemorius and Praetorian Praefect of Italy Flavius Macrobius Longinianus had to be saved from an angry mob of soldiers by Honorius and then obligingly deserted Stilicho's cause to save their lives.

Stilicho, caught unawares at Bononia (Bologna), refused the entreaties of his loyal soldiers there to revolt, and the defecting (probably bribed) Sarus the Goth led Honorian troops in a night attack on his bodyguards who were broken up and fled. Stilicho fled the town in disguise, went to the nearby naval base and trading port of Ravenna, and as Olympius' troops under Count Heraclian arrived he took refuge in a church. On 23 August he was persuaded to surrender with a fake promise that his life was to be spared, and was then handed over to a delegation of officers sent by Olympius' faction and was executed; his son Eucherius was later killed at Rome. The chief notary Peter, the court's leading bureaucrat with Naemorius, and the chamberlain Deuterius were among the pro-Stilicho ministers who joined the mass defections and the fallen commander was denounced as a 'traitor' who had planned to remove the Theodosian dynasty and hand Rome over to the Germans. His secret letters to Alaric suggesting that the latter could be made overall 'Count of the Rhine' and in a few years 'Master of Soldiers' at Mediolanum did him no favours as they were now read out to the court. Honorius publicly declared that the general had tricked him and deserved his fate, and all Stilicho's military and governmental service was forgotten – with the probability that if he had not been a (half-) German rather than a Roman he would have survived and his fatal failure was to prefer his ambitions in the East in 412 to sorting out Gaul and the Rhineland. Flavius Manlius Theodorus' son, the younger Theodorus, was made Praetorian Praefect and the younger Nicomachus Flavianus was soon made Praefect of Rome for a third term. The new 'Master of Infantry' was Jovius, and the army survived the coup with minimal disruption except for the executions of a number of senior Germans close to Stilicho; Sarus kept most of the German officers loyal but a few stayed loyal to the memory of Stilicho and managed to flee to the Upper Rhine to join Alaric who was now sacked and declared a public enemy and in retaliation in January 413 made a local aristocratic governor of noble Italian descent who Stilicho had sent off to Upper Germany as distrusted, Attalus, his puppet-Emperor.

(The fall of Stilicho occurred in reality in 408 but as part of the same crises, over German invasions and the regency of the East, as here. But this version of events omits the leading role of Alaric and his Gothic army, who in OTL were much stronger and had been at large undefeated in Illyricum since invading Italy unsuccessfully in 402. The size and effects of the German tribal coalition that crossed the Rhine to invade Gaul, in January 406 in OTL, has also been reduced. In OTL the Germans crossed the Rhine; in this version the border is at the Elbe river, not the Rhine, and the Germans have to cross that first instead so Gaul is not affected; the Rhineland alone is invaded, at a later date than in OTL. The continuing story below takes some elements of actual events but butterflies away any invasion of Italy in 409 or sack of Rome in 410 by Alaric.)

Honorius' new 'Magister Equitum' (cavalry commander) Flavius Constantius, a rising officer in his mid-thirties who had been a protégé of Stilicho, led the main Imperial army into Provence and then on to Lugdunum and Argentorate. Jovinus' Frankish general Ebodich arrived from the upper Rhine with Frank and Alemanni reinforcements but was defeated, fled to his local friend Ecdicius' estate, and was killed by him to appease the central government. Jovinus held out on the lower Rhine but was overwhelmed, captured and executed in spring 413, and Alaric withdrew into the Black Forest to avoid pursuit by Constantius' larger army and ended up dying of a sudden fever in his camp before he could be caught. His army, laden with loot and prisoners from the region around Argentorate, elected his brother-in-law Athaulf, another ex-Roman officer, to succeed him, but that leader was more canny than the over-ambitious Alaric and soon used a delegation of hostage nobles to Constantius to negotiate his pardon and offered his submission and the return of his prisoners and loot. Short of men, Constantius wisely accepted his offer and re-integrated his troops into the Roman army. But the Rhine frontier was in chaos and the loss of manpower by the armies and by the agricultural community over a wide area into NE Gaul was severe, and as a result the new Rhine frontier was fragile and staffed by forces only around two-thirds of the pre-410 army there and the region had to be given tax-remission for over a decade. Transrhenus was lost to the Vandals and their Suevic and Alan allies, though at least that opened much land there for settlement by refugees from the Huns East of the Oder, and the Empire had suffered a severe shock from major internal crises as well so the new regime was left heavily dependant on the leadership of Constantius – who in 414 was married off to the Emperor's half-sister Galla Placidia and took over as effective ruler under the vague and indecisive Honorius.

There was now also an important new 'heresy' in the West for the dominant Catholic community to face, centred originally in Rome but after the shocks of the 411–12 internal crises relocating to North Africa as their leader moved there. This was the sect of the 'Pelagians', so-called after their founder and leader Pelagius. A British student of law and amateur theologian in Rome in the last decade of the fourth century, he then settled in the city with his followers and a group of admiring young and rich Christian supporters and began to write and preach against the alleged betrayal of Christ's principles by the worldly leadership of the Church. He had turned against the oppressive and unjust secular order of society, and now denounced the selfish greed of the rich in *De Divitiis* (*'On Wealth'*). His views on the 'sin' of using your money for yourself not to help the poor were similar in some ways to those of the former Patriarch John 'Chrysostom' of Constantinople, but he acted from outside the Church not inside though he wore sackcloth, fasted, and lived simply like a monk and he tapped into the same need for idealistic inspiration as did many monastic founders and charismatic hermits and bishops. He inaugurated an early fifth-century 'heresy' that sought to deny the necessity of Divine Grace for salvation and promote the idea that Man could achieve his own perfection and conquer sin. He thus undermined the role of the clergy as intercessors with God, which led to a major confrontation with orthodox thinkers in Rome in the late 400s.

Having been active in Rome itself for over a decade and amassed a number of articulate followers with his attacks on social injustice, he was forced to flee to Africa when he was condemned for illegal preaching of subversive non-Catholic views by a commission set up by Pope Innocent after complaints about him in 410. (This is largely as in OTL.)

Settling in Carthage, he then clashed with the most prominent local exponent of the orthodox viewpoint on Divine Grace, the theologian and major thinker Bishop Augustine of Hippo (in office from 398). This former 380s Neoplatonist student of philosophers in Rome had at one time been a Manichaean too before converting to Catholicism under the influence of his equally devout and rich landed Numidian mother (St) Monica, who set up her own nunnery in Hippo once he was made bishop there. He was far from a regulation 'career bishop' who always followed official orders so that he could secure promotion and was more of a questing thinker who happened to have – finally – settled down to be orthodox in his views but who still retained much of the Neoplatonist world-view while assimilating it into Catholic theology. A vigorous and dedicated bishop and very popular with his populace for his munificence and concern for the poor, he was by 412 the leading scholarly Catholic theologian in North Africa and was now writing his masterpiece *The City of God*, in which he argued that the real 'city of God' that the Church should construct was spiritual not physical and the secular administration of the Empire was bound to be imperfect and 'sinful' so the clergy should stand apart from them and not be corrupted. Instead of setting up the Empire as the 'city of God' and making all citizens Catholic – desirable though that was- the clergy and their secular allies should perfect their souls and set a good example of holy living, influencing but not taking part in the government, and they should especially steer clear of the corrupt and faction-ridden court (which Augustine had observed with distaste as a student in Mediolanum in the early 390s). Augustine was now seen by the approving Pope Innocent as a learned and valuable ally who he consulted on matters of doctrine, and his decision that Pelagius was arrogantly non-orthodox in his theology was duly accepted. Augustine's 'party' persuaded the Papacy to condemn the heresy in 412, and his principal ally and lieutenant Celestius was condemned by a church court and driven out of Africa as excommunicated. He later preached at Ephesus, and in 413 Pelagius himself was expelled too and ended up living in Palestine and setting up a new group of religious dissidents there. (Largely as in OTL.)

Pelagius was unable to keep himself out of theological trouble, even as a guest' of the nervous and suspicious local orthodox elite in Palestine – who their own Patriarch as well as the 'central authority' of the Eastern Church in Constantinople had ordered to keep a close eye on Pelagius. They had also been sent warnings about his 'alarmingly sinful' views by the zealous Bishop (St) Augustine of Hippo in Numidia. Pelagius now quarrelled with the leading local hermit and Bible translator (St) Jerome, a highly-regarded expert on Biblical writings and the first- and second-century 'Church Fathers' who was originally from Italy but had been resident since the late 390s at Bethlehem, in Palestine. Jerome called him a fraud and rabble-rouser who ignored the most skilled and expert Christian authorities and the facts that God had allowed the rich to become rich and Christ had accepted rich or State-employed followers if they were sincere and helped the poor, and he duly persuaded most of his own 'expat' colony of enthusiastic Italian Christians living around the 'Holy Sites' (e.g. the multimillionaire heiress Melania) to shun Pelagius and not give him any money. Celestius went to Constantinople to seek support but was expelled by Patriarch Atticus. In 416 Church Councils of the provinces of 'North Africa', centred on Carthage where the meeting took place, and Milevia (for Numidia) denounced Pelagius and Celestius as heretics and asked the authorities at Rome and Mediolanum to ban all the 'Pelagians', backed by messages of learned support from senior theologians in Palestine who had been called upon to examine the accused's writings and speeches in detail by Jerome. In January Pope Innocent declared Pelagius and Celestius excommunicate unless they returned to orthodoxy. But he died on 12 March, and on the 18th the Greek presbyter Zosimus, a protégé of John 'Chrysostom', was elected Pope and he weakened official hostility to the 'Pelagians' as he placed less value on strict theological points and more on good intentions. After receiving Celestius and receiving Pelagius' letters he declared that they were not heretics, but the Catholic bishops in Africa led protests.

On 30 April Honorius issued an edict from his new principal residence at the Adriatic sea-port of Ravenna – safer than Mediolanum from attack across the Alps by either rebels or Germans – condemning 'Pelagians' and Zosimus had to agree to avoid the danger of being investigated himself. He died on 26 December 417 before he had to decide whether to expel the remaining 'Pelagians' from North Africa and ask the Palestinian clergy to expel Pelagius and his group from their new homes as Augustine and others were demanding. Next day a minority of the Roman clergy elected the youngish and radical 'anti-wealth' archdeacon Eulalius, an ally of his, but on 28 December a rival majority elected the more 'mainstream' and anti-Pelagian church official Boniface. Both were consecrated by factions, and the devout though well-off aristocratic Praefect Symmachus wrote to Honorius in support of Eulalius, as a more humble and honest man, who Honorius initially recognized. His sister Galla Placidia supported Boniface, who was eventually successful in achieving Imperial support after the Emperor changed his mind on the advice of assorted officials in April 418. The 'Pelagian'

Crisis: The Barbarians at Large Inside the Empire, and the Fall of Stilicho

leadership were condemned by his first regional Church Council later in 419 and the Palestinian clergy followed up an official request from Rome by expelling them from their province; Pelagius and Celestius moved on to Syria where they were sheltered by sympathisers. 418 also saw the arrival in the region near Antioch of the most famously eccentric austere hermit of the century – (St) Simeon 'Stylites', a skin-wearing vegetarian and water-drinker who lived on a pillar in some bleak hills all the year round and went into trances when he prophesied to his many admirers. His pillar soon surrounded by an encampment of 'fans' and assorted admirers travelling for many miles to see him and ask his blessing or seek answers to their questions, Simeon was to live up his pillar for over forty years and have a church constructed around it as a holy site ('Qalaat Simeon' in Aramaic) when he died and was buried there as a saint. As in Spain and in Gaul, the Christians thus 'captured' the rural public.

(The 'Pelagian' crisis above is largely as in OTL. The 'Hypatia crisis' in Egypt covered below is not as serious or as violent as in OTL, where Hypatia was lynched by the Patriarch's men – though modern historians think that the crisis had more to do with a political power-struggle than with 'bigoted' and 'sexist' Christians targeting a leading woman pagan academic.)

Another religious controversy of the decade saw tension between Patriarch Theophilus' nephew and (412) successor Cyril and the Jews in Alexandria, and between Cyril and pagan Praefect Orestes over the latter's arrest of a leading 'Cyrillite' troublemaker at the Games at instigation of Jews. A mob of militant Jews staged a co-ordinated massacre of Christian citizens, and had to be put down by the Praefect's troops. But at least the determined and fair-minded Orestes kept the peace as much as possible between the militant orthodox community led by Cyril and the local pagans, the latter including both the devotees of the old Hellenistic shrines in the former Ptolemaic capital and the learned Neoplatonists and Aristotleians of the 'University' at the Museion ('Great Library') site. The latter were now led by the great polymath and naturalist Sosigenes of Heracleopolis, one of the most expert writers on wildlife of the age and respected for that (but not for his religion and devotion to the god Serapis) by Patriarch Cyril. Even the bigoted Theodosius had made an exception for his rule of 'no state money for any pagans' to fund Sosigenes' research into the wildlife of the Nile valley albeit mainly to help find ways of keeping the latter off the crops and so helping to avoid famine and riots. The most famous scholar of the era was however, most unusually, female, namely the Platonist expert and lecturer Hypatia, daughter of the former (390s) head of the university Theon, who was currently its head of philosophy and was disliked by the Christian clergy on account of their theologians mostly believing that it was immoral to allow women any senior posts. As a noted ridiculer of the illogicalities of certain past Bible scholars' beliefs and an ally of Praefect Orestes she duly suffered a murderous attack in the streets of Alexandria in January 415 by a passing mob of 'Church hospital attendants' who were mostly professional anti-semitic thugs who Patriarch Cyril used to smash up synagogues and pagan statues. Fortunately a group of off-duty guardsmen rescued Hypatia as the mob started to pelt her carriage with tiles and the incident led to the Praefect ordering his troops to round up the offending mobsters of whom around thirty were identified as attackers that day and were publicly executed. But Cyril declared them 'martyrs' and refused to accept a subsequent Imperial decree backing Orestes and cutting back his staff to half its earlier size and banning them from carrying weapons.

(In reality Hypatia was killed and the rampant Alexandrian orthodox thugs were virtually out of control by this stage. This version of history also has the 'pagan' cults in Egypt surviving as a counterweight to the Church for longer, due to a less successful Christian offensive in the 390s.)

Clashes continued in Alexandria and more scholars ended up emigrating to the new University of Constantinople in the 420s to secure peace and quiet, but the Patriarch had to put up with the new 'Augusta' Pulcheria, Theodosius II's devout but feminist sister, making Hypatia the head of the University in 422 after the latter had visited her fellow-intellectual enthusiast the new Empress Eudocia (Athenais) in Constantinople at the latter's invitation. Hypatia had persuaded her to put her arguments for an 'inclusive' approach to teaching philosophy at the institution to Pulcheria. As Hypatia argued on behalf of her fellow-non-Christian scholars, they were as much 'seekers after truth' and 'teachers of virtue' as were the orthodox Catholic teachers there, and despite what Cyril fulminated about them they were not 'subversive'. They were seeking to reconcile the writings and speculations of the wisest of the 'Ancient Masters', led by Plato and Aristotle and more recently added to by Plotinus, with the theological works of the more learned Church Fathers. The great Christian syncretist Origen, the 'wisest of men' to Hypatia's fellow-scholar Bishop Synesius (a man who had a circle of intellectual admirers in Constantinople among the court nobility close to Pulcheria), had accepted that Plato and Aristotle had an overall concept of 'One Divine Force' and a majestic and mystic system of unity and harmony in the universe, so it was ignorant of Cyril and his allies to want their teachings driven out of the university. The 'pagan' scholars of Alexandria's intellectual circles were far closer to the world of Christianity than to the excesses of the ancient cults of the Nile gods with their animal-worship and mass-sacrifices.

Crisis: The Barbarians at Large Inside the Empire, and the Fall of Stilicho   61

Theodosius II's elder sister Pulcheria (born 399), a learned woman but one who shuddered at the 'idol-worship' of the Nile cults and the 'orgiastic' public festivities of the ancient gods in both Egypt and Syria, saw Hypatia's point and had a major grievance against the disrespectful and power-hungry Cyril, who sought to boss the Imperial Family around as his uncle and predecessor Theophilus had tried to intimidate her grandfather Theodosius I and her parents Arcadius and Eudoxia. Accordingly she agreed to choose Hypatia to 'guide' the University of Alexandria into a 'proper' synthesis of teaching the works of the Greek 'Masters' and of the Church Fathers as complementary and all of them promoting the worship of 'One God' – and she sent in more troops and police to the turbulent city to ensure that her decision was obeyed and the swaggering and often loutish ultra-orthodox followers of the Patriarch obeyed the law on penalty of arrest and enslavement in the mines of Upper Egypt. Under Hypatia and, after her death in 435, her successors the Neoplatonist orientation of most philosophy at the university survived, though Pulcheria created new courses and chairs in Christian theology there. The cult of Serapis survived too as it was too popular even for Pulcheria to dare close it down, it had many devoted and super-rich noble local backers who could set up a pretender to the throne if offended, and its great temple – protected by armed guards – was one of the sights of Alexandria. Pulcheria had to be satisfied with arranging for Christian scholars who were learned in the subtleties of Hellenistic philosophy in Egypt to research into the origins of the cult – manufactured as a state-sponsored new religion by its leading patrons the Ptolemies in the third century BC – to expose it as a 'political' project set up to lure the gullible Egyptian elites into a semi-Greek mixture of 'Olympian' and traditional Egyptian worship that was not worthy of serious support. This certainly worked in diminishing its intellectual and populist adherents alike in the long term, along with exposure of the money-making activities and tax-avoidance of some of its priestly dynasties; the majority of Christian bishops and abbots were careful to show that they were far more honest, modest, philanthropic, and Spartan in their manner of living, as urged by the Imperial Family, and duly won over more supporters. The cult of Serapis slowly declined in importance between c. 415 and 455, prodded by Imperial civil servants' tax-dodging investigations of its priests and its leading lay patrons.

After a visit to Constantinople to lobby Pulcheria in person in 427, where he was unusually polite and placatory to her, Cyril finally had the great cults of Amun and Osiris in Memphis and Thebes shut down as 'dens of idol-worship', their leading priests pensioned off, junior priests offered 're-training' as Christian priests in the Patriarchal theological training-colleges, and their lands handed over to local monasteries. The cult of Isis alone survived for another two decades, shorn of most of its funds and estates. The similarities between the worship of a divine 'Mother' and her 'Son' in the cult of Isis and the devotion paid to the Virgin, the 'Mother of God', in Christianity indeed kept Pulcheria in hope that many of the devotees of Isis would duly accept the Christian religion and she now launched a campaign for conversion to this effect led by great Christian civil servants and their wives in Alexandria. She used tax-concessions and grants of office as incentives; a number of well-funded Christian schools were set up in cities and the elite were ordered to send their children there (to be converted if necessary) while claims of 'tax fraud' led to a succession of important pagan schools being shut down and their assets seized while pagan tutors of the rich were rounded up on various legal excuses and deported. Banning pagans from office was not officially legalized, but was in effect in practice by 430 due to a carefully purged Egyptian civil service so that the socially ambitious and the financially needy usually gave in and converted and the proudly obstinate 'pagan recidivists' among the nobility were forced out into rural isolation and had their estates nibbled away in assorted legal cases by government-paid judges. The great shrines were preserved as monuments, but the oldest families in the Egyptian nobility now finally began to turn Christian and the Patriarch condescended to offer them lucrative new clerical jobs as custodians of orthodox shrines, often of the victims of the early C4th persecutions, to keep them from making trouble.

Hypatia's friend and former pupil (Bishop) Synesius of Cyrene was the other leading thinker and cultural figure of the era in Egypt, but was a firm if tolerant Catholic – an aristocratic orator, dilettante collector of old pagan writings, and enthusiastic scholar and author from a very old family in that one-time sixth-century BC Spartan colony West of Egypt who claimed descent from the old kings of Sparta. A dabbler in writing Hellenistic-style novels and famously his locust-plague-hit city's envoy to Constantinople in 399 to seek aid from the Imperial Court, the then young but comprehensively learned Synesius was one of the best scholars of the age in the East and built up an impressive private library which he was to leave to the University of Alexandria. But he was also acceptable to the more tolerant clerics in Alexandria (where he gave lectures on his discoveries of ancient knowledge to the University from time to time) as a man who converted to Christianity on his visit to the capital in 399. He argued for the compatibility of the ancient classics with the Bible and the similarities between certain aspects of Neoplatonism and the mystical theology of such Christian writers as Origen, who he regarded with respect as an all too rare example of a leading 'Church Father who had been prepared to study rather than just insult the 'Ancient Masters' of Greek philosophy. Origen had seen where they had – dimly in most cases – noticed and believed in a form of monotheism (albeit regarding their ancestral gods as 'aspects of' or 'junior assistants of' the One God). Synesius was a one-man 'proof' for these clerics that Emperor Julian had been wrong to declare that no honest Christian could believe in the classics or their myths so all Christians should be banned from teaching, and he was duly called on to give lectures to and write for the Alexandrian Church's trainee-priests and to convert other scholars. He was also in regular correspondence with intellectual sympathisers and allies who he had met while visiting Constantinople and/or had corresponded with on theological matters, and they duly praised him to Pulcheria and her brother Theodosius II – and later to the Emperor's new, learned Athenian wife, the woman scholar Athenais/ Eudocia – as a brilliant thinker who could draw the more learned and open-minded pagans into the worship of Christ. A degree of mutual tolerance and accommodation between (most of) the leading moderate orthodox Christian and Neoplatonist 'pagan' thinkers at the university of Alexandria thus emerged, albeit as prodded by the city's Praefecture and kept an eye on by Pulcheria and her sister-in-law in Constantinople. This decreased inter-communal tension too, though riots still flared up, and the city's business classes backed the government in this – and 'under the radar' pagan Egyptian cults survived among the rural poor.

Chapter 6

A Return to Stability? Pulcheria Rules the East, and Constantius III and Aetius Rule the West

Praefect Anthemius of Constantinople, regent of the East, died in August 414; his main legacy was to be the building of the great triple walls of Constantinople, the 'Theodosian Walls' (enclosing a larger area than the original Constantinian city by about a third) which would protect the Eastern capital from any attack from the Balkans or the sea. Theodosius' fifteen-year-old eldest sister Pulcheria took a vow of virginity and assumed control of the government as 'Augusta', with the 'Master of Offices' Helio aiding her; she turned the palace into a centre of pious endeavour and made sure that prayers and religious services had a prominent role in life there and the womenfolk weaved wool and gave generously to local charitable institutions, aided by her sisters Arcadia and Marina. She made the Imperial Family a leader in moral authority and holy works in contrast to its reputation under the worldly Arcadius and Eudoxia and duly influenced her pleasant but uninspiring brother the young Emperor to take up theology and good works too. The appreciative Patriarch Atticus of Constantinople, who she presented with a choice selection of her parents' Palace silverware to use for religious services, wrote his treatise 'On Faith and the Virgin Life' for her and her sisters, and she led the way in regular psalm-chanting and hymn-singing in the palace. But the 'downside' was her admiration for the attitude of the heretic-hating Patriarch Cyril of Alexandria, who might be too harsh on the Neoplatonists and other intellectual 'pagans' for her liking and hectored the Imperial Family on doctrine but whose loathing of 'idol-worship' was to her taste. Once he had backed away from his efforts to control the curriculum and personnel of the University of Alexandria and had accepted her ally Hypatia and the latter's fellow-Platonists' right to teach, by around 419–20, she was prepared to help him crack down on those self-run Christian groups in Egypt who dabbled with unusual and 'insulting' forms of theology that seemed to defy the teachings of the Apostles and even to deny the accepted role and nature of Christ .

All 'heretic' Christian congregations were ordered to sign up to the decretals of the Church Council of Nicaea in return for official recognition and subsidies.

With her permission he closed the theologically dubious Novationist churches in Egypt in 423, but he exceeded his authority in expelling the Jews from Alexandria on account of their 'denying the divinity of Jesus' and inciting riotous followers to seize their property in 425. Cyril's enemy, Praefect Orestes, complained to the government, was booed and pelted with refuse at a parade by Cyril's militant Nitrian monks, and executed their leader Ammonius who Cyril declared a 'martyr'. When Cyril tried to put many of his supportive street-fighting hooligans in Alexandria and Memphis on his payroll as 'Church employees' so protected by the law Pulcheria agreed to send out a commission to cut back on 'waste' in the Egyptian Church and fine the Patriarch so heavily for his 'financial extravagance' that he had to agree to sack them in return for a pardon. The majority of his devout supporters, who paid their taxes obediently and kept their spending down to avoid paying taxes on luxury goods, were infuriated by the State's 'revelations' of Cyril's 'scandalous waste and extravagance' in his huge entourage and over-staffed schools and hospitals and failed to come out on the streets and riot as his hirelings wanted. He had to back down and the grimly-satisfied Praefect Orestes proceeded to follow Pulcheria's subtle orders to set up lots of new 'Imperial' schools, hospitals, orphanages, and soup-kitchens in the cities and irrigation-schemes in the countryside to win support. From now on the 'wise and benevolent Imperial Brother and Sister, the Beloved of Christ Theodosius and Pulcheria' would be the main source of public philanthropy in Egypt as the Ptolemies had once been.

The 'Augusta' now found her easily-influenced brother Theodosius II a 'reliable' wife. In spring 421 Athenais, the daughter of the late pagan Athenian philosopher Leontius, came to Constantinople to stay with her mother's sister and argue an inheritance law-suit against her brothers, unusually for a woman by herself in open court, after they refused to let her have more than the hundred gold coins that her father had left her. Pulcheria, who was hunting for a suitable wife for the Emperor among the capital's most beautiful but virtuous young women with the Emperor's trusted friend Paulinus, was impressed when she heard her and selected her as an appropriately clever and idealistic wife for her brother, but insisted on converting her to Christianity first. Patriarch Atticus baptised Athenais as "Eudocia" and on 7 June 421 she married Theodosius II. The new Empress proved as great a patron of both learning and founding nunneries as Pulcheria, and she was generous enough to invite her highly intelligent and honest if rather narrow-minded brothers to the capital where Valerian ended up by her recommendation as 'Master of Offices' (428) and Gesios later became Praetorian Praefect of Illyricum (429–37). On 27 February 425 there followed the foundation of the ' University of Constantinople': it was based at the 'Capitol', i.e. the old acropolis in the north-east corner of the capital overlooking the Golden Horn on the North side of the new cathedral of Hagia Sophia (completed in 415). It had specially extended buildings converted from the previous mansions and homes of courtiers there, with ten "grammarians" and three "rhetors" in Latin and ten "grammarians" and five "rhetors" in Greek; there was one chair of philosophy and two of jurisprudence.

(Pulcheria's court and choice of Athenais as in OTL.)

On 8 February 421 Constantius (III), now aged around forty-five, became co-emperor with Honorius and his control of the governance of the West became official, though his wife Galla Placidia had been 'Augusta' since 418 and was also influential. In military matters Constantius now relying on Jovius' main successor as senior commander, the shrewd and energetic Count Boniface who was 'Magister Peditum' from 418, and to a lesser extent the rising provincial Italian 'new man' officer Aetius who led a successful diplomatic mission to the Huns in 422 to pay off their current leadership with gifts and enrol them to harass the unfriendly Vandals from the east. Aetius, unlike the well-connected nobleman Boniface, was a man who had many friends and allies among the young German officers 'talent-spotted' and trained by Stilicho in the 400s or by Constantius after 412, and he was more open to recruiting such men who lacked 'Roman' blood, good manners, or elegant Latin verbiage and letters as his own proteges – and he was also better able to learn their ancestral traditions and military tactics and employ these to the benefit of the Empire. His talent for choosing skilful and loyal Germans to boost his staff or take on a series of important if minor military missions on the Rhine and Danube frontiers in the 420s was duly noted by Constantius, a man who had learnt from Stilicho to choose assistants by merit not just birth but who unlike Stilicho was careful not to make his German recruits too prominent where the 'stuffier' old-fashioned courtiers and Senators would notice and resent them.

The West was at peace, which it desperately needed after the disasters of 407–13, and agriculture could recover and help tax-revenues though the flight from farms and the sack of unwalled towns in the Rhineland took longer to repair. The quiet infiltration of –loyal – Germans, especially refugee Alemanni and Franks, into the region as farmers continued albeit in a less open and controversial manner than under the politically more reckless Stilicho. There was also more raiding of western Britain, short of troops since Constantine III's 350s wars, in the 410s by seaborne Irish and new trouble from the Picts who in the chaos of 409 had overwhelmed the kingdom of the Damnonii on the Cluta (Clyde) and now ruled the region and threatened Hadrian's Wall. But in 417 on a tour of Britain Constantius with a large force of light cavalry pushed them back again and installed a new British allied king on the fortress-rock of Dumbarton on the Cluta estuary and to the East the Votadini of Gododdin helped to raid into Fife and force a treaty out of Pictish 'High King' Drest who duly became a Christian. Constantius also moved the king of the Votadini, Cunedda (OTL), and many of his warbands SW to Segontium in Venedotia (OTL: Caernarfon) to combat the Irish raiders on the coast there with fast cavalry patrols, leaving his son Tybion to rule Gododdin as a Roman ally and new Roman forts at the east end of the Antonine Wall, and in the next few decades the north of Britain quietened down again while the Saxon raiders of the east coast became a greater menace – Constantius doubled the size of the fleet and enrolled a number of ambitious Continental Frank refugee warlords and some sailing-expert Jutes from Jutland to harass the Saxon pirates in their own creeks in Frisia. (OTL: Holland)

Constantius – like his mentor Stilicho – had a different attitude to the influx of German into the Roman 'establishment' (civil as well as military) to the majority of the Roman elites, not thinking that a resolutely Mediterranean ethnic and cultural background was essential and also ideologically desirable for all 'leaders' of the Empire. The old barriers against giving men of high or at least 'middling' birth and a traceable 'respectable' social background a monopoly in high office in the Empire had crumbled in the third-century crises as even ex-farmer and ex-labourer 'new men' from the Balkans rose to become Emperor and saved Rome; and Diocletian's reforms had opened the civil as well as military 'career ladder' to humbly-born provincials. Then an increasing number of military 'new men' from outside the Empire had risen to high rank under Constantine and his sons – and under Julian, who had been fiercely protective of Romano-Greek cultural traditions but had wanted to dilute the Catholic majority of high office-holders with less 'prejudiced and Church-influenced' persons to aid his beloved paganism and so had recruited Germans as well as, in the East, Persians. The culturally as well as religiously Catholic Theodosius had kept this up for practical reasons, as his use of Argobast (born outside the Empire, which had led to Senatorial contempt for him and in 392 to the Senate backing Theodosius from the start of the year's Western crisis) as well as Stilicho (born in the Empire with a Roman mother) had showed. After the fall of Stilicho in 412 many Rome and Mediolanum aristocrats had hoped for 'no more Germans in power', equivalent to the Constantinopolitan backlash after the assassination of Gainas the Gothic general; but Constantius kept up Stilicho's pragmatic policy of ignoring his chosen office-holders' origins. He spoke German, relied on a number of ex-tribal German officers now in Roman service for advice and further Germanic recruitment, and saw his role as enabling a 'partnership' of militarily skilled and glory-seeking German warriors with the far more organised, coherent, disciplined, and militarily expert Roman 'high command' in the cause of preserving the Empire. As a man from a 'middling' provincial rural background he was as open to promoting talent that lacked aristocratic Roman blood in the army as had been his exemplars Aurelian, reunifier of the Empire in the 270s, and Constantius 'Chlorus' in the 290s (and, more quietly, Constantius' son Constantine 'the Great', Julian, and Theodosius I). But unlike Stilicho he kept most of his proteges away from Court or senior administrative ranks so the traditional Italian senatorial aristocracy and the dominant figures at Court were less aware of or alienated by them. His quietly shrewd and effective priorities in policy were absorbed by his intelligent and administratively competent wife Galla Placidia, who was to carry them on as effective 'regent' for their ineffective son Valentinian after he died in 439, and by his chief military protégé Aetius. Later historians looking back from the reunion of the Empire in the 510s were often to argue that Constantius as much as the better-known Aetius was the 'Fourth Saviour of Rome' (the first being Camillus in 390/387 BC, the second Scipio Africanus who defeated Hannibal, and the third being Emperor Aurelian in the 270s AD).

It was Constantius who gave the promotions, pay-rises, and 'pay-offs' of land and material goods – and often Italian wives of good family too – to a number of proud and touchy but talented Germans that tied them and their sons after them to the service of Rome in the 420s and 430s, at a time when traditional German tribal loyalties were in flux as many of the tribes north and north-east of the Danube lost their lands to the incoming Huns. Instead of settling down to alternately farm their ancestral lands and fight their neighbours, for their lords or for themselves, hundreds if not thousands of skilled German warriors were on the move ahead of the plundering Hunnic cavalry and were seeking safety from the latter – and Constantius, as with Aetius later, offered this to them. Entire 'peoples' like the Heruls and Scirians were vanishing as their lands were overrun either by the Huns or by the tribes who were in flight from them, and even the Vandals and Goths had entered a state of demographic 'flux' as the first wave of 'barbarian' invasions of the West after 407 had broken against the Roman defences. Indeed, a substantial proportion of the warriors who had followed their lords into the Empire in the chaos of the late 400s ended up taking service with the victorious Empire and signing up for its regiments, among them Alaric the Visigoth's brother-in-law Athaulf who was by 423 a senior aide to Constantius as 'Count Athaulphus' and who ended his career as 'dux' of Aquitaine in possession of large estates in the Garonne valley, with a noble Roman bride and half-Roman children. His nephew Theodemir, a grandson of Alaric who had taken service with the Empire and brother of the pro-Roman king Theodoric who ruled a shaky 'West Gothic' tribal kingdom in Thuringia in the 430s, was in command of a regiment largely made up of Gothic settlers in Belgica and the Loire valley under Aetius (whose wife was a noble Gothic lady, daughter of the chieftain Carpilio) on the Rhine in the 440s.

The influx of skilled Germanic sailors from anti-Saxon groupings into eastern Britain included quite a considerable community of both Jutes and the Saxons' tribal rivals from the 'Angle' (a geographical term brought into use by Roman military geographers) between Jutland and the Frisian mainland, known generically as the 'Angles'. It was set up by Constantius (and his appointees in the 420s and 430s as 'duces' of southern Britain) along the east coasts of Icenia (East Anglia), from the Tamesis (Thames) north to the Wash. They were to provide sailors for the Roman fleet – and as a 'by-product' of this they also boosted the local fisheries to provide fish for regional urbanites, packed in ice which was brought in sealed boxes from the mountains in the winter and stored in cold underground cellars and tunnels. These 'German' incomers were too fissiparous in their own Continental homeland to have acquired powerful chiefs and had no established 'royal'/ chiefly lineages there so the Roman authorities were spared the politico-military problem posed by Franks, Goths, or Vandals in their service who expected to be commanded by their own noble warlords. Instead they lived in dispersed coastal communities (as they had done on the Continent) and provided more of seaborne trade, groups of fishing-vessels, and recruits to the 'Classis Britanniae' fleet than the land-centred Iceni and Trinovantes tribes north-east of Londinium had previously done. The region's coasts as well as inland farms now became prosperous through the mid-late-fifth century and the Roman navy could send in shallow-bottomed Angle or Jutish galleys to attack troublesome Jutland coastal raiders at home by penetrating up their creeks. However the number of Germans settling there as more Continental farmers fled the threat of the Huns (or the Vandals moving towards the NW coasts as the Huns took their lands to the south-east) caused some Icenian and snobbish Romano-British landowners' resentment of the new 'barbarous' and non-Latinate speakers in what was referred to as 'Anglia'. Nor were many of the incomers Christian, though recruits to the army and navy were expected to convert (at least nominally), and the local clergy usually shunned them as 'Woden-worshipping savages'.

(This overall Roman military/ political initiative to enrol and win over large numbers of mobile and ambitious Germanic incomers, and my general 'slant' for a Romanised fifth-century Britain, gives us a degree of Germanic immigration into Britain, but not as much or as 'decentralised' as it appears to have been in – disputed in details – reality. The version of Western Roman developments in the 420s-450s, the age of the Hunnic threat, now moves ahead on the basis of substantial changes from reality – Honorius is succeeded by his adult co-ruler and brother-in-law, the competent Constantius III, who in OTL had died in 421, not by a usurper who the East overthrew in 425 and then by regents for his sister Galla Placidia's young son by Constantius, Valentinian III. In this version of Roman history we have a steady, not interrupted, line of competent military leadership from Stilicho to Constantius III to 430s-450s leading General Aetius, with a stronger and more coherent army and no German autonomous or rebel states within the Western boundaries. In our version of events, the Rhine frontier was only temporarily breached in 410 then was restored –like it was in reality in both 276 and the mid-350s.)

The takeover of the direction of political life by Constantius only formalized an effective 'direction' of it by him since 413, as the death of Stilicho had not led to any assertion of influence by the senior Emperor Honorius. A pacific and not very intelligent character, he was content to appear at ceremonies and act as a general patron of culture and appointments but lacked any political skills and privately preferred gardening and looking after his famous poultry-unit as his new palace at Ravenna – as aristocratic poets in Rome mocked. Given the danger of him being influenced by power-seeking court toadies or even his personal attendants after the way he had been panicked into getting rid of Stilicho, his sister Galla Placidia kept a close eye on who had access to him and was supposed to be employing spies in his Household to monitor Court intrigues and warn her of anything dangerous to the smooth running of government. On 15 August 423 Honorius died of dropsy at Ravenna, aged thirty-nine, after a nominal rule since 395 and effective rule (often as others' puppet) since 407; Constantius now became the senior Emperor though due to his low birth the snobbish Theodosius II and Pulcheria would only recognise him as their junior and third in rank in the dynasty. His son by Galla Placidia, Valentinian (III) who had been born in 419, was made co-emperor but was to turn out as hapless and easily influenced as Honorius. Having secured the throne and full power and seen off an abortive plot by a group of aristocratic officers at the Mediolanum military HQ of the 'comitatus' to remove him, Constantius remodelled the military structure of the northern frontier forces to give more weight to the mobile cavalry and increase their numbers and training so they were better able to catch up and destroy roaming bands of invaders. The latter had had an advantage of time and speed over armour-weighted Roman infantry columns in the chaos of the late 400s and early 410s when he was a rising commander and so had done more damage. It also enabled him to deal with the Huns more effectively when their local warlords ignored the treaty which he had agreed with their 'kings', and his success in this respect in catching Hunnic raiders of the Marcomannian (OTL: Bohemian) lowlands and through isolated Carpathian passes in the years after 423 led to the Eastern army, now under a more vigorous and adaptable half-German 'Master of Infantry' called Aspar and the aristocratic Thracian ex-stud-farm horse-breeding nobleman Caius Candidianus, to follow suit. The mobile Roman heavy cavalry units under their 'Counts' on the Rhine and upper Danube also discouraged Vandal raiding, and were backed-up by slower but useful infantry farmer-soldier 'limitanei' who mopped up raiders who had evaded the cavalry and aided any sieges of cornered invading forces. But as a social side-effect of this change in emphasis in the Western military the local legions became virtually obsolete, depending as they had done on large squares of infantry with smaller 'wings' of cavalry, and the prestige of the enlarged cavalry added to the amount of money needed to enter these units – applicants had to provide their own horses and to have had equestrian training before applying – gave a boost to the landed nobility and sons of 'service nobles' who had invested in land. A new socio-military class of cavalrymen began to emerge in the Western provinces and to take on prestige and social status, with the legal term 'equites' (Latin for 'knights') being used for the wealthier landed men who served in the cavalry as much as for the second-ranking (financially speaking) 'class' of Roman taxpayers. This extended far from the Rhine-Danube-Carpathian frontiers, to Britain too, due to them serving in the cavalry units that hunted down Irish and Pictish raiders.

In the early 420s the future evangelist St. Patrick (Patricius), from a landed family near the coast of the Sabrina Sea (OTL: Bristol Channel), returned to his apparently peaceful home in Western Britain some years after being carried off aged sixteen as a slave by Irish raiders to Leinster. He subsequently decided to join the Church and take the Gospel to his former captors, and apparently went to study at a church school in Gaul to become a priest as there were few in Britain. Later biographers seeking to show his links to the prestigious leaders of the Gallic Church connected his training to bishops Amator (d.418) and Germanus of Auxerre; the latter was a keen adventurer with a pre-ecclesiastical career in the army so he may have inspired his protégé's ambition to travel and preach the Gospel to 'savage pagans'. A community of supporters of the British/Irish Pelagius had grown up in the region by this time, possibly spurred on by the arrival of people driven out of North Africa c. 420 by St Augustine and the Council of Carthage, and this is traditionally linked to an excessive degree of worldliness and lack of interest in the poor or philanthropy by the current British bishops, men who were mostly socially well-connected associates of the local aristocracy and secular officeholders. Their bland worldliness sparked off social radicalism by a few discontented and more idealistic bishops, led by a man called Agricola, and assorted junior clergy and lay supporters, mainly in the towns of the SE, and this in turn led to appeals from worried bishops to the Gallic Church for help to suppress the spread of heresy. A mission by Germanus and his north Gallic assistants, backed by the Papacy, followed (as in OTL) to identify, question, and expel assorted Pelagians from the official Church. Germanus was also said to have impressed the until then pro-Pelagian authorities at a major town with a Christian shrine of a 300s martyr, probably that of St Alban at Verulamium, into backing him and helping him to pressurise the local Church into expulsions; several score of heretics had their property confiscated for 'subversion' and were sent into exile in remote areas of Spain.

The ex-military commander Germanus, who had once served in Britain as a junior officer, also impressed the local 'dux' into purging Pelagians from his garrisons by telling him where to ambush a roaming band of Irish pirates somewhere in the mountains of Ordovicia, traditionally near the site of the later church and monastery of 'St Garmon' (i.e. Germanus) west of Viroconium (Wroxeter) – this was less likely to have been due to a 'miraculous' revelation by a helpful angel as alleged in his hagiography than due to his knowing the region from serving there. The mission of Patrick to Ireland followed the defeat of this major raid on western Britain, probably in 431 to 433. Patrick and his staff, mostly Irish-speaking Britons and a few Gauls, landed in Leinster and made most of their conversions in the first few years there, and it is unclear if he went on to the hill-fortress stronghold of Leinster's overlord 'High King' Loeghaire (ruled c. 430 to 463) in the 430s or not until later; at some date the latter was impressed enough with his holiness and his polite deference to the secular authorities to accept that he was not just an eccentric pacifist and a 'Roman agent' but politically useful as a prop to the authority of the 'High Kingship'. Patrick was then allowed to set up his main base and his eventual bishopric at Armagh in southern Ulster, which became his seat of authority and the location of his first Irish monastery; others followed and a sub-mission began to convert the south-west Irish kingdom of Munster, ruled by Conall 'Corc', before 450. Notably, the seaborne raids on Britain petered out in the 440s and it is generally assumed that this was part of a careful plan to aid the Empire which Patrick had been instructed by Palladius or the Pope to arrange – but it may have been due more to Emperor Constantius III visiting Britain for a tour of inspection in 435 and doubling the size of the Hibernian Sea fleet. Some later Irish and British writers claimed that Patrick died in 461/3, but this has been challenged by others who would date him later or even that there were in reality two missionary Patricks, explaining how he could be active c. 430 and according to some sources have died c.490; his relics were alternatively located at Armagh or Glastonbury. (Mostly as OTL)

A Return to Stability? 73

Major religious developments and an unexpected theological challenge to orthodoxy also affected the East in these years. On 10 April 428 the energetic if erratic Syrian theologian Nestorius, youngish, charismatic, and loved for his idealism and passion for the humbler members of his Church, was consecrated Patriarch of Constantinople after a long interregnum and search for a suitable successor to Patriarch Sisinnius who had died the previous December. Assorted competent but uninspiring careerist clerics in the capital's Church had been turned down by the commission set up to find a leader by Theodosius II, who under the influence of his idealistic wife and sister was determined to reinvigorate the Church and thus win Divine support. The new Patriarch was recommended to him as a man of vision and leadership who despised 'yes-men', and he duly induced Theodosius to issue an edict on 30 May banning eighteen heretical sects. The loathed Manichaeans (believing in two not one supreme deity), who were fashionable among questing seekers after spirituality and a sense of a godly 'chosen few' but were regarded by the orthodox as a heretical cult who were not even Christian, were condemned to exile *en masse* with their religion banned and their leaders were rounded up for execution. Nestorius' friend John, Patriarch of Antioch and patron of his own 'home monastery' at Euprepios in the nearby desert, and his ally the Palestinian monastic pioneer Euthymius founded the 'Lavra' (monastic community) at Sahel, which was particularly important for converting local Arabs, this year too. Arguably the 'Lavra' at Sahel played a crucial if 'below the radar' role in Palestine through the fifth century in educating many young local Arab men, led by the sons of farmers as well as of landlords and nomad chiefs, in Latinate culture and Christianity, bringing them into the cultural world of Rome – and of orthodox Catholicism – and drawing them away from the desert tribal beliefs in assorted animist-style 'Nature spirits' and 'holy' idols. Nestorius also used Syrian Arab recruits to his theology, men used to travel across the deserts and into Mesopotamia as camel-herders, horse-dealers, and traders, as a way of spreading (his version of) Christianity East across the rural lands of Mesopotamia and far into the Arabian desert interior. But time was to show that the impressive start that the Patriarch had made as a man of vision and organizer was to be compromised by his own doctrinal innovations, whether or not he had hidden these from the Emperor in order to gain office or he developed them once he was in power and had access to the capital's large theological libraries. (Largely as in OTL, but I have extended his Arab interests.)

In 429 Theodosius moved on from setting up a university at the capital to spread learning (425) and reforming the capital's Church (428) to tackling, simplifying, and updating the Empire's legal system by having all its current laws written down in one definitive set of rules, a 'Code, so that everyone would know what they were and outdated ones could be identified and cancelled. He duly set up a commission of nine jurists, including the great law-expert and legal historian Apelles from Constantinople's 'University', to codify, revise and up-date the law-codes (last reissued c. 330) and create a vast corpus of written law, with a special commission of several hundred Imperial-funded junior bureaucrats to advise them and do the writing. This involved calling in a large body of graduates from the Empire's main law-school at Beyrutus (Beirut) in Phoenicia, which now came under close Imperial purview with extra funding allocated and in 433 was to become a formal 'University' like those of Athens, Constantinople and Alexandria. Meanwhile Nestorius now turned his attention to the Pelagians, confirmed from his theological expertise that they were indeed heretical, and wrote to the new Pope Celestine condemning their religious views but excusing them from full suppression due to their admirable social activism – provided that they signed up to the decrees of the Council of Nicaea, which he regarded as the touchstone of orthodoxy. But at Easter Nestorius lost one important original supporter, as he forbade Pulcheria entry to the most hallowed sanctuary in Hagia Sophia as she was a woman – which took precedence over the usual right of the sovereign to enter on a Holy Day. She was left outside though her brother was not, and as a result turned against him.

Nestorius campaigned against 'sin' as John 'Chrysostom' had done before him, but his secretary Anastasius caused a riot by a provocative sermon based on his recent musings on theology, alleging that the Virgin Mary – an object of devotion in the capital – could not be regarded as the 'Mother of God' ('Theotokos') as this was theologically impossible. The emerging belief by Nestorius that Christ had a separate divine and human nature and that the Virgin could only be the mother of the latter, the two having somehow fused into one person, was seen as demeaning to the nature and the worship of Mary. So as Nestorius proceeded to expand on and promote his opinions and claim that they should become part of official doctrine this led to another major split among the Christian communities both in the capital and in his native Syria – with the new theology seen from the outset as heretical and not given much if any support in the West where the Papacy never accepted it. Patriarch Cyril of Alexandria and other bishops in Egypt plus some in Syria and Palestine called for a Church Council to condemn Nestorius' religious views for heresy, particularly his denial of the Virgin Mary as 'Mother of God'. In 430 Patriarch Cyril wrote a work *'Against the Blasphemies of Nestorius'* and sent letters on the matter to Theodosius, Pulcheria, the Emperor's other sisters, and Pope Celestine. In August Pope Celestine held a synod and declared Nestorius to be excommunicate if he did not repent in ten days of receiving the decision, which quoted from the Church Councils of Nicaea in 325 and Constantinople in 381; Cyril was allowed to forward the order to him. The main Western theological expert Bishop Augustine of Hippo was also called in to write to the Emperor backing up the synod, but died a few weeks later aged seventy-six so he was not able to go to Constantinople and help in person as the Pope wished. In November 430 Cyril held a synod at Alexandria, condemned twelve named 'Nestorian' doctrines that Nestorius was ordered to denounce or else, and forwarded the excommunication.

Theodosius called a Church Council, which opened at Ephesus on 7 June 431 – away from the capital so not under pressure from Nestorius' supporters there – under the presidency of the Imperial representative Count Candidian. Patriarch Cyril opened the proceedings with Patriarch John of Antioch not arrived and Nestorius boycotting it despite Candidian's request for a delay until he arrived, and on 22 June Nestorius was condemned and dismissed in his absence. John then arrived and called the minority of dissenters to a rival synod, which on 26 June (with Candidian attending) deposed Cyril and his ally Bishop Memnon of Ephesus. Pulcheria supported Cyril out of her dislike of theological innovation, but was wary about letting the aggressive Egyptian Patriarch or any other 'champions of orthodoxy' seem to dictate to the Emperor; in her opinion the final decision had to be seen to be made by the 'Heir of Constantine' not by any bishop, however learned or energetic the latter was, and so the lay authorities had to preside at the council and pronounce – and enforce – the verdict and see that the latter stood up for orthodox beliefs. The Papal legates now arrived and declared that the first synod's decision was correct and Nestorius was a 'heretic' who should lose his post, and that was largely accepted as authentic even in Syria. However Cyril's arrogant defiance of the second synod having any legitimacy despite the Imperial representative attending caused Theodosius to declare him deposed too, probably as advised by Pulcheria; Cyril ignored him and returned to Alexandria in defiance of him and the authorities dared not arrest him due to the large popular demonstrations in his support.

Nestorius was replaced on 25 October by a harmless if uninspiring Constantinopolitan court cleric called Maximian as Patriarch of Constantinople, and was sent to his home monastery, Euprepios near Antioch, to 'repent' as a simple monk. He continued to write and preach there and his heretic 'Nestorian' sect became a major force in already heterodox Syria with local secular connivance, spreading in the later 430s and 440s into Mesopotamia, but Pulcheria organised a thorough purge of his supporters from the Church in the capital so it ceased to be a major force there. Theodosius himself retained an affection for Nestorius and respect for his zeal and his skills at conversion despite his sister's hostility to the 'heretic', and in 438 was to allow Nestorius to travel to Mesopotamia himself to assist conversion of the local Zoroastrians after the mishandling of a campaign to do this by the arrogant and theologically 'demanding' Catholic Church leadership there. The resources available to these clerics had been deliberately restricted by Julian after the annexation of the region in the early-mid 360s in order to prevent them from inflaming the local pagan religions – Sabaean 'moon-worshippers' and devotees of the old Babylonian cults as well as Zoroastrians – by pressurizing them to convert. Neither Theodosius I or the 408–14 regency had had the time or resources available to give much support to the Catholics (though the former would probably have liked to do so had it not risked rebellion). Pulcheria had reversed this at the instigation of the orthodox clergy in Ctesiphon after their delegation to her in 416, but this was causing a backlash and a lack of conversions and Theodosius believed that Nestorius, who had more local supporters outside the elite in Mesopotamia in the 430s plus a group of new schools set up by his Syrian-led devotees, would do better at persuasion (not least as his followers preached in the local languages not Greek). He persuaded Nestorius to send conciliatory letters to the 'Augusta' and the Patriarchs of Constantinople and Antioch assuring of his submission to the decrees of the recent Church Council, and the mission was allowed to go ahead to reverse the Catholic clergy's failures to make progress – in fact the men chosen (by the Praefect not by the clerical hierarchs) were all Nestorius' sympathisers. As a result the growing 'mission' in Mesopotamia, and its 440s offshoots in Media and 'Persia proper' (around Istakr and Pasargadae), ended up dominated by the 'Nestorians' – complaints about which result in the 440s were ignored by Theodosius, by then himself tiring of orthodox aggression towards the other sects. The mission was to spread onwards into Bactria and the Indus valley – establishing new cultural links with the Roman world.

(This is largely as in OTL, but the Nestorian mission in the East is different from OTL as in this version Mesopotamia and Persia are ruled by Rome from the 360s .)

Cyril was forgiven and reinstated by Theodosius in spring 432 at Pulcheria's request and turned his attention to getting the assets of the closed-down cult of Isis transferred to his see and the latter's emergence as the centre of a major missionary campaign to convert the Nubian kingdom to Christianity in the 430s as an agent of Roman cultural expansion up the Nile valley. The removal and denunciation of Nestorius was also upheld by the new Pope Sixtus, who replaced the late Celestius at the end of July 432, and reluctantly Patriarch John acquiesced too as necessary to keep himself from being sacked. He did quietly allow Nestorius to continue preaching provided that he only did so at his own monastery, but by 435 the spread of 'Nestorian' groups in Antioch itself and their noisy protests about official doctrine at various churches was so noticeable that John was forced to intervene and ask for police help to protect his intimidated priests. Nestorius died in the security of a sympathetic monastic community in Mesopotamia in 451 still insisting that he was orthodox (in OTL he had been deported to a rural area of Egypt for his non-Catholic preaching and writing), and the Nestorian communities were evicted from Antioch and several other major Syrian cities by order of Pulcheria in 451 to please the official Church but were not stopped from setting up monasteries in more remote and rural areas.

Sporadic Saxon and Irish raids still troubled Britain but not to any serious extent, as the Romans kept control of the North Sea and a fleet in the Hibernian Sea – which small but not large groups of raiders could evade. There were also 'probes' by Vandal brigands across the lower Rhine which were denied by their aggressive new king from 428 (as in OTL but there he was ruling in Spain), the ferocious Arian warlord Gaiseric who was seeking to rebuild a kingdom well away from the Hunnic threat and was offering Roman lands and loot to all who would join his army. He had now reduced most of the surviving Franks north-east of the river to vassalage and was bringing in allies from the Hun-pillaged steppes between the Oder and Vistula to add to his army; as a result, many of the Franks fled west across the Rhine to enter Roman service and were given army jobs and homes for their families by Constantius and his local 'duces'. (In OTL Gaiseric was able to lead his people to invade North Africa and overrun Rome's main grain farms there from 428; the Franks were in modern Belgium.) A similar number of Burgundians were driven in flight across the middle Rhine near Moguntiacum (Mainz) by the Vandals seizing their new lands on the upper Main river in the early 430s and ended up settled in the plains south-west of the Vosges by the Romans, scattered across too wide an area to coalesce as a threat and mixed up with local Roman military veterans as farmers on land that had been ravaged by Alaric's Goths. By contrast, after the fairly amenable and bribeable Hunnic overlord king Rua (who Aetius had befriended and hired cavalrymen from on his earlier embassy) was killed by lightning during an expedition to pillage refugee Gothic communities in the eastern Carpathians in 433 his successors, his nephews Attila and Bleda, continued to raid the Rome-allied 'East Gothic' kingdom in 'Sarmatia' every year until they overthrew it in 435. They then turned their attention to crossing the lower Danube for annual raids into Lower Moesia, their fast steppe horsemen in too large numbers for the Eastern cavalry patrols to stop them. The situation continued to deteriorate and the marshy local terrain meant that the Romans could not build a long stone wall or rampart along the riverbank in the Dobrudja to match those built earlier upstream, and commander-in-chief Aspar had to rely on creating larger bodies of cavalry, as Constantius was doing in the west, and training them in pursuit and in archery. This was to lead to a large influx of usually aristocratic young Persian noblemen, used to cavalry action and denied political power at the local 'Great King's court by the court bureaucrats, to the Eastern Roman army- though suspicious Aspar preferred to deploy them well away from the capital.

Both Persian nobles used to horsemanship on the remote Iranian plains and Alan foes of the Huns from the steppes North of the Caucasus (Chechenia) were enrolled in the Roman Danube army in the later 430s, but the Huns still had far more light and fast ponies and far more skill at archery. As Roman farms in the areas of lower Moesia fell victim to 'hit and run' raids from Huns who had crossed the Dobrudja every year Theodosius ended up sending a high-level embassy to the Hunnic kings in 438 with a gift of 100 gold pieces for each king and a promise of the same every year if they kept out of Roman territory. The Huns accepted the gifts and claimed that the raids had been by independent or disobedient chiefs out of their control, but there was a 'let-up' to some degree until Bleda was killed in a 'hunting accident' after a quarrel with Attila in 441. In 439 and 440 the Huns concentrated on expeditions to the Don and lower Volga steppes instead to collect slaves and tribute – forcing around 20,000 Alans South so they ended up moving into the Roman protectorate of northern Adiabene (OTL: Baku) and having to be incorporated into the local Roman defence-system as tributary allies.

Meanwhile the Hunnic threat was pushing the two Empires into closer alliance after some years of hostility from Constantius III to Theodosius over the latter's refusal to accept him as an equal colleague, and in 435 the West joined the East in officially issuing the huge new 'Code of Theodosius' as the joint Empire's definitive collection of current legal decrees. On Pulcheria's insistence, backed up by her brother, public pagan worship was banned – and the Jews were not to be allowed to build any new synagogues on the alleged grounds of their 'insults' to Christianity and resultant Divine displeasure with them. An Imperial marriage-alliance was now arranged, and on 29 October 437 Valentinian III, aged eighteen, married Theodosius' and Eudoxia's daughter Licinia Eudoxia, aged fifteen, at Constantinople though the bridegroom's father did not join the Western party visiting the East. The newly-weds wintered at Thessalonica before returning home, and on 22 February 439 Constantius III died aged probably sixty-three or sixty-four so Valentinian became sole Emperor of the West. A feckless and lazy hedonist like his uncle Arcadius and easily influenced by his courtiers and preferring hunting to business, Valentinian left most of the latter to his mother Galla Placidia, who was the effective ruler of the West into the late 440s, and her 'Master of Offices' Sebastian (in office 432–443). Military business was left to the West's best general Aetius who had covered himself in glory by defeating a peasant revolt and local brigandage in laxly-governed, famine-hit Belgica in 437 while Constantius III was ill and from 438 replaced Count Boniface as 'Magister Utriusque Militiae' (Master of Infantry and Cavalry). Aetius had been the mastermind behind the creation of hard-hitting, fast-moving new cavalry regiments on the Rhine to hold back Vandal raiders as 'dux' of Upper Germany in 433–5 and Lower Germany in 435–7, as commissioned by Constantius, and had then showed his skill at politics at headquarters in outmanoeuvring and disgracing Boniface who was far better-connected socially but was displaced and 'booted upstairs' to the Senate in 438 as too old and inflexible to cope with the Vandal raids or the Huns. In 442 Aetius served on a successful advisory mission to the Lower Danube to assist the harassed Aspar in tackling the latest Hunnic raids (officially denied as 'unauthorised' by Attila who had lapped up a huge annual bribe of 1,000 gold pieces the previous winter but not kept the peace as promised).

Some Western cavalry were lent by Aetius to Aspar in the East, and in 443 the two generals, having trained a large new army based on cavalry with 5000 new archers and a force of imported Alans from the Caucasus who were out for revenge on Attila, moved into Sarmatia to attack the Huns 'head-on'. But Attila just retreated out of range and burnt the fields behind him so the Romans suffered in the smoke and eventually they had to give up and head home as supplies ran short. The arrival of the Roman army had led to the Huns' Gothic vassals revolting and joining the Romans and as the latter retreated the Goths were evacuated to become Roman soldiers and farmers in raid-hit Lower Moesia and provided better resistance to the next year's Hunnic raiders than their predecessors had done. But the Hunnic problem was not solved and Aetius, who had more knowledge of the Huns than most Roman generals from missions to them in the 420s, cunningly used his old contacts among their Asiatic military noble elite to try to spark off a revolt by members of the families of former co-kings who had been deprived of their 'rights' by Attila's virtual dictatorship. The resultant revolt by junior Hunnic lords of ancient family in sub-tribes that had been pushed aside in political leadership since the early 430s failed to overthrow Attila in 444, and he defeated his assailants and executed all who did not manage to flee in time. But several thousand exiles from sub-tribes that provided crucial manpower – horsemen and archers in particular – ended up fleeing into Dacia and being added by Aetius to the Roman army there. At the same time a rebellious grouping of Burgundians, driven out of their lands in the Tatra Mountains for aiding the rebels, fled to the Vandal kingdom, were told to move on by the suspicious Gaiseric, and after a long trek into the Roman lands on the upper Danube in early 445 were enrolled by Aetius in the Roman army and given farms as 'limitanei' West of the upper Rhine. Some of these veterans, keen to get their families away from the raid-hit Rhine valley, would end up farming in the hills North of Lugdunum (OTL:Lyons) - the later 'Burgundia'.

Chapter 7

Battle for the Empire: Aetius vs Attila, Monophysites vs Catholics

The stability of the East now started to decline as the weak-minded and suggestible Theodosius II fell under the influence of scheming courtiers and began to escape from his elder sister's wise advice. His first new boon companion as a protégé introduced to government to extend this outside the circle of Pulcheria's moral and ostentatiously Christian allies was a reasonable enough character, the rising aristocratic courtier Cyrus who was ambitious and eager to build up a fortune and acquire clients. He was also both competent and a generous patron to monks as well as to his family and friends. Praefect of Constantinople in 438–42 and the builder of new public baths and sponsor of races in the Hippodrome next to the Palace, expert horseman, stud-owner, and dice-playing companion of the Emperor, and monastery-founder Cyrus had no interest in changing policy and always flattered Pulcheria to her face while encouraging Theodosius privately to take more initiatives of his own. But he also undermined the Emperor's long-term and less greedy friend Paulinus who had stood by Theodosius without seeking much for himself for two decades. Loyal and honest Paulinus, also a friend and adviser of the Empress Eudocia and one of her private circle of attendees at her Greek poetry recitals, was undermined by Cyrus for supposedly spending a suspicious amount of time alone with the Empress and writing odes to her virtues. Soon the jealous Theodosius had convinced himself that Paulinus was in love with her and his generous New Year's gifts to her were intended to win her sexual favours, and in 440 had him arrested and exiled to Armenia. The Empress' furious reaction to this in turn damaged the Imperial couple's relationship which Pulcheria could not salvage.

The ambitious and flattering new, eunuch chamberlain Chrysaphius now joined in the plotting to stir up his master's suspicions of his wife, and in 442 first Chrysaphius' original ally Praefect Cyrus was sidelined and as a 'reward for his holy endeavours to help the Church' was made a bishop in remote Cappadocia and hustled out of the capital to go and serve there. Then the Empress was tricked into believing that her husband was having affairs with not-so-holy young virgins in the circle of earnest young religious enthusiast noblewomen gathered around Pulcheria. Eudocia left the capital in high dudgeon on a pilgrimage to

Jerusalem which she had been talking of doing for years but never actually gone on, with Chrysaphius helping to fund her and giving her rich gifts to pass on to monasteries and shrines there so the Church under new Patriarch Proclus of Constantinople backed the tour. As the treacherous eunuch had hoped Eudocia never came back but settled in a palace in Jerusalem amidst congenial Church and lay sponsor company as the Holy City's greatest patron since Constantine 'the Great's mother St Helena. (This is as in OTL.) Once the Emperor was persuaded to quarrel with Pulcheria and show her that he preferred to listen to Chrysaphius' advice and appoint his friends to high office in 445 she left the court too, albeit only to live at a suburban palace on the Bosphorus some miles upstream from the capital, and Chrysaphius was left supreme at court with one of his own men, the corrupt if genial nobleman Eustratius Ancholius, as 'Master of Offices' and a succession of toadying bureaucrats to run the treasury and siphon off money to Chrysaphius and his friends. This was resented and was resisted by more independent-minded court aristocrats and bureaucratic ministers, but so far nobody dared to tackle Theodosius about the way that he naively trusted Chrysaphius as a source of 'honest' and shrewd advice.

The Emperor was currently basking in unwonted and undeserved praise for his handling of the Persian crisis of 442 when the new king Hormisdas of Bactria used a force of Turkic mercenaries to try to throw the Roman ally Yazdagerd, who had visited Constantinople in 435 and was on good terms with Theodosius, out of his kingdom and reunify the Sassanid state. The leading general Anatolius and his crack group of senior Thracian aristocratic cavalry officers happened to be in Ctesiphon at this point to reform the local military 'comitatus' and meld the Roman/ Mesopotamian cavalry regiments there with Alan refugees from Upper Adiabene and so they could take charge of a swift military 'strike' to help the refugee Yazdagerd drive his attackers out of Istakr. As Anatolius defied the pacific Emperor's orders to risk a sudden descent on the Bactrian capital of Balkh with his large cavalry force before Hormisdas, his Turkic army mauled, could get the defences in shape the Empire ended up in September 442 in possession of Balkh and its massive, well-protected Sassanid fortress-citadel plus the latter's arsenal and the person of Hormisdas. Bactria was made a Roman protectorate and its main fortresses south-west of the Oxus were taken over by a mixture of Roman troops, Arab and Alan mercenaries, and Yazdagerd's men, and as the menace of Bactria reuniting the Sassanid realm was ended nearly eighty years after Julian's great victory Theodosius was able to have Hormisdas and his officers paraded in rags and chains before him in the Hippodrome and pose as 'Persicus', a mighty conqueror of the pagan enemy and favoured by God.

The grateful Yazdagerd later visited the capital again and duly helped the Empire to keep the Turks back at the Oxus frontier while the Emperor achieved temporary appreciation from his grumbling military elite as a ruler who had some capabilities as an organizer and statesman. But now the Emperor and his vain chamberlain assumed that they could deal with Attila just as easily and in 443 they refused him the usual tribute and ordered him to pay Rome rent for his occupation of Rome's allied lands of Sarmatia instead. That was not the way to deal with a psychopathic Hun with a large horde of loot-hungry Asiatic cavalry to keep happy, and a major raid on Lower Moesia via the Dobrudja by over 50,000 Huns and their vassals overwhelmed the defence forces and led to a mass exodus of panicking farmers as the invaders put ladders up the walls of several important local fortresses at night to storm them and secure artillery to use on the local towns. All the captured Roman soldiers at the fortresses were killed and had their heads lined up along the walls to show to arriving rescuers and soon the main towns of the riverside downstream from Silistria were either stormed or else were handing over their richer citizens as slaves and all their valuables as Attila demanded. With the local 'duces' too scared to fight and a diversionary attack on the Roman 'limes' in the Beskids pinning down the armies of Dacia and Marcomannia there, Theodosius had to reassess his warlike intentions and send an embassy with three thousand pieces of gold to Attila to secure peace. The barbarian warlord insisted on the demolition of the defences of Silistria and the 'limes' of all of the Lower Moesian Danube riverbank so that his cavalry could cross at leisure to use the pastures of the Dobrudja and the Emperor had to agree, but at least this kept the peace until 447. Technically Attila became a Roman ally and promised to leave the Goths alone and to wage war on Rome's foe Gaiseric – which he did, though only on one loot-collecting expedition in 446 – so it was 'spun' as a wise Roman policy of alliance not war and Chrysaphius claimed credit for it.

On 26 January 447 the walls of Constantinople were damaged in an inopportune earthquake and panic led many inhabitants to flee the city. Equally importantly, the damage was serious enough in several major walled cities and fortresses in both Upper and Lower Moesia and on the Euxine coast to make their garrisons doubt if they could now hold back the Huns there until repairs were done. The earthquake caused the defensive wall in the Shipka Pass and some stone walls across the defensive line east of the main Balkan range, running East to the Euxine, to also partly collapse. The news was welcomed by Attila who announced that if the Emperor did not want to see the Balkans as a smoking desert and the Huns at the capital's walls he would have to pay five thousand gold pieces a year, and Theodosius hastily opened negotiations as Praefect Constantine restored the city walls with impressed local labour.

Zeno, the first important Isaurian (SE Anatolia) general, now became 'Magister Peditum' for the East (to 451) to revive the infantry regiments in the Balkans as Aspar moved aside to just run the cavalry. Soon peace was signed between the East and Attila, but on the latter's terms: the district south of the Danube from Silistria downstream, of a five-day journey's distance from the river, was to be left abandoned by both Romans and Huns and the latter occupied Silistria and were also allowed to dismantle the riverine fortresses upstream of Silistria well into Upper Moesia. The East was humiliated, though at least it held onto the Shipka Pass walls and the line of the 'Moesian Wall' from the Balkan range's Eastern end to the sea and these were soon rebuilt. The local Roman military authorities also hastened to re-position evacuated personnel from the Danube banks fortresses on the 'Moesian Wall', which was reinforced with lines of stakes in deep pits crossable by easily demolished wooden bridges and by a 'forward defence' line of earthen ramparts that would not collapse in earthquakes and would hold up raiding Hunnic cavalry for long enough for the local watch-towers to send fast riders and signals to the 'Moesian Wall' for reinforcements. The labour of building the new fortifications and the evacuation of thousands of alarmed Lower Danube valley farmers to the safety of the Hebrus valley kept those who were critical of the 'weak' Emperor too busy to stage revolts. But there were still many complaints that Aetius in the West managed defence policy better and the Western Emperor Valentinian listened to his wise chief general and his 'holy' Catholic womenfolk unlike Theodosius did. The Church joined in the rising tide of discontent about the Emperor's advisers and rumour had it that Chrysaphius had to bribe both Aspar and Zeno heavily to fend off the threat of a military coup while other officers appealed to Aetius to invade.

Patriarch Flavian of Constantinople (appointed 447) and Bishop Eusebius of Dorylaeum investigated Chrysaphius' protégé Eutyches, a septuagenarian abbot based near the capital and a former protégé of the late Patriarch Cyril of Alexandria, for denying that Christ had two natures (i.e. the new doctrine of 'Monophysitism'). This theological doctrine had arisen in Egypt in the 430s and 440s among followers of Cyril's who were devoted to the Virgin Mary as the 'Theotokos' ('Mother of God') and had been busy abusing Nestorius and his allies on that account, and they – and their ally Eutyches – had now moved on to enthuse about Christ's divine nature and the role of the Virgin in giving birth to this incarnation of God to the extent that they seemed to or in some cases did deny Christ's human nature. This view was now especially promoted by Patriarch Dioscurus of Alexandria, who was appointing clerics who held similar views across his see and was under attack on that account by alarmed orthodox clergy, who were in turn backed by Patriarch Domnus of Antoch (deposed 449). In November 448 the vigilant Eusebius of Dorylaeum denounced Eutyches as a heretic to a local synod in the capital and demanded a formal enquiry into his heresy and sackings of his allies in various Anatolian bishoprics and in Egypt. Eutyches was tried, bullied by Eusebius into admitting that Christ could only have one nature which was in contradiction of the Council of Nicaea's Creed, and was excommunicated. But Chrysaphius and Dioscurus took up his case. Chrysaphius now made a clever but dangerous attempt to bribe Edeco, the Hunnic envoy who visited Constantinople early in 448 to collect the annual bribe/tribute, to murder Attila on his return to his camp with a Roman embassy led by Maximin. Instead Edeco informed Attila when he returned to the Hunnic headquarters, but the Romans were allowed to hand over the money and leave unmolested with some sarcastic comments from Attila at their farewell interview about how their Emperor took orders from a eunuch and was no better than one himself. Attila sent his Roman (Pannonian) secretary Orestes to Constantinople with the bag containing Edeco's bribe, to show it to Chrysaphius and ask if he recognized it. But by the time that he arrived a Roman spy at Attila's court had passed on a message about the incident by carrier-pigeon to Chrysaphius' foes at the military 'high command' in Constantinople who were worried that the meddling eunuch might get one of his friends appointed as a senior commander and cause military disaster. Chrysaphius had bribed Aspar to look the other way at his politicking, but other, more junior generals were less sanguine about him and so were indignant members of the Constantinopolitan aristocracy – including those in the Guards regiments ('Excubitors' and 'Scholae'). Some of them were allies of Pulcheria and regarded the loss of her advice to her brother with indignation; others were orthodox Christians alarmed at Chrysaphius' 'Monophysite' clergy and academic friends and his enthusiasm for trying to reconcile the rival Christian factions by undermining Catholic/ orthodox power in the Church. A report on the meddling eunuch's hare-brained plan to assassinate Attila was compiled using suborned or 'persuaded' Court intimates of his who had helped him to recruit his plotters, and when the Hunnic embassy arrived in Constantinople to complain about Chrysaphius the details were sent to the Imperial 'Consistory' (Council of Ministers) to show that the Huns were telling the truth.

Chrysaphius denied sending any assassins and claimed that it was a 'fit-up' by his enemies in league with the Huns, and Theodosius believed him. But this only alienated the majority of ministers and senior generals who believed that the Empire had had a narrow escape from disaster, and a few weeks later Chrysaphius was lured to a party at a supposed ally's mansion in a remote district of a Bosphorus suburb of the capital a few miles north of the Imperial Palace and was never seen again. Rumour had it that he had been drugged and thrown in a sack into the sea, and though the frantic Emperor launched a search for him the truth was never found and the Empire was saved from a major political 'loose cannon' – and his vast fortune was soon discovered in various banks and his residence and was confiscated for the treasury as he had no heirs. But despite the hopes of assorted Court and orthodox figures the Emperor did not recall Pulcheria, who he suspected (wrongly) of encouraging the removal of his close associate, and he obstinately clung to the late minister's well-meant but politically dangerous ideas of bringing the 'Monophysites' into the mainstream of the Church – which would supposedly reconcile their anti-orthodox communities in Syria, Palestine and Egypt to the official Church. Attila was mollified as he assumed that the Empire's leadership was so scared of him that it had liquidated Chrysaphius to please him – but the danger to the Church's stability in 448–9 was not altered.

(In OTL Chrysaphius was not removed until after Theodosius died.)

Theodosius now sent his respected ex-"Master of Offices" Nomus and the senior general Anatolius on a mission to pacify Attila; he accepted their assurances with an extra gift of another five thousand gold pieces and agreed to confirm his recognition of the Danube frontier. But the theological 'fallout' of the Eutyches affair now engulfed the Empire as in autumn 448 the monk's enemies, aiming at bringing down the Monophysite leadership which he was co-ordinating, had been asking the new Pope Leo (in office since Sixtus died in 440), a respected and learned theologian, for support. He had apparently also been backed by Pulcheria. On 18 February 449 Leo wrote to Patriarch Flavian of Constantinople demanding an explanation for his failure to have Eutyches and all his Monophysite allies driven from Constantinople and expelled from Egypt too; Dioscurus' theological errors were laid out in extensive detail and he was proclaimed to be an unfit successor for the late and orthodox Patriarch Cyril (d 444), though in fact he had been developing ideas based on – and misusing? – Cyril's own writings and thought he was being loyal to him. Leo sent his formal doctrinal submission on the correct theology of Christ's two natures, the 'Tome' to Flavian for him to agree with this, which he did. Flavian persuaded the reluctant Theodosius to help, and he called a Church Council at Ephesus for June 449 to re-try Eutyches. But this was to be presided over by Dioscurus of Alexandria, not an orthodox bishop, and Pope Leo sent legates with his 'Tome' expecting its approval but had a shock. On 8 August the Council, 'packed with Monophysites', refused to accept the 'Tome' or the legates' advice, and Dioscurus of Alexandria led Eutyches' acquittal. Instead, on 22 August Flavian and Bishop Eusebius of Dorylaeum were deposed, and Flavian died on his way into exile. Leo refused to accept the verdict of the 'robber council' at Ephesus and led resistance to it as illegal across the West, but in November 449 Anatolius, a Monophysite and former priest under Dioscurus (and ally of Chrysaphius), was made Patriarch of Constantinople.

Valentinian, Galla Placidia, and Licinia Eudoxia, 'nudged' by Pope Leo, wrote in vain to Theodosius requesting a re-trial for Flavian in February 450. The situation became a dangerous stalemate with rumours of military plots in the East which it was (correctly) supposed that Aetius had sent agents to assist in the hope of avoiding more rash misjudgements by the wayward Theodosius II by making him the puppet of a 'junta' and also of avoiding an anti-Monophysite rebellion among the Constantinopolitan elite that could easily lead to a civil war. Even the feckless or stubborn Theodosius had the sense not to make further Monophysite appointments in the Church at Constantinople as most of the clergy and the populace boycotted Anatolius' services. He was probably hoping to use his authority to induce 'fence-sitters' and job-seekers in the Church to desert the 'hard-line' Catholics but the latter's ranks held firm, boosted by threats by angry junior orthodox bishops to hold their own synods and indict the new Patriarch. The majority of the Church in Egypt backed the munificent and well-liked Dioscurus and the Church at Antioch was fairly evenly divided for and against the Monophysite Patriarch of Constantinople, but the overwhelming majority of both clerics and lay people in the Balkans (plus the local 'duces' and most junior officers) backed Pope Leo.

The clergy of Illyricum, technically in the Eastern Empire, held a synod at Naissus (Nis, Serbia) in defiance of the Emperor to transfer their allegiance to the Pope and the local 'duces' declared that they would not send troops to arrest them as ordered and if pressed would recognise the orthodox Valentinian III as their ruler instead. Civil war threatened, Pulcheria fumed as alarmed ministers wished that she was in charge, and Attila looked on with satisfaction, but suddenly the situation changed as on 28 July 450 Theodosius II died from a spinal injury after being thrown from his horse in the Lycus valley outside the capital on a hunt, aged 49. Not as shrewd and competent as his sister Pulcheria (who was far better at selecting able subordinates not flatterers for office) or his grandfather Theodosius I, his reputation then stood – and stayed – low on account of the theological 'mess' that he had left the Eastern Empire in by his un-necessary sponsorship of the Monophysites. The orthodox had always suspected him as being too open to the wiles of 'dodgy' unorthodox Christian thinkers who promised to bring greater unity, such as Nestorius, and the more capable civil servants and politically interested nobles distrusted him as a man who was too open to flattery and 'chancers' such as Chrysaphius, though he meant well and thought that his proteges did so too – for which most of his courtiers forgave him though historians did not. Many in his capital's elite, even

Battle for the Empire: Aetius vs Attila, Monophysites vs Catholics

pro-Monophysites, now judged that religious 'experiments' had to take second place to unity – and that only orthodoxy would bring Western help.

Pulcheria was recalled to the capital by the ministers, and she and Aspar declared that Theodosius had nominated Aspar's former aide-de-camp Marcian, currently the 'dux' of Thrace (since 447) and formerly of Upper Moesia and Dacia, a distinguished officer of Thracian/Illyrian origin aged fifty-eight and known for his honesty and commonsense, as his successor. Pulcheria agreed to a nominal marriage with Marcian that would not break her vow of virginity and on 2 August crowned him at the Hebdoman Palace parade-ground, seven miles West of Constantinople, before a ceremonial assembly. They then married at Hagia Sophia. Marcian refused to pay any tribute to Attila, but sent him gifts; he restored good government with a massive purge of Chrysaphius' appointees and allies and seizure of their assets. The late Emperor was not openly condemned but had an abysmal reputation as the details of Chrysaphius' misrule and corruption were revealed. Anatolius was sacked as Patriarch, followed by all the Monophysites in office across the Balkans (not many) and Anatolia (rather more) who would not sign up to the decretals of the Council of Nicaea, and Marcian and Pulcheria prepared for a new Church Council to align East with West again and ignored advice from Dioscurus and a number of anxious Syrian clerics that the Monophysite faction had too strong popular support in their regions to make it wise to sack all its supporters there. Eutyches, blamed for the debacle, was abandoned by his former court allies and deported to a remote monastery in Cilicia to live as a humble monk. Domnus was restored to the see of Antioch. On 22–25 October 451 a General Council of the Church was held at the church of St Euphemia, Chalcedon, with the position of honour for Pope Leo's legates and approval of his 'Tome' as defining Orthodoxy. Christ was declared to have a dual nature as both human and divine, indissolubly linked, and Eutyches and the 'Monophysites' were condemned for heresy. The Patriarchate of Constantinople was declared equal to Rome as an Imperial city, which the Pope rejected. And 2,000 guardsmen now assisted the new and orthodox Patriarch Proterius at Alexandria against Monophysite resistance; ex-Patriarch Dioscurus was deported to a monastery in Paphlagonia.

(The change from OTL events in this scenario of the East's history in the 440s is that Chrysaphius' plot to murder Attila not only goes wrong, which it did in reality, but leads to his assassination by his enemies – who cannot trust Theodoosius II to get rid of him. In reality, he survived until the coup after the death of Theodosius in 450. The main point of the divergence from OTL here is that although he is seen as Theodosius' 'evil genius' his elimination does not alter the religious crisis of 449–50, as

Theodosius goes ahead with his switch to supporting the Monophysites – Chrysaphius's theological allies – anyway. The Emperor is thus less of a 'puppet' than supposed, which may be the case in actuality; Chrysaphius was blamed as the cause of his rash and badly-planned policies, but was more of a symptom and Theodosius had already caused one crisis in the 430s over his then ally Nestorius, qv.)

The death of Empress-Mother and 'Augusta' Galla Placidia in December 450, aged sixty, precipitated the final showdown of Attila the Hun with the West, though it was probably inevitable at some early point as he needed more loot and victories to satiate his demanding chiefs and as the East had paid him off he was left with Gaiseric and Aetius to attack. He was said to have considered Persia but to have looked at a map drawn up by his learned secretary Orestes and decided that it was too risky to take his huge army down the shores of the Caspian, short of water-holes and livestock, to attack via Adiabene. In summer 450 he was already moving his advance forces of cavalry west over the Oder and demanding that Gaiseric hand over half his lands for Hun settlement and come to his court to do homage and pay rent for the rest. Though the outnumbered Vandal king, who had little cavalry, refused to ask Aetius for help as his subordinate lords requested his own sub-kingdom of the Ostrogoths (East Goths) in Silesia, led by king Theodemir, and the rulers of the Gepids in Upper Saxony did so in secret. There was pressure on Aetius from alarmed Roman commanders in Dacia and Marcomannia to agree to this and stave off the fall of the Vandal kingdom and a huge invasion of Huns through the Ostrava Gap, where the Roman walls might be breached as Attila was constructing a force of artillery and was rumoured to be practicing using fire-laden missiles to be hurled across walls by catapults. The ambitious and restive Princess Honoria, Valentinian III's unmarried and allegedly over-sexed sister, had been refused her choice of husbands by her mother twice in the 440s and was now arguing that she should be the lynchpin of a Roman alliance to Gaiseric and lure that greedy and status-obsessed warlord into the Roman orbit by marrying his son and heir Hunneric. But the Empress-Mother had refused that idea too in 449 as 'disgusting' – Hunneric was not only a German but an Arian – and packed her off to Constantinople to stay for six months in the highly religious and moral Pulcheria's strictly controlled court.

On her return home late in 450 firstly the Ostrogoth and Gepid envoys arrived and then Galla Placidia died, but the equally snobbish Valentinian also refused to let Honoria marry Hunneric and preferred to see Attila destroy the arrogant Vandal. The uninhibited Princess developed a new idea for her future and suggested that she should marry Attila instead – he had many wives already from his allied tribes' nobility – and turn him into an ally of Rome. Somehow this suggestion got out from secret palace discussions at Ravenna, the site of the main Eastern court since 412, to a Hunnic delegation that was visiting to seek a huge bribe for Attila as a way of him funding his latest search for extra steppe cavalry allies ahead of his attack on the Vandals, and the upshot was that in early 451 the next Hunnic embassy to Ravenna gave the Emperor a nasty shock by demanding that Honoria be married off to Attila and that the latter be given all of Marcomannia as her dowry. Honoria was willing but her brother had her locked up in her apartments and refused to consider it, and with Aetius absent in Argentorate on the upper Rhine busy drawing up a secret alliance with Theodomir the Ostrogoth and a Gepid delegation he did not find out about it until later. Aetius would have counselled caution and spinning out talks at least until Attila had fought Gaiseric and hopefully suffered large losses in that war, but thanks to Valentinian's impetuosity the Empire as well as the Vandals were lined up for Attila's punishment in 451 and the great warlord announced that he would take all of Germany and the Rhineland plus Dacia anyway and if Honoria was not handed over invade Italy next.

In April 451 Attila invaded across the upper Elbe and ravaged Gaiseric's kingdom with a huge coalition of Germanic and steppe vassals including Ardaric's Gepids, the Rugians, Scirians, Heruls, Alans, and Thuringians; they defeated Gaiseric in an epic battle where the Vandals' infantry was trodden underfoot by the charge of probably 45–50,000 steppe cavalry and Gaiseric barely escaped with his life and fled into the Black Forest. The Huns then crossed the lower Main near Moguntiacum with a ready-bult bridge of boats and headed south-west for the Rhine, but Aetius had prepared a massive Roman army, both cavalry and infantry, and had trained a new army of archers too. Though he did not dare to bring much of the Marcomannian army west as Attila had left another force at the Ostrava Gap to face them he had at least 50,000 men plus the 'Salian' Franks settled on the lower Rhine, the Burgundians from the Vosges, and about half the Ostrogoths who had escaped from the debacle to Gaiseric's army. Theodoric the Visigothic king, one of Gaiseric's vassals on the middle Elbe who had had to flee west out of Attila's way towards Colonia Agrippinensis (Cologne), attempted to remain neutral and was successfully pressurised by Aetius' envoy, the southern Gallic aristocrat Avitus, to join Aetius in time for the battle that now ensued near the Rhine S of Moguntiacum – though the supposed 'Romans vs Huns' battle did in fact have large German forces on both sides.

At the crucial battle of 'Campus Mauriacus' near the Rhine on 25 June 451 a force of around 60,000 Romans and their allies met Attila and his force of around 70,000, and the Romans held back a massive Hunnic cavalry attack on their concentric circle of infantry which sheltered behind a pre-prepared chain of pits and lines of stakes and showered the attackers with arrows and flaming missiles. The expert Hunnic steppe cavalry were larger than the Roman cavalry and were eager to charge them and many were reckless for their own safety while Attila had a series of feigned retreats planned to lure the Romans into traps, but instead the Romans stayed immobile and picked off the enemy with missiles and only once the Huns were exhausted did Aetius give the order for his, more disciplined cavalry to emerge from behind his lines and stage a series of assaults on the Hunnic lines. The Roman cavalry 'rolled up' the Huns into separate groups and then systematically 'squashed' them together into smaller units until they were tightly packed and killed them, and as Roman missiles smashed the Huns' infantry as the latter tried to rescue them the Huns eventually gave up and broke to head back to their fortified camp. The latter was bombarded from a safe distance by the Roman artillery but not entered so the ambushes that Attila was preparing inside were never used, and next day Aetius annoyed his more exuberant followers and the new Visigothic king, Theodomir (son of Theodoric who had been killed in the cavalry pursuit of the Huns to their camp) by refusing proposals to assault the Hunnic camp. Instead a rain of flaming missiles continued to descend on the camp until the Huns took the hint and packed what they could salvage onto their waggons and headed back to the plains North of the Carpathians and thence to the Ukraine, though apparently Attila had wanted to resume the fight despite being laid up by a leg-injury and unable to ride and had had to be forced to pull back by his more nervous sons and lieutenants. The Huns had the discipline to keep 'in column' apart from stragglers and to preserve enough food-supplies to keep themselves and their horses from starvation, but the sight of them retreating and Attila having to ride in a wagon led to some of their allied chiefs sneaking off with their men at night to either hide in the forests or offer their swords to the nearest Roman patrols in return for immunity. It was later reckoned that Aetius gained about 10–12,000 more German tribal recruits for his forces this way, and he took care to split them up and move them in smaller units under Roman command to isolated parts of the Rhine frontier so that if they felt like defecting later this would be difficult.

Attila was allowed to retreat with his still formidable army without a major challenge and his men were just picked off in the forests as they retired to the Oder and thence the Ukraine, but he had lost at least half his army and his myth of invincibility and in the aftermath of the defeat the remaining Ostrogoths in his service deserted him *en masse*. The kingdom of the Vandals had been ravaged and had lost most of its army and Aetius was able to ignore the shattered survivors and hand over 'Transrhenus' from Rhine to Elbe to the Ostrogoths, Visigoths, Franks, and assorted Gepid and Alan defectors from Attila's army as a patchwork of Rome-allied kingdoms who paid tribute and supplied troops to the Roman army. As he rebuilt his own war-reduced army and integrated new German allied auxiliary forces into it the Huns did not resume the offensive or even dare to object as in autumn 451 Marcian reoccupied the lower Danube and rebuilt all the towns and fortresses that had been sacked or handed over.

A massive and emotional Triumph for Aetius in Rome on 25 May 452 as 'Saviour of the Empire' and 'Protector of the People of God', the 'Consul for Life', cemented his reputation as Rome's greatest general since Julius Caesar and the man who had saved Rome and Europe from Attila, though his coronation with a solid gold wreath on the Capitol at the end of the celebration procession by Valentinian did not stop rumours that the unmilitary Emperor was in reality extremely jealous of him. When the commander-in-chief started to suggest that he should have his teenage son Gaudentius married to Valentinian's elder daughter and presumed heiress, Placidia, the Emperor only pretended to go along with this and was in reality alarmed and reluctant to agree. In April 453 Attila died suddenly of a burst blood-vessel in his camp on the steppes near the upper Dniester the night after his latest wedding, to the daughter of one of his recent new Ukrainian vassal-chiefs who had been enrolled to supplement his cavalry-short army with more horsemen, and this led to a massive revolt that summer against his sons Ellac and Gerdich by many of their non-Asiatic vassals including the remaining sections of the Gepids and Alans in Hunnic service. This was mainly a German revolt and apparently emissaries had recently been sent to the chiefs who revolted by their Ostrogothic 'contacts' with gold supplied by the Western Empire, presumably by Aetius as Valentinian was too cautious and was dubious about any more success on the battlefield for his overbearing commander-in-chief. But whoever touched it off the result was a disaster for the Huns as their unprepared and still weakened army was routed in a major clash on the Dniester by the rebels, Ellac was killed, and his brother and most of the Hun elite had to pack up their tented camps and move back to the Dnieper valley to re-settle in lands that remained loyal to them.

The Huns were still militarily formidable and some of the tribes that had revolted and who now took over the Dniester region were hostile to the Empire and by the mid-460s were raiding the lower Danube again so the frontier was not at peace. But the Hunnic empire had collapsed and this was a major boon to the Romans and with Attila gone and his people moved back to the East Aetius was able to lead a Roman army though the Ostrava Gap northwards in summer 454 and reduce the loose local coalition of anti-Hun Germanic tribes, mostly Gepids and Alans plus some Heruls and Suevi, to the status of troop- and tribute-supplying Roman vassals. In effect the Western Empire now held sway as the greatest regional power and the overlord of all the tribal kings from the Rhine to the Oder and the chivalrous, honest, and personally loyal Aetius was a man who understood how to get the best out of his vassals and how to ensure his allies' loyalty, distributing gifts and favours and also inviting chiefs to send their sons to be educated in Rome and learn Roman ways – and in effect serve as hostages. As the youths were converted to Catholicism too Pope Leo, a staunch backer of Aetius, and his bishops were satisfied and a network of Roman allies was built up over the next decade while some 20–25,000 new German auxiliaries served in the Roman army and war-expired German veterans were settled as Roman farmers in the Rhineland or in Hun-ravaged areas of north-west Germany. As the Vandal kingdom was never rebuilt and Gaiseric had to make do with a small tribal lordship on the banks of the lower Vistula Aetius was also able to quietly 'Romanise' the part of Transrhenus nearer the Rhine and install some allied Frankish and Goth nobles, all former officers in his forces or at least his allies in 451, as sub-governors of small hereditary lordships under the leadership of the new Roman 'dux' there (himself always a German of noble birth). Many of these men were given the honorary Roman rank of 'Count', and were reckoned by Imperial bureaucrats as 'federates' (allies) or even (but not by themselves) as vassals. The enrolment of German officers in the Roman army and presence of Germans at court in the West was as noticeable as under Stilicho as chief minister in 405–12 but now the organiser of this was in a stronger position as a Roman himself and the saviour of the Empire from the menace of Attila, and a wise Emperor would have accepted Aetius' predominance in military matters and interest in the succession for his son if he had no son himself.

But Aetius was the target of court gossip and malevolent whispers and Valentinian was as open to the latter as Theodosius II had been in the East, and the unwise Emperor was worked on by the eunuch chamberlain Heraclius and the current Praefect of Rome, the wealthy and ambitious Petronius Maximus who was a super-rich and confident noble of ancient family linked to the Anicii dynasty. He had been serving in various honorary posts and provincial governorships since the early 420s and had built up an extra fortune to add to his inherited one from his fondness for demanding presents and favours from supplicants for his help in office. Fearful of his past illegal activities being exposed by a new finance-minister of humble birth, Aetius' Gallic protégé Agrippinus, and a current legal commission which was looking into dodgy past decisions by governors and sub-governors across Italy and Gaul and extracting large fines from offenders, Petronius used his access to the Emperor at court parties to tell him that Aetius was aiming at the throne for his son Gaudentius. Aetius would not wait for the current ruler to die but would help him on his way so that the rather vain and lazy 'Protectores' officer Gaudentius would rule as a malleable teenager and do what his father wanted. Aetius now bullied the Emperor into agreeing to marry his daughter Placidia to Gaudentius as what the Empire was expecting, and Valentinian arranged for the ambush and murder of Aetius in the Imperial Palace while the court was in residence for the early months of 455 but was detected in time by a conspirator's appalled relative who told Aetius. The alarmed 'Master of Infantry and Cavalry' agreed with a summoned meeting of his senior advisers that he could not trust the treacherous and unstable Emperor any longer, and so on 16 March 455 Valentinian, aged thirty-six, was ambushed by a group of Aetius' officers while riding in the fields north-west of Rome with a small escort and hacked to death and a 'hit squad' of officers also arrested Petronius Maximus and the scheming chamberlain who were quickly executed and had their wealth confiscated.

(In OTL Valentinian did manage to murder Aetius, and was soon killed by his late minister's supporters; disaster for the West followed.)

The public was told that the Emperor had gone insane through jealousy of his commander-in-chief and tried to murder him and that he had had to be killed to save the Empire, and as his wife Licinia Eudoxia had hated the chamberlain and his influence over her husband she gave her support to the coup unofficially and agreed that Gaudentius be married off to Placidia at once and raised to the throne. The new Emperor, aged eighteen, might widely be seen as his father's puppet and Aetius as the real ruler of the Empire, but the latter was preferable to the 'palace rule' by scheming eunuchs that had landed the East in trouble in 447–50 and in Constantinople the initially shocked Pulcheria accepted the coup on account of the similarity of the West's 'near escape' to the Chrysaphius episode. The coup left Pulcheria as the last of the House of Theodosius in the direct line ruling part of the Empire, and she continued as co-ruler with Marcian until she died in June 458, aged fifty-nine, after a forty-five year reign as 'Augusta', with her reputation then and subsequently standing high as a shrewd, capable, and idealistic Christian – and orthodox – administrator. Her admirers, led by the orthodox hierarchy of the East, hailed her as the 'female Augustus' and the 'female Marcus Aurelius' (a reference to her great learning and her high ideals); but contemporary Monophysites and later historians reckoned that she had given too much leeway to the Catholic doctrinal viewpoint at the Church Council of Chalcedon and had hindered a meaningful inter-sect reconciliation. The Empress Placidia, her great-niece and daughter of Valentinian III, was technically 'Augusta' of the West from 455 onwards as consort of Gaudentius but as a rather shallow and fashion-obsessed teenager was uninterested in governance and was politically sidelined by Aetius anyway, while Placidia's mother

Licinia Eudoxia, daughter of Theodosius II and as proud as Theodosius I, was less easily silenced and continued to drain the treasury and amass estates and jewellery. But she was kept out of politics by Aetius until one of her admirers and alleged lovers tried to interest her in a coup in 459 and she was 'persuaded' to go off on a long visit to North Africa where Aetius had her quietly locked up at a remote villa far from Carthage and encouraged to drink herself stupid. The younger daughter of her and Valentinian, Eudocia, was dangled in front of assorted ambitious young nobles as a potential bride for them if they were loyal by Aetius but was kept unmarried for a decade, and as Gaudentius and his wife had no children, the succession long-term remained a problem, with Aetius' rising officer proteges rather obviously ambitious for him to advance one of them to be Eudocia's husband and a future Emperor.

Chapter 8

Aetius (and his Son Gaudentius as Western Emperor 455–469), Majorian, and the Rise of the Anthemii in the West

With Gaudentius as the nominal ruler of the West but seen as his father's puppet Aetius had to tread warily with the civilian administration in Ravenna and across the Empire, and he also feared trouble from the nobility in Rome as he was only a 'self-made' Gallic outsider and the executed Petronius Maximus had had many friends and admirers in the old capital. On that count Aetius did not confiscate those estates and mansions that had come to Petronius' wealthy officer cadet son Palladius, as popular as his father but more lazy, via his mother and did not purge assorted members of the Petronius-allied Anicii from government either. The great southern Gallic aristocrat Eparchus Avitus, who Aetius had been using for diplomatic missions for a decade and had shown his ability in flattering and charming the lords of the Franks and Goths into helping Aetius against Attila, was invited to Rome as the new City Praefect with his Italian aristocratic wife a useful link to the local nobles. His son-in-law the Aquitaine poet-aristocrat Sidonius Apollinaris was also called in to add intellectual lustre to the new court and teach the rather boorish young officer Gaudentius some culture and social manners, and he duly presented assorted flattering odes in suitably Horatian metre for Aetius' assorted consulships for the next decade – which Aetius usually made a point of assuming in person in Rome in the antique manner to charm the local traditionalists – and for Avitus' consulship in 457. (In OTL Avitus was emperor in 455-6.)

With the army under his grip and a tightly knit circle of his senior aides, led by the men who had held command in the war of 451 such as Majorian, Count Marcellinus and his rising nephew Julius Nepos, and Aegidius, controlling the most important Western armies on the Rhine and upper Danube and in Marcomannia and Dacia the watchful Aetius had no need to fear a military revolt. His role as the saviour of Rome put would-be rebels off as they feared that soldiers would not follow them in sufficient numbers, but there was still grumbling among the nobility at all the self-made Germans who Aetius invited to join the 'Protectores' officer-cadets or to serve as 'duces' in important provinces. As the Visigothic king Thorismund's brothers Theodoric and Euric served as 'duces' in Lower Germany in the 460s and the less charismatic or 'sword-swinging' political manoeuvrer Count Ricimer became deputy 'Master of Soldiers' to Aetius in 461 wits grumbled that even if Attila had lost the war the Germans had won as many offices as if they had conquered Rome. The retort of Aetius to this was that if rich young Romans did not like this all they had to do was to join the army and show what they could do and a career based on military talent was open to all, but as he expanded the Western army by another 20,000 men on the frontiers – based in small garrisons and mobile units not large armies as the latter might revolt – in 458–60 and paid for it out of a new tax on landed estates it was mostly younger sons of rural farmers hit by drought, plagues, or locusts or small-town artisans who joined up and few nobles or 'career bureaucrats' sons did. The exception was the socially elevated and prestigious – and well-paid – cavalry regiments of the Western 'comitatus' where Romans and Germans alike mingled and even a few Hunnic deserters who did not fancy a career on the war-hit steppes after Attila's empire collapsed travelled to Rome or Mediolanum to join up. In 462 Aetius proceeded to institute an annual 'levy' of infantry from each province for the army to ensure that all, including war-averse Italians, did their duty and helped out the Empire but in practice there was a lot of draft-dodging and the less well-connected farmers and their labourers tended to have their sons called up as the rich found loopholes in the regulations (eg health problems) or paid others to take their places in the army.

In the East, in January 459 Marcian, who had been widowed for some months and had failed either to remarry or to consider the succession seriously given the multitude of potential contenders, fell ill with gout during a procession to Hebdoman to commemorate the 447 earthquake twelve years before. He died on 27 January aged nearly 71, a capable and honest man but overshadowed for most of his reign by his wife Pulcheria; the competent and ambitious Aspar, as 'Magister Peditum' (Master of Infantry) at the capital, decided not to contest the throne as he was both a German and an Arian though he was urged to it by his vain and ambitious sons Ardaburius and Patricius (who had a Roman mother). He was however determined to be as important to the East as Aetius was in the West, and he successfully promoted his former military steward Leo the Thracian, aged 49, who had served as a successful and methodical defence-restoring 'dux' of Lower Moesia in 453–5 and had earlier been a capable military commander in Dacia. Originally a Thracian peasant and said by local snobs in the capital to have been a butcher when he first arrived there, Leo was genial and incorruptible and was appreciated by his men but was not liked by the aristocratic officers who disdained Aspar as a German; however all the more well-known and respected civilian candidates were vetoed by Aspar as the Empire 'needed a military man in case of a new crisis on the steppes. The late Praefect and regent Anthemius (d 414)'s grandson, the former 'Count of the Privy Purse' Tiberius Anthemius, the 'Master of Offices' Proculus, and three past consuls and City Praefects were all ridiculed by him and his allies as never having done any military service or even visited the Northern frontier, every yard of which Leo the Thracian knew well, and the Senate duly elected Leo as Aspar wished with none of them having the support and the past military experience to be able to put themselves forward as a ruler who would be adequate in a frontier crisis.

On 7 February 459 Leo was acclaimed by the assembled Guards and officials then crowned by Patriarch Anatolius (the first Patriarchal coronation of an Emperor) in the nearby palace at the parade-ground of Hebdoman. He then returned to the capital for a ceremonial entry, a religious service at Hagia Sophia where he swore allegiance to the Councils of Nicaea, Constantinople and Chalcedon's decretals, and a fortnight of Games in the Hippodrome, and the change of regime passed off more smoothly than feared with no provincial mutinies and only one major – religious – disturbance, in Alexandria. The 'Monophysite'-persecuting Patriarch Proterius was driven out of his cathedral by angry Monophysite mobs and the City Praefect, who he had quarrelled with, did not intervene and then told Leo that a revolt would follow if the disgraced and hated Proterius was allowed to stay in office. Leo was duly panicked into abandoning him and an intriguing rival of his called Timotheus 'the Cat' (so-called for his sneaking around local churches and monasteries at night like a cat to canvass support from discontented foes of the officious Proterius) secured the Patriarchate. But although the Monophysites benefited from a lull in persecution that Aspar, who for all his faults was religiously tolerant, organised in 457–9 there were more religious clashes involving orthodox, Monophysites and Nestorians across Syria into the 460s and Leo's lack of interest in religion compared to the devout Pulcheria and Marcian was criticized in the capital.

Nor did Leo bother so much about cracking down on corruption and tax evasion, while the competent Proculus was soon replaced as 'Master of Offices by Aspar's financially dodgy court ally Decimus and Aspar's eldest son Ardaburius became 'Magister Peditum' in Thrace in 459 so he could build up a client-base in that army. As he was already married his younger brother Patricius was chosen instead to marry Leo's younger daughter Leontia and duly began to harbour thoughts about the succession. But gradually during the 460s Leo began to assert himself in alliance with the capital's bureaucracy and the city nobility to rein in Aspar, and the series of fund-raising legal commission investigations into tax dodging and bribery launched by the new 'quaestor' Miltiades of Larissa, a self-made ex-farmer Thessalian lawyer protégé of Marcian's, after 463 were used by the Emperor to undermine assorted men appointed to civilian office through Aspar's influence, governors in particular. Handing out the vacated offices to a mixture of quaestoral department officials who could be trusted to back the Emperor 'per se' as head of state, proteges and funders of local orthodox bishops (so that the Church would defend them), and rich nobles connected to the Greek, Anatolian and Syrian 'old family' nobility built up a coalition of loyalists who were slowly infiltrated into the Senate. Aspar's rival Tiberius Anthemius, married to a daughter of Marcian from his first marriage and angry at not being made emperor in 459, added his own clientele to the Emperor's support.

Aspar was more concerned to keep Hunnic and other steppe raids on Moesia and dissident Alan raids via the Daryal Pass on Iberia and Armenia in check to avoid allegations of him being incompetent to notice what was going on, while his naïve if honourable support for religious reconciliation with the growing Monophysite congregations in Syria and Egypt and refusal to allow more crackdowns infuriated the orthodox Church 'power-brokers' in both Constantinople and Antioch. His well-founded paranoia about plots in the officer-corps and among provincial commanders, who he regularly reshuffled so no general could build up a body of support in his command who would then back him in revolt, led to several capable 'duces' on the Eastern and Balkan frontiers being held back from chasing Turkic, Alan, and Hunnic cavalry raiders back into their own lands. There was a missed opportunity in 463 to stop a Sassanid pretender who had failed to overthrow the new Roman ally ruler of Istakr, Bahram IV, escaping to the Oxus and creating an anti-Roman state at Maracanda (Samarkand) backed by Turkic mercenaries, and as Aspar's eldest son Ardaburius was trusted enough to be sent to invade Sarmatia and 'play at being Aetius' (as Constantinopolitan wits sneered) in 465 but lost his way on the campaign due to poor scouts and his force was mauled in a Hunnic ambush the chances of this brash young man being named as Leo's successor dropped drastically. In order to boost the Aspar dynasty's chances the great general now arranged for his younger son Patricius to serve as the effective commander of the 'comitatus' at Ctesiphon as 'Magister Equitum' (cavalry commander) and head of a special army-reform commission there in 465–7, accompanied by his wife Princess Leontia and acting as a virtual prince. His expedition in 467 with his re-trained crack army of 25,000 armed 'cataphracts' to Persis and Hyrcania to set up new Romano-Persian military bases there to repel the rising tide of Turkic raids was successful to his father's relief – but owed this more to Patricius' capable if flashy young deputy Armatus, nephew of Leo's wife Verina, than to the hard-drinking and vain Patricius.

While the expedition was in progress and Aspar himself was on a campaign in Sarmatia as far as the Dniester to repair the accompanying Ardaburius' reputation Leo announced the creation of a new and high-profile regiment of super-tough Isaurian mountaineers and ex-farm-hands, the 'Excubitors', for the palace. He brought in the capable and ambitious Isaurian officer Tarasicodessa, renamed 'Zeno' as he was Hellenised and formerly 'dux' of Armenia and Pontus, to be their commander. Zeno was married off to Leo's elder daughter Ariadne in a surprise move and Aspar returned from his campaign to find himself with a rival in the palace, and as he tried to induce Leo to make his second son Patricius 'Caesar' and thus probable heir in winter 467- 8 monks led demonstrations against Patricius in the capital as he was an Arian and Aspar assured that he was about to convert. The stand-off lasted for over a year as Zeno manoeuvred for influence at court and a new feud between Patricius and the Empress Verina's ambitious younger brother Basiliscus, a rising ex-officer of the 'Protectores' and in 465–7 the 'dux' of two combined Thracian provinces, added another element to the intrigues. But in April 469 Leo finally struck after his quaestoral department's commissions ensnared 'Master of Offices' Decimus in a corruption enquiry and the venal minister was sacked, 'regrettably' as Leo assured the unconvinced Aspar. Some of the general's hard-drinking and indiscreet officer proteges seem to have made threats about a coup to remove Leo at parties and Patricius to have got involved out of fear that Verina was about to persuade Leo to make Basiliscus 'Caesar' and heir. But however it happened and whether or not Aspar was 'framed' the Emperor became convinced that the latter was involved in a plot and allowed Zeno and his Isaurian officers to strike against him. Aspar was invited to a secret military strategy discussion for the summer's Sarmatian campaign at the palace, intercepted in a corridor by a 'hit squad' of Isaurians, and was 'killed resisting arrest', and after this the necessity of stopping any revenge attack on the Emperor was excused as the reason for Patricius and his intimates being rounded up in the capital and killed too. Ardaburius was assassinated at his military command HQ on the lower Danube, his attackers sent from the capital with a letter which he was reading with a pleased expression when he was stabbed by them. (This was excused as showing that he was in on his brother's plot, as the fake letter was a 'progress report' on it.)

The purge of Aspar and his family plus a number of their army allies made scarcely a ripple in Eastern politics and there were no mutinies either, which was declared as proof that the government and army were secure from undue German influence and that any Arian like Aspar had minimal chances of success in a coup as all sensible generals had realized. But it did not lead to greater stability at the court as Leo had no son and Princess Leontia was now available for a new husband and Tiberius Anthemius sought her hand for one of his sons by his first marriage, to Marcian's daughter. But Leo would not allow this as Zeno was expecting to be named as heir instead and when he and Princess Ariadne had a son, Leo, in 469 this child was the obvious ultimate heir to the throne. Basiliscus was also after the throne and as an under-qualified but munificent, party-giving, and Games-funding Praefect of 'Oriens' ('the East', i.e. Syria/Lebanon) at Antioch in 470–3 proceeded to dabble in religious politics there to offer toleration to the Monophysites should he become Emperor. As Armatus had his own hopes too and was very popular in the Mesopotamian armies the Emperor had to balance between their factions and made sure of the Church's support by driving all the (mostly German) Arians who Aspar had allowed office in the army administration and land on retirement into exile in remote provinces and confiscating most of their property.

In the West, the same dilemma of overall military security but internal dynastic insecurity plagued the Empire too, and Aetius found that being the acclaimed saviour of Rome from Attila the Hun and disposing of the treacherous Valentinian had not solved all his problems. His son Gaudentius was a vain and incompetent if well-meaning character who had no judgement or political skill and was fonder of presiding at the Games, which he increasingly attended in Rome as Ravenna only had a small race-track due to it being restricted in size by the nearby marshes, than in governing, and he had no children either. Empress Licinia Eudoxia secretly sent emissaries to Constantinople in 467 and they persuaded the Eastern Emperor to intercede for her and have her released from house-arrest and allowed to go to Greece to live on her estates in the Peloponnese, and reputedly Aspar also encouraged this with the devious hope of undermining Aetius and Gaudentius and having their dynasty replaced by one of his own clients or getting an ambitious rival to transfer their activities to the West and so remove themselves as a threat to his sons. In that respect Aspar as well as Licinia Eudoxia may have been behind the successful plan at the intrigue-riven Western court to have the police-watched Princess Eudocia, Licinia Eudoxia's elder daughter, allowed to visit her mother in Greece in 468 to get her out of Italy while Gaudentius and Placidia were away on a successful Imperial tour of Carthage and North Africa. This ended with the surprise arrival of the ambitious Eastern court aristocrat and former governor of Lydia (462–5) and Phrygia (465–8) Olybrius, at Licinia Eudoxia's estate and his engagement to the much younger Eudocia.

This smooth-talking and luxury-loving nobleman, a noted holder of extravagant parties and sponsor of racing-teams in Constantinople as a young man and now nearly fifty, was a cousin of the Anicii dynasty in Rome, a descendant of the major 360s-370s political figure Petronius Probus, and had in fact been born and brought up in Rome itself and he was angling for the throne of the Western Empire as a protégé of Leo or of Aspar. Though the suspicious Aetius would not allow him to go to the West after his marriage 469 saw a major upheaval in the West as well as the East as in April 469 Aetius died suddenly, aged 71, after over fifty years as the major military figure in the West and fourteen years as the 'Emperor-maker'. The loss of his father and chief organiser left Gaudentius without the man he relied on to run politics and decide on major appointments for him, and as he let the great general's most respected lieutenant Majorian become 'Master of Infantry' but balanced him against the ageing General Marcellinus' ambitious nephew Julius Nepos ('dux' of Illyria in 466–9) as 'Master of Cavalry' his fear of them both as potential coup-leaders grew and scheming courtiers who resented the huge military budget and land-taxes encouraged him to rein in the army leadership by force.

The soldiers had respected Aetius as their heroic leader and would accept his orders however much hard work this entailed but they despised his 'amateur' soldier son who had never served on a major campaign and had only been a guards-officer due to family influence not talent. As Gaudentius sought to juggle military appointments to reshuffle grumbling HQ officers away from Rome and part spy-reported grumbling regional 'duces' from their commands discontent came to a head in an unlikely way. While Majorian was questioning the Emperor's more unjust transfers of capable commanders from their posts openly the seething sacked 'Master of Infantry' Ricimer, his predecessor, privately felt that his new and very remote command as a regional 'dux' in faraway Mauretania was an insult to his honour, and whether or not at his instigation his part-Burgundian nephew Gundobad and a group of his fellow-officers ended up assassinating the Emperor on 18 July 469 at a party at one of his villas near Tibur in what initially appeared to be a spontaneous drunken brawl. The death of Gaudentius left the throne up for grabs and had Olybrius been in Italy he would have stood a good chance of winning it as a 'legitimate Theodosian' claimant via his new wife, but instead the senior officers at the 'comitatus' HQ at Mediolanum proceeded to agree on Majorian as the much-needed experienced 'strongman' who would have the necessary military confidence and stave off civil war and the Senate and senior palace bureaucrats reluctantly agreed when they were asked to do so.

(In OTL Majorian was merely one of the ephemeral Western rulers who were first raised up and then deposed by the German-dominated army after the assassination of Valentinian III and the sack of Rome by the Vandals in 455. He ruled from 457–62, came close to reviving Roman power in an epic reassertion of central control, but was defeated in an attempt to invade Vandal North Africa in 462 and executed by his chief general, Ricimer. With more resources and luck he could have done much more and possibly saved the Empire; my version gives him this chance. I preserve a successful and stable line of Western Roman commanders in the early-mid-fifth century which was broken up in real life – Theodosius I, Stilicho, Constantius III, Aetius, and Majorian.)

Majorian, aged fifty-four, was duly elected and was raised on a shield at the 'comitatus' parade-ground and later crowned by the bishop of Mediolanum to symbolise Church support, and he proved as strong a ruler 'in front of the curtain' as Aetius had been 'behind the curtain' and continued his effective predecessor's military priorities and army- reforms. He had no children or near male relatives and so the identity of the next heir was unclear, but he was in good health and had full military support and as the Senate and palace bureaucrats hoped for a proper senatorial election of a civilian 'next time round' he did not disabuse them of this possibility. He chose to cut back on Imperial formality and non-essential ceremonies and pose as an informal, approachable 'First Citizen' as the first such emperor since Julian. He was however, careful to keep up public good relations with the orthodox Catholic church hierarchy in Rome, whose mostly honest and hard-working diocesan officials earned his respect and were often invited to help out the City of Rome administration and its civic public works projects and serve on commissions though he had no interest in theology and Pope Hilarius was only invited to the Palace for church services and dinners out of the resulting good publicity. Turning over the great – and currently vacant since Theodosius I threw out the priests – former Temple of Cybele on the Esquiline to the Church to be transformed into the new Church of Mary Magdalene and setting up a chain of Imperial orphanages across Italy jointly funded by Emperor and Church in the 470s kept the Church 'on side'. But even the latter had its practical uses as the Emperor ordered his administrators running the project to select bright (male) pupils and direct them into the Palace and civic bureaucracies.

A large collection of palace furnishings and Imperial jewellery amassed by the House of Theodosius that Majorian had no use for was sold off at an ostentatiously munificent Imperial public auction and the proceeds used to set up army orphanages. The philanthropic Emperor – who was a Catholic but was uninterested in theology – was popular with the Church as honest and committed to helping the poor and also spent much more of his time than his predecessors either in Rome, where he usually resided rather than in Ravenna, or on tour. In Rome the old Imperial palace on the Palatine, used from time to time by Valentinian III and by Gaudentius when he had been presiding at the races in the Circus Maximus, was renovated for the Emperor's use. The size of the Imperial Household was cut back by a quarter and all the Eastern eunuchs were sent packing, the Emperor relying on a personal staff of his own ex-officers and a corps of young aristocratic pages on secondment from the now expanded 'Protectores' officer-cadet school. With the palace in Mediolanum closed down and half of it pulled down and sold off for the value of its building materials in 470–1 there was a general air of retrenchment at court and a subsequent sale of more Imperial villas across the West including most of the Theodosian dynasty's luxury complex at Baiae and estates around Mediolanum. Majorian preferred to keep estates strictly as hunting-lodges and in that capacity would hold convivial hunting-parties for his senior officers there (mainly in northern and central Italy) each autumn and invite regional 'duces' to attend so he could assess them personally, and this and his regional tours – Spain in 470 and 472, Gaul in 471, the Rhineland in 473, Rhaetia and Noricum in 474, Illyria and Dacia in 475, and North Africa in 476 – meant that he had as much knowledge of the Empire and its leading military personnel as Aetius and could move commanders around and summon promising junior officers to his HQ out of personal acquaintance.

His heavy taxes on the landed nobility to fund his army and his regular commissions into official corruption were not exactly popular with the office-holding and non-serving nobility and he also made sure that the laws of the 'Theodosian Code' were being observed across the Empire with roving Imperial inspectors investigating the judicial processes in each province and trying and sacking the corrupt or incompetent. But all this earned him popular and Church support and the less vindictive of the nobility, even in the snobbish circles of the Roman 'old families', had to accept that he was not appointing as many Germans to senior command as Aetius had done and that capable young nobles had a reasonable chance of senior military posts. Although the new Emperor had the army behind him and the backing of even the most well-regarded and well-supported of his former boss Aetius' lieutenants who might have been a threat to a younger and less military ruler, led by Marcellinus (d 472) – who had been 'Master of Infantry and Cavalry in Illyria/Pannonia' in charge of the middle Danube army in 459–67 – and Aegidius (d. 474) – who had been 'Master of Infantry' on the Rhine from 458–63 and in Marcomannia in 464–8 – he was wary of obvious rivals and preferred not to run risks. Olybrius was kept out of the West on various excuses and had to scheme from the safety of Constantinople, with Majorian paying Zeno to keep an eye on him, and the same applied to Tiberius Anthemius and at first his adult sons too. The rump Visigothic kingdom in Transrhenus passed in 466 to the Roman ex-'dux' and trusted ally Euric who built a (wooden) Roman-style mansion and stud-farm at his dynastic headquarters near the middle Elbe and governed as a semi-Roman ruler with Roman contractors and officers at his court, and the same applied to the kings of the Ostrogoths further South in Hesse – Theodemir to 473 and thence Theodoric 'Strabo' – and the Franks in Westphalia (Childeric son of Merovech). (All were OTL post-Roman tribal rulers, within the Empire.)

The only kingdom resistant to Roman influence and bribery was that of the resurgent Vandals on the Vistula, now governed by Gaiseric's son Hunneric who still hankered after Princess Eudocia and built up an anti-Roman lordship far from the nearest Roman frontier which the Empire did not bother to tackle. There was still sporadic trouble from Saxon raiding on the eastern coasts of Britain during the 450s to 470s, and Aetius' employment of a brilliant 'Jutish' mercenary commander from Jutland, the warlord Hengest ('The Stallion', a nickname), to lead small and mobile patrols of the 'Classis Britannia' fleet across the North Sea to raid their marshy homelands on the Frisian Islands did not work long-term. It led to complaints that the German-loving Roman military supremo was indulging his German allies again and let Hengest get away with stealing recovered loot and using it to buy up land for his family in eastern Britain, specifically in Canticia (Kent) where he and his son Aesc ended up as major landholders. (Hengest in OTL was legendary king of Kent.)

But at least the dynamic new 'Count of Britain' from 458, Aetius' former officer Ambrosius Aurelianus who was related to the family of the late Emperor Magnus Maximus' wife Helen's brother in Armorica in north-west Gaul, was a capable and vigorous cavalry officer and battle-strategist who kept the raiding Picts at bay in the north and in the mid-460s launched successful attacks on their lands between Forth and Spey while in the West of the island the Irish were less troublesome as more were converted to Christianity and gave up raiding. In 476 Majorian used his tour of North Africa to launch the Empire's first major trading-military initiative beyond its frontiers for decades as a mixed force of regular infantry, camel-riding auxiliaries from local tribes, and Roman traders marched south across the Sahara across the line of oases from Leptis Magna (where Majorian saw them off) to the Lake Chad region to secure trading-concessions from and regular contact with the local pagan kingdoms and then sent a smaller force across to the east into Darfur to establish links with the tribes to the south of the Eastern Empire's neighbour Nubia. The mission was heavily enough armed to fend off any bandits and set up a chain of small Roman forts along the route to make it safe, and a local 'Count of the Garamantes', named after the ancient but now extinct local tribe who had featured in classical geography books such as Ptolemy's guides, was appointed to take charge of a mixed force of infantry garrisons and mobile camel-riding patrols and was usually a Tripolitanian who knew the area. One of the main lures was the rumour of gold-mines far to the South, in distant forests, as implied by impressive gold 'objets d'art' being sold on to Roman/ Garamantian traders.

Finance ministry officials were keen to acquire a new source of gold for coinage – and poorly-armed African tribes might be easily bribed with Roman trade-goods or threatened with force. Adventure-seeking army officers were sent off to investigate.

(Ambrosius is the OTL 'last of the Romans' who apparently revived the Romano Britons' fortunes against incoming Germanic settlers in the later C5th, as testified to by 540s historian/ polemicist Gildas. Count Marcellinus is the OTL final Roman warlord ruling the western Balkans for the Western Empire in the 460s and his nephew, briefly Emperor, was Julius Nepos. My German tribal rulers are the OTL kings of these tribes at this time, though here only ruling in central Europe beyond the Roman frontier as the Empire's allies. The Saharan campaigns are my invention, but a logical pursuit of new revenue for the Empire. The events in the Eastern Empire in the 470s and 480s in my version are a slightly different version of what happened in real life; Tiberius Anthemius is an altered version of a real, unsuccessful Western ruler of 467–72 but his son Titus II is invented.)

The Church in Carthage was allowed to send along missionaries in return for helping to fund the expedition and duly set up a small mission at the trading town of Bornu on Lake Chad in the late 470s, and trade-goods from further South were soon trickling up the new route into the declining towns of Tripolitania to add to their revenue. This was only part of the thoughtful and wide-seeing Majorian's exploration of ways to add to the Empire's 'reach' and revenue although he was careful to give the credit to his trainer Aetius who had used similar missions to build up links with the Germans north of the Danube and Carpathians (mainly to establish an anti-Attila coalition until 451/3). As he had the central 'comitatus' headquarters' staff expanded to include experts on the kingdoms and tribes beyond Rome's boundaries (many of them travellers and merchants) and also had the written guides to the Empire's geographical layout by Ptolemy in the early second century AD updated a number of leading geographers from the Museion and University at Alexandria were called west by him with Leo I's permission to advise him and work at the new military staff headquarters for the Western army, at Mediolanum. At the request of Ambrosius Aurelianus in Britain the first official political missions were sent to the current 'High King' of Ireland, Aillel 'Molt', in 471 and 477 to establish regular diplomatic and trading relations, set up a Roman 'entrepot' for trade at the mouth of the River Liffey near Tara (Ireland had no towns as yet), export cattle and pigs from Ireland to the Empire to improve local breeds, and ransom slaves and hostages taken in raids. In the coming decades the gifts and goods flowing into Tara helped to boost the prestige of the 'High Kings' as the dispensers of Roman patronage and thus a more powerful ally to be sought out by ambitious local tribal lords than their rival kings in Leinster, Munster, and eastern Ulster. Aillel himself was a lord from distant Connacht in the west who had achieved power by force of arms over the usual group of lords from the family of his great early fifth century-predecessor Niall 'of the Nine Hostages' (d. 405) who usually monopolized the 'High Kingship', but after his death in 482 power returned to the family of Niall, the 'Ui Niall' ('Grandsons of Niall') in Midhe in the East, and they became internally more stable rulers and Roman allies.

The subtle and yet militarily ruthless Ambrosius, seen by British poets as the man who tamed both Irish and Picts and the epitome of the Christian Roman gentleman, was kept on as supreme commander in Britain by Majorian for most of his reign. Similar long terms of office marked the tenure of equally successful commanders on the Rhine and in Marcomannia, and it was seen as a tribute to his confidence and the belief of the army in him that he could give a series of senior posts to his one-time potential rival Julius Nepos and others to Aegidius' son Syagrius, one of the eponymous Syagrii dynasty of Gaul and so rich and well-connected, without political concern. Majorian also initiated a regular series of 'Military Games', contests in athletics and various other Ancient Greek sports plus military prowess at sword-fighting, archery, and the Persian cavalry sport of polo, for his soldiers at Rome every two years, commencing on his return from North Africa in 476. After his tour of southern Gaul and Spain as far as Gades (Cadiz) in 478 he also created a new naval academy at Reggium to train naval officers in sailing all types of vessels so that he could call on a substantial body of suitably expert men to man the North Sea as well as Mediterranean fleets and could expand the Hibernian Sea fleet to patrol as far north as the Orcades and intimidate the Picts.

In the East, the succession-crisis came to a head when Leo I died in Constantinople on 18 January 474, aged 64 or 65. His grandson Leo II succeeded, aged five, under his father Zeno's regency, and on 9 February Zeno was crowned co-emperor in Hippodrome by Patriarch Acacius (in office 471–89) on the Senate's formal request. But Zeno was unpopular as a semi-educated Isaurian mountaineer who might be of local noble descent but had not even spoken Latin or Greek as a boy and was sneered at by the capital's aristocracy, and the boy-emperor's grandmother Verina had wanted to be regent and 'Augusta' and started to plot against Zeno with her brother Basiliscus. The sudden death of Leo II on 17 November meant that Zeno succeeded as sole Emperor and as he made his Isaurian friend and adviser Illus, a dashing and rather thuggish but

Emperor Julian. (*Coin or portrait bust from Wikipedia entry*)
'Julian, the last ruler from Costantine the Great's family and also the Classical philosophy enthusiast who tried to turn back the tide against Christianity. Venerated by admirers of his Neoplatonist beliefs as the man who could have constructed an alternative State religion to the intolerant Church, and loathed by the latter as 'The Apostate'. He was killed during his invasion of Sassanian Persia/Iran – but what if he had won his campaign and had decades to build up his new systems?

Emperor Magnus Maximus. Gold 'aureus', 383-8. (© *CNG*)
The first challenger to the new Catholic emperors Gratian (West) and Theodosius the Great (East) in 383-8, and as commander in Britain long remembered as 'Macsen Wledig' in Welsh folklore. Evidently a charismatic commander, he deposed and killed the inexperienced Gratain but was brought down by the latter's brother-in-law Theodosius ansd executed.
He also inaugurated executions of 'heretic' Christians for dissident beliefs, an ominous sign for future Catholic tolerance – which my narrative arc will minimalise.

Bas-relief of Theodosius and his sons at the Games, at the Hippodrome, Constantinople. 'The last ruler of a united Roman Empire at its full extent, who died in 395 aged only 47. After his death the German tribal armies began moving into the Western Empire and became crucial and increasingly autonomous players in its politics, gradually detaching its provinces and starving it of revenue. Theodosius' military reputation as the man who held them back for his lifetime was tarnished by his autocratic and legalistic imposition of Catholic Christianity as the only allowed state religion, closing and taking property from pagan temples and banning sacrifices. He is seen as the harbinger of a new era of Christian intolerance – but what if he had had to act with a surviving powerful Julianic pagan elite and choose another path? Or his survival had prevented or delayed the rule of his incompetent sons?'

Theodosian Walls of Constantinople. Theodosian Walls of Constantinople. (© *A. Savin/ Wiki Commons*) The massive triple land-walls of Constantiople, which kept out the marauding 'barbarians' in the Balkans from the Eastern Empire's capital for as long as the Empire's foes lacked sophisticated artillery. Built by Anthemius, Praefect of the city and regent for Theodosius the Great's eponymous grandson from 408; completed by the latter's highly capable sister Pulcheria. The West's capital lacked this impregnable bonus and its slaves opened the gates to the Goths in 410 – but what if the West had been as militarily strong as the East?

Constantius III. (© *CNG, ie Classical Numismatic Group*)

'The almost-forgotten Western Roman general who rebuilt the Empire's armies and confidence after the disastrous purge of Stilicho's officers and the sack of Rome – and brought the Goths under control. Rescuer of and married to Honorius' sister Galla Placidia, he became co-ruler in 421 but then suddenly died – leading to more factional feuding at court. But what if he had survived for another decade or two and ruled instead of his inept son Valentinian III and feuding generals, keeping the Vandals out of North Africa and maintaining the strategies of his mentor Stilicho?'

Mausoleum of Galla Placidia, Ravenna. (© *Petar Milosevic/ Creative Commons*)

'The almost forgotten daughter of Theodosius and half-sister of Honorius, married to Constantius III, who was arguably as crucial a bastion of stability and wise governance in the West as her cousin Pulcheria was in the East. After her husband died she was evicted from power by her brother and a usurper, but restored her young son Valentinian III to the throne with Eastern help. She chose and put her trust in the military strongman Aetius, who restored the Empire's military fortunes and built up the vital Romano-Germanic coalition which defeated Attila's steppe empire at the Catalaunian Fields in Gaul in 451. Her death then led to the fatal showdown between Aetius and her fearful son and the disasters of 455 which wrecked the Empire's resources and viability. But what if she and her allies had had as much luck and success as Pulcheria and her husband Marcian did in the East, and Aetius had been the victor in Court politics?'

Emperor Valentinian III. Gold 'solidus'. (© *CNG1*)

'Valentinian, as feeble and wayward a son of a great military leader as was Honorius, followed the latter in having the warlord who had saved his throne murdered at the behest of his Court rivals – and so precipitated disaster. His reputation stands very low as a result, though it is impossible to know if Aetius really intended to replace him with his own son Gaudentius as a puppet-emperor. Given the results, the Western Empire would have been served better had Aetius won and kept up his Romano-German coalition – and might the Empire have even forged a large and stable enough military machine to survive as a great power for the next century as the East did?'

Emperor Petronius Maximus. Gold 'solidus', 455. (© *CNG*)

The multimillionaire aristocratic minister to Western Emperor Valentinian III who in real life is said to have inspired and/or led the plan to murder his commander in chief Aetius in 454, a fatal blow to the Empire's power and unity. He then overthrew Valentinian in turn and became emperor, but was attacked by Gaiseric the Vandal's fleet from Carthage, fled Rome, and was caught and lynched. But what if this disaster had been pre-empted and Aetius not Petronius had triumphed – and there had been no Vandal kingdom in North Africa due to a stronger West?

Emperor Majorian. Gold 'solidus', Arelate, France 461–2.

'One of Aetius' best officers but now forgotten, the valiant and charismatic commander who took the Western throne in 457 and did his best to rebuild the shrunken Empire after the shock of the sack of Rome by Gaiseric the Vandal. Lacking resources or luck and overshadowed by his powerful Germanic commander Ricimer, his resurgent control in Gaul and Spain was offset by his failure to regain North Africa from the Vandals and he was killed in a coup in 462. But with more resources and as the deputy and then the successor of Aetius, what more could this final Western Imperial strongman have done?'

Emperor Anthemius. Gold 'solidus'. (© *CNG*)

'In real life, an ambitious and capable but militarily ineffective Eastern Roman courtier aristocrat who was chosen by Emperor Leo I in 467 to spearhead a military attempt to take over and revive the Western Empire. Installed in Rome and the last ruler to have some success in intervening in Gaul, he was left stranded by the failure of the Eastern navy to destroy Gaiseric the Vandal and was later deposed and murdered. If the Western Empire had survived to this point as the equal of the East due to an unbroken line of successful military leaders, could this under-estimated ruler have done more if the lack of an heir for Majorian had given him a chance of its throne?'

Emperor Julius Nepos. Gold 'solidus'. (© *CNG*)

One of the regional military strongmen who emerged as the final commanders of Roman troops and provinces in the collapsing Empire in the 460s, succeeding his uncle Marcellinus as ruler of Illyria (the Serbia/ Croatia region). Nominally loyal to the weak emperors in Rome, these ex-aides to Aetius held back the encroaching German warlords – and in 474 Julius Nepos briefly took over Italy too and ruled precariously in Rome for a year. He was then chased out, and survived the 'fall' of the West to hold the Imperial title in 'exile' until murdered in 480. But what if he had had a much stronger regime in Italy able to command his loyalty as a 'normal' Roman frontier commander?

Coin of Zeno, Eastern Emperor 474-5 and 476-91.

'The wily and ruthless South-Eastern Anatolian ('Isaurian') tribal warlord who was brought to Constantinople by the son-less Emperor Leo I to marry his daughter, provide grandsons to rule under his regency, and use his fierce regiments of rural mountaineers to rally and control the weakened Eastern armies. A strongman comparable to Stilicho and Aetius and similarly resented as a 'barbarian' but less of a general than a politician, he won out in his struggle with the civilian administrators and scheming courtiers and kept the encroaching Ostrogoths as well as his own rebel officers at bay. If the West had had similarly successful 'outisder' leaders, would Mediterranean history have been drastically different?'

Pevensey Late Roman 'Saxon Shore' fortress, Sussex, Britain. (© *Peter Jeffrey. Creative Commons*)
'One of the most impressive survivors of the system of coastal fortresses set up on the South-East coasts of Britain in the later third and early fourth centuries to keep watch on loot-hungry 'Saxon' raiders from north-western Germany. Historians now debate if this shore was called 'Saxon' because of the regional military threat or because the Romans had to call in Saxon settlers to help their understaffed army, and the so-called 'Anglo-Saxons' ma well have been settling in as well as trading with Britain before 'Roman withdrawal' in 410. But if Roman rule had survived, how far would this immigration have gone – and how 'Saxon' or 'Romano-British'/Welsh would Britian have been?'

Dumbarton Rock, capital of the post-Roman kingdom of Strathclyde. (© *Lairich Rig/ Creative Commons*)
'The fortress-capital of the post-Roman Brittonic kingdom of Alt Clud or Strathclyde, dominating the region North-West of Hadrian's Wall and predating on newly Christian Ulster in the fifth century. The kingdom was reputedly set up as a vassal ally by the final Roman commanders in Britain pre-withdrawal, so would have been a crucial player in Northern British politics had the Empire kept control of Britain. But would it and its fleets have been friend or foe?'

Abbey of Iona, Hebrides, founded AD 563 by St. Columba. (© *David Dixon/ Creative Commons*)
'The great Christian spiritual centre of the post-Roman kingdom of Dalriada in Argyll, founded in 563 by evangelizing Irish aristocratic missionary St. Columba/ Columbcille. Would a surviving and strong Western Empire that had utilised the coversion of Ireland to wean its restive warlords off raiding Roman Britain have adopted the same tactic with Columba's mission to tame the threat from Argyll?'

Priory of Lindisfarne, Northumberland, founded by St Aedan AD 635. (© *David Dixon/ Creative Commons*)
'The first centre of Christian evangelization in then-pagan Anglian Northumbria, straddling the pre-410 Roman frontier of Hadrian's Wall. Founded by the Iona-based Gaelic missionary St.Aedan, in a tradition of hermits and wandering missionaries far from the neat, bureaucratically-organised Roman Church. Under continuing Roman rule, there would have been no pagan kingdom of Northumbria, though possibly still Anglian immigrant warriors to bolster the denuded Roman army – but Lothian was a restive vassal ally of the Late Roman Empire so could Iona have been asked to help Christianise and tame it? And would the austere Iona monks have shown up the morally lax, worldly clergy of Late Roman Britain and provided an alternative model for Christianity?

capable commander on the lower Danube, 'Master of Infantry' in the Balkans to prop up his regime and brought more Isaurian guards to the capital to join the palace regiments this stirred up anger from passed-over Roman officers. Verina plotted against Zeno on behalf of her lover Patricius, the sacked ex-"Master of Offices" who Zeno had persuaded Leo to get rid of in 473 and who was out for revenge, and won over Illus and his brother Trocandrus, a senior commander in the 'Excubitors' regiment of Isaurians. With Patricius and his wealthy Constantinopolitan noble wife 'on side' Verina could start raising funds for a supposed new summer mansion on the nearby Princes' Islands but in fact to bribe important officials and give to the capital's horse-racing clubs ('Demes') who ran the races in the Hippodrome where the rival 'Blues', 'Greens', 'Reds', and 'Whites' competed. The vain and ambitious Basiliscus was 'conned' that Verina wanted to make him Emperor instead of Patricius, found out that she really backed the latter after he bribed Patricius' steward and mistress to spy on him, and double-crossed her in turn. In January 475 Verina instigated riots in Constantinople and persuaded Zeno to flee the apparent imminent danger of attack on the Palace across the Bosphorus to Chalcedon. Once he had gone she and her allied nobles then instigated a coûp; the populace were armed by Verina's associates and massacred the Isaurian soldiers who tried to put down the rioting, and Zeno fled to Isauria with a small force.

But the Senate chose Basiliscus not Patricius as Emperor (19 January) as he had had time to spend large bribes on prominent members, and Verina was excluded from power; Basiliscus then executed Patricius. Basiliscus made his wife Zenonis " not Verina 'Augusta' and his spoilt teenage son Marcus "Caesar". His nephew Armatus, a capable but vain general, massive spendthrift and gambler, and Zenonis reputed ' lover, was made "Master of Soldiers" which alienated many of the senior officers given his ability to make enemies by his cutting wit. Basiliscus now favoured the "Monophysites" in a gamble to pose as the champion of religious toleration and neuter the Church under Acacius which had hoped for the munificent hospital- and school-funder Patricius as Emperor. Patriarchs Timotheus 'Aelurus' (' the Cat') were restored to Alexandria and Peter to Antioch on promises to work for toleration, exile the worst orthodox polemicists, and return all Church property held by Monophysites in their dioceses as of 449 to them. Basiliscus issued an encyclical letter condemning the Council of Chalcedon and the 'Tome' of Pope Leo I as divisive and theologically suspect. In doing so Basiliscus made himself a hero for the Monophysite populations of the Levant but infuriated the Papacy which refused to recognize him as Emperor and induced Majorian to declare that Zeno was the legitimate ruler. Basiliscus now favoured the visiting 'Monophysite' Patriarch Timotheus 'Aelurus' of Alexandria in summer 475 and allowed him and the other Eastern Patriarchs to declare autonomy from the authority of Constantinople. Patriarch Acacius was furious and draped Hagia Sophia in black, and the orthodox resisted Basiliscus with riots in the capital as the local Monophysites were invited back from exile and had their old churches restored, protected by Imperial guardsmen. Acacius boycotted the palace and did not let the new Emperor or any of his ministers and court attend his church services at Hagia Sophia, and Basiliscus dared not have the cathedral stormed – which duly persuaded hard-line guards devotees of the rule that 'the Emperor is always right' that he was a weakling and would lose the coming civil war.

Zeno held out at Salmon, Isauria, and was joined by troops from the command at Antioch whose 'Master of Infantry' Jovianus and 'Master of Cavalry' Perdiccas did not like the low-born Zeno but hated the 'fop' Basiliscus more so they sent help to Zeno, and though much of the command at Ctesiphon was supportive to the Monophysites or else had Nestorian sympathies and hoped for toleration for them too they could not risk a civil war and stayed out of the clash. The vindictive and oppressive new Sassanid king Firuz of Sogdiana/ Maracanda had launched a persecution of the rich and unpopular Jewish mercantile community in his kingdom in 473 to win loot for a war on Rome and their co-religionists along the 'Silk Road' in Susa, Ctesiphon and Edessa had appealed to Emperor Leo I for aid so a major Roman army was currently invading Sogdiana over the Oxus in 475. The denuded troops at Ctesiphon dared not march West to aid Zeno or Basiliscus, so their generals just recognized the latter for the moment as the man in possession of the capital and stayed quiet but let local orthodox nobles who disliked Basiliscus send money and volunteers to Zeno. In spring 476 Illus and Trocandrus were sent against Zeno by Basiliscus but, encouraged by letters from ministers in capital, deserted to Zeno who also now had a large treasury of funds sent by his Eastern supporters and was doling out bribes to all who defected. Zeno received and pardoned his old allies, and marched on the capital as the reinforcements from the lower Danube who Basiliscus had sent in a 'second wave' behind Illus' army deserted too. In May 476 Basiliscus recalled his ecclesiastical edicts to conciliate the people and sent Armatus against Zeno, but Zeno offered Armatus the role of 'Master of Soldiers' in the high command at Constantinople for life and the 'Caesarship' for his young son and he avoided Zeno's army and marched out of his way into Phrygia to give him a clear run to the capital. Zeno invested Armatus' son, the younger Basiliscus, as 'Caesar' at Nicaea and once this was done Armatus joined him.

In August 476 Zeno entered Constantinople unopposed with the support of and an official welcome from Patriarch Acacius, and Basiliscus was captured fleeing by sea towards Greece with his family, sent to Cucusus in Cappadocia in exile as he was promised his life, and was killed a few weeks later, aged forty-eight. His wife Zenonis and son Marcus were also killed. Once Zeno was securely on the throne Armatus was assassinated in October in a 'hit' in a street of the capital on his way to dine with the Emperor, allegedly at Illus' instigation, and his son Basiliscus was soon made a monk at the church and monastery of the Virgin Mary at Blachernae (he later became Bishop of Cyzicus). Illus now became chief adviser to Zeno and "Patrician" and 'Master of Offices', and Basiliscus' 'Monophysite' supporters were exiled; Verina was pardoned but was soon at odds with Zeno after apparently trying to turn his wife Ariadne, her elder daughter, against him. The suspicious Emperor also asked the Western Emperor Majorian, who congratulated him on his successful restoration, to accept his supposed supporter Tiberius Anthemius, who had led his clients to help the pro-Zeno coup in the capital in August 476 despite his elder two sons (by Marcian's daughter) being held hostage by Basiliscus in the palace, as his ambassador in Rome in order to get this potential plotter out of Constantinople. In spring 477 Majorian obliged. Thus Tiberius Anthemius and his second wife and their two sons, the teenage Titus and Heraclius, were despatched on an 'honourable' mission but in effect into exile in Italy. Although Majorian kept them all under initial surveillance and did not let them join his court but gave them some remote estates in Marsium (Marsii tribe's lands, NE of Naples) to live on he was sufficiently confident of them by 480 to invite the two boys to join the 'Protectores' and do military training and in 482 Tiberius was belatedly given the consulship and the first of a series of prestigious but politically minor court posts. The loyalty of the latter to Majorian was doubted by some of the Imperial generals but it is probable that Tiberius, a shrewd operator, was aware that any coup by him (even if he bribed enough nobles and senators to secure the administration) would end in military defeat by the generals so he was playing a long game as a loyal subordinate instead. Certainly he had other hopes, namely of the Eastern throne too for his family, and in the chaos of 476 Tiberius had forced the desperate Zeno to accept his eldest son Marcianus Anthemius marrying Leo I's widowed daughter Leontia (widow of Patricius the son of Aspar) and from 477–9 Marcianus served as a senior minister to Zeno despite the latter's doubts of his loyalty – as Tiberius' terms for his support?

Verina was more of an immediate threat to Zeno, and in spring 478 she suborned the Praefect of the City (Constantinople), the great noble Epinicus, to have Illus assassinated. The attempt, by hired thugs disguised as palace attendants with forged palace security passes, in a passage from the main buildings of the palace complex (the 'Daphne Palace ' built by Constantine 'the Great') to the Imperial Box ('Kathisma') in the adjacent Hippodrome, was foiled by Illus' quick reactions and the intervention of his bodyguards, though he was wounded. A captured assassin implicated Epinicus under torture, and the

Praefect was sacked and sent to a fortress in Eastern Anatolia as a prisoner. But during a military tour of inspection to the Caucasus in summer 479 Illus secretly visited the exiled Epinicus, who confessed about Verina putting him up to the plot. The Emperor was more concerned currently with Marcianus Anthemius as a threat to him and the latter was sacked in early 479 under the cover of a 'reshuffle' of ministers and was sent off on a time-consuming commission to inspect the administration in Antioch and look for financial cuts there, but when Illus complained about Verina and presented a written statement by Epinicus she was arrested and sent to an Isaurian fortress as a nun, guarded by Zeno's countrymen. But after an earthquake in Constantinople on 17 September 479 caused panic, the returned and brooding Marcianus struck against Zeno, claiming that his wife Leontia should be Empress instead of her elder sister Ariadne as she was born when Leo I was Emperor, and as he showered money on a crowd outside his palace and encouraged them to march on the Augusteum and seek the Patriarch's support to depose the Emperor his brother Procopius led anti-Isaurian riots. A large crowd tried to march on the Palace in a coûp and the loyalist guards were defeated, but Acacius stayed out of the riots and next day Illus brought in Isaurian troops from a barracks in Chalcedon and the revolt was suppressed. Marcianus was arrested and sent to Cappadocia as a monk to serve in a remote monastery, but Procopius escaped by ship and fled to the West where he died in suspicious circumstances in Sicily a few weeks later. He was said to have been poisoned by Zeno's agents or else by Western police agents sent by the Western Emperor's security-chief Germanus to stop him using his large treasury of evacuated money to revolt against Majorian.

In spring 481 Illus, fearing assassination by the increasingly nervous Zeno who was annoyed at his claiming the credit for putting down Marcianus' revolt, was transferred to Antioch at his own request as 'Master of the Infantry in the East'. The Eastern army at Ctesiphon had occupied Maracanda (Samarcand), the Sogdian capital, in 477 to chase out the anti-Roman king Firuz and halt his persecution of the Jews and the latter had been restored to their property there with a Roman puppet Sassanid prince from Persis called Diran taking over as king. But he had been driven out by Firuz and his Turk allies in 480 and now Zeno was planning to restore his reputation by annexing Bactria and Sogdiana and so extending formal Roman rule to the Oxus. Sympathetic to the Monophysites (at least to the extent of seeing no reason to ban their worship and seize their property just to satisfy the orthodox Church) and currently working with a commission of moderate orthodox bishops and veteran theologians in Constantinople for a religious compromise that would overturn the harshly anti-Monophysite tone of the Council of Chalcedon in 451, Zeno had more concept and understanding of Levantine religious complexities than most Constantinopolitan clerics or civil servants. He was aiming for long-term reconciliation of the rival churches, by Imperial 'fiat' if necessary – and the secular counterpart of this was to be final victory in Persia. In that context he was sending more troops to Ctesiphon in 480–1 ahead of a major advance on the Oxus and had summoned assorted senior nobles from great families in Persis and Hyrcania – some dating back to Achaemenid times – to his capital. Zeno intended to lavish gifts and hospitality on them and win them over as his clients in the future, occupied but 'devolved' provinces of Persis and Hyrcania which would be run by a mixed Romano-Persian civilian elite and Persian civil and Roman military governors. (Possibly the idea owed something to Majorian's plans for Transrhenus, and were given to him during a friendly Western embassy to Constantinople in 480.) Illus was hankering to be given the high command for the expedition to the Oxus – but in fact Zeno had no intention to allow this as if he won the war he could use his army to claim the throne and attack the capital. He just 'strung Illus along' with flattery about his being trusted and invaluable until he was ready in March 482 to send his senior Balkan general Justus Evagrius, who had served in Lower Mesopotamia as 'dux' in the early 470s before transfer to Upper Moesia and had a high reputation with the office-corps at Ctesiphon, to succeed Illus' rival John 'the Scythian' as 'Master of Infantry' at Ctesiphon and take over the campaign.

In autumn 481 Zeno, advised by Patriarch Acacius and the veteran Egyptian theologian and Biblical history expert Peter Mongus, promulgated the new compromise 'Henoticon' doctrine in a letter to the Church of Egypt. This was then sent round to all the East's regional churches for approval ahead of a formal promulgation as official doctrine by a Church Council at Constantinople the following spring. (This was only a regional Council for the sees under Constantinople's religious control, i.e. not those controlled by Antioch, Alexandria, or Jerusalem, as Zeno feared that a General Council of the East would get out of hand and refuse his orders; the other Churches were expected to fall into line.) The doctrine was a careful compromise, declaring the Councils of Nicaea (325) and Constantinople (381) sufficient for the ratification of correct doctrine and excluding the more hard-line doctrine of Chalcedon (451); it denounced the 'Nestorians' and criticized recent innovations made at Chalcedon which were declared to be unacceptable as based on insufficient evidence. It thus opened 'wriggle-room' for a compromise which the Catholics had stopped in 451 – reflecting Zeno's local knowledge of anti-Catholic passions in Syria and Mesopotamia. The Monophysites were largely satisfied and their local churches across the East were allowed to hold meetings to ratify it and then had their pre-451 property restored, but in the West Pope Simplicius (in office 468–83) denounced it, not least for its having an Imperial not a proper Papal/

Patriarchal decision on doctrine. The clerical elite in Rome thus backed the clerical elite in Constantinople against 'heretical' provincials. Emperor Majorian did not bother to interfere.

In spring 482 the orthodox Patriarch Timotheus 'Salophaciolus' ('White Hat') of Alexandria, who Zeno had installed to replace Timotheus 'Aelurus' in 477 after local orthodox pressure to fend off more riots, died and there was a 'moderate vs extremist' orthodox struggle over the succession. The more hard-line John Talaia, who was opposed to the 'Henoticon', was consecrated as he had majority support and the Praefect backed him, but in June was evicted by the Imperial candidate Peter Mongus who was sent by Zeno with a contingent of troops and orders to the Praefect to accept him. John fled to Rome to appeal to papal authority. Pope Simplicius died on 10 March 483 after backing John as legitimate and attacking Acacius for accepting the 'illegal' deposition; on 13 March the equally orthodox 'Catholic' deacon Felix was elected Pope under supervision of the 'Praetorian Praefect' Basilius. He denounced the 'Henoticon' and received John, whose removal was declared illegal again; Acacius was summoned to Rome to explain himself but won over Felix's legates sent to summon him and they accepted that he had nothing to explain so he need not go, for which Felix then sacked them. (Largely as in OTL, but in real life Rome was by now ruled by the German Odovacar.)

In January 484 Illus revolted at Antioch and proclaimed Leo I's son-in-law Marcianus Anthemius, who he summoned from his monastery, as Emperor and Zeno a heretical usurper. He rescued Verina from her Isaurian prison fortress and at Tarsus she proclaimed that she was the rightful ruler and proclaimed herself as 'Augusta'. But to Illus' disappointment her choice as her co-ruler was the local noble 'Patrician' Leontius, a former Praefect of 'Oriens' in the late 460s and now her regular visitor and supplier of luxuries at her prison, to whom Illus transferred his allegiance a few weeks later. He abandoned Marcianus, who fled from expected arrest and headed off to Cyprus by ship but was drowned in a storm as he made his way to Italy. Questions were duly asked, by Zeno among others, if Illus had lured him into acting as his 'front man' to assess if he was a viable Emperor and then abandoned him when it became clear that Verina had more support in Cilicia and Syria or if he had always intended to betray him. A large donation of money sent east by Tiberius Anthemius for his son Marcianus' cause, whether or not with Majorian's blessing, had already arrived in Syria and was now used by Illus, but a second sum of money was recalled in time and some of Marcianus' aristocratic allies in Constantinople who had been intending to join Marcianus now left Illus alone and either funded Zeno instead or fled west to Italy. The deaths of Tiberius Anthemius' older sons opened the way for their half-brother Titus.

Illus and Verina entered Antioch in March and Patriarch Calandrio crowned Leontius, but Zeno sent the army at Ctesiphon under 'Master of Infantry' John 'the Scythian' west and the Oxus expedition was abandoned though the contingent of Eastern Roman troops that had already occupied Hyrcania (483) now set up the planned Roman province there with a local Persian (Zoroastrian not Christian) civil and a Roman military governor. Illus' pagan followers such as the leading Syrian 'Hellenist' enthusiast Pamprepius, a learned former professor at the University of Constantinople sacked for paganism to appease the Church in 477, could be used in Constantinopolitan Church propaganda against him, but it is unclear to what extent he genuinely appealed to the local aristocratic pagans – mostly nobles – or if he was just after their money to fund his army. The rebels were defeated in battle near Zeugma in July 484 by John's army and fled north-west to the mountains to be besieged in a remote Isaurian fort, Cherris, where Verina soon died but Illus held out until January 488 when he had to surrender after food-supplies by mountain paths from his local sympathisers were cut off and he was arrested and executed (largely as in OTL).

Leontius was taken to the capital for a public execution and assorted officers at the fortress, mostly Isaurians, were executed too but the refugee Syrian 'high command' officers who had had little alternative to supporting their harsh and vengeful commander in 484 were mostly pardoned. The rebellion had little impact on the East – not least on religion, as the majority of Monophysites were backing Zeno in 484 over the 'Henoticon' and steered clear of it and even the extremist orthodox had no reason to trust Illus. The 'Henoticon' was generally accepted in Syria and the Mesopotamian provinces though there were riots by the orthodox hard-liners in Palestine and a new Patriarch had to be installed in Jerusalem to enforce it. As the extremist Monophysite congregations in Egypt did not regard it as going far enough and their representatives told Patriarch Peter at a meeting in June 484 that they needed further concessions he had to disabuse them of this idea and rely on the moderate orthodox clergy and their tame crowds of urban enthusiasts to stop the Monophysite radicals from attacking their own moderates. Egypt remained in a ferment through the mid-late 480s. But at least in the capital the action of Pope Felix's latest, more hard-line legates in 486 in excommunicating Patriarch Acacius and pinning a document announcing this to his vestments during a service in Hagia Sophia won him majority support from his Church and the Papacy was in turn declared to be 'in error' and refused recognition. This 'Acacian Schism' caused much anger and anguish in the Church in Rome, but was more or less ignored by Emperor Majorian who blamed the Pope for pushing matters to an extremity in defiance of his advice and the embattled orthodox faction in Rome in turn accused him of secretly backing the 'Henoticon'. The majority of the Western bishops showed no knowledge of or sympathy for the Eastern leadership's need to balance large and obstinate rival Church factions – but neither did their Emperor. Some Western ministers were indeed pleased to see religious controversy weaken the East. ('Henoticon' controversy in East is largely as in OTL.)

There was also trouble in the Patriarchate of Ctesiphon in Mesopotamia, where the Zeno loyalist Patriarch 'Mar' (i.e. 'Abbot') Barbawai/ Barbinius, a converted ex-Zoroastrian whose Christology was under suspicion already by orthodox zealots, backed the 'Henoticon' through the 480s and sacked opposing bishops, both real or suspected Monophysites and Nestorians as well as the obstinate orthodox. Some sees ended up with two or three rival bishops claiming the 'official' properties and their congregations engaging in physical struggles over possession. Zeno at first favoured the 'mainstream' majority of the Monophysites as they were more supportive of the 'Henoticon' than the orthodox and so ordered his officials and troops to assist them over possession of churches, monasteries, and estates. An uneasy alliance between Barbawai's authorities in Ctesiphon and the Monophysite community's majority in Mesopotamia during the Illus rebellion saw a rapprochement between offended anti-'Henoticon' orthodox clerics (and their lay supporters) and the growing Nestorian community, the latter based on the theological school at the 'Blessed City' of Edessa set up by the controversial former Bishop Ibas (in office 435–57, disputed) and now headed by the formidably-learned scholar Bar Sauma. The fact that the sometimes theologically speculative Ibas, who had been distrusted by many of the mainstream Catholic theologians during his lifetime, had been exonerated by the Council of Chalcedon in 451 after writing 'official' letters attacking Nestorius was used by his followers to argue that he had been fully orthodox. Thus they were too and they should be accepted by the Catholic hierarchy as legally entitled to their Church offices and possessions. This 'truce' did not last. The Nestorians, who were a majority in the community of the ancient (second century AD origin) 'Assyrian Christians' in northern Mesopotamia around Nisibis, Mosul, and Arbela and who included a large number of refugee Syrians from Nestorius' original Antioch-based 'sect', dominated the remote and austere monastic communities of the 'Assyrian' hills around Nisibis and Mosul. They used this period to extend their congregations and politico-economic influence as well as their control of sees and monasteries, and after the end of the civil war Zeno could or would not rein them in for fear of provoking a new revolt. He duly avoided appointing any of their harshest critics to sees or abbacies in Mesopotamia, and allowed the majority of Nestorian clergy to survive without harassment, as his (often Nestorian) lay officials and military officers in the region advised him to do. The most that he would do to satisfy angry orthodox demands to stamp out the 'heretics' was to purge the school and see of Edessa –

closer to Syria and easier to control – of religiously dubious 'suspects', Nestorians in particular. This led to Bar Sauma relocating himself and his students to the more laxly-supervised theological college at Nisibis where a 'parallel community' of Nestorians now had more wealth and Church property than the precariously-supreme orthodox bishop and community. The Patriarchate of Ctesiphon was secured from Nestorian influence after the death of Zeno led to the end of the 'Henoticon' and a 'moderate'/ 'hard-line' orthodox reconciliation in 491 – but the Church in Mesopotamia remained divided between the communities and that in the Roman protectorate of Media to the East came under Nestorian control by around 500.

(In OTL the Nestorian expansion in Mesopotamia and Persia was in Sassanid Persian, not Roman lands and at risk of Zoroastrian persecution. Ibas, Barbawai, Bar Sauma et al are OTL; the local Assyrian Christians lasted until the C21st rule of ISIS.)

(In OTL the last Western emperor, Romulus Augustulus, son of Attila's ex-secretary Orestes, was deposed by the German commander in chief Odovocar in 476; he technically recognized Zeno as his Emperor but really ran a separate kingdom of Italy. This was then taken over by Theodoric the Ostrogoth, migrating from the East at the latter's suggestion, in 491/3.)

The religious crises in the East enabled the shrewd and ambitious Tiberius Anthemius to pose as the champion of orthodox Catholicism, and after the incumbent 'Master of Offices' Paulinus died suddenly in April 487 he managed to persuade Majorian, who had been ill recently and was recuperating at his villa near Lorium, to name him as the new holder of that office. The elderly and ailing Emperor seems to have given up on combating the rich and popular Tiberius and accepted him as his inevitable successor as none of his generals had enough support to avoid the risk of civil war if he named one of them. Crucially the charismatic Julius Nepos chose to marry off his daughter and heiress to Heraclius, the younger son of Tiberius, in 484 and enter his extended family network – possibly after allegations that he had threatened an 'impertinent' Imperial legal commissioner of low birth with a flogging for investigating his accounts as 'Master of Infantry' in Marcomannia and Dacia (479–83) led to the offended Majorian sacking him and withdrawing his favour. Tiberius lavished hospitality on and made promises to many of the great Roman nobles and his officer-cadet elder surviving son Titus, tall, impressive-looking, charismatic, and a natural soldier, was hugely popular among the 'Protectores' and hosted huge hunting parties at the family's estates in Sabine country but was trusted by the Emperor. It is likely that Majorian now considered Titus, who had signs of military 'flair' and ruthless ability on the battlefield and who had no qualms about employing Germans as well as Romans in his entourage if they were capable and loyal, as his successor – certainly as the Empire's next military 'strongman', possibly as Emperor too if he could persuade Tiberius Anthemius to stand aside in his favour or make him co-ruler. (If not, Titus would succeed Tiberius, as in fact happened.) Titus, like Majorian, also had no interest in arcane religious controversies, except as an irritating bar to State unity. He did not pose as a champion of Catholicism unlike his father Tiberius, though he was as ruthless a believer in order and obedience as Constantine the Great.

Titus also served successfully as a junior regimental commander in Britain in 486–7 under Ambrosius Aurelianus and won plaudits for his dealing with Pictish attacks on a campaign in the Caledonian mountains and then in 488 served as deputy 'dux' in Marcomannia where he rescued some soldiers from a snowstorm at great personal risk. He also had the advantage of a close-knit network of his own ex-fellow-cadet friends now serving in either the Guards regiments in Rome or in middle-ranking posts in provincial armies. He was known to and respected by their, usually Italian aristocratic, families as a 'true Roman' of impeccable and aggressively war-loving sentiments who gloried in the past heroics of famous Roman military heroes and had a near-veneration for men such as Camillus, Scipio Africanus, Scipio Aemilianus, and the First Emperor's general Agrippa and relation Germanicus – so plenty of opportunities to gain loot and glory would come if he became Emperor. His religious sentiments were also less orthodox and less interested in Catholic theology than his father and he was more appreciative of the 'world-view' of the Emperor Julian than any of the Theodosian dynasty had been so residual pagans or semi-Christian traditionalists rallied to him and he had plenty of Senate support. His fondness for the great military heroes of the Roman Republic as his exemplars was useful in that it rallied 'traditionalist' senators and writers to support him, whether their own ideal was a Catholic Christian (Constantine 'the Great') or a pagan-style (Julian) ruler. But he could not be accused of paganism himself despite a few disgruntled Catholic nobles talking in dark terms of needing to keep him off the throne or the 'military rule' and 'disregard for the August Fathers (i.e. the Senate) and the Pope' of Aetius and Majorian would continue. Titus, like Julian but like Constantine too, regarded the Emperor's primary role as securing justice and peace – but he was not as religious as either of them. In fact Titus was as ruthless as Augustus.

When Majorian died suddenly in a villa near Naples on 23 July 488, aged seventy-two, the senior administrators and a commission of senators met quickly in Rome and on the 29th elected Tiberius as Emperor, aged sixty-four,

Aetius (and his Son Gaudentius as Western Emperor 455–469) 117

as the best candidate available. This was not challenged by any of the provincial armies as the central comitatus' came out in Tiberius' favour, and it was Prince Titus, quickly made 'Caesar' on 5 August and aged 26, who was the lynchpin in securing army support for the new regime. Titus was a stronger personality than his scheming politically-expert father, a more direct and dynamic character, and more (openly) ruthless, and though his religious views were unknown he had had orthodox Catholic tutors and was not likely to challenge the prevailing orthodox religious consensus in the West and he did not extend his private friendships with openly pagan young aristocratic fellow-cadets to any Julian-style threats to 'turn back the clock' in religious matters and aid the pagan religion. The new Emperor backed the Papacy in the 'Acacian Schism' but this was more of a political move to win Catholic support and embarrass Zeno, though Tiberius did encourage the Church to set up new shrines to past 'martyrs' in Rome to which he contributed generously and he welcomed preaching itinerant priests and monks and nuns on pilgrimage to his court. His own church foundations were mostly outside Rome, such as in the now rather neglected Ravenna (where a relative of his was bishop) and in Naples, than in Rome itself. Tiberius' own financial dealings had been questionable in the past and he had built up his already extensive fortune in the West during the early-mid 480s to make himself extremely rich, owning estates across a huge area of Italy and southern Gaul, he now kept up Majorian's 'anticorruption' commissions into the Imperial administration to ensure popular support and also sent out new roving legal commissions to look into miscarriages of justice and listen to appeals in all the provinces. The mastermind behind this, the late Emperor's final 'Quaestor' Julius Secundus from Arles, who Tiberius kept on and have extra staff, and his coterie of zealous – often moralist Christian – deputies were backed equally firmly by the strict but just Titus, who in his first speech as 'Caesar' to the Senate said that restoring ancient Republican standards of justice would be his watchword and his model would be Cicero.

Though Tiberius presided at the usual round of ceremonies at court (more extensive than under Majorian but at Julian's rather than Theodosian levels of grandeur) and was assiduous at doing business and signing papers it was Titus who was the regime's strongman and in that capacity went on tours of inspection of the provinces every summer and autumn – to Gaul in 489, the Rhineland and Rhaetia in 490, Britain in 491, Spain and Mauretania in 492, and Illyria and Dacia in 493. His scholarly younger brother Heraclius, his presumed heir as Titus only had two daughters by his heiress wife Paula, acted as the regime's main cultural patron and ran a literary and philosophic circle in Rome and Campania that included a number of pagan Antiochene refugees from the 484 rebellion. It was Heraclius' ultimate intention to open a non-denominational

University at Rome that would teach pagan philosophy and mysticism and the theology and mystical writings of all the Christian factions without any Church interference and to that end the Papacy would have to be neutered as a force for persecution and control of public thought. But the wary and politically-minded Emperor would not touch such an idea as he relied on Papal support so the Prince, who publicly assured that he believed in pagan philosophy's value as a 'spiritual pointer to the Truth' (i.e. Christianity) by the 'semi-enlightened wise men' of the Greek world led by Pythagoras, Socrates, Plato, and Aristotle but was in private more sceptical about the theological intolerance shown by most of the Christian theologians, had to make do with his private circle of philosophers. He had more support from Titus, who was privately fuming at the disrespect which Pope Felix (who came to office in 483), unlike his more urban predecessors Hilarius and Simplicius, showed to Imperial authority.

All citizens had to be equal under the Law in Titus' mind and that applied to the Church too, and his personal friends from his youth in the East who paid visits to him in the West after 488 – often paid by Zeno to report on what he was up to and intended to do once he was Emperor, as he was well aware – were instructed to take the Eastern ruler his private good wishes and support for the 'Henoticon' as an instrument of toleration. As 'Principes Iuventites' (Princes of Youth') from 489 like the young heirs of early Emperors, an ancient honorary rank restored by Tiberius II as a goodwill gesture to the antiquarian pagan nobles in Rome who had helped him in the 480s, Titus and Heraclius led revivals of the old parades of horse-expert young aristocrats at the 'Troy Games' on certain Roman race-days when they were in Rome. Titus became an expert in ancient Roman customs which he revived as much as possible, carefully shorn of pagan ritual associations, and generous donations to new monasteries in Italy kept the local Church happy. But Titus insisted that really patriotic Romans should join the army not become monks and he also began to recruit more restless young German nobles from the kingdoms of Transrhenus to his entourage of officers as Majorian had done. With his father's permission he helped to avert a Frankish civil war in Westphalia in 493 by ensuring that when their king Childeric died and a trio of princes from the 'Ripuarian' branch of their people, i.e. those residing on the east bank of the Rhine, challenged his son Clovis for the succession a friend of Titus' who was deputy 'dux' of Lower Germany brought Roman troops to the Frankish royal 'vill' (estate/ palace) to help Clovis drive off a rebel attack.

Clovis was secured on the throne and remained a loyal Roman ally for two decades and as he was Catholic and let in missionaries from Belgica to convert his people the Church was pleased with Titus for once. But the neighbouring Ostrogoths were more obstreperous under renegade and expansionist warlord

Theodoric the Amal, who had overthrown Theodoric 'Strabo' the ally of Majorian in 484, and their depredations down the Elbe into Saxon lands led to a major exodus of Saxon 'boat people' from their burnt farms to seek refuge on the 'Saxon Shore' in southern Britain where some of them had kin in the Roman army. Ambrosius Aurelianus had been retired by Tiberius II as Count in 490 and it was his less urbane or civilized Western British 'self-made' man ex-farmer successor and distant relative Artorius who had just taken over and had to round them up and intern them after illegal landings on the marshes of Trinovantia (Essex) near Camulodunum (Colchester). But at Titus' request the Emperor agreed to settle them on under-used farmland along the south coast of Britain to increase corn yields and tax-revenues and so that part of the 'Saxon Shore' was to end up more inhabited by German-speaking Saxons than by Britons as some 10,000 more settlers flooded in during 493–508, driven out of their homeland by Theodoric and led by lords such as Aelle and his son Cissa. (Aelle and Cissa are OTL semi-legendary Saxon leaders in Sussex; Artorius is the legendary 'King Arthur' who some see as a post-Roman British general.)

Part III

Reunification. 491 to 542

Chapter 9

The Road to Union: Titus II in the West, Anastasius in the East, to 516

(The reign of Anastasius is largely as in OTL – except that the Catholic rebellion of his general Vitalian, which forced him to abandon reconciliation with the Monophysites, in 514–15 was in reality without any Western assistance. In OTL Vitalian forced the Emperor to back down but was not chosen to succeed him in 518 and was later murdered; in this version it is the West's emperor Titus who aids Vitalian and brokers peace between him and Anastasius in return for the succession to the latter.)

On 9 April 491 the Eastern Emperor Zeno died at Constantinople, aged sixty – a better ruler than allowed for by his later reputation from Roman historians as a devious master of intrigue, and an 'outsider' from a village in the remote Cilician mountains who had seen off better-placed and in some cases better-educated rivals. Despite the claims of his brother Longinus, a senior and fairly respectable Isaurian former guards-officer who had commanded the 'Excubitors' regiment in 479–87 and was now a senator, the election-meeting called by the Senate supported his widow Ariadne who proposed to make her own choice, as advised but not mandated by them. On 10 April she appeared to the capital's crowds in the Imperial Box ('Kathisma') at the Hippodrome to announce that she would choose a new husband and Emperor. The Isaurian Praefect of the city, Gaetulicianus, was arrested by 'Master of Infantry' Callistus to prevent a coûp as he was resisting this and making aggressive speeches to the guards. He was replaced by the politically neutral Bithynian bureaucrat Julian; Ariadne chose as emperor senior 'Silentiary' (Palace administrative official) Anastasius of Dyrrachium, around Zeno's age, who was well-known as a sensible and hard-working character of no strong political or religious affiliations. He had worked well with assorted rival factions during Zeno's reign without offending any of them and had been a masterly chairman of the committee of palace figures set up in 484 to reshuffle appointments as Zen purged alleged supporters of Illus. Now a senator as of 489 as a mark of Zeno's trust and with two young and capable officer nephews in the 'Scholae' (or 'Schools') palace regiments with Constantinopolitan noble heiress wives,

Hypatius and Probus, he was brought to the Palace and acclaimed. But as he was rumoured to be sympathetic to the Monophysites and to have encouraged Zeno to go further in his reconciliation-plans than the 'Henoticon' the new Patriarch Euphemius, who had recently succeeded Acacius' German successor Fravitta (in office 489–90), made him sign a statement of orthodoxy.

On 20 April Anastasius married Ariadne in the palace church of St Stephen and was then crowned by Euphemius in the 'Kathisma' before the crowds. Longinus promised to behave if he could keep his posts but broke his word and angrily stirred up riots by the racing-factions who his allies lavished money on, and he was arrested and exiled to Egypt. About a third of the Isaurian soldiers in the capital's regiments and some in the Balkan army were dismissed in case of revolt, and many of them turned down the offer of farms in faraway Epirus and returned home to join a revolt in Isauria that summer. The rebels set out for the capital but were defeated at Cotyaeum by the new 'Master of Soldiers', John the Scythian, and the rebellion was soon ended and Anastasius secured on the throne. However he had no real link to the elite of ex-officers and mostly self-made careerist administrators from the provinces that had backed Zeno and his religious sympathies for toleration and resulting hostility to the hard-line orthodox made many of the latter dubious about him. As he sought support from the West the determined Tiberius agreed to lend him military help to keep an eye on the grumbling Balkan and Lower Moesian army but in return required the cession of Epirus and the provinces of eastern Illyria as far as Lake Ochrid, plus the military HQ and regiments at Sirmium, to the West. The latter was arguably better able to stabilize this region's army than the unknown civilian Anastasius and could help him that way and so Tiberius' ambassadors successfully argued, and after the cession the Western 'Master of Infantry' on the upper-middle Danube, Count Alexander, duly moved to Sirmium as the new 'Master of Soldiers' there. He purged the local armies of potential troublemakers including Isaurians and ultra-orthodox soldiers, installing reliable Rhinelanders.

Titus made a tour of inspection there in 494 which included military manoeuvres and a vigorous expedition by the Dacian and Danube armies over the Carpathians to punish raiding Heruls, but the orthodox in Constantinople and Syria were not mollified to have the East relying on Western troops and a not noticeably fervent 'Caesar' of the West for support. As Titus visited Anastasius in Constantinople in winter 494–5 after a nostalgic tour of famous sites of Ancient Greek history and literature in Greece there were rumours that he had bullied the Eastern ruler into nominating him in secret as his heir. Even at this early date it was said that Titus, an aggressive enthusiast for the days of the Early Empire who after the Herul expedition had himself acclaimed as the 'new Trajan', wanted to reunify the Empire under himself and would give the orthodox Church short shrift, and when Tiberius II died in Rome in February 496 aged seventy-one Titus succeeded smoothly to the West aged thirty-four and mollified the suspicious Pope Felix with a magnificent Church-led coronation in St Peter's Basilica in the Vatican. However, he also carried out a modified and sacrifice-free Christian version of the old Imperial inauguration rituals at the 'Shrine of the Genius of Rome', aka the former Temple of Jupiter, on the Capitol with the Senate in attendance and then hosted a month of races in the Circus Maximus and traditional wild-beast hunts in the Colosseum. The new Emperor virtually abandoned the fifth-century imperial residence at Ravenna to live in Rome most winters and from 498 was building a new and grand 'Marble Palace' in the style of the old Palatine palace's grander halls on the Pincine Hill at the North end of Rome, incorporating the older local gardens of the first and second century AD nobility. He also renovated the abandoned temple of Minerva on the Capitol as the new 'Shrine of the Divine Wisdom' and installed statues of Pythagoras (who was claimed by some Christian thinkers of Neoplatonist leanings as a mystic forerunner of the Church Fathers in his search for the Divinity through the study of numbers), the early Greek philosopher Thales of Miletus, Socrates, Plato, and Zeno of Citium the Stoic founder there, along with statues of Moses, Isaiah, and Jeremiah and the third-century Church Fathers Origen and Tertullian. But he was talked out of installing a statue of the Persian hero/god Mithras despite the worship of him by many soldiers as this would offend the Church and the same argument applied to his proposed statue of the Persian religious founder Zoroaster. In public Titus was Catholic; in private he supported all 'civilised' faiths.

The transformation of the near-derelict Temple of Vesta in the Forum Romanum into a 'Shrine of the Divine Flame' was less contentious as this could be Christianised, with a team of nuns to tend it in place of the Vestal Virgins. He also turned the Temple of Castor and Pollux nearby into a shrine to the victories of the early Roman Republic on the grounds that it had been set up after an alleged appearance of the 'Divine Twins' after the battle of Lake Regillus in 498 BC. Frequently seen in the Forum with his entourage en route to presiding at the local law-courts when in Rome, Titus indeed liked to pose as a traditional Roman magistrate, but he did not neglect Greek culture either and from 498 he held an annual Drama Festival in the capital usually at the Theatre of Marcellus, where the classics from the fifth and fourth centuries BC were re-enacted. He funded his own private theatrical ensemble of actors and made sure that the Eastern Emperor allowed them to attend a regular drama festival at Epidaurus in Greece, run by local nobles, which he part-funded. When he was not in Rome for the festival his brother Heraclius presided at it, and both of them encouraged new dramatists to write plays about mythological subjects in the old tradition – and Christian writers to write dramas about the martyrdoms of the victims of Diocletian and Galerius who Titus was content to have abused as 'tyrants' and the wrong sort of emperors. (In 506 the new play 'The Triumph of Constantine' by an Imperial court poet won the Rome festival prize after presenting a propaganda play about the correct sort of Emperor, i.e. a just and sternly virtuous Christian warrior who punished misrule and kept both Germans and Persians in their places.)

Titus usually wore a toga like an old Roman magistrate not the usual post-third century robes of a 'Diocletianic' emperor, got rid of many of the Persian-sounding ranks and offices at the court in favour of more traditional Latin names for them, and made his young corps of Roman (mostly aristocratic) pages and junior officers the centre of his household as had Majorian. In the mid-late 490s the work which he had already induced his ailing father to commence under his guidance earlier to create new Imperial commissions of legal supervision for the administration and legal system was extended and junior senators were drafted into it to 'earn their keep' by working for the Emperor before they achieved high rank. Extra law-courts were created in Rome and the capitals of the Western 'vicarates' to speed up justice. New courts of appeal were also created while a new legal college at Bononia (Bologna) trained lawyers to staff them and promising lawyers in the provinces were 'talent-spotted' by Imperial officials there and called in to staff the extra courts and at an older age teach at the new college. An overhaul of the Western Empire's tax-registers to bring them fully up to date and formally list who owned what estates across the entire Empire was also ordered in 497 with the officials in each province's governorate ordered to carry it out but being checked by special commissioners sent round from other provinces after they had done this, in 498, to ensure that they had taken in all the details correctly and to correct any mistakes. As Titus had suspected, some dodgy officials had taken bribes from or had voluntarily helped greedy local aristocrats to under-estimate their estates so they would not be rated at their full value and this was now exposed. The correct rates of tax for each estate could thus be charged once the resulting finalized details were submitted to their local tax-departments and copies transmitted to Rome in 499–500, and quite apart from this enabling the Emperor and his advisers to estimate their resources accurately and so improve tax collection the annual budget could be drawn up more easily and the poor were jubilant at the – loudly publicized – Imperial 'drive' to see that everyone paid their fair share of tax. The Emperor could pose as the defender of all his citizens and of just dealing – and emphasized this in the lettering on his coinage to get the message across.

The worst offenders for fiddling the census were dismissed and/or fined and the purge duly scared corrupt officials into behaving, and the amount of taxes on luxuries and employing 'unnecessary' servants were increased substantially while the land-taxes were altered from 505 to encourage the owners of multiple estates in several provinces to sell off or rent out land to more landless farmers – who were encouraged to apply to a new Imperial 'Land Fund' to borrow money to buy or rent farms. The main intention, duly met, was to bring back unused land into service and increase agricultural production both to feed the army and to stave off famine, and special financial grants encouraged buying land to set up stud-farms to breed horses for the army. The Emperor also stimulated trade as advised by his 'Count of the Sacred Largesses' from 497–508, ex-merchant turned senator (from Syracuse) Quintus Augerius, who had travelled far afield to Ireland, Transrhenus, and the Sahara in pursuit of markets for his expanding trading company and who now recommended to Titus that the problem of harsh and rigorously meticulous hunts for tax-dodging aristocrats causing dissent and plots – a difficulty under Majorian – could be avoided by creating greater trade opportunities and taxing imported goods. The richest pickings for trade lay in the East and there after 491 Anastasius was having similar tax-raising ideas to expand the Red Sea trade via the Himyarite kingdom (Aden) at the mouth of the Red Sea to India and up the Nile to Nubia. But in the west Titus could increase trading journeys by British, Gallic, and Spanish merchants to Ireland for agricultural products and via the North Sea to the Baltic for timber, rope for shipping-rigging, and amber (a luxury object for the rich) and with the expanded 'Classis Britannia' already helping pre-496 to keep Saxon piracy down Titus now ordered naval ships to escort trading-voyages to Jutland and the kingdom of the Geats in southern Sweden.

Some of the Saxons driven out of their marshy Elbe-mouth lands by the Ostrogoths to settle in Britain already knew the area – including from past piracy – and were recruited to serve as merchant navy captains and crews. This duly stimulated the growth of Londinium and the new Icenian (Suffolk) port of Harvicium (Harwich) as trading-centred in the early sixth century along with that of new ports in the pirate-raided and formerly declining Continental province of Gallia Belgica. Austendium (Ostend) on the North Sea coast and Aventerium (Antwerp) up the river Scheldt to the east grew up as new trading-ports in the early sixth century and Roman/ Belgican/ Saxon merchants began to move into new trading-posts on Jutland and later in Scania, where Geatish kings Hygelac (d 518) and his nephew Beowulf (d. 540), the latter later known in local myth as a heroic 'monster-slayer', became gift-laden Roman allies and distributed Roman goods and money to their lords. An alternative trade-route of 'caravans' escorted by Roman troops by land north from the Ostrava Gap into semi-friendly German territory was created for annual missions to the lower Vistula and the lagoons to its east to collect amber and wagon-loads of timber from the local tribes. But this new interest by Rome in the region, which also led to many ambitious young warriors taking the path to the Empire to enrol in the army where the younger sons of Frankish king Clovis became senior military aides to Emperor Titus after c. 510, also led to the paranoid but highly skilled anti-Roman king Theodoric of the Ostrogoths fearing that Rome was out to encircle him and bring him down as it had done to Gaiseric the Vandal. After the new and luxury-loving Vandal king Gelimer, lord of the lower Vistula, signed up as a Catholic and a Roman ally and married a Franco-Roman noble bride in 520 Theodoric was to invade Jutland and sack the main Roman entrepots there, carrying off the less mobile goods stored there as loot.

The Gothic attack on Jutland led to the local Danish king Hrothgar calling in Roman troops from Belgica to help his ravaged kingdom and build a 'Danish Dyke' ('Danevirke') to keep out the Ostrogoths, but it also sparked off a large migration by the decentralized and militarily weak lords of the Angles, in the 'Angle' between the Elbe and the Jutish peninsula, to escape the invaders who burnt their farms and enslaved their menfolk. In the 520s several thousand Angles sailed to Britain to take up farms in eastern Icenia, serve as tenants on the Imperial grain-growing estates of the Fens, or settle in the Romano-British administrative region of 'Linnuis' around Lindum (Lincoln). The movement of assorted military settlers and their families as 'limitanei' to the under-manned north-west regions of Britain around Hadrian's Wall (hit by Irish raiding in the later fourth century to the mid-fifth century) by Ambrosius Aurelianus under Majorian had left the east of Britain short of farming manpower, tax-revenues were falling, and the government had noticed. The Angles duly filled the gap in manpower although there were grumbles by older noble families in Britain that the new settlers, who continued to speak Anglian as well as Latin and referred to their settlements as the 'North Folk', 'South Folk', and 'Lindsey', were not trying to become British but treated the region as an extension of their homeland. But the trade-boom and extra revenue were what mattered to Titus and his advisers, and similarly he put money and military effort into building up the trans-Sahara trade-route to Lake Chad to bring in exotic goods to Carthage and the other regional ports from the Sahel and enterprising local traders soon started to import slaves sold to them by tribal kings in the Lake Chad region who were only too happy to get rid of their enemies' captured manpower. Roman traders, on Imperial orders, also started bribing local chiefs with Roman luxuries to acquire and pass on quantities of gold from the distant forests to the South-West. Small at first, this regular trade was boosting the Western Imperial currency's stability by c. 520.

Some Roman traders at the town of Bornu got hold of gold mined in the distant lands of the Ashanti people on the Gulf of Benin coast in the mid-490s and this news duly reached Rome where the Imperial finance ministry was always keen to acquire new gold-mines. The source of gold had been located – but it was too far to send troops across a good thousand miles beyond Lake Chad for an undetermined amount of precious metal and instead one of Titus' imported geographers from the Museion at Alexandria, who had read a copy of Himilco the Carthaginian's fourth century BC account of his voyage down the west coast of Africa, suggested to the Emperor that he send a naval expedition to the Gulf by sea. This appealed to the restless Titus and as he already had captains trained in serving in the Atlantic waters at his naval academy stationed at Gades (Cadiz) he sent a small naval flotilla of five ships SW from the Pillars of Hercules down the coast in 500, accompanied by local tribal interpreters from the mainland tribes south-west of Tingis (Tangier). Roman traders had been travelling sporadically across the west Sahara to the River Niger for many years but had no idea of what was on the coast, and the expedition reached the mouth of the River Senegal and beyond that the mysterious 'Mountains of the Moon' once seen by Himilco but found no trace of gold-mines and in 501, after a winter encamped on the 'Monkey Coast', loaded up with apes, exotic plants, and timber and returned to report that the route was impractical and far too expensive to be worthwhile. The Emperor was then distracted by events in the east, but he kept up occasional trading-missions to the new Roman base set up at the mouth of the River Senegal and in 508 a ship blown off course was to accidentally discover the Canary Islands which were immediately claimed to be the lost 'Hesperides' visited by Hercules before he came to the site of Rome on his Twelve Labours. The Emperor was thus created the 'New Hercules' and 'Lord of the Hesperides' by the obliging Senate, and a small Roman military post was set up on the islands with their wildlife and plants occasionally featuring in Imperial entertainments in Rome – and captured and forcibly 'Romanised' local tribesmen even spoke of a mysterious land beyond the 'Far Western Sea' which the Carthaginians had once visited but which the Emperor did not believe to be worth trying to reach.

In summer 496 Titus sent a Papal embassy to Constantinople in an effort to sort out the problems over the non-recognition of Acacius as Patriarch, his father having failed to pressurize the determined previous Pope Gelasius (in office 492–6) to be more conciliatory but Titus having arranged for the Imperial administration to arrange the election of the more emollient bureaucrat Anastasius to succeed him. The new Pope however only agreed to recognize Acacius' appointees as legal, not him, and insisted that he could not go back on his predecessors' refusal to accept Acacius or trust his statements on his faith. However, the Roman and the Alexandrian church representatives at the synod that met during Pope Anastasius' delegates' visit to Constantinople, as prodded by chief delegate and Imperial confidante Bishop Paulus of Ravenna, worked out a declaration of faith close to the "Henoticon". This revised the terms of the Chalcedonian decretals on the nature of Christ to 'explain them in greater detail' without explicitly changing them – the latter would have been unacceptable to the hard-line Catholics. Emperor Anastasius agreed to recognise the Pope and his predecessors as legal and put their names in the Eastern liturgy in return for acceptance of the 'Henoticon' as a legally acceptable statement of doctrine, and also made promises to refrain from further expulsions of either orthodox or Monophysite hard-liners from their churches. But opposition in the Papal bureaucracy in Rome and in other hard-line Catholic episcopal strongholds was heightened after the Pope received a pro-Acacian deacon who had been attacking the Catholic position on Chalcedon as erroneous in his writings, Photinus from Thessalonica, and he was then invited to Titus' court to give sermons and hold services over winter 497–8.

In 498 Anastasius launched financial reforms of his own, in the East led by his new chief minister and fellow-ex-palace-bureaucrat Marinus and the new 'Count of Sacred Largesses' John. This featured the abolition of the unpopular sales-tax on commercial business transactions, the "Chrysargyon", and stimulated the economy by giving higher profits to businessmen; the deficit was made up by higher land-taxes and luxury-taxes but these were not raised too steeply in order not to stimulate any plots. A new copper coinage was also issued, with a new set of mines in Dacia ordered by Titus as 'Caesar' in 494 coming 'on stream' and supplying metal for coins to both Empires by mutual arrangement. Assorted Isaurian brigands and former members of Zeno's army arrested in the suppression of the last local revolts and guerilla attacks there in 496–7 were sent to these slave-mines by arrangement with Titus, who also sent convicted corrupt officials to the slave-mines there and in the Cantabrian mountains of Spain from 498 as a warning to his State servants to behave properly. Taking up Titus' ideas of legal reform, Anastasius also created the new post of *Vindex Civitatis* ('defender of the city') for his capital and other major cities (498) and later towns (504), a new position of the State-controlled supervisor of local tax-collection, to decrease corruption. The free issue of soldiers' rations and equipment was replaced with more generous allowances to cover the cost of purchase.

But the Eastern Empire remained in a politically and militarily uncertain state under a ruler with few military links and in 500 his military 'strongman' and chief adviser on military appointments, John 'the Scythian', was lured away by Titus with a large salary to work for him in reforming the Marcomannian and upper Danube armies to create new Romano-German regiments. John was then to overhaul the armies in Gaul and Spain to merge the local armies of those provinces away from the Rhine into flexible and mobile regional regiments and abolish a number of no-longer-needed garrisons in cities that were not under threat from German attacks. (This duly led to a number of regional 'ducates' in non-frontier provinces being abolished altogether in 502-4). Titus could afford to cut his troops' numbers and military administration away from the frontiers and only keep troops where they were needed, though he continued to recruit soldiers locally in every province on the principle that the Empire's citizenry needed to participate in not just benefit from their defence. But the East had no such luxury as even in externally unthreatened Syria and Egypt the local religious communities were feuding bloodily, though the 'orthodox vs Monophysite' riots were now decreasing in Palestine as the orthodox gained numerical predominance and a grip on the local sees and their resources after a purge of pro-Illus Monophysites by Zeno after 484. (This was the era of the founding of such iconic and well-founded and pilgrim-visited orthodox monasteries as that of St Sabas at the 'Great Lavra' in Judaea in 502.)

The Sassanid kingdom of Sogdiana had survived the crisis of the early 480s thanks to the Eastern Roman civil war and was now in the hands of the capable and aggressive King Kavadh who had recruited a mercenary force of Hepthalite Huns from the Jaxartes steppes, and he had designs on Bactria. In January 503 Persian soldiers scaled the walls of the regional Roman capital, Balkh, at a place where drunken monk guards were asleep and stormed the city, massacring the population, and the Sassanids and Huns swept into Bactria and on into Hyrcania that spring. Other sieges along the Caspian coast failed as the Roman garrisons were now alert and had supplies and artillery ready, and Anastasius sent an army of around 52,000 men under his nephew Hypatius and generals Areobindus and Patricius to collect the main force stationed at Ctesiphon and move north via Media while the 'Master of Soldiers' at Ctesiphon, Secundinus, kept the Huns out of Persis with his armoured cavalry army and drove them back to Alexandria-in –Arachosiea. But the vain and over-confident Hypatius and his generals quarrelled over their campaign-route towards Balkh and they split up so the Persians could respond effectively; Areobindus ended up trapped and besieged in Zadracarta and the others had to halt and rescue him. As Hypatius had made all sorts of mistakes and was excoriated by his fellowcommanders Anastasius recalled him and sent out his –civilian – chief minister Celer, at the head of a commission of generals from HQ in the capital, to take charge of the 504 campaign. (In OTL the Sassanian surprise attack was in Mesopotamia.)

But despite military worries Celer listened to advice and proved competent and in that year the Romans retook Balkh and set up a new chain of fortresses along the Oxus. Kavadh, nervous of his Hun allies overthrowing him when his money ran out, sent an embassy to Celer to negotiate and the 'status quo' was restored, but the Empire had had a narrow escape and the reputation of Anastasius suffered over his cost-cutting in the garrisons in Hyrcania and Media leaving them exposed to attack and his failure to note the implications of the pre-war alliance of Kavadh and the Huns; by contrast, Titus kept a close eye on events on his adjacent steppes and had regular missions sent to 'check out', bribe or threaten dangerous tribes on the Dneister and Dnieper. Domestic disorder also raged in the east, and in 507 faction-rioting in the circus at Antioch was not reined in by the ineffective but Imperially-approved, costcutting Praefect. The famous and multi-millionaire charioteer Porphyrius, the greatest sportsman of the era and the subject of numerous honorary regional statues and the 'guest of choice' for drooling Antiochene socialite hostesses, led a raid by an armed mob on a Jewish synagogue at Daphne to deal with apparent cheating by a Jewish racing-team- sponsor and his betting-ring by a mass lynching, and the city's Jewish community had to arm themselves and fight or flee as the Imperial troops did not protect them in a week of riots. Anastasius sent a commission of enquiry and later dismissed the "Court of the East" (i.e. Syria) Basilius for being too frightened to act; however his successor was expelled from the city and the police-chief Menas was lynched in new riots, and the local Irenaeus had to be made 'Count' instead to calm down the rioters. The nobility and troops looked on and muttered that Titus would have kept order better and stood no nonsense.

Anastasius now endeavoured to repair his reputation by sorting out the trouble between orthodox and Monophysites more forcefully than the distrusted Zeno had done, and was able to utilise years of unofficial talks with local Monophysites in the capital and his personal contacts with their clerics in Syria via missions by sympathetic clerics in the capital's church bureaucracy. In 511, at the instigation of his Monophysite adviser the minor cleric and veteran theologian Severus, Anastasius ordered a synod to depose Patriarch Macedonius for 'Nestorianism' as he was standing in the way of a major offensive for reconciliation that Anastasius was arranging and was refusing to call a regional Church Council. He was succeeded by the more conciliatory Timotheus. In summer 512 Anastasius' finance-minister Marinus persuaded him to make pro-'Monophysite'" changes in the liturgy at the aforementioned Council when it met, to bring moderate Monophysites into the regional Church and its offices – which now a large number of Macedonius' faction were boycotting. On 4 November severe rioting in the Hippodrome followed, as normally rival "Blues" and "Greens" from those two racing-clubs joined orthodox demonstrators. A mob at the Forum of Constantine, up the 'Mese' avenue West of the Hippodrome and the 'Augustaeum' square, proclaimed Areobindus (husband of Theodosius I's descendant Juliana Anicia, daughter of Valentinian III's daughter Placidia by Olybrius) Emperor and stoned the minister Celer and the 'Master of Soldiers' Patricius as they tried to address the crowds. On 6 November Anastasius appeared without his crown in the Hippodrome and offered to abdicate, and after he had promised to retain the existing liturgy and defend the Council of Chalcedon's decretals the rising subsided. Macedonius and assorted orthodox nobles were suspected of being behind the riots and rumour had it that Areobindus was a 'stalking horse' for Titus who feared that Anastasius was lining up Hypatius as his successor not him. The Eastern Emperor pressed ahead with his religious plans away from the capital where there was less risk of him being overthrown. In November a synod at Antioch replaced Patriarch Flavian of Antioch with Severus, a leading Monophysite, and a purge of obstinate orthodox from the local clerical posts for refusing to recognise him followed. (The events of 512 are based on OTL.)

This sparked off military mutiny and in spring 513 Vitalian, the orthodox 'Count'insert space of the (German and Bulgar)'Federates' mercenaries in Thrace, led his troops in rebellion against Hypatius the Emperor's nephew, now "Master of Infantry" there. He declared himself the champion of orthodoxy; Hypatius was deserted by his troops, not least as his officers resented this pampered court show-off and unsuccessful commander in Persia in 503 being foisted on them, and fled to the capital. The army of Lower Moesia under Count Candidian now backed orthodox too, as did the military headquarters at Thessalonica under regional 'Master of Infantry' Cassianus and 'Master of Cavalry' Saturninus – both former junior officers in the West under Titus in Dacia and rumoured to be in touch with if not paid by him to embarrass Anastasius. The coastal towns of Odessus and Mesembria were forced to surrender; peasants joined Vitalian's army and he advanced to the suburbs of the capital where 'Master of Soldiers' Patricius mediated. The rebel's lieutenants were received by the Emperor and were told that he would call a full Church Council to redefine and reaffirm orthodoxy and that the Western Church would be invited to participate and assist with its theological expertise – which under Pope Symmachus (in office 504–14) would be expected to be firmly orthodox. The majority of senior officers declared themselves satisfied, the arriving Cassianus and Saturninus at Adrianople did so too and swore allegiance to the Council of Chalcedon to the noisy satisfaction of the crowds in the capital. The unsatisfied Vitalian had no option to agree and retired into Thrace to await the Council. But once more Eastern troops from garrisons in Anatolia had reached the capital Anastasius sent out an army to attack Vitalian's force; the first commander, Cyril, was murdered as he ordered his men to attack Vitalian and then Hypatius took over but was defeated and captured. In spring 515 the 'Praefect of the Watch' was killed in riots in the Hippodrome as the orthodox crowds in the capital rose again; Vitalian gathered an army, was joined by the until then equivocal Cassianus and Saturninus and a fleet from the naval base at Callipolis (Gallipoli), and set out for Constantinople. Anastasius sent envoys to meet him at Stenum; it was agreed that a Council of the Church would be summoned to Heraclea, Thrace, under the new Pope Hormisdas' presidency, and a truce was established. In the West, Emperor and Pope were agreed that they not Anastasius would mediate – and assert their power in doing so. For Titus, clearly he had the succession – and reunification – in mind. Vitalian, his temporary ally, probably had other ideas.

Vitalian was made 'Master of Soldiers' in Thrace and Hypatius was ransomed. Anastasius invited Pope Hormisdas to come and preside over the Church Council at Heraclea, but Vitalian did not believe the Emperor's sincerity and revolted again with a demand that he co-chair the Council as 'Protector of the Church'. He marched on Constantinople with the Thracian army, and set up his camp at Pera across the Golden Horn harbour from the city. This may have been due to rumours that Titus had decided to take a hand in matters and intended to use his army, which was gathering at Sirmium for an alleged campaign in Dacia to 'help' the East by driving back a major raid that spring by marauding Utrigur Huns from Sarmatia on Upper Moesia, to march on Constantinople so he could chair the Church Council himself and pressurize Anastasius. But if Vitalian had been hoping to scare Anastasius into accepting him running the Council and even making him his heir this failed, and as the Eastern Emperor held out a Papal embassy arrived at Constantinople in early August with Hormisdas' terms and his learned opinion on what doctrine was correct; the Pope himself had landed at Dyrrachium and was heading by land for the capital. No agreement was reached or a Church Council formally called on account of Hormisdas insisting on acceptance of strict orthodoxy as determined at Chalcedon and the condemnation of Acacius.

But Titus now crossed the eastern frontier with his full army of 50,000 men and headed for Constantinople to allegedly arbitrate and 'help' his fellow-Emperor and Cassianus and Saturninus declared their acceptance of him as arbitrator, and as the army at Antioch was busy putting down more orthodox riots there and did not move Anastasius was left with a choice between Titus or Vitalian and chose the former as his ally. The demoralized troops in the capital did not want to fight and the Western navy now moved East from Syracuse to Athens in early September while a second Western army landed at Dyrrachium. As the main Balkan commanders all announced their allegiance to the 'Emperors of undivided Rome, Anastasius and Titus' (the Eastern ruler had been on the throne longer so he counted as being more senior) Titus entered Adrianople on 2 October and reached Selymbria near the capital on the 18th. Anastasius had to give in and go out to Hebdoman to welcome his co-emperor to the capital as Titus requested, and on 24 October Titus and some of his regiments entered Constantinople through the Golden Gate to proceed along the 'Mese' avenue to the palace, greeted as the saviours of orthodoxy by the crowds. Anastasus kept his throne as his generals (except the furious Vitalian) wished, but from this date Titus was formally co-emperor of the East and as he spent the winter in the Eastern capital he was able to put the armies of the Balkans and the central command at Constantinople to out his own men in charge, Cassianus as 'Master of Infantry' in the capital. For the moment, the Antiochene and Mesopotamian armies were not altered as they recognized him as co-emperor.

Pope Hormisdas now arrived with his delegation, led by Bishop Germanus of Capua and Bishop John, at Constantinople. They celebrated Christmas in the cathedral of Hagia Sophia with the two Emperors using the Chalcedonian liturgy, and detailed discussions followed with delegations from Antioch, Jerusalem and Alexandria. On Titus' insistence, the rival groups in each of these sees were all invited to the talks but as Hormisdas would not meet the 'heretic' representatives in person his juniors did so and when the Council met the orthodox claimants were admitted as the rightful Patriarchs and their rivals had to sit in an annex of the council-room and send in delegates. On 25 March 516 the bishops were all welcomed to the capital by Titus, Anastasius, those Eastern HQ military commanders certified as orthodox led by 'Excubitors' regimental commander Justin the Illyrian, and Anastasius' nephew Pompeius. Next day Pope Hormisdas read out his own theological 'resume' of the legal situation, backing the full orthodoxy of the Council of Chalcedon; the new (514) Patriarch John of Constantinople refused to accept this over its repeating accusations against the late Patriarch Acacius. On the 27th the accusations against Acacius and the leaders of the Church in Constantinople in 512–15 were listed by senior deacon Dioscurus, and the majority of the delegates declared themselves satisfied that the accused, including Acacius, were guilty of heresy.

On 28 March Titus and the reluctant Anastasius signed the "Formula of Hormisdas", recognizing full Chalcedonian orthodoxy and condemning Acacius and his successors, and required the Council to do so. The bishops signed up or if they did not were dismissed, which latter result covered most of the 512–15 Constantinopolitan Church leadership and their Eastern allies; Church unity was duly restored. A synod in Antioch restored orthodoxy to the Church there. Patriarch Severus and 54 other Monophysite bishops were deposed; Severus dodged orders to report to Constantinople for trial and fled to Egypt where Patriarch Timotheus III, a 'Monophysite' but too powerful to be removed, gave him sanctuary. The leadership of the Monophysite Church in Mesopotamia either followed orders from the capital to sign up to the Council's decretals or were removed from office in November, and in December the new 'Master of Soldiers' (Infantry and Cavalry) Anatolianus arrived in Ctesiphon. He added his use of military force to the local orthodox Church's officials' manpower as they dispossessed the Nestorian Church too – at least in the regional capital, as most of their local monasteries in the rural areas of Assyria and Atropatene were not confiscated and some local clerics survived the purge too with episcopal support.

Chapter 10

After Reunion in 516: The Dynasty Of Titus II

In Constantinople a triumvirate of Anastasius' chief minster Celer, Titus' appointee as 'Master of Infantry' (for all the East) Marcellus the ex-commander in Noricum, and Western civilian administrator Honoratus (of a metropolitan noble dynasty of early fifth century 'service nobility' origins and son and cousin of past Eastern consuls) assisted Titus. He was crowned co-emperor of the East by the new Patriarch John in Hagia Sophia on 22 March 516 and thereafter was the effective ruler as Anastasius was treated with honour but required to submit his plans to his colleague. Once the Church Council in the capital was over and Titus had remodelled the administration and left for a tour of Asia Minor and Syria the triumvirate exercised power, and the arrival of Titus and 40,000 Western troops in Antioch a couple of months later duly warned off any potentially rebellious or autonomist local commanders. More of his troops and half his fleet remained in Constantinople for the rest of 516 while the other half of the fleet under admiral Nebridius, of Alexandrian palace 'service nobility' origin, sailed to and took over Alexandria and replaced the Praefect with a Sicilian general called Dioscurus of Catana, and apart from assorted extremist Monophysite riots as orthodox clerics in Alexandria had their churches restored the East remained quiescent. Titus moved on from Antioch to Edessa for a series of re-modellings and military manoeuvres of the Mesopotamian army and then marched to Ctesiphon to reside in splendour in the old Sassanid palace there for winter 516–17 and to receive both assorted local Persian nobles (including from occupied Persis and Hyrcania) and the Sassanid client-rulers of Bactria. These key 'lynch-pins' of local collaboration with Rome were piled with gifts and new estates and were lured into agreeing to act for the Emperor who to their relief promised more toleration for their usually Zoroastrian beliefs and their client priests, the 'Magians' among them, than the recent Eastern Emperors had shown. He also gave under-governorates to noble Zoroastrians to win over the landed gentry.

Titus did not care about orthodoxy as long as people obeyed the Emperor and paid their taxes and this duly benefited the local Nestorians, Jews, and Zoroastrians and even the pagan sect of the 'Sabaeans' around Edessa and

Carrhae, the ancient moon-worshippers who had their old temples guaranteed. The only sect to suffer from his dislike and have their assets seized were the Manichaeans who Christians and Zoroastrians alike regarded as 'heretics' and hated and who he abandoned to their foes' administrative victimization. The Emperor's toleration for Mithraists and return of seized Mithraist shrines and treasures that the orthodox Pulcheria and Marcian had seized in a gesture to the orthodox in 451–9 secured their goodwill and that of a large number of covert Mithraists in the army in particular. Indeed the way that he 'balanced' between rival religions and sects in complex, multi-faith Mesopotamia and Persia in 517 made the region's elite less likely to feud and more loyal to him than they had been to any Eastern regime since the 440s – and duly offset the dislike of extremists of rival Christian factions for his regime in parts of violence-riven Syria. He also stimulated trade to bring about prosperity and distract the local elites from feuding – and to increase tax-revenues, with a visit to Charax (Basra) to build an extended new port there, the building of a Persian Gulf anti-piracy fleet, and a new series of mercantile missions to India by sea. By land assorted Romano-Persian caravans were escorted by local cavalry from Ecbatana and Tabriz across Bactria and sullenly submissive Sogdiana to the Indus valley to extend the 'Silk Road' link to distant China from 518. In September 517 Titus sailed from Antioch back to the West to take over from his deputy and (April 515) 'Caesar' Honorius in Italy, but as events turned out Anastasius, who had been widowed when Empress Ariadne died in March 516, died on 9 July 518 aged eighty-eight and the 'triumvirate' and the Eastern guards-commander Justin the Illyrian quickly arranged a ceremony in the Hippodrome where Titus was proclaimed sole 'Emperor of the East'.

The new regime was accepted with swearing-in ceremonies in Antioch, Alexandria and Ctesiphon as Titus had arranged in 516 and there were no revolts even by the extreme Monophysites in Egypt, half the guards-regiments and police in Alexandria having been replaced by Westerners since 516, but to be sure Titus despatched more troops by sea to Constantinople in August 518 and in October he followed in person to spend the winter at the Sacred Palace there. It was unofficially understood to satisfy Eastern autonomist sensibilities that in due course Titus, like Constantine 'the Great' in the 320s–330s, would create new 'Caesars' to divide up the Empire and one of his brother Heraclius' sons (Anastasius, born in 496, and Nerva, born in 498) would take over in Constantinople. But this did not immediately happen and as time passed it became obvious that Titus intended to keep real power in his own hands and make sure this time that the Western Emperor, based in Rome, remained senior to any junior relatives elsewhere and the latter and any mutinous provincial governors had not enough troops to revolt successfully. In the Eastern capital

Celer served as 'Master of Offices' to 522 and was then replaced by Justin the Illyrian's ambitious and ruthless nephew and aide, the rising Illyrian farm-boy turned learned bureaucrat Petrus Sabbatius (OTL Emperor Justinian 'the Great'), and the problematic Vitalian was bought off with the rank of 'Master of Infantry' for Thrace in 516–20, then given the 520 Eastern consulship and sent off in 521 on a military inspection-tour of the Caucasus defences to strengthen the fortification in the new inland Iberian kingdom of zealous Christian ruler Vakhtang 'Gorgeslani' (the 'Wolf-Lion'). The honoured and gift-laden but dangerous Vitalian then had a mysterious 'accident' in a mountain-valley avalanche near Mount Elbruz in August 521 and rumour had it that Titus had had him disposed of to be rid of a rival. (In OTL Justinian appears to have killed Vitalian.)

But the Eastern army remained loyal and no plots ensued – in any case, most of Vitalian's senior officers from his rebellion had been transferred to the Rhine or Britain since 516 – and the union of East and West continued smoothly. The Emperor could now use a culture-pursuing tour of Greece in summer-autumn 522 to announce that his Western 'Military Games' to keep soldiers fit and active and regiments busy with healthy rivalry would be extended to the East with annual Games at Thessalonica from 524 and that he would revive the defunct local Isthmian and Nemean Games too (for locals) and would attend the 524 Olympics in person. Those clerics who objected to 'immoral' Greek athletics as obnoxious secular-minded hedonism and nudism were mollified by the banning of nudity at all Games and appropriate religious services at their opening and conclusion but some angry preachers and hermits who were not satisfied ended up tried and deported to remote monasteries for insulting the Emperor. The latter was determined to incorporate the best of ancient Greece in the new Christian Rome and would not accept any criticism by Christians who thought themselves above the law, and the triumphant orthodox clergy who had won the arguments in the 515–16 religious overhaul of the East now found that they had not won the right to behave as arrogantly as they had done to the State authorities in the fifth century and that the new Emperor had more in common with Julian than they had suspected at the time.

Titus used his 524 visit to Greece for the Olympics, following a tour of Spain, Lusitania and Mauretania in 523 and winter 523–4 at Rome, to 'invite' (in effect order) the leading members of the nobility in the region, Asia Minor, and Egypt to come to the Games where he lectured them on the need to keep up Classical values and the compatibility of Christianity with the ideals of Plato and Socrates. He also stressed that the self-denial, striving for perfection and dedication to the glory of their home cities or towns of athletes was similar to that of soul-improving ascetic monks and patriotic soldiers, and was hailed as the 'Athlete of Christ' by the sycophantic but sincere bishop Leonidas of Corinth who ended up as archbishop of Athens by his master's orders in 529,, transforming the Parthenon to be the new cathedral of the Virgin Mary with an appropriately large statue made in silver (as cheaper and easier to sculpt than gold). Titus also used the tour to rebuild parts of neglected ancient towns in the Peloponnese in the style of the fifth century BC and to import new farmer-settlers, many of them Slav refugees from the Huns and now the Bulgars on the western steppes, to rebuild a prosperous agriculture in emigration-denuded Achaea, Elis, and Arcadia, giving generously of his own funds and establishing an 'Imperial Greek Land Fund' to keep the project running. His argument that a prosperous Greece full of sturdy farmers and able young soldiers had kept the barbarian Northerners at bay in the fifth and fourth centuries BC but emigration in the Hellenistic era had led to the 270s BC Gaul invaders having a 'walk-over' into a declining land had military as well as statistical merit. He encouraged his provincial 'duces' on the Danube and in Dacia to settle time-expired soldiers in Greece and help agriculture there further. Towns were revived and craftsmen given subsidies to move from overcrowded places in Syria and Egypt to Athens, Megara, Corinth, Argos, and Thebes whose populations were all to nearly double by 550, and in turn the new farmers in the countryside were encouraged to have large families by Augustan-style tax-relief for having more children. At least one son of each family with two or more sons was to enter the army and so boost the manpower – and its Romano-Greek component – of the armed forces in the Balkans and Dacia with new local regiments being formed there to concentrate loyalties on specific, historic locations. (By 540 Titus had created special 'Spartan', 'Argive', 'Theban',and 'Achaean' regiments in the Lower Moesian army.)

A similar venture to both settle farmers from time-expired military veterans and raise locally-named regiments from their families was launched in Ionia and Lydia as Titus proceeded to spend several months in the area after winter 524–5 at Constantinople, and historic towns in Ionia were funded by him for rebuilding in the ancient styles and a new regional legal college was set up at Ephesus. Across Greece, Macedonia, Thrace, and Asia Minor Titus ordered his roving commissions to examine the foundation-documents and allied legal transactions that had set up all the region's monasteries during 525–6 and all such arrangements that were questionable for reasons of slipshod administration, bribery, embezzlement, or undue influence dating back as far as 330 were cancelled and the land seized and handed over either to existing tenants as the new owners or to new tenants. The regional – mostly orthodox hard-liner – bishops also had their land-grants investigated and many of them cancelled so Titus was able to hold this investigation over them as an implicit threat to punish all who did not go along with his assertions of Imperial power and religious toleration. With the Eastern armies flooded with loyal Western troops and extra Oriental trade bringing new tax-revenues and a suitable boost for military spending any fuming bishops or abbots who tried to foment rebellion got nowhere and ended up reported by Titus' spies and sacked. But the Emperor had no objection to Churchmen who toed the line and after a tour of Galatia, Phrygia and Cappadocia in summer –autumn 525 to stimulate agriculture (stock-raising in the former two and corn-growing in valleys in the third) he proceeded to Antioch for the winter to hold military and chariot-racing Games and charm the public with extravagant expenditure but expel assorted obstinate extremist orthodox clerics and abbots for fomenting riots. The populace and rival factions of Antioch were now supposed to divide up the city's Church property between them in an equable manner and live together peacefully and the Emperor set his troops on anyone who protested and several fulminating 'stylite' monks up their pillars who called him rude names were 'invited' to move to more remote locations in the desert and perfect their austerity there. As a result several noisy bearded, rag-clad holy men who proclaimed themselves the heirs of St Anthony, driven out into the wilderness by the 'new Diocletian', were able to found long-lasting and well-subscribed monasteries on the desert fringes of the Euphrates and Orontes valleys but lost their influence in a suddenly pacific Antioch.

The surviving local Monophysite community, driven out of their main churches and monasteries by the purge after Titus' agreement with Pope Hormisdas and Anastasius on this in 516, were invited back to most of their property in 526, and as a result a new confidence saw them starting to convert the uncommitted and the opponents of the harsh orthodox triumphalism of 516–18, led by their new bishop Jacob Baradeus who was said to have preached to Titus himself at a local synod in 526 and who later went secretly to Constantinople to set up a new community there. (His principal funder was supposed to be 'Master of Offices' and from 526 Praefect of Constantinople Petrus Sabbatius' ex-'showgirl' wife Theodora, a former Hippodrome erotic performer and a Monophysite noble's lover while living in Egypt.) (OTL: Empress Theodora, Justinian's wife.) The Eastern civil tax-registers were overhauled on the lines of the Western ones and the landed aristocracy were required to pay a fair rate of tax and stop hiding their assets from the taxman by an Imperial commission set up in 526 and, as with the Church, they were powerless to do anything about it. But the main impact of Titus' winter residence of 526–7 at Alexandria was in the Red Sea region as he was determined to extend its trade revenues as he had done in the Persian Gulf and he now ordered the rebuilding of the 'Canal of Necho' to link the Red Sea to the Nile near Memphis. In 525 a major Roman naval expedition down the Red Sea to the Himyarite kingdom, following an appeal by persecuted Christians in the region to the Patriarch of Alexandria against their oppressive Jewish King Caleb, had led to the Romans equipping and transporting an army from the adjacent Christian kingdom of Abyssinia in North Africa to the Arab side of the Sea to overthrow and kill Caleb, who had famously been cornered on the seashore after a battle and had ridden his horse into the sea rather than surrender. As the Abyssinians had occupied Himyar and now ruled both shores of the Red Sea Titus was able to detach a new Roman fleet there to patrol the Sea and aid the Abyssinians, who had few ships, to put down piracy and extend the trade-route over the Indian Ocean to India.

(The Abyssinian campaigns in Yemen at Roman instigation are real, but altered to fit greater Roman involvement and resources than in OTL.)

In 527 Titus reviewed his new fleet on the Red Sea before sailing back from Egypt to Rome, and on his orders the Roman fleet occupied Aden in 528 and set up a garrison to protect trade there and in the next decade Roman captains not only sailed directly from the Nile to India to bring back Oriental goods but explored South down the African coasts beyond the Somali deserts to Kilwa and Mombasa. Titus had a vision for a 'World Empire' and thought that this would bind the East in prosperity to the West and distract ambitious men from internal politics and plotting revolt as they made money out of trade, but he also had a passion for justice and good legal order that he shared with the late orthodox emperor Theodosius II as well as with Julian. One of his 'discoveries' in the administration of the East during his mid-520s tour who was invited back to Rome to work for him was the learned but still young jurist Tribonian, a former law-lecturer at Beyrutus University who was an expert on Roman and local Greek law and had his own collection of generations of legal codes. In 529 Tribonian became the new 'Quaestor of the Sacred Palace', senior legal minster of the Empire, and was commissioned to collect and update all the Empire's laws, and in autumn 530 he and his commission of lawyers started to collect all civil laws issued in Roman Imperial history since the time of Augustus and the relevant Republican laws from the first and second centuries BC. Tribonian was assisted by Dorotheus, head of the law school at Beyrutus, the 'Magister Libellorum' (head of Imperial letters, i.e. the man whose department handled the correspondence to and from the Palace) Constantine, the Constantinopolitan lawyers Theophilus and Cratinus, Anatolius from Beyrutus, and Jovinus and Marcellinus from Syracuse University, and all laws that were either outdated or at odds with later legislation were duly noted and sent to the Senate for cancellation.

On 16 December 533 Tribonian's commission's great collection of all Roman jurists' law was issued as 'The Digests'; it was accompanied by a new official law textbook for legal schools, 'The Institutes', and the collected laws were also copied into new books to be issued to all lawcourts and copies were kept at the Quaestor's department in Rome and the Empire's universities. Regarding himself as on a mission to boost the Empire and its traditions and keep up the intellectual level of Roman-Greek culture, as much for his own use in obtaining expert advice as for his subjects' own welfare, Titus now backed his brother Heraclius' long-term plans for a new university at Rome itself to stimulate learning in the West. Scholars who he had recruited in Greece, Asia Minor, Syria, and Egypt during his mid-520s Eastern tours, often marginal figures from minority communities, were invited to Rome by him in 528 for a conference on Ancient Greek scientific and philosophical studies at his Marble Palace while tax money was allocated for building-work on a university modelled on that at Constantinople. A government –sponsored 'Consul for Learning', Athenian veteran Hyperamnes of Cos (ex-tutor to Heraclius' sons Anastasius and Nerva in the 510s), was appointed to take charge, and from 529 to 532 the new buildings were erected in the south-eastern suburbs of Rome beyond the Esquiline Hill with regular Imperial visits.

New departments for teaching the liberal arts, philosophy, rhetoric, poetry, the law, science (based on the work of Aristotle), architecture, Greek art and sculpture and their principles, mathematics, and Christian theology were established and teachers assembled from across the Empire. Titus also ordered that a programme of copying important old books on these subjects and distributing copies to this and other universities be set up due to his concern at all the losses of libraries to fire and civil disorder in recent centuries which he had been told about on the Eastern tour. (The collapse of many buildings in Antioch during a major earthquake in 526, destroying much of its Seleucid heritage, was probably the main impetus for this, along with reports of inter-faction burning and looting by rival Christian groups in Alexandria in 518–19.) Much of the contents of the Museion libraries at Alexandria and the former Attalid kingdom's royal library at Ephesus were now copied and moved to Rome, and though it was not true as local scholars later alleged that Titus 'pillaged' the literary heritage of the East and moved it to Rome as Constantine I had moved the artistic heritage of Greece to Constantinople the Emperor certainly believed in centralization and concentrating heritage at the capital as Constantine had done. He also now allocated a significant proportion of the non-military budget from 530 to the task of training teachers for the many, almost all privately-run schools in the Empire and ensuring that as many as possible were graduates of the Empire's universities. But only graduates with a suitable certificate received extra tax-remission in careers as teachers and he could not insist that all teachers had to be graduates as he and his brother would have liked – and in order to add extra graduates to the teaching profession he also had to allow Church theological and monastery schools' graduates to have similar tax-privileges. The staff at the new university in Rome were mostly 'middle-class' professional scholars and many of them were from the East or the originally Greek areas of southern Italy, but they also included a 'leaven of either pagan or moderate Catholic Romans of ancient senatorial families who had pursued learning as part of their scholarly and 'civilised' heritage and then turned to it professionally, sometimes as amateur writers and manuscript-collectors.

There were also a number of learned Imperial administrative staff or honorary post-holders in the higher ranks of the 'cursus honorum' in Rome involved in the plan, often from Titus' own social circle, and the most notable of these was Quintus Boethius, an amateur scholar and expert on Plato, Aristotle, Plotinus, and Proclus (the learned head of the 'Academy' in Athens in the 460s-80s). Boethius, from a major senatorial family had served as a middle-ranking City official in Rome from his twenties, in the 490s, and ended up as City Praefect in 520–28 and consul in 525 and 529. The acknowledged master of scholarly 'otium' (dignified and learned leisure, concentrating on dinner-parties, house-parties, and private research and publication) in the tradition of great Roman 'Hellenists' and an enthusiast for reviving the priorities of Late Republican and Augustan aristocratic scholars, Boethius was a great favourite of the Emperor and wrote extensively and expertly on Greek philosophy including a four-volume 'Concordance' to Plato's works and a two-volume one on Plotinus. He was also a leading exponent of the idea of morally virtuous and incorruptible Platonists serving as a sort of 'moral council' to the Emperor to keep him on the paths of virtue and just rule and also taking part in senior governmental activity. This would be a form of 'rule by philosophers' as recommended by Plato and would keep the Roman government moral and free from vulgar populism or political scheming, and the impressed Titus often had Boethius address and read out his works to Imperial dinner-parties and in 528 made him head of the 'philosophy department' at the new university – where Boethius then taught until his death in 538. His actual influence on the Emperor and on governance was however limited.

(In OTL Boethius was an executed victim of the paranoid elderly Gothic king Thedoric of Italy, his ex-patron, probably out of fear of his contacts with the expansionist Eastern Empire. The latter was now led by 'Justinian', aka this version's Petrus Sabbatius – his original name – from 527 to 565 and launched the reconquest of North Africa from 533 and Italy from 535.

The main commander of this was Belisarius; I give him a different but no less important career. His wife Antonina and Justinian's wife Theodora, with the latter's Monophysite links, are taken from real life. So is the Western scholar and civil servant Cassiodorus.)

As with Maximin and Julian and their desire for all pagan priests to be trained and to 'sing from the same hymn-sheet' in their rituals and philosophy, Titus the centralizer wanted the teachers of the Empire's (male) youth to have a basic education and series of values in common. He and his more far-sighted advisers among the staff at the new Rome university did contemplate an Empire-wide system of education for the under-sixteens with proper organization and supervision in each province – many 'schools' were still haphazard open-air affairs run in local marketplaces or gymnasia by 'pop-up' masters with enthusiasm or money – but did not have the time or resources to take this to its logical conclusion. At least Titus did see that more educated men were appointed to the episcopate and do his best to work with 'enlightened' and learned bishops who were more interested in moral education of the populace than in abstruse theological disputes, though this only took off once the Empire was reunified in 518. After the death of the aggressively anti-Monophysite Pope Hormisdas in 523 Titus secured the election of three successive Popes who were more tolerant in religion and were dedicated to education – John II (d 526), Felix IV (d 530), and John III (d 535). After them one of Titus;' closest religious allies, the veteran theologian and literary enthusiast of noble birth Agapitus who was one of the first senior tutors in Catholic theology at the Rome university from 530, was elected Pope and although he only lasted for three years was a major link between the Rome city clergy and the university. He proved of valuable aid to the Emperor in getting most of the clergy to support the institution not undermine it as a 'den of pagans and heretics' as their extremists had been urging until then. Agapitus and his senior palace bureaucrat friend, the Emperor's learned aide Cassiodorus (a major Roman noble bibliophile who from 526 to 530 was engaged in using his own money to have Alexandrian manuscripts copied and brought to Rome), who had been 'Count of the Privy Purse' to Titus from 512 to 520, were the Emperor's closest Catholic allies in his work on the university and also proved crucial in organizing funding to set up new and less bigoted theology colleges in major cities (usually bishoprics) in the West in the 520s and 530s. Students who treated Platonic philosophy favourably were to be backed for Church jobs.

It was also Cassiodorus who was most influential in persuading the suspicious Titus that monks need not be seen as anti-learning religious fanatics who practised extreme austerity, insulted philosophers, and preferred burning books to reading them – Titus had had poor experiences with fanatical monk preachers at his father's court in the 480s – and that monasteries could and should be centres of learning. Under Cassiodorus' vision for a chain of monasteries across the West to run not attack schools, train teachers, and maintain useful libraries the Emperor took this up from 530 and under Pope Agapitus a 'Consul of Monastic Learning' was set up to co-ordinate and provide funds for monastic schools and libraries and see that local bishops appointed learned men as abbots and that ultra-austere and moral but bigoted monks were vetoed from posts of monastic power. Once Agapitus had died (538) and a younger generation were running the Church in Rome, now led by the less learned and more 'political' Imperial ally the ex-diplomat Pope Silverius, Cassiodorus retired from the Palace to set up his own monastery in inland Campania, on one of his estates, and rule it as abbot to establish a major library and school there and show the way to other monastic founders and leaders. The most prestigious and venerated abbot of the era was not a major figure of learning or indeed an educated noble but the forceful and well-organised ex-hermit (St) Benedict of Nursia, an austere abbot from the upper Sabine hills who started off living in a cave c. 500 and later persuaded his noble admirers to fund a new monastery which he ran as abbot. But he did believe in study as well as prayer and hard labour as part of his daily routine for his monks, albeit less important than the other two. The sackcloth-clad, water-drinking vegetarian Benedict (d. 545) was the leading monastic figure of the era and his belief in self-control and hard labour won the Emperor's respect so Titus ended up funding and visiting him (the latter in 536) and building him a chapel at his monastery despite his antagonism to pagan learning, with a whole 'monastic order' of 'Benedictine' monasteries later following Benedict's rules for monastic life.

But it was Cassiodorus that was the Emperor's own chief monastic protégé and his monastery had close links with the Imperial Family for the next century while the pattern of educated monks with in interest in (Christian) scholarship was to spread over the next generation as far as Britain, where a former fourth-century community of hermits at Ynys Witrinus in Dobunnia (Glastonbury) was to become a major monastic and scholarly centre after the 540s, and Ireland where the so far mainly 'missionary' monasteries set up by St Patrick's heirs across Ireland now began to take an interest in scholarship too. The main monastic centre outside Armagh pre-500 had been the remote and freezingly cold island hermitages on the western Aran Island beyond Connacht, founded by St Enda c. 490; now a series of new and learned monasteries in the central lowlands, e.g. Clonmacnois (founded by St Ciaran) and Clonfert, were set up c. 540–50. In Britain scholarship was also important at the island monastery of St Piro at Caldey Island in Demetia (Pembrokeshire) and the lowland exestate monastery of St Cadoc at Llancarfan in Siluria (Glamorgan), and the British monks were instrumental in converting the rather uncivilized and rural Brittonic expatriate community in Armorica (Brittany) to Christianity and cultured Roman ways after c.500 under Ss. Samson and Paul Aurelian, both from Siluria (South-East Wales (All OTL)). The Britons were notably reluctant to bother with the obstinately pagan Saxons in the SE of the island who still tended to worship their old gods, e.g. Woden, and were regarded by the local bishops as 'heathen mercenaries' not worth bothering with. Despite the efforts made by the Rome-backed archbishoprics of Trier and Colonia Agrippinsis (both held by German-speaking ex-missionaries from the 490s onwards on Titus' instructions so as to prioritise converting Germans beyond the Rhine) and the bishoprics of Belgica, there were also notably lower amounts of conversions of allied Germans in the Rhine-Elbe-Oder region away from the lands of the pro-Roman Franks, with the latter being led by Titus' ally Clovis until he died in 521 but no converted rulers in the Saxon, Danish, and Angle lands. The kings of the Vandals and Ostrogoths were Christian but Arian and were hostile to what they perceived as 'Catholic persecution' of their co-religionists post-518. Titus had abandoned the Arians in the Empire to the aggressive 're-conversions' of them planned by the post-518 Papacy, and this duly had an impact on how he and the Popes were seen by German Arian rulers.

Titus' first years as sole Emperor saw a high-level 'dialogue' with 'Monophysite' clerics summoned to the Marble Palace in Rome from Egypt (led by their Patriarch Theodosius of Alexandria, who was denied recognition by the local orthodox Church but could now lead his own rival hierarchy with official churches and estates) and Syria (led by ex-Patriarch Severus, a charismatic ally of and nominee for his see by Anastasius). Moderate Catholic theologians at the Imperial Court like Cassiodorus backed this and to some degree sponsored it as a means for reconciliation. This failed to achieve agreement with the capital's orthodox leadership by 534 despite years of long-winded discussions on a 'Formula of Reunion', and Titus secretly backed the moderate Monophysites, as more amenable than the orthodox, to continue to run schools and monasteries across Egypt and ordered his Praefects and local governors there to protect them. But it was not as if reconciling these two bodies of theologians and administrators in the Marble Palace debates of 526–34 would have 'solved' the problem, as both groupings faced problems from irreconcilable 'hard-liners' – Theodosius had been driven out of his cathedral in Alexandria shortly after his election by a rival group of 'Julianist' Monophysites, radical enemies of any compromise, who regarded him as a heretic, and had had to rely on Titus to send the eunuch general Narses with troops to re-install him by force in 533. He and his extremist rival Gaianus then consecrated rival bodies of clergy who would not recognise each other, and the inter-Monophysite schism continued. In the case of the orthodox Chalcedonians the main problem lay with the Papacy and its hard-line Western bishops who threatened to declare a schism and depose any Pope who signed up to a compromise, with the Cisalpine Gallic bishops (as heirs of St Ambrose of Milan) and some of the Gallic and Spanish bishops the most determined. Titus' efforts to get these to agree to his new, less offensively anti-Monophysite declaration of 'official' faith of March 530 were stymied. The Papacy had already noisily opposed attempts at orthodox/Monophysite reconciliation by Zeno and Anastasius and had backed up 'ultra' orthodox protesters in the East, so trouble was to be expected from thence and any Papal compromise might lead to trouble for a Pope who let his zealot followers down. (Their 'line' on opposing Monophysites had been 'set in stone' by Pope Leo 'the Great' with his definitive statement on it, the 'Tome', in the 450s so a major Papal move towards moderation was unlikely.) (In OTL this hard-line Catholic attitude faced Justinian.)

There were also a number of , 'lower-key', Imperial efforts to lure the large and truculently anti-Chalcedonian community of 'Nestorians' (the term was usually used of them by their opponents by c. 470 to 'smear' them to the orthodox but slightly erroneously, as strictly speaking their theology followed that of the late Patriarch Nestorius' less 'heretical' early C5th inspiration Theodore of Mopsuestia) in Mesopotamia, Media and Persia. Zeno had had to leave them alone and allow them to continue to amass followers and property and found new schools and monasteries after the end of the 480s rebellion by Illus to keep them loyal. Anastasius had done so out of a mixture of natural tolerance and understanding of their theological differences from the Monophysites – after all, their then leader Bishop Ibas of Edessa had been examined by and theologically 'approved' by the orthodox Council of Chalcedon in 451. Those tolerant or theologically subtle advisers who had backed Anastasius in this pre-518 were now working for Titus or still advising the authorities in Constantinople (now led by the Praefects), and Titus duly sent a series of religious envoys to the Nestorians to explore the possibilities of a theological formula to readmit them to the official Church – despite Papal disapproval. The obstacles to creating such a doctrinal compromise proved too great, mostly from the Catholic side, but Titus allowed the Nestorians to continue to found new religious institutions. His reign saw the foundation of a number of major rural monasteries around Mosul and Arbela on the upper Tigris by the energetic and charismatic 'Mar' Aba, a converted ex-Zoroastrian who toured the monasteries of Syria and Palestine picking up ideas (and manuscripts) for his own monasteries in the late 520s and early 530s and from 538 was the Catholicos of Mesopotamia, i.e. its Nestorian religious 'head' with authority over Media and Persia, based in Ctesiphon. Another revered monastic founder and scholar was Abraham of Kashkar, who founded monasteries (and their accompanying schools) around Nisibis, the seat of the main Nestorian-run theological 'college', mainly on Mount Izla. The 'golden age' of the foundations of schools and monasteries by the Nestorians in these regions was from c. 520 to 560, under Titus and his successors, and their success duly alarmed the orthodox hierarchy in the region who had possession of the 'official' church property and the adherence of the majority of the senior official elite but were short of non-Imperial funding compared to the far more popular Nestorians. The latter were seen as more in line with local Mesopotamian religious culture; the orthodox were seen as alien-led 'yes-men' of unfeeling and contemptuous hierarchs in Constantinople and Rome. Titus' toleration indeed stimulated loyalty to the ruling dynasty among ordinary citizens – and Nestorian or Zoroastrian nobles. None of these had religious links to (usually orthodox) regional military commanders; this undermined the threat of regional rebellion. (The Nestorian leaders are OTL figures.)

Titus was in fact both more knowledgeable of and sympathetic to the subtleties of cultural and theological differences between the intellectual worlds of Syria/Mesopotamia than was believed by those at the Papal offices in Rome who assumed that they were more expert – as was their responsibility as clerics – and had the right and duty to dictate to the lay powers on theology. Titus was not only learned in Christology as well as in Platonic philosophy; in 519 he imported to Rome the era's most notable and prolific hymnodist, Romanus 'the Melodist' (d. c. 550) (OTL figure), a musical expert and composer of many liturgical hymns (from Beyrutus but as of 518 working as composer-in-residence at a church in Constantinople) Romanus created many of the chanted hymns sung at the overnight vigils before 'holy day' services that were to be used by the orthodox in the East for over a millennium. The greatest of his hymns, the 'Akathistos' to the Virgin Mary, and some of his other pieces for vigils and services were also used in the Western Church following his time in the 520s and 530s as the resident composer and choirmaster at the Imperial (i.e. Marble) Palace chapel in Rome. These had an influence on the development of the 'Benedictine' chanted hymns in Italian and Gallic monasteries in the sixth century but were less used in those regions well away from the cultural influence of the Imperial and Papal chapel practices (e.g. Spain and Britain).

Titus was a devotee of his passionate and deeply spiritual music and did his best to load this modest and unassuming man with honours, calling him a man who could open up a window on the Divine, and though the more workaday and 'puritanical' Catholic administrators frowned on his work as too mystic and so probably 'heretical' he was the main Levantine culturo-religious contributor to the Imperial Court's culture in the early-mid-sixth century. He made Imperial chapel services more intensely and emotionally spiritual – and built up a major choir which survived for centuries. Titus seems to have looked on Romanus as a figure who could bring the squabbling Christian factions together in harmonious devotion to God via the spirituality of his Church music even if theology could not unite them, and hailed him as an architect of Christian unity in the united Empire. His quest for a united culture was also seen in another of his proteges, the learned historian John Malalas (OTL), who was brought to Rome to teach history at the new University in the mid-530s and was commissioned to write a grand *Imperial Chronicle of World History* that combined Egyptian, Old Testament Israelite, Babylonian, Persian, Greek and Roman history from the third millennium BC to the 500s AD. This work was to continue under Titus' brother and successor Heraclius, a scholar who gave his protégé Malalas a seat in the Senate in 544 and called him 'consul of the historians' – but Titus' interest in the project was more ideological, as a symbol of and herald of the Providential' march of events' under Divine guidance towards the summit of human achievement in the reunited Roman Empire led by himself.

(Romanus 'the Melodist', Popes Agapitus, Silverius, and John, Patriarchs Menas and Theodosius, and other figures who appear here are real but with altered careers from OTL.)

'Popes John II and John III were not unsympathetic to Titus' efforts to reunify the Catholics and Monophysites, which the Emperor insisted was carrying out a duty to God as well as to the Roman state by putting disparate groups on an equal footing as citizens of one Empire, and Patriarch Anthimus of Constantinople (from Trebizond), in office from 528, went further and was converted to Monophysitism. But within a couple of years the next Pope, the self-confident aristocrat Agapitus, had reversed the initial Papal position of accepting Anthimus after his own hard-liners held a rival synod at Mediolanum in 530 and threatened to depose him. In 532 he persuaded Titus to sack Anthimus in favour of a staunchly orthodox Patriarch (Menas) and send the Monophysite leader Severus packing from Rome for backing Anthimus. Theodosius was duly arrested too for refusing to accept Menas as Patriarch, shut up in a monastery near Rome with his delegation for insulting the Emperor, and threatened with incarceration until he converted to Chalcedonianism but they were later released; Titus presumably realised that intimidating them into reunion would only be denounced by the 'grass-roots' Monophysite clergy in the Levantine provinces. The main problem over the failure to secure a compromise in the 530s may be assigned to Papal obstinacy rather than Titus' own lack of realism, though probably he underestimated just how entrenched anti-Monophysitism was in the Western Church – and his resort in 539 to deposing the new Pope Silverius as an obstacle to a settlement indicates that he thought that he could intimidate the Church into following his orders. Even supposedly pliant Popes such as the new appointment of 539, Vigilius, were more scared of their own 'hard-liners' than of the Emperor, and any compromise could be denounced in Italy as abandoning the hard line' of the venerated Pope Leo I in the 450s.

The East also faced military problems in the early 530s due to a resurgence of attacks by the Hepthalite Huns on the weak Sassanid realm of Sogdiana, which their local candidate Bahram took over in 529 with the late ruler Kavadh's pro-Roman Persis/ Hyrcanian bodyguards having to flee for their lives back to Roman Bactria. An attack on Balkh by a horde of Huns followed while more steppe raiders on fast horses raided into Hyrcania and isolated Zadracarta and several other fortresses from help for some months, but a new Roman hero, the rising Thracian officer Belisarius (OTL), was luckily in command at the Roman garrison-town of Merv in reach of Balkh and once he had heard of the siege of that city he put together a rescue-force and led it there. The refugee Sassanid prince Khusrau (or 'Chosroes' in Greek), a pro-Roman figure educated at a Roman military academy for local nobles and self-made volunteers at Ctesiphon in the 510s as a semi-hostage and also an enthusiast for Plato and Plotinus, fled from Sogdiana to help Belisarius as Bahram wanted to kill him and offered himself as a replacement. Once Belisarius had cunningly caught the Hepthalite force sent to intercept him in a trap in a valley in the hills SW of Balkh and wiped them out he marched on Balkh, set up a camp out of reach of the attackers' artillery and horses in a high hilly position, and launched a series of guerrilla raids on the besiegers that kept them on the defensive.

(The Persian rulers here are real from OTL; but Khusrau was a far greater ruler of a far larger realm in real life, from 531 to 579.)

Not used to Roman-style siege warfare and with their hired Sassanid Sogdian siege-artillery destroyed in Belisarius' raids, the Huns were soon demoralised and were kept busy trying to fend off the Roman commander's ingenious tactics, and despite small numbers and dwindling food the Roman garrison of Balkh was able to hold out until a larger Romans rescue-army arrived from Mesopotamia next spring led by Titus' trusted general Hermogenes. The latter was prepared to listen to Belisarius, who by now knew the vicinity of Balkh like his own back garden, and take up his ideas for luring the Huns into a trap and attacking them from three sides at once, and as a result the over-confident, reinforced horde of up to 30,000 steppe nomads were 'minced' by a Roman 'textbook' attack on several sides and lost most of their manpower in the battle that led to the relief of

Balkh. As ordered by Titus the Romans then advanced over the Oxus to besiege Maracanda and thanks to Belisarius and his roaming cavalry raiders the Huns could not rescue the city and in May 530 it fell to Rome, but though Bahram escaped via a tunnel to continue the war and there was still resistance in the Ferghana valley and the nearby mountains the Emperor had ordered a 'no risk, minimise the cost' withdrawal leaving a Roman puppet-king in charge with a small and mobile Roman garrison and Belisarius' plans to take over Sogdiana and turn the war-wracked region with its rival brigand lords into a peaceful Romano-Persian province were ignored. Hermogenes sent Belisarius back to the West, put his ally Khusrau on the Sogdian throne with a small supporting force, and left the Huns and Bahram at large, and as a result the latter were able to depose Khusrau again in 532 and all that had been done to pacify the region in the 530 campaign had to be done again – as Belisarius had warned the Emperor in a memorandum at the end of the 530 campaign. Rumour had it that his jealous rival Narses (OTL), an Armenian eunuch general who had gone from Anastasius' to Titus' service in 516, wanted to run the next Sogdian war himself and then become 'Master of Infantry' or even 'Master of Both Services' in Mesopotamia so he had persuaded Titus to ignore Belisarius' ideas as too financially costly and the result of a fondness for grandiose schemes that he did not have to pay for. But Titus had his own grand strategies in politics and war and was not incontrovertibly averse to spending money though he preferred not to build up any too-successful generals in the East lest they revolt. Once the Huns were in control of Sogdiana and pillaging passing Roman and pro-Roman Persian caravan-trains on the 'Silk Road' in 532 he acted and called in Belisarius to assess him and his plans. As a result he decided to trust the young general and in 533 made him 'dux' of Lower Mesopotamia (the Charax/ Basra province) with 'imperium' over Persis and Bactria and ordered the commanders in Ctesiphon, Hyrcania and Media to assist him in invading Sogdiana.

The 'Master of Infantry' Marcellus and 'Master of Cavalry' Sosigenes in Ctesiphon were sent off on a campaign to northern Atropatene to strengthen the defences of Baku and block the Eastern end of the Caucasus range to Hunnic attack, and meanwhile Belisarius with a striking-force of 25,000 men and some 10,000 Persian allies invaded Sogdiana, retook Maracanda, drove the Huns back after two more brilliantly successful if unorthodox victories by Belisarius, and set up a new chain of Roman garrisons linking Maracanda to the Roman positions around Balkh. Khusrau was put back on the Sogdian throne, Bahram was hunted down in the Pamirs and killed, and the methodical Belisarius undertook the first sustained Western campaign to take every major and most of the minor Sogdian hill-forts and set up European-style fortresses there since Alexander the Great's 329–8 BC expedition there. As 10,000 more

Roman troops – mostly Armenians and Caucasian Iberians used to mountain fighting – were brought in to man the new forts and the local nobility had to collaborate or face expulsion Belisarius was hailed as the man who had finally 'solved' the Sogdian problem. Relying heavily on young Persian nobles from Persis, Media and Hyrcania (plus a few from Bactria) who had been educated as semi-hostages in Roman schools and military training camps in Mesopotamia, especially at Ctesiphon, Belisarius in fact imported a substantial section of ethnic Persians as well as Westerners to take up lands in Sogdiana and his new 'Roman' rule there was as much Persian as Roman and included many Zoroastrians and a few Nestorian Christians to the horror of the Church. But Titus backed him up and his friendship with Khusrau led to that new king of Sogdiana, aided by a mixed Roman and Persian military council and Roman (usually Easterners) civilian council, establishing Sogdiana as a relatively secure Roman sub-kingdom once the surviving brigand lords in the high mountains had been hunted down or forced to submit by Belisarius, who remained in the province until 537, and a new chain of Roman fortresses had been built on the Jaxartes to keep the Huns back with mobile cavalry patrols. Belisarius also led large but mobile and self-supporting cavalry armies over the Jaxartes to attack the Huns and chase them for hundreds of miles across the steppe in 535 and 536 and the Romans managed to catch up with and loot assorted caravans of retreating Hunnic civilians and loot to take many prisoners.

But unlike the average arrogant, nomad-despising Roman general Belisarius treated his prisoners well, did not dishonour Hunnic lords by raping their captive wives and daughters, and usually offered the refuge menfolk their women back if they would come and surrender and take oaths to 'Augustus Titus and the king Khusrau' and in return he took oaths to protect the Huns and pay them subsidies provided they supplied him with hostages. He duly acquired a high reputation for fair dealing and many junior Hun chiefs abandoned their warlike seniors to sign up to his demands. Though some inter-clan wars and raids continued by 538 the majority of the Huns had learnt to leave the Sogdian frontier alone and Belisarius had even been offered the throne of one ancient Hunnic tribe – which he politely turned down but which led to one of his officers, a spy for his rival Narses, writing this detail in a letter to Narses who gleefully told the Emperor.

After Belisarius was recalled and sent off on a Western campaign as 'Master of Infantry' on the Rhine in 539–40 to punish the current Ostrogothic king, Theodoric's drunken grandson and successor Athalaric (OTL), Titus kept on one of his equally adaptable and fair-dealing commanders, Mundus (OTL), to be 'dux' of Sogdiana and help Khusrau keep order until 545 and the Jaxartes frontier remained stable, but the Roman advance now pushed their boundaries up against the former eastern Sassanid lordships of the Hindu Kush, now local mini-states, and the mid-late 530s saw raids from this area on Bactria and some damage to the land trade-route that as a result tended to move North via Kabul to Balkh and Merv instead. The eastern frontier of the Empire was fluid and Arachosia passed to and from pro-Roman lords and after his successful Ostrogothic war in 540 Belisarius, who had ravaged the Goths' lands and driven the incompetent Athalaric to surrender and accept deportation but had then had to fight and defeat his successor Witigis, came to Rome to urge Titus to emulate Seleucus if not Alexander and take over the lands to the Khyber Pass. This would protect the eastern borders and secure a trade-route by land from the upper Indus W to Kabul and then south-west to Kandahar and Istakr, but Titus judged this too expensive and this plan would not be followed by the Empire for another eighty years. The Bactrian plan was also hindered by the Emperor's unexpected logistical need to attend to a major famine in 537-8 after widespread harvest failures – probably caused by volcanic dust weakening sunlight.

Instead, Titus packed the restless Belisarius off to the upper Nile to invade Nubia and force the aggressive new local king to rescind his higher taxes on Roman merchants and Roman imports. As a result Belisarius ended up marching up the Nile to the junction of the White and Blue Niles in 541 and imposing an annual tribute and levy of troops on the Nubian kingdom but also hiring guides to explore up the Nile into Abyssinia with his officers in the hope of establishing a new and quicker land-route to the Abyssinian capital, Axum, than over the deserts south-east from Meroe. The Emperor's elder nephew Anastasius was with this expedition as a senior officer to obtain military experience after four years serving on the lower Rhine and one in Britain and he came under the charismatic general's influence, with Belisarius revealing to him his plans for a major expansion of Roman power in the region with Nubian help. This would extend a 'protectorate' as far as the marshes of the far upper Nile and on the Red Sea coasts set up Roman military and naval posts right along the Red Sea as far as the narrows at its southern end, bringing in Abyssinia as a means to subdue the tribes of the Somali coasts and inland Yemen. But in the event, the death of Titus on 27 February 542, aged seventy-nine, after a reign of forty-six years in the West and of twenty-five years in the East held up plans, as the Prince was recalled to Rome by his father Heraclius who now ascended the throne aged seventy-four.

Having reunited the Empire by determination allied with both political and military skill and personal charisma, Titus left it in the hands of a less dynamic brother instead of passing it directly to one of the latter's sons (or both of them as colleagues) as some of his nervous ministers and generals had advised. But his reckoning that Heraclius was perfectly adequate at the task of holding his achievement together despite his lack of military interests and skills was correct – and the rule that Titus had laid down of the Imperial Family acting together as a unit, all loyal to one another and complementing each other's abilities and interests, continued to hold. In any case, he had created a whole group of capable and communally motivated ministers to act under him as his civilian Council, plus a 'high command' of generals and retired frontier commanders who saw the overwhelming necessity of avoiding civil war or even a peaceful division of the Empire. Under these 'top layers' of leadership lay neat bureaucratically-organised 'pyramids' of civilian and military officials. There were tensions behind the scenes and undoubtably some of the other generals were jealous of Titus' own personal 'favourite' Belisarius, the only frontier commander who he had permitted to make his own decisions without close supervision – and who had the charisma, the string of past victories, and the level of public admiration to have been able to launch a military coup against the Emperors after 542 (the civilian Heraclius or the controversial Anastasius) with a chance of success. Those civilian leaders of the Empire who were loyal to the long-standing governmental principle of civilian /Palace supremacy over the danger of ambitious and well-supported military men launching revolts as an endemic threat to the state – what might be called the 'nightmare of the 250s' (after the number of military coups then) or the 'Magnentius/. Maximus threat' (after the Western coups by Magnentius in 350 and by Maximus in 383) had been warning Titus about Belisarius as a potential 'loose ballista/catapult' for decades, to no avail. Titus trusted Belisarius and the latter trusted him, and their visions of an expansionist but law-promoting and 'just' Rome dominating both the Mediterranean and the Middle East as far as the Oxus were similar – and both could be reckoned to be the 'heirs of Aetius' in their fair treatment of Germans as well as Romans in terms of promotion. Nor did Titus listen to warnings that Belisarius, or indeed any other general who had a similar run of successes, could challenge his brother or nephews as they all lacked his own huge prestige as the man who had reunited Rome. Titus trusted his 'team', civilian and military alike, and they repaid his support with total loyalty to him if not to each other, and his 'semi-pagan' cultural values. His ruthless way of treating the Church as a department of State may have annoyed powerful and devout Catholics but they lacked the means to do anything about it – not least due to his careful use of a regular group of highly-trained bodyguards to protect himself from assassins and his marginalization of intrigue- or bribe-prone Court / Household officials.

Thanks to his long and stable reign, and a hiatus in the pressure on the Empire's Northern frontiers between the Huns in the mid-C5th and the Avars in the later sixth century the Empire was now set on a new course.

After Reunion in 516: The Dynasty Of Titus II

Some ministers would have preferred to divide up the Empire and let the military-minded and ambitious Anastasius, an enthusiast for conquering the Germans and bringing direct Roman rule as far as the Baltic, govern the West under his father as his 'Caesar' and the more scholarly legal enthusiast Nerva rule the East. But this had been vetoed by Titus in his pre-announced plans for the succession in 539 and it was his belief, backed up by Heraclius, that only one Emperor should reign at a time. A 'Caesar' could be appointed but not with a defined territory to govern or an ambitious prince could then start a civil war, and Heraclius, crowned in St Peter's Basilica in Rome by Pope Vigilius on 21 April 542 (the annual commemoration of Rome's presumed founding on 21 April 753 BC), kept to this plan and did not even make Anastasius, who was forty-six already, 'Caesar' until 544 and then gave him no territory. As it was still deemed necessary to keep up the notion of an 'Emperor of the East' to fend off allegations of the region being neglected Heraclius was officially recognised as Eastern Emperor from his accession and as soon as practicable the Praefects of Constantinople (Petrus Sabbatius), Antioch (Damaratus), and Alexandria (Hipparchus of Cnidus) all journeyed to Rome to swear allegiance to him and hand over the signed oaths of their senior officials and the Eastern military commanders.

Part IV

Expansion, 542 to 641. The Conquest of Eastern Persia and Bactria: To the Indus

Chapter 11

Heraclius I 542–559: The Scholar

Titus II the reunifier was succeeded by his younger brother and long-term deputy Heraclius. As it was still deemed necessary to keep up the notion of an 'Emperor of the East' to fend off allegations of the region being neglected Heraclius was officially recognised as Eastern Emperor from his accession and as soon as practicable the Praefects of Constantinople (Petrus Sabbatius), Antioch (Damaratus), and Alexandria (Hipparchus of Cnidus) all journeyed to Rome to swear allegiance to him and hand over the signed oaths of their senior officials and the Eastern military commanders. Though the new Emperor was in uncertain health and was less alert and hard-working than Titus had been at a similar age he made his way by sea to Constantinople in spring 543 for his Eastern coronation on 25 May and then spent the summer at the Sacred Palace before going on a cultural pilgrimage to Athens, Corinth, Delphi, Epidaurus, and Olympia in Greece – and to Mycenae where he ordered a regular festival for the reciting of Homer in competitive renderings to be held every four years. Heraclius was back in Sicily for winter 543–44 in Syracuse and in April 544 he returned to Rome, and notably his ambitious elder son Anastasius was not allowed to govern Rome in his absence but a committee of ministers advised by Cassiodorus did so while the prince had to go off on a military inspection tour – short of troops for his entourage in case he thought of revolting – to the Marcomannian and lower Danube frontiers. His younger son Prince Nerva was also away during 543, on a lengthy legal commission across the western provinces to see that the 'Codex Titi' (as the codification and updating of laws by Tribonian was generally known) was being properly enforced, and after his similar tour of the East with the Empire's top jurists in 544 he reported to the Emperor and some modifications of the Code were issued. The legal practices of the Empire's vassal-states in Transrhenus (Germany), Geatland, the Danish kingdom, the Sarmatian steppes, Nubia, and the Persian states were also written down and formally codified by Rome-taught commissions of their own legal experts later in the 540s on Nerva's advice, and Heraclius also expanded the extant law college at Beyrutus to train more legal experts for the future with jobs assured in the expanded Imperial legal bureaucracy. Rome was to stand as the fountainhead of and civilised world leader in the 'Rule of Law' – and written law at that, with orderly cases lodged and judged in lawcourts though in less literate societies (e.g. Transrhenus) customary law memorised by 'lawmen' was to be accepted until more men were able to read. The Eastern half of the Empire could use Greek not Latin, out of practical necessity though some high officials (e.g. Sabbatius) argued for full use of Latin by all to spread the language for unity.

Generally Heraclius proved as determined a centraliser and upholder of Roman tradition as his brother if in a less energetic manner, also stressing his role as upholder of justice (in a moral and usually Christian context) and in that context sacking some of his brother's more aggressive and vindictive ministers who had been relentless in their pursuit of injustice but also of every last minor bureaucratic rule-infringement (and relentless in seeing that all fines were paid in full). Several unpopular and obsessively legalistic 'enforcers' in senior ranks fell foul of Heraclius after complaints were made about them as he actually listened to the latter, and the most famous of these was his brother's humbly-born and brilliant but oppressive finance-minister in the 530s, 'Count of the Sacred Largesses' John the Cappadocian. He had not only combated corruption and tax-evasion as Titus had mandated, but had insisted that all fines to the treasury had to be paid on time and with the due interest and anyone who did this late would be taken to court and reduced to beggary for alleged corruption – with the local courts required to act even if the accused were important provincial figures. A lot of 'tax-dodging' and duly ruined great nobles' estates had ended up in the hands of John or his family and friends under Titus, and now in 543–4 Heraclius had the minister investigated by a major committee of junior 'legal eagles', university men and provincials rather than government lawyers who might be in awe of or bribed by John. After a ten-month enquiry John was found guilty and forced to resign and hand over all his assets as did his family and friends. The minister, the former owner of estates across the Mediterranean, ended up living in a humble shack in a village in Upper Egypt as a tenant-pig-farmer under police supervision and Heraclius made the most of this to show that nobody was above the law, and as assorted corrupt Church officials and legacy-hunting abbots also ended up ruined the more moralist monkish writers and preachers and zealously austere stylites and other hermits duly hailed Heraclius as a model of Christian virtue and humility despite his pagan literary and philosophic leanings.

(John's career and disgrace are real events of the early 540s, though altered here; the Gothic kings who I refer to, especially Witigis and Totila, were also real but in OTL were involved in a ruinous war across Italy against the Eastern armies.)

His austere lifestyle and passion for justice plus his disdain for the luxurious life of great courtiers made the new Emperor stand out among the Imperial elite and he was hailed as a 'new Augustus' like Titus but this time for having his wife weave wool for his clothes and his plain living not for administrative work or international achievements. Notably he also cracked down on the lifestyles of his senior ministers and Palace guards officers who were required to set a good example, gaming and prostitutes being banned from all Imperial properties and drunkenness at Imperial parties being not only unfashionable but fatal to careers. The literary-minded and learned Emperor was all for reviving the atmosphere of the great philosophers' literary meetings of fifth century BC Athens or the Ptolemaic courts in the third century BC, but his 'symposia' were much shorter than those on alcohol and young nobles reported for drunken fooling around in Rome, getting girls pregnant, rape, beating up the poor, or running over people in their chariots were packed off on military service to toughen up. The one-time roisterer Prince Anastasius had sobered up somewhat and learnt to be cautious by the time his father became Emperor but the latter still disapproved of him and his boozy circle of officers and saw to it that he spent most of the reign out of Rome on military tours of inspection. Heraclius was heard to lament several times that loyalty to Titus' memory prevented him from removing Anastasius from the succession but he was sure that Nerva, sober and hardworking, would be a better Emperor while Titus' younger daughter Princess Aelia (born 497), a learned and highly skilled poet who wrote odes in assorted classical Greek metre and starred at her Apulian landowner husband Paterculus' literary soirees, would have made a better Emperor than Anastasius too. The intelligent and dignified Aelia, who also wove wool for her family clothes and was an amateur architect who had designed some of her family's holiday villas in Sicily and Corcyra (Corfu), had been a favourite of Titus' but as a traditional Roman he could not think of advancing a woman in the succession and her business skills were semi-wasted though he did use her to help with his regional estates' accounts.

Under the less formal and traditionalist Heraclius the Princess was at court more and offered advice on promotions and new laws and after her husband died in 545 became the Emperor's unofficial chief secretary, aiding with his correspondence and arranging his schedule with his chamberlains. Anastasius was said to loathe her and to fear that she intended to become 'Augusta' and succeed her uncle with his connivance and then pass the throne to her children, but he was unable to get her sent away from court and he had to be content with (probably) being behind her guards-officer son Gellius Paterculus' disgrace for womanising and despatch to a remote garrison in Mauretania as a trainee officer in 549. Anastasius himself was sent on a rare Imperial 'state visit' out of the Empire to attend the inauguration of the new Irish 'High King' Diarmait mc Cearbhall (OTL), a vigorous centraliser who was keen to rein in his obstreperous regional sub-kings and their nobles with the aid of a Roman mercenary bodyguard, in 548. This was so successful that in 549 Anastasius was sent to lead a mission to Nubia to arrange a joint slave-collecting expedition to the savannah tribes between the Upper Nile and the mountains of western Abyssinia. The extra slaves were then used to boost corn-growing on Imperial (ex-Ptolemaic royal) estates in the Nile valley, whose irrigation-systems were checked and updated by a task-force of Imperial army engineers by the Emperor's orders in 545–6.

But Heraclius would not let his heir near an army for fear of his ambition, and instead it was the scrupulously loyal and trusted general Belisarius who after four years as a senior staff officer training 'Comitatus' officers in military tactics was recalled to active service in 546 for a new Arabian military mission. This time the brilliant commander was called upon to take 15,000 troops acclimatised to the heat of Arabia (mostly Syrians and Palestinians and a few Arab mercenary tribal contingents) to the weakening Himyarite kingdom in Yemen to stave off the threat of civil war or a dispute over the throne threatening the Abyssinian dynasty there, who had never been popular. The Abyssinian ('Axumite', from its capital at Axum) King Kaleb had crossed the Red Sea after appeals for help from the local Christian community, aided by the Roman navy, and had defeated and either killed or expelled the locally unpopular Jewish king of the Himyarites (Dhu Nuwas) to conquer the kingdom in the 520s in what was seen as a major Romano-Axumite Christian offensive. However the new Abyssinian-backed ruler, an enemy of Dhu Nuwas from the Himyarite royal dynasty, had become unwilling to act as an Abyssinian 'puppet' and had been replaced around 531 by the local Abyssinian commander Abreha, as a formal Abyssinian viceroy. This had led to 'targeted' local nobles and tribal leaders fleeing to Roman lands in Palestine and Syria to seek help – which was now granted once Roman attitudes to their insubordinate Abyssinian ally hardened. Belisarius, as a man who had campaigned in Nubia commanding Arab regiments, had Arab officers and personal friends, and spoke Arabic, was chosen as the man to command the expedition, and with his usual thoroughness drew up detailed plans first with merchants who had been to the region advising him on the geography, climate, and local 'strongmen' – and Roman agents, mostly Red Sea merchants, contacted those of the latter who had fallen out with the Abyssinians so that they sent troops to aid the Romans as they landed. The Abyssinian viceroy Abreha faced a large-scale mutiny of his local troops at the town of Timna in the Qartaban region as he marched on a rebel tribal coalition, and as he was left with only his own Abyssinian troops plus a few loyal locals he chose to withdraw in haste to the coast and 'hole up' in a fortress near Hodeidah to await rescue from Abyssinia. But a Roman fleet sent down the Red Sea kept the king of Axum from sending any help to Himyar, and as Belisarius won over most of the local chiefs by promising to keep the Abyssinians out and end their harsh, tax-exacting rule Abreha had to give up and flee back to Africa. The restive former vassals of Himyar in the eastern Hadramaut also allied to Rome due to resentment of recent plundering raids by loot-seeking Abyssinian armies, and mostly signed up to become Roman clients after Belisarius offered them access to the Roman-controlled Red Sea trade and jobs for their young warriors in the new Arab regiments that he was now raising for the Roman army. These were to be stationed right up in the north-west region of the Arabian peninsula in 'Ammonitis' (OTL: Amman region) to protect the Roman agricultural regions of eastern Syria and Palestine from raids, which also served to keep these potential Hadramauti rebel warriors out of their homeland long-term and so aid Roman control. The main coastal ports of the Himyarite kingdom passed under permanent Roman military control, which was 'sold' successfully to their oligarchic merchant and commerce-involved-tribal-leaders elite as giving them customs-free access to the massive world of Roman commerce in the Mediterranean and protecting them from inland tribal warlords' plundering. Most were too glad to be rid of the oppressive Abyssinian army to argue, and the charismatic Belisarius personally won over many of their leaders and enrolled useful local 'key figures' in his and Rome's service.

After stabilising the Himyarite state by replacing the client-king and most of his elite for incompetence or misrule and imposing an under-age relative as the new Roman puppet-king, aided by a council of pro-Roman Christian nobles and senior merchants, Belisarius, never one to be conventional, set up his own force of local – pagan, Nature- spirit-worshipping – Arabs as 'bucellarii' (bodyguards). He now advised Heraclius to annex the southern part of the Himyarite lands, the mountains from Taif to near Aden, as a new province, and offer gifts and titles to the restive semi-autonomous Arab lords along the coast eastwards. He believed that the 'alien' Abyssinian presence in Arabia had been so unpopular that the Himyarite dynasty had lost most of its support and would face revolt before long so the Romans should pressurise the more 'local' new regime which he had installed at the prestigious Himyarite inland capital, Marib, to cede its southern and south-eastern lands to Rome. The latter would then have the local 'presence' and support – provided that it governed well as the bringer of justice and stability, which to Belisarius was its main political role – to intervene in Himyar and annex it all, in a decade or two if possible, which was wiser than a risky immediate annexation which would lead to complaints by the proud local lords that Rome was no better than Abyssinia. Nor would Belisarius follow the advice of enthusiastic (mostly Egyptian) regional 'expert' Christian clerics who urged him to annex the entire region and push for mass-conversion to Christianity to help their religion fend off any new 'persecution' by 'pagan' rulers in the manner of Dhu Nuwas' actions – though he and Heraclius had agreed to boost funds and personnel for the Himyarite Church which was, as planned, aided to set up new bishoprics, schools, and monasteries.

Belisarius believed that Rome should set up a new province of 'Arabia Felix', centred on Aden and including the Sana'a and Taiz inland regions – and if a trading navy was built up at Aden the Empire should lure the great men of the region into making their fortunes by trading to India instead of fighting each other. This was duly done in 547–9 as Heraclius had full trust in Belisarius and so the dream of Augustus for a province of Arabia Felix to corner the regional trade-routes in the 20s BC was fulfilled. But the cost of building a major port at Aden and setting up Roman garrisons in the region was not popular in the treasury in Rome and the number of marginalised Monophysite laymen in Egypt, victimised by the Chalcedonian elite there, who ended up serving in the army in or as merchants and administrators in southern Arabia in the later 540s and the 550s led to complaints to Rome by the Alexandrian authorities. Belisarius was supposed to be favouring heretics and spreading their doctrines across Arabia and on to India and the hard-line Chalcedonians called for a purge of them, but tolerant and trade-minded Heraclius would only allow orthodox bishoprics to be set up at all in Arabia out of a desire to keep the Church 'on side' and he forbade any compulsory conversions of either 'heretics' or those of other religions, Jews included. The angry ultra-doctrinaire Catholics at the Papal chancery in Rome forced the dithering Pope Vigilius to take a stand on their behalf and complain to the Emperor about the 'blasphemous' toleration of Arab animists by Belisarius in 550 and this duly led to his recall after he deported some missionaries from Aden for smashing up local pagan shrines. But the Emperor sent out another tolerant 'dux' to take over plus a new governor who had Monophysite relatives and was rumoured to be one himself. The wise policy of toleration certainly kept the local Arabs loyal – to the extent that some tribal notables even journeyed to Rome to ask for Belisarius' recall to be their 'dux' of the Arabia Felix province in 551 and their sons joined new military training colleges, which Heraclius had agreed to him setting up – one at Lutetia (Paris) for citizens of the North-Western provinces, and later also one in 560 at Emesa (Homs) in Syria for the East.

Fortunately the militant expansionist Anastasius was no more inclined to back the Catholic hard-liners than his father was and his own religious interests were minimal with some saying that his admiration for Julian made him really a pagan, and the ageing Emperor turned his own attention in 549 to setting up a 'Great Library' in Rome to rival that in Alexandria. He had his niece Aelia design the building for the south-eastern quarter of Rome beyond the Caelian Hill and ordering the network of cluttered minor roads and large blocks of flats ('insulae') in that area of Rome cleared to create a new avenue that would lead East from the square by the Colosseum past the new library out to the road to Antium. The Emperor's hope was to have a copy of every book in the Empire either collected or copied for the library so it would serve as the state's main research and cultural centre and so eclipse the inconveniently (for the West) distant library in Alexandria that was a shadow of its former self anyway as parts of the Museion complex were annexed for other activities or left to fall into disrepair, and this work had to involve sending out new commissions of scholars to find and register the books and then getting other people who knew the relevant languages hired to copy them. This duly led on to the Emperor setting up new schools in Rome and Constantinople to teach bright teenagers languages such as ancient Aramaic and Egyptian to help the process and a revival in learning Greek in the far West and Persian (and Babylonian) in the former Sassanid lands of Mesopotamia.

The Emperor sent a special commission of scholars to the great library of the former Attalid kingdom at Pergamum in Ionia, still huge and important despite many of the best manuscripts having been carried off to Rome in the first century BC, to assess the material there and arrange for a mixture of copying manuscripts and removing the originals to Rome or copying them and taking the copies to Rome, and in 547 during his Imperial tour of Asia Minor he called in at Pergamum to take a look at the process and ask if the scholars needed anything. He collected more documents himself on his subsequent tour east to Antioch, where he presided at a fortnight of Games and ordered that troops should now protect all property of all the rival Churches from rival sects' arsonists and vandals. But due to illness he was unable to go on to the great library of the former, Greco-Aramaic kingdom of Osrhoene there and instead his attendant scholars did this later and collected a haul of documents. While in Antioch, Heraclius ordered that all ancient temples and other monuments should be preserved and that looting of stone for building should be prevented, and as the post-526 earthquake rebuilding-programme at the city had not bothered to rebuild a number of important Hellenistic structures from the Seleucid era he ordered this to be put right and had several new buildings which had replaced revered older ones to be demolished and replaced by replicas of the originals at the expense of the city council and the owners. The Praefect of the city was accused of accepting 'gifts' from leading commercial entrepreneurs to let them have the sites of ruined public buildings for private use and was sacked, and Heraclius was for once as forceful as Titus in seeing that his wishes were obeyed. The Emperor also generously declared that a 'universal' library should include Jewish learning and ordered copies of the great Jewish studies of the Torah and their fifth- century religio-legal compilations made in Galilee to be collected too, which infuriated the Church. As senior Torah scholars joined a conference of philosophers that the Emperor hosted in Rome in spring 551 even the controversy-dodging Pope Vigilius had to decide whether to obey his Emperor or his clergy and as he was more afraid of the latter ordered all clergy and church school employees to boycott the conference on penalty of being excommunicated and dismissed.

Chapter 12

Anastasius II 551–559: The Maverick

The Emperor was unable to attend much of this conference due to declining health, and he died on 8 August 551 aged eighty-four. His elder son Anastasius II succeeded to the throne aged fifty-five, and though he was as energetic and as devoted to justice and tradition as much as his uncle and revered model Titus II he was a cruder, less subtle, and harsher character who was supposed to be embittered by his father's preference for his brother Nerva who he despised as too consensual. As he had told his courtiers at a dinner while his father was bedridden and visibly declining, Nerva would be ruled by his elite and not dare to step out of line with past policy but he himself would do what was right for Rome as Titus had done. Though he was not a pagan like his most admired Emperor, the authoritarian Diocletian, and disliked semi-republican thinkers he was more aggressive than any ruler since his Eastern namesake (and godfather) Anastasius I to the Catholic/ orthodox Church for putting promoting their own doctrine above their duty to their Emperor. Pope Vigilius was soon arrested for speaking his mind to the Emperor about the new Imperial orders of September 551, issued days after the coronation on 21 September at the Basilica of St Peter in Rome, requiring the protection of all ancient temples across the Empire and making the local Church authorities financially responsible for repairs if they were vandalised by orthodox mobs – a minor problem in the West but a large one in Egypt.

The Pope was sent off to Corsica for six months to cool his heels while services in St Peter's and the Lateran Basilica were suspended until the papal treasury had paid for the rebuilding of several important Roman temples pulled down and replaced by churches in the fifth century. Though the Emperor had the sense to see that the magnificent (and still intact) ex-temple of 'Venus and Rome', now the dynastic monument to the family of Augustus and their 'ancestor' Aeneas of Troy, could not be turned back into a temple or have sacrifices of incense like some of his pagan noble friends advised he did allow annual celebrational services there. At these, pagan poets could mention Venus and the 'divine' ancestry of Aeneas and hint that the success of the Augustan 'Caesar' family was due to divine backing, and a current literary 'cult' of the great first century

BC poet Vergil, friend of Augustus and writer of the 'Aeneid', was now backed by a regular Imperial financial grant. There was also a new annual 'Festival of Vergil' at the ex-temple where his works were recited in competitions, teenagers competed to remember the 'Aeneid' by memory and the winner received a laurel crown from the Emperor, and imitations of Vergil by new poets were sought out and recited.

The Emperor also ordered a laudatory commission to investigate the history and records of the defunct worship of Osiris and Isis in Egypt in 552–4 and write up accounts of these for the Great Library in Rome, arguing that it had historic importance as the cult of a 'Mother Goddess' and her son (Horus) had been a foreshadowing of the cult of the Virgin and Child – and it might show God's hand in revealing a hint of His 'Truth' to the wise Egyptians. As this sparked off orthodox rioting in Egypt about rumours of an In this context it is spelled imminent restoration of paganism large mobs besieged and tried to demolish the shut but intact Temple of Serapis in Alexandria and had to be kept out by the city's troops – whose bold commander was then promoted to a major 'ducate' and given a medal as a 'hero of Rome' by the Emperor. As more pagan shrines in Egypt were sacked in a wave of vandalism in 553 the non-interventionist 'Augustal Praefect' (over-governor of all Egypt), a timid if bureaucratically efficient scholarly friend of the late Emperor Heraclius called Delphinius, was sacked and a brutal ex-officer called Justus Janustinus was installed to lead a crackdown. The upshot was that over 1,000 rioters and vandals, some of them clerics or monks, ended up in the slave-mines of Upper Egypt and the Emperor held Egypt down by martial law for five years and had the usually unpunished orthodox 'rowdies' crushed by force – to the benefit of the Monophysites who had carefully stood aside from helping the attacks as friends at court in Rome had told them what the Emperor would probably do to the perpetrators.

The punishment of the Egyptian rioters and a simultaneous purge of the Church in Rome to deport about a third of its staff to the outer provinces, take over and demolish a number of churches whose construction-permits were not in order, and cut the State grant to the papacy by half were not challenged by the intimidated Vigilius. But many local priests and a few bishops across Italy, Gaul, and Spain denounced the Emperor as 'Nero' and a conspiracy was launched to murder him by Christian nobles in Rome, men now banned from Anastasius' court and denied all office as 'subversives' who did not show appreciation of his policies in public and/or made rude speeches in the Senate. The ex-governor Atilius Lampadius of Lucania and his group of rich malcontents planned to murder the Emperor and put either the just and 'reliable' Nerva, who paid court to great nobles of ancient blood out of a sense of tradition, or his elder son

Gallus (born 537), an idealist who was said to be devout, on the throne. How serious some of them were was unclear and though Lampadius had a murderous hatred of Anastasius some of his friends may just have been grumbling with no serious intentions, but once they started to 'sound out' officers in the 'Protectores' officer-cadets and the 'Scholae' guards-regiments who had Catholic Christian beliefs someone soon leaked details to the police and in February 554 most of the plotters were rounded up and tortured into confessing. The descendant of six consuls Lampadius and several other plotters from families dating back to the first century AD in the Senate ended up at police headquarters on the rack and having their backs flogged to ribbons and once they had confessed they were dragged before a special new tribunal for 'maiestas' (treason) and convicted and then were thrown off the Tarpeian Rock on the Capitol as an appropriately traditional punishment. After this shock had reverberated around the Empire Anastasius was obeyed if not honoured or liked by the great Christian nobles and the Church and he had the courage to put openly pagan ministers, mostly nobles from traditionalist Roman or Italian families or 'revivalist' scholars, in office and purge a number of senior archbishops across the West from office for preaching against him.

Ironically the dilemma of having legally to obey an 'unjust' and 'heretic' or 'pagan' Emperor stimulated some current Church theologians who dared not write or speak against the Emperor to argue 'in code' in favour of a more consensual government and rule by a sovereign who listened to his people and as such they linked up with some idealist Platonist and Neoplatonist university thinkers who regarded the impulsive Anastasius as a despot like Plato's employers Dionysius I and II of Syracuse. But this was all done 'under the radar' and the Emperor was invincible in political terms and also retained the loyalty of the armies as a man devoted to military order, high military expenditure, and aggression against Rome's enemies. As such he was able to order that his late uncle's daughter Aelia, his old rival, leave Rome for exile in a remote area of southern Spain under police supervision after the 554 conspiracy, though any links to it by her were never proved, and later in 554 the ultra-Christian 'strongman' Praefect of Constantinople Petrus Sabbatius (OTL: Emperor Justinian), who had virtually ruled the city and the vicarate dependent on the Eastern capital since the mid-530s, was summoned to Rome and escorted there by Imperial troops and a far more pro-Monophysite official, Helio of Gordium, replaced him and cracked down on the orthodox crowds and clerics in the city. It was supposed that Petrus Sabbatius was in trouble for links to the plot and might end up executed too and certainly the Emperor had his suspicions and a commission from the finance ministry trawled through twenty-five years of his employee's accounts and made him hand a large sum back to the state. But in the event Petrus was exonerated and was even called in to assist the Emperor with plans to force the Catholics to accept a new theological 'formula' that would accommodate the Monophysites and cancel the inflammatory language (as Anastasius saw it) of the 451 Council of Chalcedon. The theological expert Petrus had much to offer the Emperor on this given his own private talks with clerics of all sects and the links to and patronage of the Monophysites by his late wife Theodora (d 548), who as an ex-actress and multi-millionaire had also been funding several theatrical troupes and a theatre festival (at Epidaurus) and as such had had the previous and current Emperor's goodwill for cultural work. Anastasius was duly inspired to call together a private committee of 'moderate' theologians from all the main Christian sects in Rome in 555 to work on a formula that would then be put to a Church Council of East and West. The new way to reconcile with the Monophysites was to be centred on condemning the "Three Chapters", i.e. the works of the strong-minded and doctrinally aggressive orthodox writers Theodore of Mopsuestia (d. 428), Theodoret of Cyrrhus (d. 458 ?) and Ibas of Edessa (d. 457), which Monophysites regarded as offensive and virtually "Nestorian" but had been backed by the Council of Chalcedon in 451.

As a first 'shot' to test the response Anastasius ordered an edict to be issued in early 555 condemning these works and required that all Patriarchs and the Pope required to endorse the edict; although Menas of Constantinople did under protest Pope Vigilius refused and was deported again, this time to Sicily, and Patriarch Dionysius of Alexandria was even more resistant and ended up deposed and replaced by a regional cleric from the Nile Delta who was the only senior official in the orthodox Church in Egypt to dare to defy his boycott of the government. More riots in Egypt followed and were put down, more orthodox ended up in the slave-mines, and hundreds of clergy fled to remote orthodox monasteries and were sacked. As a third of the Church's assets in the region were now confiscated as a punishment several objecting abbots tried to send in monks and tenants to occupy confiscated estates and had to be besieged in their monasteries and dragged out by troops. The money acquired by the purge was given to the Army to fund new barracks and training-camps plus military manoeuvres and the Emperor was safe from any more plots as only the elite in Rome could try to get at him and he was too well-protected by his troops, but he was from this point even more detested by the orthodox and his new Church Council in 557 did not help. Vigilius was intimidated by a board of Imperial commissioners into agreeing to attend the Council and accept its formula if this fitted the 'Word of God', and the Emperor was talked into accepting this compromise and letting him resume his functions as Pope to stop a threatened illegal council of the Gallic and Spanish churches meeting in secret in the Pyrenees to anathematize and depose him and elect a rival Pope.

On 5 May 557 Anastasius' "Fifth General Council" of the Church opened at Messina, well away from Rome and any Catholic riots and surrounded by troops to 'protect' it with a board of specialist expert university theologians, all vetted by the Emperor to assure their loyalty to his plans, in attendance to offer advice. Once it was clear that the Council, led by the new and moderate Patriarch Eutychius of Constantinople who was too committed to reconciliation with the Monophysites to bother about dodgy theology, would back the Emperor's plans to 'amend' the Chalcedonian formula on the nature of Christ and the Virgin Mary and attack the 'Three Chapters' Vigilius boycotted it, and on the 14th he issued a compromise 'First Constitution'. This proposed alternative solution condemned sixty propositions attributed to Theodore and others of Theodoret's, leaving out the most pro-orthodox of their works which had been approved at Chalcedon. This was a compromise by his terms and perhaps two-thirds of the Western Bishops backed it, but Anastasius refused to respond and revealed Vigilius' secret letters condemning his 'official' Papal position on these matters as nonorthodox and only a political manoeuvre that he would condemn openly later. This amounted to double-crossing the Emperor. Vigilius' name was struck from the official 'diptychs' in each Patriarchate recognizing Church leaders, but personally not as Pope. The Council anathematized the 'Three Chapters', and Anastasius gaoled Vigilius' assistants for putting him up to his manoeuvre and refused to release any of them until they signed up to the Council's verdict; some stayed in gaol for the rest of his reign (two years). Vigilius eventually signed up to the new formula early in 558 and was allowed to go back to Rome as Pope but faced trouble for giving in to the Emperor from the majority of the Spanish and Gallic churches. Although the majority of the Eastern bishops and their churches obeyed the Emperor the Monophysite communities in Egypt and Syria (that in Palestine had largely been driven out or forcibly converted in the past two decades) were still debating whether to accept the new Church Council's verdict and hold councils to rejoin the official Church when Anastasius died in 559. The planned reunion thus collapsed as his successor Nerva II reversed the Council's verdict to appease the Catholics and reunify the Western Church, and Anastasius' crude and overbearing use of threats of force at the Council did his reputation no favours despite his temporary success and indeed helped to alienate his nephew Gallus, in attendance as an Imperial commissioner, from him. Gallus politely officially pretended to support the Council's decisions as did most of the Constantinopolitan nobility and orthodox community and the majority of the Christian elite in Rome. To Anastasius, uninterested in doctrine and regarding unity as paramount, discipline and obedience mattered more than consciences – and forcible sectarian reconciliation was necessary to stop the endless inter-Church quarrels. The Emperor would decide on doctrine, not the clergy – after all, Constantine had behaved similarly. (In OTL, the 'Three Chapters' controversy was a real attempt to solve doctrinal disputes, handled equally forcefully by Emperor Justinian.)

As a military expansionist Anastasius was determined to keep up Titus' work and indeed followed the advice of some of his generals, consulted months before his accession, that if Rome kept up its momentum of expansion malcontent officers who might be contemplating a Catholic revolt and restive neighbours like the Ostrogoths and the Epthalite Huns would be kept on the defensive. The East had far more commercial potential and the locally experienced Belisarius and the well-connected Narses, the latter with relatives in Ctesiphon dabbling in the 'Silk Road' trade as part of the expanding Romano-Persian mercantile community there, advised Anastasius that if Rome cornered the 'Silk Road' trade by land and sea it could pay for its army and administration much easier and keep taxes down. This would entail either an advance by land in the South from Persis or Alexandria-in-Arachosia East to the lower Indus to take control of its ports, backed by a naval escort loaded with supplies if the desert route near the coast was used, or an advance by land to the north across the Hindu Kush via Kabul to the Khyber Pass and the upper Indus at Attock. That would also entail the occupation of the rich land of the upper Indus with the local Buddhist kingdom of Gandhara – and would emulate Alexander. Belisarius advised it as feasible and offered to lead the necessary campaign – and he had sent out scouts and emissaries to the Khyber tribes during his Sogdian war to annotate and map the local passes and rivers for a future war and had paid the tribal chiefs off to cut off arms-supplies from the kingdom of Gandhara on the upper Indus to Sogdian rebels.

In 552 Anastasius read the accounts of Alexander's wars there and of Seleucid ambassadors to Gandhara and the Mauryas and considered a war, but a challenge to Rome by dynamic king Totila of the Ostrogoths in north Germany intervened. The latter, who had rallied the loot-hungry warrior nobles to evict the pro-Roman king Witigis who was in the Empire's pay, now helped Frankish king Chlodomir the Merovingian to evict his Rome-allied brother Chlotar. The Arian Totila also sent Catholic priests and Roman mercenaries and mine-contractors packing from annexed Roman frontier lands, so for once the Emperor and the Church were on the same side as evicted Roman missionaries from Belgican monasteries and cathedrals arrived in Rome to lobby Pope Vigilius for a war to save Catholicism in crumbling Transrhenus. Anastasius did not care about the Catholics (he was allowing Church-demolished pagan German shrines to their gods Woden, Freya and so on to be rebuilt by local pagans in the eastern Rhineland forests to keep non-Christian German locals who supplied troops to Rome loyal, eg the Alemanni) but he did about Rome's prestige, so in late 553 Petrus Sabbatius' 'showy' but pragmatic and meticulous aristocratic Christian nephew Germanus, 'dux' of Dacia since 546, was called to Rome to be given the job of removing Totila and an expedition was planned. In spring 554 Germanus, as the new 'Master of Infantry' in the Rhineland, led a mobile force of 40,000 mixed regimental troops and 'limitanei', mostly infantry due to the forests and with plenty of artillery to smash down wooden German fortress walls and set fire to their buildings, into the Merovingian realm near the lower Elbe to systematically destroy the Ostrogoth occupation forces and aid Chlotar's partisans to regain control. After two major defeats in open battle Totila took his troops into the forests and Elbe-mouth marshes far from the nearest Roman roads and launched a guerilla war.

This' hit and run' war was no more than a nuisance to the Romans who had greater numbers and far better armour and in addition mobile cavalry, but the Franks usually fought in smaller groups on foot and used ancestral-style battleaxes and short swords so they were worse affected and they had to be taught to use Roman weapons and tactics – particularly to manage a tactical battle not just fight as individual warriors – to stand a chance against the versatile and imaginative Totila. After reoccupying most of the kingdom of Chlotar Germanus moved on to invade Totila's own realm and sacked his towns and fortresses one by one, and later 554 and 555 saw the Romans occupying the Ostrogothic realm from Elbe to Oder and setting up a chain of fortresses on each new, slave-built Roman road back to the Elbe plus more fortresses on the Baltic coast east of the 'Danevirke' dyke as far as the mouth of the Oder. More Roman troops moved north from the Ostrava Gap to cut off the Ostrogothic refugees' retreat east to the Vistula and over 40,000 of their people were captured and ordered by the Emperor to be taken to the Mediterranean provinces and sold off as slaves, to the disquiet of the Church. But though this left the smoking ruins of the Ostrogoths' towns and local villages in Roman hands and new fortresses being erected there Totila abandoned his Frankish campaign to march home and try to save his surviving subjects, who were in hiding, and as he avoided open battle against a far larger Roman army it was late 556 before he was cornered and killed by Germanus. Anastasius now annexed 'Ostrogothia' as the province of 'Germania Ulterior', from Elbe to Oder, and set up a fortified 'limes' at the latter river, but this land was mostly forested and infertile and lacked the mines of inland central Germany and it was a drain on Roman finances for decades, not many volunteer farmers moving in from the Rhine as Anastasius had hoped so he had to bring in army veterans whose grants of land on retirement from the Western armies from 557 tended to be in the new province. Many of them were of German ethnic origin and as Anastasius annoyed the Church by allowing them to keep their pagan religion and set up their own shrines, banning conversions, he duly attracted large numbers of traditionalist pagan German tribesmen who were serving in the army to this area. But Roman urbanization was slow to develop as there was not much to export except livestock and timber and the province was privately regarded as a waste of money by many generals, Belisarius included.

Meanwhile a war between 'expatriate' northern Irish pagans from Ulster who had been moving into Epidaii territory in Argyll across the 'North Channel' since the 520s – largely to escape demands by the expansionist 'High Kings' of the 'Ui Niall' dynasty in southern Ulster and Midhe – and the local pro-Roman tribes had been going on without Roman involvement in the early-mid 550s as Anastasius had called off most of the British frontier troops to the Ostrogothic war and regarded Britain as a backwater. In 558 the defeat of the Epidaii led to Comgall, the Irish king of 'Dalriada' as the Irish colony in Argyll was called, driving the tribespeople out of their lands and settling a large group of his Ulster kin on them. The Epidaii took refuge with the Picts to the east and the latter's new king Bridei enrolled them for his expanding army, and as pro-Roman tribal chiefs were evicted from Angus and Buchan by the Picts in 558–9 Anastasius was called on to intervene and save the entire network of Roman allied north of Hadrian's Wall from disaster. Local king of the Votadini (i.e. Lothian) Morcant and the king of the Selgovae to the West, Tutugual, asked the Roman 'dux' of 'Brigantia', the northern British province ruled from Eburacum, for help as the 'Count of Britain' Mailcunus/ Maelgwyn, a local general from the Venedotian regional command (Gwynedd) and kin to Morcant, was away fighting in Ostrogothia to mop up guerillas and they journeyed to Rome to ask for aid in January 559, but before they arrived, on 20 February, Anastasius had a stroke and so any possibility of war was delayed – and was to be sidelined as his heir Nerva, a pacific character, had other priorities. (Named British and Irish rulers are OTL figures.)

Despite Anastasius' attempts in his bedside directions to his ministers to get his nephew Gallus not the 'Church-loving pacifist' Nerva chosen as regent the latter was elected by the ministerial council on 2 March 559, and as Anastasius was too weak and confused to rule the regency became permanent and on 18 April Nerva was proclaimed co-emperor as 'Nerva II'. The conciliatory manner and astute political manoeuvrings' of the latter, seeking consensus rather than imposing his will on all using the power of the State, was to see him regarded then and in retrospect as a 'better' Emperor and a 'better' man than Anastasius, whose confrontational religious policy of deciding on a 'line' and then enforcing it had led to bitter disputes among those Christians who took doctrine seriously. Those members of the politico-social elite who believed in untrammelled Imperial power and trusted the Emperor to make decisions and his subjects to obey them regarded Anastasius in a better light as an honest man doing his best while wistful admirers of the 'tolerant' and 'doctrine-free' pre-Christian Empire looked on him as a worthy successor for his uncle Titus II and an imitator of Trajan or Aurelian. Indeed in later centuries Anastasius was to be held up for admiration as an efficient administrator and a man who believed in Greco-Roman civilizational values but treated the Germans and Persians fairly and recruited more of them into his army and his administration. He had loyal defenders among his civilian and military proteges as Titus II had done, and did not spark off a civil war despite some angry Catholics' desire for one – and both Belisarius and the other military 'star' of his reign, the more 'acceptable' aristocratic Germanus, remained loyal to him. But where Titus had usually headed off confrontation, Anastasius headed deliberately into it – was this necessity or arrogance?

Chapter 13

Nerva II 559–570: The Man of Justice

The succession was delayed as Anastasius did partially recover in the summer of 559 after a long recuperation at his villas on the Bay of Naples, but he could not handle any business except in short bursts and Nerva had removed his most anti-Catholic ministers and recalled Princess Aelia and other exiles so he was a political nullity and lacked the energy to protest at this. Vowing to rule as his namesake had done, as a reconciler and upholder of justice, Nerva – who took over as sole ruler when Anastasius died on 12 December 559 aged sixty-three, after a banquet to celebrate the visit of some of his top generals to him in Rome proved too much for his fragile health – cancelled all his controversial brother's religious legislation in July 559 and duly received the plaudits of the Church. But as he did not restore many of the expelled and sacked archbishops, bishops, or abbots (let alone the removed Patriarchs) and he declared that monasteries that had resisted Roman troops had broken the law and could not be pardoned the orthodox Church in the East, especially Egypt, did not recover its pre-551 position of dominance. The local Monophysites retained what property Anastasius had returned to them provided that Nerva's new commission of roving legal experts confirmed that they had owned this property legally as of the 440s. The majority of orthodox exiles, including most of those who had taken refuge in the deserts, were able to return home and the persecutions ended with assorted over-eager police officials investigated and sacked by Nerva's commissioners so by and large the Catholics backed him. But the official restoration of the decretals of Chalcedon by Church Councils in each Patriarchate in 560 were accompanied by a new 'addendum', required by Nerva and the new and moderate Pope John IV, that no offence was intended to the Monophysites' beliefs and that the 'merged' personas and wills of the Divine Christ and the Human Christ, born as one person of the Virgin Mary, were indissoluble and equal in status.

Nerva's main concern was to repair the damage that his rash and aggressive brother had done to the reputation of the Imperial office and its seeming impartiality, and as stated in his first speeches to the Senate he stood above the political fray and acted as an arbiter rather than pressing on with his own policies no matter what the cost or controversy. He sacked nearly all of Anastasius' ministers for abuse of power and offensive treatment of petitioners and junior civil servants, though almost none could be touched for corruption so their foes were disappointed of hopes for a series of trials, and a body of second-ranking and uncontroversial civil servants and respected aristocratic senators took over most of the ministries in Rome while the aggressive and anti-orthodox 'Augustal Praefect' and most of his senior staff in Alexandria were sacked in a massive purge by a judicial commission headed by a board of three 'Imperial Censors' in spring-summer 560. A traditionalist though not a Catholic-hater like his brother and just as fond of the works and ideological legacy of the poet Vergil, Nerva kept up Anastasius' 'Vergil Festival', published his late brother's personal and private literary work on the 'Aeneid' which Anastasius and his cultural aides had been writing for a decade, and also kept up the late ruler's interest in and patronage of the theatre, calling the Empire's top theatrical companies to perform 'revivals' of the Roman comic playwright as well as the classical Greek tragedies and comedies in Rome in alternate winters (560–1, 562–3, 564–5, and so on). He also set up a new 'Board of Censors', consisting of venerable and respected jurists from all over the Empire, to receive petitions about and deal with cases of alleged abuse of power and corruption by officials in 560. The board sent roving commissions to each province to check up on cases and hear appeals against past 'biased' judgements though they themselves sat in Rome, in the Basilica Aemilia in the Forum Romanum until a new 'Forum of Nerva II' and its attendant basilica was completed east of the main Forum in the late 560s. Nerva himself issued coins and made speeches stressing the Emperor's role as the guarantor of law and justice, and hired expert legal advisors who could help him select trustable and honest judges to preside over cases – and in doing so he made the Emperor seem less of a remote and unapproachable figure and more of a moral protector to ordinary citizens (or at least those literate ones who could afford to bring lawsuits). He sat in judgement himself in cases more than his predecessors had done, and news of this was duly spread by visitors to Rome to the outer provinces – with some supportive bishops (relieved to be rid of Anastasius) playing up his role as the 'new Soloman', which his ministers approved of as uniting all Christian sects behind him and avoiding contentious theological quibbles.

As a result of the recommendations of the touring legal commissions to him in 564 that the Imperial bureaucracy across the Empire was overstaffed Nerva set up a commission to decide how to remedy this and they looked into reports from each province. Once they had reported back to him some 1,200 officials, mostly junior ones, across the Empire had their posts terminated – either immediately or on their retirement – from 567 and in that year Nerva also merged some dozen provinces in the central Mediterranean region, mostly in Italy and the Balkans, with their neighbours and kept on only about 75 per\ cent of the officials in them. The cutbacks aided the Imperial budget and were popular with the majority of the public and with the army, though not with officials except for underpaid provincial junior ones who were now given a pay-rise (which meant that the impoverished and more honest ones could afford to avoid taking bribes). In 568 Nerva felt confident enough to announce on his second summer stay of four months in Constantinople – the first had been in 561 – that as the Empire did not need so many fully-staffed palaces the 'full complement' Imperial staff at the Sacred Palace would only serve when the Emperor was in the Eastern capital and the rest of the time they would have to serve in local civil service jobs or work for the city's bureaucracy (which meant that 20 per cent of current jobs in the latter could be shut down as not needed). The Emperor had the shrewdness not to listen to austere Christian preachers and cost-cutting finance department advisers who wanted him to sell off a large proportion of 'unnecessary' Imperial estates, including land confiscated from plotters by Anastasius II, and instead those lands that the Emperor did not need directly or visit were often leased out on long and expensive leases to local nobles and entrepreneurs – who were thus enrolled as the Emperor's grateful clients and whose rent-money added to the treasury's income.

There was also an unexpected and long-term, if not immediately apparent, bonus to the treasury in 565 as a group of Nestorian monks from Mesopotamia who had gone on a combined mercantile and conversion expedition to the divided realms of China a few years before had discovered the secret of making silk and this year they returned to Ctesiphon with a collection of invaluable silkworms hidden inside their hollow walking staffs so they could get round the Chinese ban on exporting silkworms. They set up a small workshop for the silkworms to produce wilk and when they had done so successfully reported this to the Praefect and did a demonstration, and in 566 they and some of the silkworms were sent on to Rome to do a demonstration for the Emperor and as a result Nerva agreed to set up a special 'Silk Production Unit' in the grounds of the Marble Palace on the Pincian Hill, his main residence. Silk was duly produced for Imperial robes to add to the glory and majesty of the Emperor and from the 570s silk started to be sold off to courtiers and then to other great nobles too, adding to the Emperor's income, but it was more of a 'prestige' project than a major commercial breakthrough for the moment and more revenue was produced by the expanding Red Sea and Persian Gulf trade by sea to the Indian sub-continent, Nerva keeping up his brother's interest in this and in 564 sending an ambassador with a trade-mission to the king of Taprobane (Ceylon). With his eyes on the East the Emperor was indeed initially unaware of the greatest potential discovery of his reign and dismissive once he did hear news.

The end of Anastasius' reign had led to the cancellation of his plans to assist the embattled Irish 'High King' Diarmait (OTL) against a growing coalition of his discontented vassal-kings who were annoyed at his interfering in their territories, and with Rome preoccupied the latter struck in 561 to rebel against their overlord, successfully. A rival branch of the 'Ui Niall' dynasty in southern Ulster led by king Ainmere (OTL), ruler at the fortress of Ailech, were inspired and given spiritual backing by the latter's cousin Bishop/Abbot Columbcille of Derry (St Columba, OTL), and they defeated Diarmait and his Roman mercenary bodyguard at the battle of Cuil Dreimhe.

Though the 'High King' saved his throne by promptly opening negotiations and offering to rule through a council of his vassal-kings, which was accepted, his power was broken and with it the centralised government (such as it was) of Ireland and he had to send his mercenaries back to the Empire and rule by traditional Irish law as administered by the socially conservative professional jurists, the 'brehons'. The Empire preferred to deal with one man as an allied ruler not a band of squabbling provincial kings and refugee nephews of Diarmait turned up in Rome in 562 urging an invasion to restore him, but peaceable Nerva agreed with his bishops that this would be a 'sin' and he did not think it advisable to prop up an unpopular ruler who would need a large Roman army and probable occupation of crucial fortresses to keep him in power. Diarmait had been bullying the Irish Church for years, so both the somewhat maverick Columbcille and the more respected senior cleric of the Irish midlands, Abbot Ruadhan of Lorrha (OTL), had been asking Pope John to back the rebel coalition to defeat 'tyranny' and the Emperor was told of Diarmait's dubiously legal arrests, executions, and new tax-demands of livestock on his vassals. Nerva agreed to the new regime being recognized, and when Diarmait died in 564 the two elderly nephews of the early C6th 'High King' Muirchertach Mac Erca (d 534) succeeded (as in OTL) as in effect the nominal 'front-men' for a 'senate' council headed by Ainmere. As one result of the civil war the turbulent Columbcille was ordered by the next Irish Church Council in 564 to go abroad for a decade and win new souls to Christ in expiation of the bloodshed that he had caused, and he set off with a band of his followers to the Irish kingdom of Dalriada in Argyll where he founded a new island monastery at Iona and started to convert the locals to Catholic Christianity – a mission which the Papacy 'sold' to the Emperor as a way to turn the fierce and anti-Roman Dalriadans into peaceful allies and so to avoid the cost and 'sin' of invading them. This duly served as Nerva's reasoning in the mid-late 560s for not intervening in war-hit Caledonia and letting the Dalriadans and Picts fight it out.

But the other main religious outcome of the Irish civil war was more important to Rome in the long term, as disillusioned midlands abbot Brendan of Clonfert

(OTL), who had been hearing for years from travelling missionary monks about the mysterious and semi-magical 'Northern Isles' to the north-west of Scotland, had heard in 562 from a group of voyagers who had apparently been on a year-long journey over the Atlantic Ocean and had discovered a 'Land of Promise' there. Apparently an angel had promised it to the Christians, so Brendan and his own monks made a voyage there by coracle in 564–5 to investigate and find a refuge from the war-hit and (temporarily) disordered Ireland and on their return reported that they had seen the island and it was real and huge. The earlier voyagers' 'islands of sheep' and 'islands of ice mountains' had meanwhile been identified by a group of experts at the University in Rome, on a visit there by some of the voyagers (to give thanks for their safe return at the shrine of St Peter), as the mysterious islands of the north leading up to 'Thule' on the Arctic Circle which the Greek voyager Pytheas had discovered and written about c. 300 BC. But the reports from (St) Brendan and his monks of a vast and fertile land some months' voyage beyond 'Thule' was regarded by the Roman 'experts' who heard it in 566 as fantasy or a 'sales pitch' for an island that was actually much nearer and smaller and they advised Nerva that even if there were real islands there the commercial prospects from any Roman exploration would be small. The lands were apparently uninhabited and the only significant produce of the region seemed to be wood while the bleak northern islands were cold and useless and the seas' teeming fish and whales would cost a lot to 'harvest', so the monks were not summoned to Rome to tell their story. The episode faded from memory except among some of the more adventurous British merchants trading with Irish ports who heard of it in 566 and ended up sending some fishing-boats from Hibernian Sea ports up to the 'islands of sheep' (the Faroes) to look for fish and set up small summer camps there.

(Alleged voyage of St. Brendan to the Americas is an OTL mystery.)

The commander and officers of the Hibernian Sea fleet were more interested in the war between the Dalriadans and the Picts and as long as neither were raiding Roman lands they were not interested in ventures to the far islands or even as far as the Hebrides, and as the new Dalriadan king Conall mac Comgall (d 574) (OTL) proceeded to use his Irish mercenaries from Ulster to push back Pictish king Bridei (OTL) in the late 560s the Roman commanders, forbidden to intervene by Nerva, sent secret mercenary help to the latter and stabilised the situation. The main Roman officers involved included some of the Venedotian cavalry coastal patrols who normally watched for Irish pirates or smugglers, including the late commander Mailcunus' son Rhun (OTL) and one of the Carvetian (Cumbrian) coastal anti-piracy patrol commanders, the aristocratic

Urien (OTL) whose Roman commander great-grandfather Coilinus (Coel) had been 'dux' of Brigantia in the 430s; their exploits were turned into heroic poetry by his attendant bard and cousin Llywarch (OTL), a passionate exponent of traditional Romano-British 'sung' as opposed to written poetry who was later written of as the 'British Homer' for his poems of this war. Columbcille, who had been trying to convert the Dalriadans to the ways of peace and had had reinforcements from the British Church as offered by the Pope in the 570s but only a few of these men as they needed to speak Gaelic, had had a struggle converting many of the Argyll settlers. He only had a major boost to his mission when his local ally prince Aedan mac Gabhran (OTL) succeeded to the Dalriadan throne in 574, and from then on conversions multiplied and the Dalriadan kingdom became more stable and was confident enough to open relations with the Empire via Columbcille's Church links.

(The Irish, North British, and Dalriadan/ Scots events are based on those of reality, with real rulers of the correct dates – but in this version a 'centralised' Irish High Kingship is supported by Rome.)

As the crisis in northern Britain passed the Emperor lost what little interest he had in this bleak and cold frontier and concentrated on his Red Sea and Persian Gulf trading-fleets and the need for Rome to prop up the faltering rule of the Abyssinians in the Himyarite kingdom. The latter land was restive under the alien Abyssinian yoke and animist and Jewish Arab tribes as well as pillaged townsmen were chafing under the exploitative rule of an elite from Africa, and the withdrawal of around half the Roman forces there in the 550s to take over garrison duties from Eastern troops sent to the Ostrogothic war had reduced the Roman embassy's ability to coerce the Abyssinians. The current Abyssinian viceroy, Abraha (junior, son of his eponymous father Abreha the Elder') ignored advice from Nerva's man in Aden, Belisarius' old military colleague Archistratus who was now the civil governor there, to ease up on those of a different faith to his regime's idiosyncratic version of Monophysitism (the developed version of the faith brought to Abyssinia by the Alexandrian monks who had converted it in the 330s). A purge after an unsuccessful plot to kill Abraha in 565 led to many civic leaders in Marib, a city in decline since the 490s breaching of its famous dam that had long irrigated a large area of fertile lands around it, fleeing to Aden via the rebel-held town of Taif, and as Archistratus refused to hand them over as demanded Abraha invaded the Roman province of Arabia Felix in 566 and demolished some mud-brick frontier forts. The first inter-Christian war in Arabia embarrassed the king of Abyssinia, who was currently receiving a Roman trade-delegation and had to explain to them that he had not sanctioned the attack on their countrymen. Nerva did not want a war, but the sight witnessed by passing traders on the great camel-route north from Yemen to Mecca of naked Roman soldiers being dragged in chains along the dusty road to Abraha's capital to be put in cages in the marketplace inflamed feeling in the Senate when it was reported to Rome and in effect the Emperor was forced to declare war by militant senators and ex-ministers of Anastasius' stirring up huge demonstrations in Rome. With a crowd of up to 30,000 in the Forum Romanum demanding vengeance and a noisy group of young nobles intent on war, the 'Sons of Camillus' club (led by the son of one of Anastasius' late generals), camping out at the statue of Rome's 390 BC rescuer Camillus on the Capitol issuing up pagan prayers to him and Jupiter Optimus Maximus to come and rescue the dishonoured Empire in November 566, Nerva had to appear at the forthcoming Circus Maximus races before an ominously silent crowd and promise to act, which was seen as being as humiliating a reversal as Anastasius I's climbdown over religion in the Eastern capital in 514–15. He sent a delegation to Marib to urge Abraha to give in and release the captives and pay the demanded compensation while another delegation sped up the Red Sea to the Axumite port of Adulis to head for their capital and ask King Yekuno to order his viceroy to give in, but the Romans reached Marib to find the heads of the leading hostages decorating the main gates and they were then taken prisoners too and told they would be killed if the Empire invaded.

Abraha had plenty of troops to hand and was confident that they could hold out against 'soft' Mediterranean troops in guerilla warfare even if the Romans had the men and firepower to take the main towns of the Himyarite lands, but a few weeks later the rag-clad, starving diplomatic mission was rescued from their cell in a tower in the capital in a daring midnight raid by the knife-wielding members of an Arab trading delegation from the ancient town of Mecca up the trade-route North, as directed by the delegation's leader Al-Abbas, a junior member of the powerful Umayyad clan who dominated the town's mercantile business. Abraha's 'minister for trade' (in reality his extortionist crony) had just demanded too high a bribe for agreement with the Meccans and that presumably turned them into enemies and drove them to help the Empire lest Abraha invade their city next, but for whatever reason the Romans were helped to escape disguised as Arab servants – and stained brown to look like Arabs – as the delegation left for home and back at Mecca they could contact the nearest Roman troops as the latter headed down the Red Sea on the invasion-fleet to the port of Jeddah. The Meccans added details of the defences of Marib, and as the Roman ships (said to number 600) bombarded Jeddah into submission and rained fire down mercilessly on the main Abyssinian port in Arabia the wary Yekuno did not dare intervene lest Rome turn on him next. The survivors of the garrison of Jeddah surrendered and the Roman commander Sallustius had the entire town demolished and its population driven out into the desert as a warning, and as the camel-riding warriors of Mecca and the other main trading-town on the 'spice road' north to Petra, Yathrib, brought more men and supplies to aid the Romans they marched on Marib apart from one column that curved off to the south to take the highland towns of Sada and Sana.

The out-numbered and out-equipped Himyarite/ Abyssinian army retreated and destroyed all the supplies and blocked all the waterholes en route to Marib, but the Romans pressed on and in late April they arrived at and started to bombard Abraha's capital. The aged tyrant held out for a month hoping for an early and blazingly hot summer to save him, but the Romans had brought desert troops from Numidia and Tripolitania who were used to heat and had plenty of camels plus some 'Garamantian' tribesmen and 5,000 Nubian warriors – the latter's Christian King Gadran was hoping that Yekuno would try to rescue his viceroy and Rome would attack him next so the Nubians could loot his kingdom. Eventually the Roman catapults, hauled across the desert in pieces by trains of camels and Arab desert horses, broke holes in the city walls and on 3 June 567 Marib fell to Rome, its civic officials surrendering to prevent a massacre despite Abraha's orders, and as the viceroy held out in his fortified citadel it was rained with fire in a two-day relentless attack and collapsed in crumbling ruins and flames. That was the last that was heard of Abraha, though he was never found and might have escaped, and as his main commanders were dragged off in fetters and forced to walk barefoot all the way to Jeddah to be put on galleys bound for Rome and execution there Sallustius proceeded to have the ruins of Marib demolished as an example and then a new town was built there on a Roman grid pattern as 'Civitas Nervarum'. The rest of the province was soon annexed to form the new Roman province of 'Arabia Oriens' and 20,000 Roman and Nubian troops garrisoned its strongpoints, an occupation that the Emperor had not wanted but did not dare to scale down in case of a successful revolt. The Roman ambassador sent to king Yekuno to have the annexation confirmed replied to his request for 'his' province back by presenting him with the twisted and mangled door-lock of the Marib citadel front gate and telling him that 50,000 troops would bring the rest of the city gates if Yekuno so desired, plus the heads of his viceroy's executed ministers, but would then take over the Axumite coastal province of Eritrea and the capital, Axum, until 100 million denarii 'war reparations' were paid. After that Yekuno had to give in and accept the annexation and pay all that the Romans demanded, handing over two of the main Axumite ports to Rome on 50-year leases, but although Rome now controlled the entire south-east coast of the Red Sea it was too difficult to hold the Hejaz to the north, which was handed over to local chiefs as Roman vassals, and Rome and its new ally, the mercantile oligarchy of Mecca led by the Ummayads, jointly policed the 'spice route' from Yemen to Petra while the inland desert oases and tribal wilds of Himyar were in effect autonomous apart from a few Roman garrisons.

As in the tribal lands of Germany, many local warriors joined the Roman army in the next few decades and the peace imposed by Rome on Himyar was not welcomed by all, feuding Arab warlords in particular, but restless young nobles in a quest for glory or loot could always join the Roman army. The first two Roman 'duces' of Arabia Oriens were Syrians with experience of the Arab trade-routes and personal links to north Arabian tribal chiefs from their time as desert garrison commanders so they understood the proud and battle-loving sort of lords who led the regional tribes and required success and loot to keep their menfolk loyal. The Roman alliance to Mecca also brought Roman embassies and gifts to that growing city, the centre of a major local animist cult of the sacred 'Black Stone at the 'Ka'aba', and as Al Abbas' brother Abu Talib acted as the first official Meccan ambassador to Rome in 570 the sneeringly superior courtiers who laughed at the simply-clad Arab desert lord were rebuked and countered by the courteous Emperor himself. To the pacific Nerva the idea of annexing a major region of Arabia and causing massive destruction just due to the arrogance of one minor local potentate was nothing to celebrate and he refused to take the title of 'Arabicus' as offered by the Senate, but the war did his reputation much good with the grumbling army 'high command' and he was no longer written off as an inferior ruler to his late brother. His success in Arabia, though undesired by him, also countered the grumbles that he was letting Anastasius' conquest of Germania Ulterior go uncompleted by not bothering to annex the Merovingian, Rome- allied Frankish kingdom which was unstable due to plots against its King Sigebert (assassinated in 575). The latter's brother and successor Chilperic (d 584), youngest son of Chlotar I, then died and a boy, Chlotar II, succeeded, but Nerva's son Gallus, a local commander in the later 560s – and by then Emperor – did not annex the weakened kingdom despite having personally served nearby and knowing its leadership but just hired more of its warrior elite to serve as officers in his Rhine armies. Nerva did not bother either about the latest convulsions east of the Oder where now the assorted ex-vassals of the Ostrogoths had been overrun and forced into submission by the latest arrivals from the steppes, the Langobards under King Alboin.

(Merovingian rulers and Alboin are OTL.)

It was Gallus, another classical enthusiast and as fond of Vergil's poems and sense of Roman mission as his late uncle Anastasius but less brutal, who used his years of military training as an officer on secondment to the army of the 'Master of Soldiers on the Rhine' (566–72) Tiberius Constantine, and carefully navigated his way between militaristic expectations of Roman glory and his father's pacifism to punish Saxon brigands in the woods and marshes of the region between the lower Elbe and the Frisian coast in the late 560s. He carried out daring exploits but did not provoke a major war with the semi-independent and proudly pagan warlords of this region, and the locals were taught to respect the power of Roman arms but also the generosity and honour-bound codes followed by leaders like Tiberius Constantine (OTL: Eastern Emperor Tiberius II) and above all the charismatic Gallus – a man who even spoke the Saxon tongue and hired Frankish and Saxon aides. He also had a personal friendship with the later Frankish regent after 584, Merovingian prince Childebert, and as Emperor acted as godfather to his sons. His daring and generosity in his deeds earned him Saxon respect as well as Roman poets' praise and generals' hopes that he would become a new Anastasius II without the late ruler's confrontational habits, and when Nerva unexpectedly abdicated on 12 March 570 after an illness, aged seventy-two, to devote his remaining years to philosophic and legal studies Gallus became Emperor aged thirty-three and was immediately made 'Saxonicus' by the Senate in honour of his achievements in Germany.

(The Abyssinian/ Arabian crisis is based on real events; Abu Talib is the uncle of the Prophet Mohammed.)

Chapter 14

Gallus 570–582: The Warlord

To Gallus' credit, he was embarrassed by this and declared that he had not won a war against the Saxons as a race but had merely kept the peace with and among them so he turned the honour into the title 'Protector Germaniae et Pacificator Saxonicus', and he even invited assorted Saxon chiefs who he had exchanged vows of 'guest friendship' with as an officer to his modest coronation in June, a low-key ceremony carried out at the end of a special 'High Mass' in St Peter's with the crowning followed by him taking a vow to protect justice and religious and inter-communal toleration. The coronation banquet involved inviting representatives of the poor of Rome, chosen by lot, to attend along with the usual civic worthies, which inspired his idealist eldest son Rillanus in his own interpretation of the Imperial office's role, and won the plaudits of austere hermits and abbots across the Empire though assorted aristocrats in Rome sneered at it as a public relations gesture. His month of races in the Circus Maximus were as splendid and full of expensive prizes as ever and as a connoisseur of horseflesh with his own studs he took a keen interest in who won, and indeed it was his shared love of riding, racing and breeding horses with his officers and a circle of younger Roman nobles rather than his military reputation that was his main 'channel' to and reason for support from the sort of military aristocrat who had thought Nerva a weak pacifist and were looking for more wars under Gallus but were to be disappointed.

Not a law-book-reading antiquarian or enthusiast for idealistically regulated justice like Nerva, Gallus was nevertheless another believer in the need to return to the old values of Cicero and other great 'public servants' of the Late Republic who had put the State above personal ambition. In that respect his reign was to see as much of a conscious attempt to choose 'worthy' as well as experienced office-holders to head his ministries as Nerva had done. He was content to keep his father's exhaustively learned 'Quaestor' since 566, Julius Rusticanus the Ligurian author of a massive tome on the works and ideals of Cicero, and the austere cost-cutter 'Count of the Privy Purse' Hellanicus in office for most of his reign. Though he was young most of his senior ministers were as old and experienced as the men Nerva had chosen – and if not so often law graduates, still usually with a higher education as well as experience in office. He created new 'under-quaestorships' in Rome in 571 to handle the work of the roving judicial commissions set up by Nerva, which were kept in being, and he also set up a 'task force' commission of experienced former public works superintendents from across the Empire, headed by elderly but vigorous former 'aediles' who had served in Rome since the 530s. They were to keep an eye on spending on and where needed speed up work on various Imperially-ordered projects currently underway and start more – mostly roads, bridges, public buildings in major towns, and ports as usual but also new schools and hospitals. It was his aim to ensure that every town in the Empire had adequate schooling and medical facilities and he was deeply disapproving of the habits of many nobles in the past two and a half centuries of evading their 'civic responsibility' to pay for new buildings in their local towns and spend the cash on their own estates and mansions instead. Normally the wiser (or craftier) hedonistic nobles paid the local Church as well as the civil service to keep quiet by funding new churches or monasteries and in return getting a chapel at the said buildings for their own family mausoleum or monument. But Gallus decreed in 571 that the old Augustan orders that nobles should not only have houses in their local towns but help to pay for their civic amenities should be enforced, not just kept on the statute book in the Codes of Theodosius II and Titus II. The rules still continued to be dodged, but this was harder and when Gallus made his inaugural tours round Italy and Sicily in 572, Gaul and the Rhineland in 573, Spain and Lusitania in 574, and Illyria and western Greece in 575 he checked up that the laws were being carried out and civic work was being done and being funded properly. His inaugural visit to Constantinople was by sea in April-June 571, during his tour of southern Italy and done by sailing from Brundisium and returning to Syracuse, and he dispensed with the formality of a coronation as a waste of money and satisfied the populace with more races in the Hippodrome.

Happily married with three sons, Rillanus (born 559), Carus (born 563), and Claudius (born 568), Gallus was a handsome and popular young man and was by some regarded as a 'new Germanicus' as he not only had had similar German triumphs to that first century AD Augustan heir but looked like him. But despite his earnest devotion to justice and tradition like his father he was an outspoken admirer of the Emperor Julian and a critic of the Church's wealth, if not its principles. Although he had too much sense to renew Anastasius II's doctrinal controversies he regarded the Catholics with irritation for their hostility to the Monophysites and Nestorians and their belief in the power and prestige of the Pope – in his mind, a rival to the Emperor in his own capital and the heir to an executed 'troublemaker'. He regularly made barbed comments about clerics who did not live up to the austere and democratic lifestyle of leaders of the early Church. At least the current Popes of his early years in office, John (d 575) and Pelagius (d 579), were respectable, restrained, and modestly-living men from well-off civil service families with a sense of dedication to the Church and their congregations who avoided doctrinal controversy and did nothing to which Gallus might take exception. But he was as hostile to the wealth of the Papacy and as keen to keep an eye on this as Anastasius II and he tended to favour the more earnest and austere monastic leaders, e.g. the current abbot of St Benedict's monastery at Montus Cassinus near Naples, over the well-paid and high-living great bishops. In 575 he even held a major Church Council for bishops from both East and West in Rome which concentrated not on doctrine but on tightening up and enforcing rules on poverty, communal living, and chastity for priests and bishops and he required church property to be visibly used for communal benefit and that of the poor not for boosting the lifestyle of the higher clerics.

It was firmly stated that the bishops were in office to benefit the public and save their souls, not least by setting a good example, and Gallus was most impressed by those bishops who either lived like hermits and sold off their robes and palace furnishings (most common in the East and in idealism- affected remote regions like western Britain) or who used their power to investigate corrupt judges and oppressive officials and invited the poor and the needy to take refuge each harsh winter in their churches and palaces. The austere, grass-eating, water-drinking ex-hermit Bishop David (d 589, OTL) of Siluria in western Britain, who moved his see from the wealthy agricultural town of Caerleon to the remote village and shrine of Menevia on the Hibernian Sea, and the learned and justice-pursuing Bishop Leander (d 589, OTL) of Augusta Sevilla in Baetica in the Iberian peninsula, who compiled huge dossiers of official misdeeds to pass them on to the Emperor's commissioners and hid runaway 'wrongly accused' people in his palace, were Gallus' sort of churchmen not fat and greedy careerist clerics. They were duly praised by him at the Church Council and given financial help for their campaigns. The wealthy bishops of southern Gaul, careerist aristocrats from great noble families who had often monopolized running certain sees since the mid-C4th, were condemned by Gallus as not living in the manner of the great local monastic founder St Martinus of Turones, whose shrine he visited and honoured on his visit to Gaul. But the contemporary era's greatest Christian historian, Bishop Gregorius of Turones itself (d. 598), OTL, escaped censure due to his meticulous and honest historical works and his helping the poor. In revenge the seething clerics – required now to show Imperial commissioners each year how they had helped the local poor and to fund schools and hospitals in their dioceses – had Bishop David's outspoken preachings investigated for religious unorthodoxy and sent an accusation of Pelagianism (in his attacks on the idea of Predestination damning the 'idle poor' and 'thieving beggars' to Hell) to his local archbishop in Londinium in 576.

Thanks to the Emperor pressuring the Pope to see that this great holy man was acquitted the charges were dismissed, but the austerity that he had sponsored and made fashionable continued to spread at British monasteries, backed up by visiting monks from the Irish hermitages on the Aran islands and by encouragement from the equally austere Columbcille (d. 597) on Iona in Dalriada. The Gallic bishops' attempts to stop eager (mostly young) monks there walking out on 'slack' monasteries to set up their own, more rigorous ones were to lead to years of clashes with the authorities as they tried to get the 'runaways' arrested and returned by force but firstly Gallus and later his sons backed the runaways. An itinerant Irish missionary out to reform the 'slothful' Gallic church, Columbanus, and some British monks from the Demetian monastery of Ynys Pir (Caldey Island) and others from Ynys Witrinus (Glastonbury) also became involved in this push for greater austerity and less worldliness in monasteries in the north-west of the Empire in the later sixth century. Though the zeal of these perfectionist reformers irritated many high-up clerics as a reproach to their own lifestyles the reformers had a more sympathetic reception from 579 in the new Pope Pelagius II (in office 579–90). He was a humbly-born administrator from a part-German family in central Italy who Gallus chose not (as some said) as a 'yes-man' but as an honest character who had had to struggle to succeed and was a foe of the well-born young nobles who had clerical relatives and relied on them to help their smooth careers.

Anastasius II had been committed to meritocracy in the army and Nerva to it in the civil service and now Gallus kept up both and tried to bring it into the Church too by making sure that young men of humble birth were promoted to major bishoprics fairly young and careerist nobles were left by the wayside. In alliance with this campaign he also let some of his father's less well-connected philosopher friends, provincial graduates at top universities, talk him into having a commission set up in 575 to investigate the standards of teaching at schools across the Empire and combat the practice of anyone with the cash, not necessarily good teachers or organisers, setting up unregulated private schools that might either have poor resources or useless teachers and so not make the most of their pupils. By and large church schools were reasonably well staffed, resourced and motivated but the pagans in Nerva's old circle only argued that that meant that Christians, antagonistic to their pagan philosophy, had a head start in educating boys and brainwashing them into their own bigoted beliefs. Gallus accordingly set up his commission to look into Empire-wide education to the age of fourteen and report on abuses and in 579 this body reported on assorted scandals including drunk, abusive, or incompetent people running and teaching in many schools and boys who had the bare essentials beaten or bribed into them and gave up learning with relief. This was not the way to create that state run by philosophers that Plato and then Julian had believed in, and Gallus duly arranged to set up and fund a trial training college in Rome to produce better educated and better supervised teachers and appointed Nerva's old friend Philistarchus of Cnidus, a leading expert on 'ideal' ancient Athenian education, to run it and also serve as his formal 'consul for education' for a period of five years. The plan was for a whole system of such colleges to be set up across the Empire and for their graduates to be flooded into and improve secular education. But in the event the Emperor's death in 582 was to halt this though the teaching college was to continue in existence and make some improvement to Roman education as it sent out a hundred or more graduates each year and also provided funding for those new schools that its personnel approved of after examining their plans and their personnel's abilities.

Without being explicitly anti-Catholic Gallus clearly had some idea of reviving Julian's desire to wrest education from the hands of narrow-minded Christians, and in a similar vein he lavished funds on the Universities in Athens and Syracuse that were largely run by and for either pagans or tolerant Christians. He also created new official competitions for boys from across the Empire to go to Greece to compete in reciting the works of their great poets 'in situ' at appropriate venues each year, funding specific 'poetry festivals' dedicated to various poets and sending his friends there with his prizes to represent him – and in 577 using his inaugural tour of eastern Greece, Macedonia, and the Aegean islands to attend and preside at part of the annual new 'Homer Festival' on the island of Samos. It was his vision to restore the world of both epic 'narrative' and domestic/ pastoral poetry of the Augustan era and as such he was fascinated by the heroic sagas told around the fire at Saxon halls which he had heard while he was serving in Germany and the narrative bardic poetry of the 'Celts'. In tune with that he summoned both assorted Saxon travelling poets and British bards – most notably the famous Llywarch, friend and commemorator of the wars of the Venedotian captain Urien, and his fellow-bard Aneirin – to his court to give recitals in the 570s and encouraged younger Roman courtiers with poetic interests to take up poetry as a major art–form and become the new Horace or the new Vergil. This was to culminate with his foundation of a private school and archive for poets in Campania in 581 which he ensured had enough funds and enough teachers to outlive him and his abortive plans for a similar school in Greece were eventually realized by his second son Carus' devotion to his memory and plans in the mid-590s. But the main organizational impetus and probably the original idea came from his Vergilian enthusiast courtier friend Camillus Posidonianus, from a wealthy Greco-Italian landed dynasty in Calabria and rich enough to run his own poetic house-parties on his estates before the Emperor took up his ideas, and after Gallus died Camillus returned to being a private patron and was seen as the 'new Maecenas' well into the 620s.

The Emperor also honoured his father Nerva's cultural and his grandfather Heraclius' philosophic interests by sending learned commissioners (mostly from Rome, Athens and Alexandria universities) to the East in 572 to examine the possibilities of setting up a new university in the Levant/ Mesopotamia. They were to acquire knowledge of the philosophical studies of the past in the former Sassanid lands, hoping to incorporate the works of Hellenic-descended teachers in Parthian and Sassanid Mesopotamia and even Zoroastrian thinkers at the Sassanid court in Istakr. They duly carried off a valuable haul of manuscripts to the university in Rome and the 'Great Library' there, which Gallus got his experts to examine and report on to him. But no foundation of a university followed, not least as some of the commission (mostly Catholics) were antagonistic to the group talking to and acquiring material from the Jewish community in Ctesiphon and 'heretic' Christian monks in Assyria and reported this to the Church hierarchy who duly protested. With some Christian scholars in the Levant who the commission had approached about working at a new university there regretting that they had been told they would lose all their Church jobs or funding or face heresy charges if they joined an institution with Jewish links and 'insulted Christ' even the furious Gallus had to decide to back off. This added to his antagonism to Church obstreperousness and in 577–9 a major legal enquiry into Church lands and financial activities followed in Italy, Spain and North Africa, targeting bishoprics that had protested at the university/ Jewish links plan. Gallus became increasingly interested in Julian's means of reining in the Church thereafter though he was too cautious to act quickly. His attitude was mostly noticeable in his promotion of ceremonies in Rome and new literary works that played up the roles of virtuous pagan heroes of the old Republic who could rival the great men of the Church for their moral achievements, e.g. the austere and incorruptible Cato 'the Elder' and the consuls who had fought off the Gauls and Hannibal. A three-day-long festival of music, poetry, recitals of the historical works of Livy, and new plays about the great moments of the epochal 'Second Punic War' of 218–202 BC when Rome faced annihilation by but defeated Hannibal was staged by Gallus in Rome in spring 581 with the Theatre of Marcellus serving as the main venue for the drama and rich prizes luring in the Empire's best, mostly university-educated playwrights and poets. Gallus hoped to coax yet more men into writing plays and poetry and bringing back the great cultural age of Augustus and made sure that his elder two sons Rillanus and Carus were 'on side' and were seen to appear at the events and provide prizes too – his third son Claudius was only interested in warfare.

The Emperor was, however, becoming more irascible and suffering from a mixture of ailments and a surprising series of minor memory lapses or sudden collapses, and as his health began to go downhill in late 581 he began to rail at the Empire's adoption of Christianity as a betrayal of its traditions and as handing over too much power and influence to a rival institution that threatened Imperial power. It was up to the Emperor to be the moral guardian and principal source of emulation for the public, not the bishops or (in the West) the Pope, and if the court and administration did not look out sharply they would find that any policy antagonistic to Church interests would be impossible due to a mixture of private pressure and outright civic disobedience and intimidation. The public should look to the moral leadership in the past of an Augustus, Trajan, Hadrian or Marcus Aurelius not to the Church Fathers and though Diocletian had been a centralizing tyrant he had had a point in tackling the Church. The Emperor began to exclude all Catholics who would not condemn the primacy of episcopal moral leadership from court and senior office and to start to direct his legal teams to investigate all the Papacy's lands and its network of financial funding. The bishops needed to be reduced to proper 'apostolic poverty' in his opinion, and in spring 582 his commissioners delivered a report on dodgy financial practices and tax-evasion by the Papal estates' administration that led to series of court cases, mass confiscation of assets, and the Pope being required to have his private finance records audited and a large amount of Church plate seized as allegedly acquired by dubious and probably forged wills by wealthy Romans. As the Church in Rome faced financial ruin the Emperor was denounced by bolder clerics from the pulpit for 'persecution' and they in turn faced arrest and trial for insulting the Law and encouraging defiance, but on 25 May 582 Gallus collapsed and died suddenly at the races in the Circus Maximus, aged only forty-five, and the Church boldly declared this to be Divine vengeance which only increased the antagonism of sections of the administration and the army to its 'disloyal' behaviour.

Chapter 15

Rillanus 582–590: The Idealist

The heir, Rillanus, aged twenty-three, was as antagonistic to the 'thought control' exercised by aggressive Catholic theologians and bishops and the pretensions of the Papacy as his father but was a more emollient and democratic person. He had indeed toyed with becoming a monk and serving the poor as a teenager rather than do the two years' military service as a trainee officer mandated by his father so he was not so hostile to the Church *per se* and he had assorted 'holy men' and wealthy Italian noble philanthropists among his friends. His multi-millionaire heiress wife Dionysia, from a superrich landed family in Sicily and connected via her mother to the Constantinopolitan Christian courtier nobility, had not provided him with children as intended by Gallus when he had arranged the marriage in 574 (partly as a way of providing a political link to the ex-Eastern capital's elite and using her complex network of cousins there as senior, trusted administrators there). But she was a fervent and austere Christian who had wanted to be a nun, worshipped her senior Bithynian abbess aunt who had partly educated her, and wore sackcloth next to her skin, fasted, had herself whipped regularly, and spent part of her time serving as a kitchen-helper and charwoman at an orphanage under an assumed name to keep herself humble and she duly helped to persuade Rillanus to reconcile with the Church, not keep up his father's feud.

The new Emperor did not abandon all the prosecutions of the Roman Church administration or personnel for financial irregularities but he did call off the ones for sedition and let the matter of anti-Jewish pressure on the would-be Eastern university personnel drop. After his coronation at St Peter's on 28 July 582 he proceeded to make it clear that he would govern for all his people not 'target' any communities or institutions and that he would seek to show that the Emperor was the 'first servant of the people' not their 'lord and master' (a rebuke for the aims of Diocletian who he loathed as a tyrant as did the Church). Rillanus intended to get the Imperial office back to the relative simplicity of the era of the 'First Citizen' and in that regard proceeded to have the court and its offices overhauled during the rest of 582, leading to cuts of around 30 per cent in its personnel, and he also made a point of almost always wearing a traditional toga and requiring the Senate and ministers to do so in public too while his wife wore simple dresses with Greek-style 'stoles' like a classical-era wife not rich robes, rarely wore more than a few pieces of jewellery, and held an auction of over half the Imperial jewellery collection to raise funds for her favourite orphanages.

The Empress Dionysia created a new role for the Empress as a leader of charity fundraising and went on many morale-boosting visits to charitable institutions across Italy rather than being the main leader of the capital's social life as many of her predecessors had done though to some degree she had had a predecessor in that role at Constantinople in Pulcheria in the fifth century. She also made a point of putting funds into new schools for girls and insisting that they needed education too if they were to be model and inspirational wives and mothers and in this vein set up her own 'trust' to which she encouraged leading society ladies to contribute – though there were very few female teachers and many ladies as well as men were nervous at letting men teach girls so progress was slow. The Emperor backed up his wife, citing the role of Livia under Augustus, and so did a number of more enlightened Rome society hostesses and leading abbesses across Italy and some of her Constantinopolitan female relatives joined in too and created a number of girls' schools for the elite in the city in the 580s and 590s. But to most of the Senate and the court – and the Church – the idea of teaching girls to do more than basic reading and writing and sewing/weaving was anathema and they could cite Roman and Greek tradition too. Against that, when challenged by preachers the Empress cited Pulcheria as her model and also spoke of the roles of Livia and of Septimius Severus' C3rd wife Julia Domna. When the more easy-going or liberal-minded poets in the late Emperor Gallus' circle, who Rillanus continued to back and fund, cited the example of the seventh century BC pioneering female poet Sappho that led to angry Church remarks about her reputation for 'unholy' sexual practices and the leading Roman Church theologians and their allies in the East also quoted St Paul on how women should stay silent and not presume to dictate to men. But Rillanus was as determined to extend the benefits of Roman culture and society to women as to the poor and under his rule the idea of female education, though limited to individual experimental schools in a few great cities if there were enough funders and teachers available, did at least emerge as part of the Imperial agenda – though in turn this helped to halt his initial 'honeymoon' with the Church and Pope Pelagius and assorted austere abbots who otherwise backed him were antagonistic to his wife and refused to associate with her or help her fund-raising.

One of the main funders of girls' schools in Constantinople was indeed also the first notable woman poet for centuries apart from the 420s-50s Empress Eudocia, the well-educated aristocrat Hegistrata of Nicaea who had been known to the Empress Dionysia and shared lessons with her as a girl. She was a devout and ecstatic Christian mystic who wrote about her experience of 'divine union' with Christ and the Virgin after fasting and praying so Patriarch John of Constantinople reluctantly approved of her work and inspiration to Christian devotion and helped her funding once she set up a nunnery in her mansion with herself as abbess in the late 580s. Her own work as abbess, educator and poet lasted through to the 620s and after Emperor Rillanus died his wife became an abbess herself and regularly visited her old friend, technically contrary to rules on abbesses leaving their convents, but the majority of bishops and theologians still regarded her and her work askance and frowned on educated women in general.

Rillanus himself did his best for education and regularly poured funds into setting up new schools in all those provinces – mostly the poorer and remoter ones – that were identified by his commission into education of 583–4 as needing them. He also required those schools once run by pagan temples in the classical era that had not been remodelled at conversion into Christian schools but shut down to be reopened under Imperial, Church, or private sponsorship so it should not be said that Christianisation had spoilt education. He regularly took promising boys from schools that had connections to the elite or the personnel of government (i.e. ones that could have their pupils' potential easily notified to the civil service and court) into service as junior clerks in the Imperial bureaucracy so they could advance to success and wealth if they were talented enough. Under him Rome was groping towards the idea of an Empire-wide examination system like that in China and the Emperor's 583–4 commission did recommend a series of quantifiable rules for recruiting boys to the civil service that could identify and estimate intellectual quality, but it was not until a Roman trade-mission to reunited Sui China in the 600s that this idea was to be transmitted to Rome, too late for this ruler. In the meantime Rillanus made sure to be available in person three afternoons a week on the judge's tribunal in the Basilica Julia in the Forum Romanum to receive petitions on injustice and hear from the complainers or their representatives in person, for which there were long queues – a haphazard and slow process, but meant to show him doing justice in person like a traditional Republican magistrate and with his clerks instructed to 'fast-track' the poor and visibly distressed to the front of the queue. (Once the public got wise to this, as wits mocked, clever litigants would dress in rags and fake collapse or bring along hired droves of 'their' children, the disabled, or elderly relatives.)

Rillanus attended the Games and theatre regularly but rarely bothered with court parties, abandoned many 'wasteful' court events, and refused to go hunting as it was cruel to animals. For most of the summer months he was away on extensive and exhausting tours of the provinces – Gaul in 583, the upper-middle Danube region and Marcomannia and Dacia in 584, Greece and Thrace in 585, Asia Minor and Syria in 586, and North Africa from Alexandria to Carthage and Numidia in 587 – where he also made himself available to the public and his other main concern was checking up on public works. He had doubts over the cost of the huge Diocletianic bureaucracy, not to mention its habits of self-satisfied obsession with rules, pay, and promotion and lack of responsiveness to the public. Thus the reforms carried out by his predecessors to cut inessential jobs were speeded up as a new commission investigated the system for effectiveness and speed of response to problems in 583–4 and as a result some 20 per cent of lower-ranked jobs were cut in the next decade. Most of the jobs lost went with the great regional 'vicarates', the rank of over-governors between the 'praeses' (provincial governors) and Praefects since the 290s, which were abolished in 586 though most incumbents were allowed to serve out their (usually five-year) terms. Many sacked junior officials were redeployed to work for new trusts that managed public works so that even bureaucrats did not end up starving. Rillanus would have liked to cut the army too but did not dare, not least as his brothers Carus and Claudius spent most of the 580s as rising army officers (Carus was 'dux' of Upper Moesia in 586–9 and Claudius ditto of Media in 586–8 and Lower Mesopotamia in 588–92) and might stir up a mutiny if the Emperor was too unpopular with the troops. Instead he played up the roles of the past soldiery as protectors of the public not expansionists and stressed how the army had saved Rome from the Gauls, Hannibal, the Seleucids, Mithradates of Pontus, Arminius in the reign of Augustus, the Sassanids and Goths in the 260s, and the Huns in the 440s and 450s.

The army continued at full strength and Rillanus was aware of the need for competent leadership and so 'fast-tracked' boys recommended as school 'stars' (but as fit and ambitious too) into the 'Protectores' as trainee officers. But he had no plans to extend the Empire despite the continuing disruption of the land 'Silk Road' across the Hindu Kush by brigands and invading steppe raiders and occasional clashes with the resurgent Hepthalites and other Turkic marauders in Sogdiana. Claudius and his circle of aggressive young officers wanted Rome to advance over the Hindu Kush to the Indus to remedy this and elements in the regional 'high command' at Ctesiphon agreed, but Rillanus regarded them as glory-seekers. He was not pleased when some pacifist local monks and preachers exposed them to him in a detailed petition in 587 as having secret interests in the local slave –trade (workers were needed to run the large 'latifundiae' corn-growing plantations of lower Mesopotamia) and wanting to get their hands on hundreds or thousands of Turks and mountain tribesmen as cheap slaves. The sea trade from Charax to northern India and from Aden to south-west India and Taprobane was flourishing and bringing in revenue and enriching merchants in Mesopotamia and Egypt so the tax-revenues from the region were healthy. Rillanus duly ruled out a new war and even agreed to hand back leased ports on the lower Red Sea's west coast to Abyssinia early as a goodwill gesture and banned Roman merchants in Nubia from shipping slaves to Egypt and so undercutting the price of labour in the Nile valley farms. In 588 he visited Egypt again for a journey up the Nile valley a year earlier than planned after reports of locust-caused distress among the starving poor there and organized the distribution of imported corn that he had brought along on his own galley and on its escorting fleet. His wife acquired new inspiration from the region's austere monasteries (except those that would not admit women visitors, even an Empress) and set up a new trust run by female as well as male nobility to create a new system of girls' schools in the province, pointing out that this was the land of female rulers Hatshepsut, Nefertiti, and the Cleopatras so this was nothing new. Rillanus met the king of Nubia on the frontier south of Aswan for a 'summit' and arranged a joint exploratory mission of geographers and soldiers up the Nile to look for its source – and to crack down on the local slave-trade. After Christmas in Jerusalem, where the Emperor joined his wife to tour religious sites and lavish gifts on them but was more interested in seeing that the religious custodians used the money they took from tourists for the poor and not for themselves. Rillanus sold off most of the Imperial estates in Palestine to pay for relief for the locust-plague and earthquake-hit rural inhabitants of Samaria and Galilee. He headed to Beyrutus to check on rebuilding there after an earthquake in 576, and then he sailed back to Rome without bothering to attend the spring military manoeuvre's in Syria as expected, in order to deal with a reported bullying scandal in an important privately-run orphanage in Veii whose owners had been leasing their inmates out as cheap labour to local farms and mines.

Rillanus was even more popular as the 'People's Emperor' after he had the victims of the 'scam' adopted by himself as his proteges and educated at a new institution at his own expense, and the offending officials ended up with the choice of begging on the streets or labouring in the mines themselves. But as he started to turn his long-term egalitarian Christian rhetoric to attacks on the selfish greed of the rich in the manner of St John Chrysostom (d. 407), the late Patriarch of Constantinople, and mused openly about how the rich had acquired their wealth, rumours were spread that it was not only tax-evaders that were at risk of his commissions. It was said that he intended to take on the 'get rich quick' mercantile success stories of Roman trade and business in general, driven by an urge to be the 'new Tiberius Gracchus', with redistribution of at least some over-large estates in the future. There was also trouble with both the Church and ultra-patriotic Roman authoritarians and revivalists when

Rillanus announced in early 590 that he intended to right the wrongs done to the pacific majority of the Jewish population by Hadrian's eviction of their ancestors from Judaea by giving all Jews the right to settle anywhere in their traditional lands, Jerusalem included, and restoring their confiscated holy sites. But the Emperor was undeterred and his sackings of various local officials in Palestine who his commissions had discovered had been using dubious (often forged) documentation to hang onto former Jewish property opened the way for a plethora of Jewish legal claims and for the indignant resignation of the provincial governor of 'Palestine I' (Judaea). Assorted police officials in Rome and major Italian cities were now investigated for dodgy practice after alarming cases of them 'framing' the poor to get conviction-rates improved were brought to the Emperor's attention by his young and earnestly moral commissioners. It is possible that angry police officials or associates of the sacked or resigned Palestinian officials were involved in the plot that seems to have developed at the end of Rillanus' long and exhaustive summer tour of Sicily, Epirus, Dalmatia, and Cisalpine Gaul in May – August 590 where he made a point of having dodgy legal documentation for the ownership of large estates investigated and rack renting by landlords reined in, producing more enemies with grudges to add to a long list.

On 18 September a supposed 'crazed lone assassin with a grudge' produced a hidden knife and killed the Emperor, aged thirty-one, as he was listening to supplicants at one of his justice sessions' at the Basilica Julia in Rome. His officials soon confirmed to the assembling and angry populace of the city that it was a 'one-off' attack by a ruined minor trader who had had an earlier legal appeal against a wealthier rival's bankruptcy claim on his property turned down due to inadequate evidence. But there were rumours that the man had been put up to it by police officials, anti-Jewish clerics, ruined landowners, war-hungry officers in the 'Scholae', or even a clique of nobles who regarded his quiet, unobtrusive, and cautious next brother Carus as a much more biddable ruler. The Emperor's bodyguards had not managed to intervene in time either as another litigant had been causing a disturbance elsewhere in the Basilica and that was rumoured to be no accident, but nothing could be proved and as Carus, on a state inspection tour of military facilities in Dacia, was recalled hurriedly to Rome the ministers insisted that there had been no larger plot. The sporadic riots that broke out in Rome, with several police posts and disgraced rich nobles' homes burnt, were put down with exemplary executions.

Chapter 16

Carus I 590–615: The Bureaucrat

Carus, aged twenty-seven might not be known or popular but at least he made a good and very moving address at his brother's state funeral and had a special mausoleum constructed for him near that of Augustus and Rillanus was proclaimed posthumously as 'Pius' and 'The People's Emperor', and as the coronation was kept very low-key and the public were mostly won round by a month of special Games the army and the Church greeted the new ruler with more enthusiasm. The respected and philanthropic new Bishop Gregorius of Rome (OTL Gregory 'the Great'), a long-standing church official and inter-Patriarchal negotiator who had made his name as a smooth and wise conciliator (and was a former noble of ancient family who had set up his own monastery in his family mansion until Pope Pelagius lured him to work for the Papacy in the late 570s), helped to ensure that the Church was duly sorrowful for the loss of the late Emperor and distanced itself from all the anti-Jewish rants by its personnel. It was clear that Gregorius, respected for his morals and austerity by Rillanus, had not had anything to do with clerical ravings about the late ruler as a menace and a heretic. As he kept up a tradition of philanthropy in his new role as Bishop the angry poor of Rome slowly calmed down and only a few of the local clergy who had been especially hostile to Rillanus in public faced attacks on their churches and needed bodyguards for months. But the police were targets of assault and arson for a long time and even the careful and emollient Carus had to replace those senior officers who were known to have hated the Emperor for having lazy or corrupt policemen sacked. Some loud-mouthed anti-Jewish and anti-Rillanus nobles were advised to leave Rome for a while and/or set up public works programmes in the late ruler's name to show their remorse. Carus kept on his brother's ministers and officially kept up all his projects too though in reality many of those aimed at large estates and dodgy businessmen were soon toned down. He was helped by the support of Dowager Empress Dionysia, who stayed in the Marble Palace to assist him until autumn 591 and then moved out to take over her own new convent in Perusia as abbess, and by his own beautiful socialite heiress fiancé Aurelia Drusilla who he married in spring 591. She turned out to be another 'public success' as Empress albeit more of a 'Society' leader and hedonist than her predecessor with a large collection of jewellery and another of dresses.

The new Emperor had done some military service with a degree of competence if not distinction, was regarded as more trustworthy in terms of his ideology and commitment to the Empire's expansion than Rillanus by his generals, and was advised by the latter and the 'comitatus' 'high command' of retired military men to unite the Empire by military success so people would forget the controversy about how and why Rillanus had been killed. That event was now leading some radical egalitarian Christian as well as pagan writers and speakers to allege that the court, the senior bishops, and the Rome police had conspired together to be rid of an embarrassment. Accordingly Carus held largescale military manoeuvres for the 'comitatus' near Mediolanum in summer 591 and had Claudius, now 'Master of Soldiers' in Mesopotamia, hold an Eastern series of manoeuvres at Edessa in spring 592 while military recruiting was increased and the antipiracy patrols of the 'Classis Britannica' and 'Classis Hibernica' were redoubled to catch Saxon, Danish and Irish pirates who were carted off in waggon-loads in chains to Rome for public execution at the Games for the delight of the populace. The demands that Claudius made for a major Eastern war to stop the 'hit and run' raids on Bactria and Sogdiana from both East (the Hindu Kush tribesmen) and North (the steppe nomads) were considered seriously and in 591 an embassy went to the current Hindu 'maharajah' ('great king') of the Gujarati peninsula to seek aid for a joint Roman and Indian 'pincer movement' on the restive and raid-sponsoring minor princes of the lower and middle Indus. But in the event the Eastern project was put aside as the current Ukrainian nomad power, the Avars whose 'Kagan' had overthrown the Utrigur Huns' hegemony in the early 580s was now in the position to threaten Roman interests and, like Attila, had need of loot and success to keep their warriors happy and loyal. The pro-Roman 'rump' state of the semi-nomad Bulgars in the Dniester region, usually referred to by antiquarian-minded Roman specialists and writers as 'Scythia' during the sixth century, had been defeated in battle by the 'Kagan' in 588 and many of its warriors had fled to the lower Danube or the Carpathian passes seeking refuge in Roman lands while others headed East to the Don out of the way of the Avar cavalry warriors. As this was not a threat on the scale of the Goths' arrival in 378 the humanitarian Rillanus had granted them refuge and so brought some 18–20,000 new horseback warriors (and their valuable herds of tough steppe horses) to the Roman army and many farmers to settle in the Danube valley. The district around Singidunum indeed now became known colloquially as 'Bulgaria', with its initially tent-dwelling pastoral nomad incomers with their herds of horses and sheep alien to the settled, Latin-speaking Roman farmers (many of the latter descendants of fourth-century Goths and fifth-century refugees from Attila) who despised and clashed with them. Nor were they quick to convert to Christianity and the local bishops, almost all of them urban sophisticates from the upper gentry or merchant families, ignored them and were duly criticized by the earnest poor-loving philanthropic hermits and preachers of Constantinople and the new monastic community of austere monks on the Bithynian Mount Olympus near Bursa. The threat of an Avar attack on the lower Danube was rising as the 'Kagan' sought to emulate Attila and show off to his warriors, and in 592 after unsuccessful Bulgar and Kutrigur Hun 'rebels' fled to the Empire the Avars pursued them over the Danube near Silistria and clashed with Roman forces.

That particular area of the river was currently short of Roman fast cavalry and archers due to a large contingent of men being absent at manoeuvres in Dacia so the Avars had the best of the clashes and for good measure looted farms and carried off slaves, and as Carus' subsequent complaint embassy to the 'Kagan' was jeered at and sent packing war followed. In 593 a large Roman army was assembled to raid north, carrying their provisions and stocks of arrows with them, to the Avar nomad camps on the Dniester and Dnieper. Carus delegated the rising Cappadocian commander Mauricius, a 'steady' and unflappable general (OTL: Eastern Roman Emperor 582 to 602) who had earned praise as 'dux' of Armenia in the mid-580s and had then put down maverick Alan raiders of north Atropatene as their 'dux' in 588–91, to take charge and locate and destroy the Avars. As a second large Roman army was ferried to the mouth of the Dnieper and thence moved on Avar territory from the east the Avars faced several columns of fast-moving Roman cavalry, a 'rearguard' of cavalry-protected infantry escorting artillery on a mission to attack any fortified camps, and mobile patrols of fast cavalry (some of them Arabs from the Arabian peninsula) ready to attack any Avars who sought to launch 'hit and run' raids. The Avars were larger in numbers due to all their steppe vassals having been summoned to send aid but lacked Roman firepower or armoured cavalry and had to retreat far up the Dnieper and evacuate their civilians in trains of waggons escorted by their flocks. But although Mauricius only made contact with a few smaller groups of the Avar rearguard he defeated them decisively and the Imperial spin-doctors' made the most of that and proclaimed the Avars to be defeated and in helpless retreat. The expectation that the Avars would sue for peace was not met and after returning to Constantinople for the winter Mauricius, now joined by the experienced Sogdian provincial cavalry commander Xenodorus with his Sogdian regional steppe nomad mercenaries and another 10,000 Arabs, had to repeat the 593 campaign in 594. But this time he had enough supplies to march and ride his men right up to the central Dnieper region and several of the Avars' junior sub-rulers lost heart and deserted their 'Kagan', who had fled into the Russian forests to hide his main forces there, and came to do homage and hand over hostages and some recovered Roman loot. This was played up as a great success and Mauricius was authorized to set up these warlords as Roman vassal-rulers on the lower Dniester as a 'buffer' to the main Avar empire, aided by Roman mercenaries and Roman money. New Roman fortresses were erected at the mouths of the Dniester and other, minor rivers and were supplied with enough artillery and food to be sure of defeating any Avar siege so the enemy was in effect – temporarily – put on the defensive. Carus also agreed to Mauricius' idea to set up a special command under a new 'dux' at the allied vassal-state of Cherson on the Crimea, a princely trading-city of fourth-century BC Greek origin, and arrange for a new Roman naval base to be built nearby at the harbour of 'Sebastopolis', 'August City' (OTL: Sebastopol) where Roman troops could now land regularly. From Cherson a series of Roman cavalry missions over the next few years proceeded to help the Avars' restive Eastern vassals on the lower Don attack the enemy each year and so keep them preoccupied. The Avar problem was however, not solved but only contained and as the new 'Count of the Avar Frontier' Mauricius, based on the lower Danube with authority over Cherson and the Dniester-mouth fortresses, proceeded to insist that his soldiers had to fight with their nomad allies against the Avars every summer and even winter (in small numbers) at their settlements to help protect them. This showed the dubious nomads that Rome was a trustworthy ally but annoyed the soldiers at all the hardship involved for which their abrasive commander did not bother to reward them.

> (The Avar and Lombard wars are based on reality, but are in different locations as demanded by the extent of the Empire in this TL. In reality the Lombards had started conquering war-ravaged and tax-hit Italy from 568.)

As well as the Avar war, Rome had to cope with a new outbreak of raiding over the Oder by the Langobards in the early 590s as their new warlord Agilulf disposed of several pro-Roman rivals who Emperor Gallus had subsidized to keep the peace, drove out their Christian missionaries as 'Roman agents', and tried to unite his perpetually feuding people with a war against the Empire and its Frankish clients. (In OTL, Agilulf was the king of the Lombards who had settled in northern Italy, 'Lombardy', by this time and spent the period fighting the Eastern Empire central Italy.) The late pro-Roman ruler Authari's Catholic widow Theodelinda managed to escape from being held hostage thanks to some fellow-Christians and fled across the Tatra mountains to the Carpathians to seek help from Roman frontier troops and was sent on to 'dux' Romanus of Dacia so the Emperor could pose as protector of the 'oppressed majority' of the Langobards in her name and portray Agilulf as a crazed despot keen for loot and driven by anti-Roman paranoia like Mithradates of Pontus in the first century BC. The king was the main *sotto voce* target of the winning, propagandist play 'The Threat of Mithradates' at the Rome theatrical festival in June 593, written by the classical enthusiast dramatist Leon of Megara (d. 625) whose re-interpretations of great events of the Late Republican era dominated theatrical competitions in Italy and Greece in the last two decades of the sixth century and the first two of the seventh century with Imperial support. In 594 a large-scale Roman expedition led by 'Count of the Rhine' Stratocles marched from Colonia Agrippinensis across Transrhenus, picking up Frankish mercenaries *en route*, to the Elbe to reinforce the main garrisons of 'Germania Ulterior' which had been holding out since the previous autumn's large-scale Langobard invasion, their fortifications too strong for the poorly-armed 'barbarians'. The Langobards were routed as they tried to prevent the relief of the fortress-town of 'Colonia Portilana' (Potsdam) and lost so many men in a wave of charges that they had to retreat across the Oder. A second Roman army from the Dacian region then crossed the Carpathians Northwards to complete the rout, led by the generals Cometiolus (OTL) and Marcus Plautius. Elite bodies of Roman cavalry occupied the main Langobard strategic points on the upper Vistula, burning the wooden Langobard forts and halls there, to clear the area and drive the locals into the forests to hide; Roman infantry then arrived to build new fortifications (earth banks, wooden palisades and trenches not stone as the latter was hard to find). The undefended or poorly-defended towns, villages and farms of the province had been systematically devastated and looted by the Langobards and the surviving residents had either fled or been enslaved, Agilulf handing thousands of them to his steppe allies as a reward for their help in the invasion. As a result the carefully-created Roman rural and urban structure of the new province, populated by a mixture of Romans and Germans, had been wrecked and there was no enthusiasm by the refugees who had streamed into Tranrhenus in 593 to return despite all the Roman propaganda about victory.

Agilulf had escaped to the steppes and the Romans could hardly occupy the whole of the large Langobard (and vassals') realm that stretched from the Oder east across the Vistula to the Bug and the Pripyat. Though a few strategists at the 'command HQ' of the 'comitatus' in Mediolanum were advising Carus to put an end to the German menace for good and annex all their territory to the edge of the Russian forests, i.e. the Pripyat marshes, he blanched at the likely cost and it was too ambitious for this essentially timid man. The economy of Germania Ulterior was ruined and new settlers would have to be found and Carus judged that that was a large enough problem, so in 595 the Romans were instructed to evacuate the occupied Langobard territories by their Emperor and in place of the expected new Roman province a submissive cousin of Agilulf who he had tried to murder and driven into hiding, Grimoald, was installed as the new puppet-king, married off to Theodelinda, converted to Christianity, and persuaded to sign a treaty of vassalage and accept a mercenary bodyguard of 6000 Romans (mostly of Germanic origin and family connections and speaking German as well as Latin) to garrison his wooden 'capital', Posnonia (Poznan). The fear that Agilulf had aroused by his purges of the squabbling nobility meant that a significant part of the latter signed up to become Roman vassals and Catholics and to help keep Grimoald on the throne and this unlikely king lasted for three decades with Roman help so the war was to some degree successful. But the 'official' Langobardic kingdom now only reached as far East as the forests beyond the Vistula as the east of the realm broke away and was later taken over by Agilulf (598) and Carus notably failed to evict him or risk starting any new wars. The ethnic 'make-up' of the devastated province of 'Germania Ulterior' sharply altered following the war of 593–4 as very few Romans would now live there and it was mostly handed over to Germans, mainly a mixture of Franks, Goths, and surviving Vandals, who were by now mostly Catholic but were only imperfectly Romanised and mostly had beards (still rare in the Roman Empire except the Levant and Persia), wore trousers not togas or short tunics, lived in wooden halls, and listened to elaborate heroic sagas as they quaffed their outlandish drinks at boozy feasts. Indeed the horror-stories of Langobards committing cannibalism on captured Romans and sacrificing their soldiers to their pagan gods were so widespread that the naïve Carus found that all his speeches and written calls for 'civilised Romans' to move to Germany and carry the frontier of 'Romanitas' North to the Baltic in the 590s and 600s were ignored and even some of the Roman settlers in Transrhenus who had fled in the panic of 593 never returned.

The Christian mission in Langobardia succeeded in affiliating a new network of bishops and priests to the Church in Rome and most of Grimoald's court converted thanks to the great work carried out by Queen Theodelinda, who visited Rome as her husband's envoy in 601 and was treated with great honour. But the only concrete territorial gains of the war for Rome were a string of fortresses set up in the upper Vistula region, centred on the rock of Cracovia (Cracow), to watch the region for more trouble and stop attacks from the 'rebel' east of Langobardia on Grimoald's regime. But the grateful king did send a regular 'tribute' of 500 boys a year to be trained as Roman soldiers on the Danube and join the Roman army and many of these later returned home as agents of Romanization in the 620s and 630s. In the short term the 'failure' to annex Langobardia, financially wise but annoying to the militaristic public as well as the more aggressive generals, damaged Carus' reputation and he was seen as the man who had let the region slip out of Roman hands. Though it is probable that those chauvinist senators who made rude speeches in the next few years complaining that an elective not 'primogeniture' process for selecting the Emperor would have chosen the more capable Claudius to rule were put up to it by the latter, rumours about his loyalty spread.

Nor did the Empire bother to intervene in trouble within the Merovingian Frankish vassal-state after the death of its queen-regent Fredegund in 597 as assorted nobles fought to control the government of her under-age son King Chlotar II. In 599 the Gothic princess who had been thwarted of the throne when the late king Chilperic married Fredegund not her, the ambitious Brunhilde (named after a legendary heroine from Rhineland myth), returned from two decades away in Gaul making her fortune to use her money and bodyguard to seize power. The widow of a prominent Romano-German business tycoon and vineyard entrepreneur in the Moselle valley who had died suddenly (suspiciously, some said) leaving her all his fortune and leaving out his kin, Brunhilde had made a big impression as a generous philanthropist and founder of girls' schools in Gaul at the court of Rillanus and convinced his wife Dionysia of her credentials and piety so her foes had failed to get hold of her husband's money in the courts. Now she was a friend of the Empress Aurelia Drusilla, but her blatantly illegal coup and purge of her enemies at the Frankish court left some senior generals in neighbouring Roman provinces keen to use this chance to annex the Frankish kingdom and make up for the disgrace of losing out on Langobardia. They and nobles keen to win estates in an annexed new province were probably behind the stories that Carus had been bribed by Brunhilde to look the other way while she took over the kingdom. All this added to his growing unpopularity, and he blithely ignored advice from the blunt and practical Mauricius in winter 601–2 to let him annex some of the 'Sarmatian' steppes around the Dniester for Roman farming, protected by a network of forts, to restore his military prestige as a 'conqueror'. Indeed only months later some of Mauricius' troops at the mouth of the Dniester mutinied against his harsh orders and parsimony and sent him fleeing for his life so his plans to use them to annex a large swathe of territory were probably as unrealistic as Carus reckoned.

(Chlotar and the other Frankish elite are real people, from the Merovingian Frankish kingdom which in OTL was in Gaul not northern Germany. The 'Victory Riot', below, is inspired by the OTL 'Nika Riots', 'Nika' meaning 'Victory' in Greek, against Justinian in Constantinople in 532. This part of the timeline was created by me aged around eleven, along with the names of the sixth- and seventh century- Emperors.)

The simmering discontent with the Emperor, fair or not, erupted into a famous and unexpected outbreak of violence in Rome itself on 18–20 September 602 in the 'Victory Riot' (so-called after the catchphrase shouted by the rioters). The annual 'Ludi Romani' Games had seen not exactly new but worse than usual cheating by the rival racing factions based at the Circus Maximus, the four 'Demes' (Blues, Greens, Whites, and Reds), and for once Carus tried a crackdown as he had a popular charioteer disqualified for allegedly paying a groom to put doped potions in the feed of a rival so that he won with a new and untried team of horses and his backers made a fortune in bets. The shady business and courtier backers apparently feared that their 'patsy' charioteer would talk about who had paid him to save his career so they had him rescued from the police and spirited out of Rome. But Carus blamed his racing-club, the Blues, and banned them from appearing at the rest of the Games or the next due public racing-days until the errant charioteer handed himself in to the authorities. Their supporters then rioted in the Circus and climbed down onto the race-track to block the course and stop the rest of the races. For once their rivals the Greens supported them, possibly to frighten the government off a current investigation into a betting-scam at their own club, and a large mob started to abuse the Emperor and shout that he had let Langobardia slip from Roman hands and his wife had been bribed by her friend Brunhilde the Frankish queen to leave her takeover of the Merovingian kingdom go unchallenged. The Emperor sent in his guards from the 'Scholae' to clear the Circus of rioters and re-start the races, but the task took most of the day as the racing-factions' toughs and volunteer hooligans fought back. The evicted rioters were still battling it out in the streets outside the Circus when the factions' refusal to race again for the rest of the Ludi led to the audience being sent home and getting caught up in the battle. Some civilians were killed accidentally by a police 'hit squad' that was trying to isolate and capture leading rioters and those who tried to rescue them were attacked too, so next day a large and angry crowd of poorer civilians aided the faction rioters in setting up barricades in the streets East of the Colosseum. They were chased out of there in a few hours of fighting as more Guards arrived but then fled up the Caelian Hill to erect more barricades.

 With the rioters throwing tiles onto the Guards' heads the latter had to retreat, and as fires were started most of the wooden buildings on the Caelian and other buildings downhill to the north were burnt down with the 'Vigiles' (fire service/ watchmen) unable to put the fires out. The riots were eventually put down after two days of fighting as the Guards charged the mob on horseback and retook the occupied area house by house, but a large area of Rome around the Caelian was left in ruins and over 2000 people were killed and the disaster shook the Empire with lurid stories of a mass popular uprising and most of Rome in flames. (In fact most of Rome was unaffected and as built of stone or marble would not burn anyway.) The capital fell into peace out of sheer exhaustion and Carus and his wife launched a large-scale public relief effort to feed the homeless and then organized the rebuilding of the ruined area, in efforts worthy of the 'People's Emperor' Rillanus. The clearance of badly-planned houses and narrow streets east of the Colosseum enabled the Imperial city-planners to extend the 'Mese' avenue West to the Colosseum Square and erect a large new 'Baths of Carus' and 'Hospital of Carus and Aurelia Drusilla' on the Caelian to show Imperial munificence.

Architecturally Rome was improved by the new area built after the riots and the local slums were cleared, but wits still joked that the town-planner Emperor had had this ancient area of Rome burnt down deliberately by the Guards during the riot so he could show off his abilities as a planner, like Nero with the 'Great Fire' and post-fire building in AD 64. Rumour had it that Claudius had heard that his brother had been deposed by the Senate after he fled Rome in a panic during the riots and he had been on alert to rush from the east to Rome and take over. Despite all his relief-efforts and his giving pensions to the widows and children of civilians – except those working for the racing – factions who had started the riots – killed in the fighting Carus' reputation did not recover from the riots. It was openly said in the Senate that he could have regained control earlier had he been more ruthless or more careful on the first day of the battles, and the police who had inflamed the riots by accidentally killing civilians who had 'got in the way' of their initial charges onto the rioters were never prosecuted. Nervous Praefect of Rome Honoratus Anicius, a bumbling member of an ancient family whose illustrious career owed more to 'networking' and his ambitious and clever wife than to his own competence, argued to Carus that this would be bad for morale. As the capital was largely hostile and Carus' banning of all public races for six months (to allegedly balance the budget due to the cost of rebuilding) did not help either he spent most of 603 on a large-scale tour of Gaul, the Rhineland, Rhaetia, and Noricum and spent the winter in Vindobona (Vienna) taking personal charge of the resettlement of nervous Transrhenus refugees from the 593–4 war who still had no long-term homes on new farms. He also required his 'ally' Queen Brunhilde to admit more excluded members of the Frankish elite, foes of her regime and/or allies of the late Queen Fredegund, to her government so that she could have a more stable basis for her rule and was not seen as so 'tyrannical'. This was a move which in the long run benefited the Empire by bringing the young and talented, Rome-educated Frankish nobles Pepin of Lamden and Bishop Arnulf into the government. With the young king Chlotar II now proclaimed adult and his regent forced to retire from that role and share power Carus stabilised the problematic ally and by receiving and giving more aid and civilian advisers to Queen Theodelinda of the Langobards during that winter at Vindobona he also helped the Langobard vassal-state stabilise and hold back the incursions of raiders loyal to the exiled Agilulf. But he did not receive any thanks from the militant expansionist poets or generals back in Rome and as a Rome-allied king of Abyssinia fell to a coup by rebel generals angry at his country's 'vassalage' to the Empire in 604 and a major Avar attack occurred on Rome's new steppe allies on the lower Don in 605, both without any reprisals, Carus was regarded as a hopelessly cautious bureaucrat by swashbuckling officers in army bases across the Empire.

The major civil initiative of the final decade of Carus' reign was seen at the time as being a typical bureaucratic manoeuvre by this careful and 'plodding' ruler, and to later devotees of Imperial centralization and dynamic government as not going far enough in reform. But it was in practice a major shift in emphasis for the recruitment and 'career structure' of officials in government with a move away from the old practice of buying offices, both in the form of entering junior (or more senior) posts in the Imperial bureaucracy and in subsequent promotion. A trade and orthodox/ catholic missionary delegation had been sent by sea to the capital of the new centralised Sui dynasty government of China a few years earlier, with Rome university geographers and junior Imperial bureaucrats accompanying them to make reports on what they saw and the layout of the region's states, their governments, their major imports and exports, their military structure and practices, local agriculture, and other important or potentially useful matters. This returned to the Empire via Aden and Alexandria in 604 and reported to Carus in Rome that winter. The Emperor and his vigorous – and self-made, humbly-born – 'Master of Offices' Livius Secundinus were particularly interested in the Chinese examination-system whereby students from all the provinces of the Empire, of all backgrounds, were encouraged to apply for and sit examinations in basic knowledge and the essential 'Classic' texts of the Chinese liberal arts in an annual round of such tests in the provincial capitals. The results were then marked and the best-placed contestants were enrolled as junior civil servants and trained to serve in the nation-wide bureaucracy, at least in theory. In fact the practice of local governors recommending their 'best' young scholars (not always selected on examination-results, more often a matter of personal recommendation of proteges) had been common though not universal for centuries and a formal, examination-results-based universal 'system' was a recent innovation by the Sui. The more successful and competent duly progressed by promotion every few years up the 'cursus honorum' (as Romans would call it) to senior office, and could end up in charge of one of the half-dozen or so senior ministries in the capital, Nanjing in the Yangtze valley of southern China – later to be moved north to the old Han capital in the north, Chang-an, by the Tang dynasty. The new system that the Sui ministers showed off to the Roman embassy struck Secundinus as ideally suited for Rome's bureaucracy too and a way to weed out favouritism, promotion by bribery or using your family wealth, and complacency by those who sought an easy life at a junior level with family money to support them and did not bother to carry out their duties competently or else paid their clerks to do the real work. He pointed this out to the Emperor – with a reminder that he and Rome had paid dearly for the failure of the local bureaucrats in Rome to get a grip on either betting-scandals in the Circus Maximus racing-factions (which were supposed to be supervised by the City government) or the brutality and laziness of the police before the 'Victory Riot' in 602.

Accordingly Carus set up a commission to look into the question of a Roman examination-system for recruiting junior civil servants in 605, and on their approving report to him two years later he introduced a 'trial' system of examinations. This was in the essentials of learned Latin writing, arithmetic (much improved by the adoption of Indian numerals as now recommended to the Imperial Council by traders, '1 to 10' etc, to replace 'I to X' etc. and to introduce the zero in the 580s), basic knowledge of the Roman political system and history, and cultural literary 'classics' in Italy, Gaul, Spain, and Illyria in 608. This series of annual examinations, judged by a panel of recommended senior teachers and where possible university lecturers in each of the provinces involved, then led to a list of successful candidates being 'adopted' for the Imperial bureaucracy and awarded junior posts in their home provinces before transfer elsewhere on promotion and if so recommended an invitation to work in Rome. With around 300 candidates being taken up for posts as a result of the first round of examinations it was also arranged that the so far rather haphazard of timetabling promotions should be made more regular and more centrally controlled to enable the capable and successful to stand a reasonable chance of advancing to relatively high rank in around fifteen years. It was resisted by the lazy, slack, and work-averse and also by those who regarded a bureaucratic post as a respectable but not too onerous way of earning money to supplement a dignified and ostentatious lifestyle as a 'gentleman', a 'vir honestiores'. The new system was slow to advance genuinely capable young men who passed the first series of examinations to senior office – some of the 608 successes did not reach high rank until the late 630s. There was also the problem that candidates had to have a reasonable level of education and knowledge to stand a chance in the examinations. As schooling in the Empire was haphazard and mostly down to private initiative (or by the Church) the middle and upper classes stood a far greater chance of passing the examinations and very few poor boys could pass unless they had had luck in acquiring a good education – also a problem in China, and not noticed by the Roman embassy there as it drew up its report. But it was a start and it introduced a greater degree of meritocracy into selections for the civil service and speeded up promotion, and with a special 'Board for the Examinations' running the examinations and the subsequent appointments at Empire-wide level and issuing orders to the local examination-boards the system was judged successful enough by Carus and Secundinus in 614 to be extended to the other Mediterranean provinces and to Mesopotamia which had high urbanization and more schools than the outer provinces in the west and north of the Empire. The system was also kept up by Carus' brother and successor, Claudius III, despite its cost, as he was a fan of meritocracy and hated lazy and pampered upper-middle-class 'amateur' officials who did not bother to work hard.

In retrospect the new initiative was a great success, though it was seen by most traditionalist observers and angry great nobles at the time as a bizarre and un-Roman innovation and some poets and wits condemned it as either 'Persian' or else a hangover from the bureaucratic system of Ptolemaic Egypt on which some of Carus' learned Alexandria university advisers were experts. It gave a new sense of purpose to a government shaken by the 'Victory Riot', and the same could be said of the conquest of the fertile lands of the Danish and Jutish peoples in the Jutland peninsula in the late 600s which Carus now launched to acquire more fertile agricultural land for Roman and local German settlers reassuringly safe from more steppe incursions from the east (a factor which was impeding settlement in war-ravaged Germania Ulterior). The formally stable Danish kingdom of late sixth-century ruler Eric of Odense had been broken up among his three sons around 600 and they were engaged in a series of wars while uncontrolled local coastal warlords had been raiding Britain again. To the South the Saxon-Jutish lord Ceawlin (OTL: Ceawlin, king of Wessex in England), son of a returned 'ex-patriate' soldier in Roman service in Britain (and with a British mother) and in possession of Roman military skills and his British relatives' gold, had been building up a new kingdom and forcing the local Saxons on the Frisian coast into slavery so some of them had fled to Roman lands to appeal for help. The war-hungry Prince Claudius was recalled from the east to take charge of the war with the aid of 'dux' John 'the Frank' of Lower Germany and the 'Count of the Rhine' Pacatius. In 605 a large naval expedition was carried by the 'Classis Britannia' from Londinium to western Jutland to land in the creeks north of Ceawlin's realm and join up with rebels against his authority while more troops were taken into the Skaggerak and landed on Fynen island to back up one of the three rival Danish kings, Harald, who had seen the advantages of coming to terms with overwhelming Roman power and offering to be a vassal-ruler if he could be helped to remove his anti-Roman brothers. More Roman troops under Claudius with artillery, backed up by local Franks under Chlotar's loyal aides duke Fredegar and Pepin of

Lamden and assorted Saxon mercenaries who feared Ceawlin's potential as a foe, crossed the 'Danevirke' dyke into Jutland and took Ceawlin in the rear while he was fighting the north-west Jutland landing. As Rome had overwhelming superiority in weaponry and numbers plus wide-ranging and fast armoured cavalry the Jutish realm soon crumbled and Ceawlin was killed in battle with his son Cuthwine, his nephew Ceol having deserted to Claudius in return for a promise of lands and gold.

The Danish kingdom of Harald's brother Guthrum, centred on the town of Aarhus on eastern Jutland's coast, was next to be overwhelmed. Once the king had been defeated in open battle despite his force of 'berserkers' (suicidal naked warriors drunk and driven by a promise of eternal glory in the halls of the Otherworld's home for dead heroes, Valhalla, to throw themselves at the Roman front line) the open farmland was overrun and the wooden triple-lined fortifications of Aarhus were burnt down by bombardment. By the end of 605 the Romans had all of Jutland in their hands and the brutal Claudius had ordered 8,000 captured Danish warriors and 2,000 Jutes to be taken off as slaves to work in the mines of Marcomannia and various Roman provincial bridge-building projects for ten years – survivors were then to be released (as a sop to the Church whose Pope Gregorius disapproved of slavery) and sent off to work as tenant farmers far from Denmark. The surrendered prince Ceol the Jute and various leading Danish nobles who had come over to Rome were allowed to keep their lands as encouragement for others to defect. But the rest of Jutland was opened for settlement, mainly to Romans and Germans who were in need of land but unwilling to settle in Germania Ulterior. A network of small farms were set up there and later on Fynen too, the menfolk serving the Roman army part-time as 'limitanei' to assist the new Roman occupation-force and farms with at least three sons having to send one of them to join the Roman army overseas. To please the Church – though Claudius was at most a formal Catholic and he did not like either social egalitarianism or pacifism and regarded monks as 'draft-dodgers' – the Danish and incoming German populations had to become Catholic like the Romans and a network of bishops and priests were set up. But the Church acquired very little land or other wealth as Claudius and his first civilian governor of 'Dania', veteran Rhineland administrator Cassius Conidianus, wanted small farmers serving part-time in the army to dominate the province and also very few towns were set up as trading-prospects were poor except in agricultural goods and few Roman traders bothered to move there.

The rebuilt Aarhus, as the new town of 'Augusta Arhanorum' with a new Roman fortress and naval base there, and Harald's wood-built capital of Odense (annexed with the rest of his kingdom on his death in 628 and renamed 'Civitas Danorum Odensium')were turned into Roman towns with a square 'grid' layout and the usual Roman buildings and civic amenities. But the rural Danes and the mostly rural, farm-dwelling incoming Germans were not attuned to urban Roman life and the region remained mainly rural and a noted cultural backwater for centuries though the Church managed to set up a successful network of schools that produced a higher level of male literacy than in Germany, sending off many ambitious boys with no farms to inherit to work in the Roman civil service and trade across north-west Europe. There was also interest in the national cultural tradition of heroic warfare sagas that produced such literature as the local eighth–century epic 'Beowulf'. Meanwhile the relentless and glory-seeking Claudius went on in 606 to land on the main, eastern Danish island of Zeeland and reduce its king, Harald's ruthless and defiant brother Sven, and his lords to vassalage or slavery with military defeat, the burning of their wooden halls, and occupation of the entire island. The king surrendered once he had lost two battles in succession and was allowed to keep a third of the island as a puppet-ruler, minus all fortified positions and most of his army, but ended up deported to a remote farm in Dacia in 612 when Claudius heard that he was plotting revolt; the majority of the farmer nobility were also deported and Roman or German farmers acquired their lands in small estates.

The former royal hall and fortified town / naval base at Cobnhavn on the East side of the island was razed and turned into the new capital of Dania from 610, the Roman town and military base of 'Claudiana', and with Danish sailors impressed to help build a new Roman naval base and fleet nearby and 200 Roman 'dromones' (oared galleys) and 100 sailing-ships based there to create the new 'Danish Straits Fleet' the Romans now dominated the entrance to the Baltic. Merchants could move in to export amber, furs, tar, and timber from the upper Baltic by sea without having to rely on the previous route of dubious roads and tracks north from the Carpathians. Refugee Danish warriors fled across the Sound to Scania and tried to interest the king of the Geats, Wigmund, and his neighbour the king of the inland Swedes at Uppsala (Olaf 'the Virtuous') in fighting on. But after what had happened to the Danish kings neither of them was interested although it took crude threats of invasion and annihilation by Claudius to get Olaf to surrender the refugees at his court. With Roman embassies signing trade-deals with the two kingdoms their elites accepted Roman gold and a regular subsidy of cheap luxury goods in return for surrendering the Danish 'trouble-makers' to be taken off to Rome for Claudius' victory Triumph in 607. The Romans annexed a new town and military base at Malmo on the Geatish side of the Straits to keep an eye on the Geats and the Swedes and sporadic raiding across the Straits for loot and slaves by bored warlords soon resumed, but for all practical purposes Claudius had secured the Danish kingdoms intact to join the 'Pax Romana' and the 'civilised' Roman world and after the setbacks of the 590s in northern Germany this success made him hugely popular, not least with the Church for his gaining of extra people for Christianity.

Pope Gregorius (OTL: Pope Gregory 'the Great'), rebuilding his Church's and his own see's reputation with the civilian elite after the setbacks of the 580s as a shining exemplar of moral leadership and keeping out of politics, made a point of personally redeeming Danish and Jutish slaves in the slave-markets of Rome and presented the war as extending Christianity and enabling heathen Danes who sacrificed their war-captives to Woden to turn into model Romans. But Carus was more equivocal about giving all the credit to his ambitious brother and though he only had one son (Carus, born in 602) and his health was declining under the effects of arthritis and a lung condition he refused to let his brother talk him into becoming 'Caesar' and was said to have determined to live until his son was adult to deny Claudius the throne. He certainly took great care of his health and spent much of his time from the later 600s visiting provinces with health spas, spending time at the medicinal baths of Augusta Viciorum in southern Gaul in 606, Aquae Sulis in Britain in 607, and Spalata in Dalmatia in 609 during regional tours and in winter 609–10 starting a regular habit of wintering in Sicily or Corcyra not Rome. But Claudius was allowed no access to power and after his 607 triumph had to stay in Dania as 'dux' and 'Count of the North Sea Provinces' until 610 and was then sent back to the eastern Mediterranean and Euxine to collect troops and mount an invasion of the Avars' homeland from Cherson in 611.

This latest attempt to respond to Avar raids on 'Scythia' and the overthrow of Rome's puppet-rulers on the Don by marching 40,000 Roman infantry and 20,000 cavalry across the steppes to the middle Dnieper was no more successful than the last one as the Avars evaded battle again and burnt the steppes behind them so the Romans had to march across miles and miles of smouldering grassland without a sign of the enemy. But at least they kept their supplies intact and only lost a few men to ambushes and the lightweight Roman war-galleys that Claudius had brought along could be lifted out of the water at the Dnieper rapids and carried above the latter to be re-launched, enabling the Roman navy to head upstream as far as the rocky eminence of what the local Slav farmers (Avar tributary vassals) called 'Kiev'. The Roman commanders despised the disunited and unmilitary Slavs, who had tamely given up their independence to fight for and supply food and troops to the Avars, as no use as allies and Claudius duly decided against enrolling them as a new ally and setting up a Rome-aided local kingdom to undermine the Avars. But he did agree to letting hundreds (later thousands) of young and impoverished Slavs who were short of land and tired to being exploited as serfs by the Avars march down the Dnieper to the Roman ports at the river mouth and be enrolled as Roman soldier-farmers. In the next decade many of them were resettled as 'limitanei' in lower Moesia or in new fortified settlements North of the Danube in 'Scythia' to boost the Avar-ravaged, disheartened local Germans and Kutrigur Bulgars there. Another Roman army under the rising general Heraclius of Cappadocia, son of the 600s' governor of North Africa/ Carthage, had meanwhile marched up the Don hundreds of miles to the NE of the Sea of Azov and linked up with the Avars' local foes, the Khazars, and this proved of more military worth as the latter were more militaristic and also had large cavalry forces and they were more than happy to aid Rome in fighting the Avars who had been harassing them for a decade.

Thanks to this 611 expedition and a 'follow-up' one by Heraclius' deputy commander Petronius in 612 the Khazars agreed to supply Rome with fast-moving steppe cavalry and attack the Avars from the east each year. From then on the Avars were kept busy by the Khazars and their attacks on the Empire decreased with Rome supplying them with weapons and gold up the Don from their new fortress at the north-eastern end of the sea of Azov, 'Heraclea Romana', and Heraclius himself served as 'dux' of Cherson from 612–20 with Claudius' full confidence as virtual viceroy of the region. The orthodox conversion of the Khazars to Christianity also commenced and by the early 620s a bishopric had been set up at their camp-style main 'town' at the mouth of the Volga onto the Caspian Sea. But once the Avars had been contained Claudius abandoned his interest in the steppes north of the Euxine and, denied another triumph by his suspicious brother, did his best to pressurize the latter into allowing him to start a Sogdian war to march to the Khyber Pass on the excuse of suppressing banditry and protecting the 'Silk Road' land-route to India. Carus was not interested and tension between them resumed after a failed military 'planning summit' at Mediolanum after the grand military manoeuvres for sections of all the armies in the west there (Claudius' idea) in summer 613, but on 28 April 615 Carus died suddenly of a heart-attack after a day at the Games in Rome, aged fifty-two, and as his son Carus was only thirteen, the hastily summoned ministers agreed to Claudius succeeding as Emperor and had him elected by the Senate on the 29th. (Heraclius, the OTL Byzantine emperor in 610-41, and other generals are OTL.)

Chapter 17

Claudius III 615–630: The Conqueror

Aged forty-seven, Claudius was not universally popular given his brash and autocratic character and his fondness for autocratic solutions and military-style discipline, but his foe Pope Gregorius had died in 612 and the Empress Aurelia Drusilla, not interested in politics so not a potential 'Augusta' Pulcheria, agreed to his succession provided that he would proclaim her son Carus as 'Caesar' and heir. As Claudius had no son he went along with this and pretended to honour his late brother's memory despite being known to have despised him for decades and made assorted disloyal noises about the army having a duty to depose him if he vetoed any more wars. His wife Marcia Drusilla, younger sister of the previous Empress, was a moral and well-meaning woman and a traditional Roman aristocratic lady of the less assertive variety, more interested in her family (they had four daughters hut no son), religious festivals, philanthropy, and displays of piety than in politics, and the brusque and hard-nosed Claudius was less of a philistine than he seemed – or pretended to be. He also kept on most of his late brother's more competent ministers but was obsessed with detail, order, and obedience and sought to turn the Empire, like the army, into a smoothly-running machine where he and his advisers made the decisions and everybody else did what they were told. He had no time for argument or slackness after a decision had been made but was open to quite radical ideas until that point if they seemed likely to work, and he was also a meritocrat like Rillanus and had no more time than that ruler had had for the corrupt and lazy though he was far harsher and more unforgiving. His personal models were said to be the blunt, efficient, and pragmatic emperors Vespasian (d. AD 79) and Trajan (d. 117), and he was certainly as effective but brutal as them in warfare.

Keeping on the late ruler Carus' experimental examinations system to recruit civil servants and extending it slowly over more, literate provinces through the later 610s and 620s and recruiting more examiners and assessors each year, he saw the point of using it to bring talented working-class men into the government. He did his best (not altogether successfully) to stop dim upper-class candidates bribing others to sit the examinations for them and then switching the results This was a major problem but one which generally was covered up by 'paid off' junior examiners who needed the money that they were given in bribes, and he also increased the pay of and honorary ranks given to the middle-ranking Rome and provincial civil servants to encourage aspiring young men to apply to join the service and when he was in Rome presided in person at annual ceremonies to give out awards and titles to those who were successful in securing promotion. He also did his best to see that competent teachers were recruited to those schools that the government had some influence over (e.g. as financial sponsors or if they rented government buildings) and he bullied the Church into selecting senior teachers and headmasters for their schools on the basis of competence not just piety. But his plan to make sure that the Church co-operated in this by setting up a 'Religious Education Commission' board to oversee recruitment of Church school teachers and conduct inspections was not liked. It was often subverted by its members working with the local Church, and he could not rely on the Popes and the regional Patriarchs to assist him either despite his constant stream of official letters to them on this and his all-Empire 'Church Councils' – called to create new and enforce new and old disciplinary 'canons'/ rules, not to alter doctrine – in winter 616–17, 621–2, and 626–7. He was unaware until one humbly-born senator told him that schools in poorer urban areas or rural villages rarely had good enough teachers to educate boys to examination standards, and was shocked at this though he blamed the teachers for lack of motivation. His informant wanted more universities and the Church to use resources to train teachers, but Claudius did not trust their competence and disliked 'pacifist' monks as 'un-Roman'. He famously declared that the main agents of creating the ideal, dedicated and obedient Roman citizen working for the Empire should be 'bread and the birch' (i.e. plain food and the fear of physical punishment), starting at school. Slovenly soldiers should be sent off to 'penal' work in junior roles at isolated outposts if they did not live up to their duty or evaded carrying out what was expected of them. Though his harshness caused some grumbles, he was relentlessly fair in seeing that all soldiers had adequate food, clothing, and weapons on campaign or in garrison-duties and that they could rely on their officers to obey the regulations so mutinies were scarce.

Claudius also believed in the 'mission' of the Empire to extend its rule and its civilizing role, cut down the proud and the aggressively un-Roman, and bring justice and civilization, as set out by Vergil, and in that cause now he had full control of the reins of power he reversed Carus' military caution. He arranged for the long-delayed Eastern war to commence quickly with troops and supplies being sent east later in 615 and his 'General Staff' at the 'comitatus' HQ in Mediolanum 'war-gaming' possible scenarios and going through intelligence reports in the meantime. The Avars were capable of finding out that the Empire would be distracted in Asia for years and attacking the Roman clients in 'Scythia' or the Khazars on the Don in the meantime so in 615–16 Heraclius at Cherson led a large-scale military 'embassy' to Itil to supply weapons and mercenaries to the Khazars and enable them to fight off any Avar attacks. New fortifications were constructed on the lower Dniester as an 'early warning system' to hold up any Avar attacks on the lands to the south-west of the river, the garrisons containing enough cavalry to harass any Avar forces who tried to bypass them and head on towards the Danube. A military force from Marcomannia and Dacia aided the Langobard kingdom of Grimoald in raiding Agilulf's 'rebel' state to their east to keep that foe of Rome on the defensive and the allied Geats and Swedes were called upon to land troops in Lituwa (the tribal lands of the Lithuanian pagans at the east end of the Baltic) and attack Agilulf from the north-west. So with the main potential foes of Rome duly cowed in winter 616–17 Claudius resided at Constantinople to hold military manoeuvres for his Balkan armies there before heading east in the spring to Antioch. Other troops from across the Empire were shipped by sea to Antioch's port Seleucia Pieria, Beyrutus, the nearby ports of Byblos and Tyre, the new Phoenician port of Tripolis, or Ptolemais in northern Palestine and marched into Mesopotamia while the Alans supplied mercenaries via Adiabene and the Persian provinces' levies, trained in the Roman manner apart from their own equestrian and archery specialities, assembled at Istakr and Zadracarta and the Bactrians gathered at Balkh.

In July 617 Claudius led an army of some 80,000 East from Ctesiphon to Alexandria-in-Arachosia where the local troops, led by 'dux' Marcellus of Bactria and 'dux' Xenodares of Sogdiana (of Mesopotamian Greek descent and with a Persian mother and local noble cousins to supply family connections), had already anticipated his arrival by heading into the Hindu Kush foothills to take some bandit strongholds and erect new forts nearby. The Emperor, a skilled horseman, led the main cavalry force on Kabul with 'out-flanker' forces of horse and foot protecting each flank of his advance from ambush and scouts milling around to keep the countryside empty of attackers. As a result tribal warriors gathering to ambush his siege-train were soon spotted and a task force of Roman infantry with archers and skirmishers, some of them skilled Saxon and Langobard 'berserkers', intercepted them. The tribesmen were annihilated in a clever move of luring them to attack a seemingly bumblingly unprotected Roman column laden with supplies who in fact had their own well-armed associates in hiding a few miles to either side of their route of march in quiet valleys. Once the would-be tribal ambushers had been dealt with Claudius had a clear route to Kabul and headed there at top speed to catch the local prince, a Sassanid cousin called Azdak whose great-grandfather had fled there from Roman attacks in the mid-sixth century, outside the gates reviewing his recent reinforcements from the Indus rajahdom of Gandhara. The Roman cavalry charge nearly caught Azdak and he only just got back into the 'Bala Hissar' citadel in time, but his following warriors were caught jamming the nearest gate into the city by the Roman vanguard and slaughtered and as ferocious German champion fighters stormed the gate, hewing at the fleeing Afghans with their axes, the gate was taken and the legionaries behind the Germans could enter.

The need for a siege of the walled city was thus avoided and it was swiftly occupied, with piles of artillery and food collected there for months captured, and due to this piece of luck the Romans were not forced to camp outside Kabul all winter and bombard the thick walls as Claudius had planned and his huge artillery train and piles of rocks and inflammable material were not needed in Kabul. The Romans settled into the largely intact city and used their equipment to bombard the Bala Hissar instead while part of the army went on to secure the western approaches to the Khyber Pass. But the near-impregnable Bala Hissar still took four months to fall and only surrendered in ruins as most of its walls had been levelled and the starving survivors inside faced the final attack by ten times as many Romans in a snowy January, 618. Azdak was found dead in the ruins, and reportedly threw himself off a wrecked tower, or was pushed by his rivals, rather than surrender; the cousin who had admitted the Romans to a postern gate was given a local estate belonging to his family as a (small) reward but not control of any fortified buildings and the brigand ruler's surrounded bodyguard were given a choice of service in the Roman army in distant Armenia then lands there or ten years in loincloths and chains in a mine in Sogdiana. By the point when the fortress surrendered the Romans had erected 'ready-made' fortresses, initially of wood as digging up and moving stone would take too long, along the main road back to Arachosia. Once the snows had melted Claudius systematically reduced all the fortresses around Kabul that were still holding out but left the task of clearing the 'rebel'-held Panjshir valley to the north-west, ruled by Azdak's younger brother and full of refugees from Kabul, to a picked force of Caucasus and Alpine mountaineers who had to take it village by village and took months to do so.

Roman mountaineers climbed up to various 'impregnable' forts around Kabul once artillery had hurled rocks up to blast holes in the walls and fiery missiles had set the roofs on fire and one by one the fortresses fell. In the meantime Claudius marched his main army, surrounded by a 'screen' of protective scouts and mountaineers who climbed up each hill and mountain to either side to clear ambushers out of the way before the army advanced, to the Khyber. There had been less rain than in many years so the rivers were not in flood and the Romans were only held up by blockages of rocks piled in the narrower parts of the pass. But while the Afghans were waiting behind the rockpiles for head-on attacks the Romans headed round goat-tracks to either side, guided by scouts who had either been bribed or had relatives held captive in Kabul (mostly from the time of the city's fall). The soldiers certainly appreciated Claudius' showing the Afghans that any trickery would mean dire revenge by organizing mass-executions every time a scout played him false and having their captive womenfolk handed over to his troops as prostitutes to shame their families though stories of what he had done later reached Rome and were fuel to the anger of those nobles, literary men and Churchmen who regarded him as a thuggish tyrant. By May 618 Claudius was at the great rock of Attock, now a garrison for the rajahdom of Taxila (the great Buddhist university city to the east which had once hosted Alexander the Great), and organizing its siege with thousands of captives dragged all the way from Kabul and assorted impressed Sogdian and Bactrian peasants piling up ramparts of earth and stones for him to have his artillery hauled up to the walls. Once the work was complete – in eight weeks – the Emperor launched a devastating 24-hour-a-day barrage that reduced parts of the wall to rubble in a few days. The Indian garrison fought to the last in the hope of their local rajah, Bindusara of Gandhara, sending rescuers in time and the fortress was a pile of smoking rubble and unuseable by the time that it had been taken, virtually room by room. Claudius ordered that it be abandoned and joined his advance-guard who were waiting on the banks of the Indus with a 'bridge of boats' that had been carried all the way from Bactria in the (correct) expectation that the Indians would pull down the bridge on the Kabul-Punjab road over the river and wait on the far side.

The waiting Indian army had to pull back from the riverbank and let the Romans cross and land as they were showered with missiles by the artillery on the west bank, and then on 5 June the Emperor defeated Bindusara's huge army in a classic 'set-piece' battle where the Indian reliance on elephants was deflected by the Romans launching a 'barrage' of foxes with burning faggots tied to their tails at them and then sending forward men rolling burning logs. The elephants panicked and fled back into their own ranks and as chaos spread the Roman cavalry charged at them and began to carve swathes in the enemy ranks into which wedges of infantry then poured. With flanking Roman wings to either side of the battlefield closing in and raining arrows on the retreating Indians the latter, never as disciplined as Romans, broke up in panic and lost most of their experienced warriors and almost all the rajah's nobles (who had been in the vanguard as appropriate for their honourable rank). Bindusara was knocked off his elephant and killed, probably trampled underfoot though not by Claudius in person as was claimed in the latter's victory medal. With the Indian army destroyed and the late rajah's son Arjun in retreat across the Sutlej to seek aid from the greatest ruler of northern India, his father's rival Harsha the 'Maharajah' (i.e. 'over-king'/ 'great king') of Thanesar in the eastern

Punjab who now ruled the upper Ganges region, Claudius could occupy the undefended Taxila. The city was reprieved out of respect for its historic past – it had been ruled by the Indian kingdom of the expatriate Bactrian Greeks as recently as the first century – and it duly became a major Roman garrison and capital of the province of 'India Claudiana'. With the Emperor in possession of the second –century BC palace of the great Greek ruler Menander, lord of most of NW India, he had the temptation to go on like Alexander but was too practical to listen to his more ebullient advisers, even those generals who had feared Bindusara and his elephants but seen the latter fall into simple traps. To the sensible Claudius, now hailed by his troops as 'Indicus', there was no point in taking territory that would require many thousands of soldiers to hold down and in addition the garrison could spawn rebellion as it would be so large and so far away from reprisal from the main Roman eastern armies in Mesopotamia. He ordered a halt at the River Beas and sent an envoy, appropriately attended and mounted on a huge war-elephant taken from Bindusara's collection of them, to Harsha at Thanesar to say that the 'Augustus of West and East' would be content with the river as their border and if the Indian ruler was willing to set up Arjun in a buffer-state in the central Punjab Rome would not interfere.

Some Roman merchants used to the Silk Road who had been to and had contacts in Harsha's capital accompanied the embassy and helped to secure a treaty and the Beas was duly arranged as the border and a chain of Roman forts were set up there, and through the rest of 618 and into 619 Claudius campaigned down the Indus as far as the Arabian Sea to reduce the local towns and create a new Roman province of the lower Indus. He built a new Roman port of 'Alexandria Indica' at the nearest point of the lower Indus practicable to the river-mouth (which itself was deep in mud and marshes and unuseable for building). The plan was to use the Roman control of the entire length of the Indus up to Attock to cut off the remaining bandit tribes in the Quetta region from their potential helpers in the Punjab and Gujarat and settle the river's fertile plains with warlike veteran Roman soldiers as 'limitanei' ahead of a final conquest. In the meantime the Indus valley towns had the choice of surrendering and being 'Romanised' with a large contingent of new settlers from the west or being destroyed and sown with salt, as happened to a large number of them in 619 as the extent of forced Romanization became clear – with around 20,000 veteran Roman soldiers already in Arachosia and Charax poised to move in at the imminent end of their military service and set up 'readymade' Roman forts and fortified settlements along the river. They would then create arable farms along the riverbanks.

The Emperor had talked to local experts, mostly former 'Silk Road ' traders, in detail for years and had his plans for Romanization drawn up in detail and knew approximately how long each 'phase' would take while Roman geographers knew what sort of crops to plant there and make money and suitable animals were ready to be shipped there by sea from Charax and used on the farms. But he had anticipated rather more Indians collaborating and the settlement of his western 'limitanei' was to take longer and suffer more losses than he had planned – as was to become apparent in the 630s. But with the main Roman army of occupation, around 12000 regular soldiers in a small 'comitatus' based at Taxila plus 15,000 more in garrisons and around 10,000 more 'limitanei' in the countryside, in the north ready as of late 619 to meet any attack from the Punjab and a picked cavalry force of 8,000 steppe nomads from Sogdiana at large to intercept any bandit attacks from the unsubdued mountains South of the Khyber Pass the northern province was secure. It had a clear route of 'contact' via the Khyber and Kabul to the Roman lands around Alexandria-in-Arachosia to retreat along if needed, and this gave the new administration confidence.

Claudius chose officers who were personally loyal to him to command there and was sure that none would dare to revolt. Messages would take a long time to reach Mesopotamia, even with carrier –pigeons now in use, and help would arrive even slower and the sea-route to the mouth of the Indus was fraught with difficulties especially in the monsoon season. But the Emperor had chosen his commanders wisely and no trouble occurred beyond a constant 'pin-pricking' of bandit raids from the mountains and the new safety of the 'Silk Road' land-route via Kabul to Sogdiana and Bactria soon revived that road as a regular route for merchants once Harsha in the Ganges valley gave them permission to use it. The increased tax revenues soon paid for the cost of the garrison of the Taxila area if not that of the heavily fortified and Romanised Kabul and despite the sneers of wits in Rome the province of 'India Claudiana' did not go the same way as Alexander's province of northern India and have to be abandoned. But the restive rural population and the frequent floods in the lower Indus area made that province distinctly less useful or successful and as rumours of its harsh climate, floods, and hostile natives spread few military veterans volunteered to move there. By 628 Claudius was facing mutiny from time-expired troops in Mesopotamia who were due to go there compulsorily despite his generous offers of ten years' tax-remission and free Indian slaves to till the land. The garrisons were under attack every year and the Romans lacked the men or the money to tackle the bandits in the hills beyond Quetta while the Emperor's 'white elephant' port on the lower Indus (as it was called in tribute to a custom of the distant Cambodian empire of Angkor of venerating but not using white elephants) was half-built and hit by floods. In the end Claudius had to admit in 629 that he could not set up a large Roman landed colony of small farmers as he had done in strategic areas of other frontiers (eg Denmark) and he would have to import a system of a few, armed and ruthless entrepreneurs from Mesopotamia to use Indian peasant-farmers as serfs on 'latifundiae' estates growing cash crops and also ask his ally Harsha to loan him some experienced, land-hungry Ganges valley Indians who knew local agriculture and trade in the long run, this introduced Indian vegetables and later rice to the Empire.

But for the moment as of autumn 619 the Emperor had added two large new provinces to his Empire and had silenced his critics, and he sailed back from the mouth of the Indus with the core of his army to Charax to spend the winter in Ctesiphon, extending the Persian Gulf fleet to set up a regular supply-route to the mouth of the Indus and arranging for an expedition of Arabs used to the deserts to head for the wilds of Gedrosia and reduce it in 620. (This was the first expedition of his Meccan Arab 'find' as an inspirational general with an instinct for the lie of the land, the swashbuckling Khaled, and for the Ummayad dynasty's young noble commander Ali, son of Abu Talib.) In spring 620 Claudius headed on to Ptolemias (OTL: Acre) now a rising trading-port for Arab exports from the Yemen-Mecca-Petra-Galilee trade-route, to set sail for Rome and as events turned out never returned to the east apart from winter 622–3 at Constantinople. But he kept up his interest after his grand Triumph in Rome as the 'New Alexander' and he ensured that a steady supply of Western European troops and Langobard, Frank, and Gothic mercenaries had experience of military service in the Afghan mountains as the struggle continued to subdue the 'rebel' bandits in the high mountains south of Kabul, a war that lasted for decades. It was not over even when the Romans had set up new forts in a secure chain around Kabul and were fighting to the north of the city as well to control the heights of the Pamirs and to the north-east to secure the valleys of Swat and Malakand. The Emperor sought to use his new 'North-East Frontier' there as a means to toughen up young officers and introduce them to the realities of harsh military campaigning in guerilla-prone mountain territory and so a regular 'rota' of officers and even cadets from the West were to be sent there for decades to come as a series of major and minor forts were built and the local tribes had to 'Romanise' or were deported to Bactria and Mesopotamia.

Slowly the security of the roads west from Taxila via Kabul to Persia improved though this took several decades to make a major difference and in the meantime the long 'Romans vs Indian rural guerillas and mountain bandits' wars in the lower Indus valley made the land-route south from Taxila to the river-mouth much less safe than it had been in the sixth century. This diverted trading caravans north and also increased traffic by sea. Claudius was also to recruit a regular levy of younger sons of tenant-farmers of the great landlords in the Persian plateau (whose poor fertility meant that it could not sustain a large population or divided-up inheritances of farms) plus volunteers from the nobility across

Persia for new Roman regiments to man the riverside and roadside forts and to serve as 'scouts' in the Oxus region of Sogdiana – replacing troops who had been moved to the Kabul region and the Indus. These men were to be taught Roman military tactics and thoroughly culturally 'Romanised' as Claudius saw them to be a means for building up Roman culture as well as manpower there – but his strict requirements of imposing Latino-Greek cultural norms on them were to be diluted under his less Eurocentric successors. The tone of the expanding (with peace and security for trade) existing towns and of the newly-founded 'strategic sites' towns on roads and at river-crossings and oases, which Claudius now arranged to be built by his military engineers and impressed local labour once the new forts had been constructed, was to be Latinate too according to his orders. But some skilled Mesopotamian urban planners (mostly of long-resident Hellenistic Greek descent) who he and his successor Carus II hired to do the planning-work in the next twenty years or so were either used to working on regional Greco-Iranian urban models, in the Sassanid tradition, or else reused old Hellenistic town-planning documents as a guide – and round Sassanid-style towns and Sassanid-style buildings were to emerge in 'Claudian' and 'Carian' planning in the new provinces too. Military buildings were always erected on time-honoured Roman plans, but the influence of the traditions and tactics of the former Sassanid 'cataphract' cavalry regiments, now part of the Roman army (and in Mesopotamia part of the Roman army since Julian's conquests in the 360s) were also notable in the new regiments and garrisons in seventh-century Sogdiana, Transoxiana, Kabul, and Gandhara. This was not Claudius' plan, though he was prepared to adapt Persian and local Sogdian/ Gandharan military tactics when needed – his was a culturally 'Western' vision, for which later regional military tactics-book-writer and historian Artemidorus Arsennatius was to call him 'the heir of Seleucus not of Alexander or Menander' in his masterly study of the Claudian campaigns in the 820s. But this was to be reversed by his more 'Iranophile' successor Carus, who for one thing had Persian nobles at his court – and spoke Persian to them, as well as reading Sassanid manuscripts that Julian had carried off as loot to his library in Constantinople in the 360s.

With the main fighting over Claudius now turned his attention to an overhaul of the 'comitatus' training-'college' at Mediolanum and its lectures and military manoeuvres and in 622 created a new Eastern 'staff college' at Antioch to train officers from the eastern provinces as thoroughly. Another 'staff college', concentrating on training Persians, Armenians, and Arabs, was to be founded at Ecbatana in Media in 628. Though he had a number of well-off contemporaries of his from the Italian nobility (who had been in the 'Scholae' when he was a young officer and had known him since his late teens) among his hard-drinking circle of intimates and he also had major connections with the nobility via his wife he remained suspicious of the majority of well-off young officers who regarded the army as a well-paid basis for social advancement and travel rather than a serious career and did his best to open up the 'Scholae' to new, lower-class recruits too. In his informed opinion, and that of senior tutors at the staff colleges whose works he read, the 'amateur' noble officers had time after time brought Rome near to disaster, as when Flaminius the elder had been crushed by Hannibal in 217 BC, Metellus had failed to defeat Jugurtha in North Africa in 110–109, Caepio's army had been destroyed by the Cimbri and Teutones at Arausio in 106, and Varus had been defeated by Arminius in the Teutoberg Forest in AD 9.If Rome was to continue its mission successfully it needed to sideline these over-confident incompetents; accordingly he made very few senior appointments of 'hereditary military family' nobles whose rich ancestors had been in senior military roles for centuries and where they were called on for advice by him it was mainly on breeding horses for the cavalry or the rising new sport of polo which Persian and Sogdian nobles had introduced to their Roman counterparts in the East in the fifth century and which had now reached the Imperial cavalry in the West with annual tournaments. Where Julian, Stilicho, Constantius III and Aetius had given high rank to capable 'immigrant' Germans, Claudius now selected many competent ex-'farm boys' and rural provincials – and chose senior trainers from similar backgrounds at his military colleges to keep up his work. As he reminded his officers, Danubian ex-peasants Aurelian, Maximian and Constantius I had helped save the C3rd Empire.

The Emperor judged that the Empire needed some years of stability and reorganization to absorb its new provinces and see how their financial viability developed, so he proved as cautious in effect if not in rhetoric as his brother Carus from now on and ignored the opportunities to advance Roman power up the Red Sea or the Nile that were offered by ambitious local commanders and traders. He ignored the provocations towards Rome offered by the increasingly assertive Abyssinian realm or the 620s civil wars in Nubia where the ancient realm's temporary break-up into three feuding kingdoms led to calls for Rome to intervene and annex them in the name of security. Obsessed with the need to control and monitor his 'lazy' and 'embezzling' ministers and their careerist juniors, Claudius embarked on a series of lengthy audits of each ministry in Rome by specially-selected boards of commissioners (mostly humbly-born outsiders from the provinces who would not be likely to be bought off or intimidated by powerful Rome civil servants) in 620–24. He had any senior figures who were found to have been pocketing cash or neglecting their duties put on trial and forced to disgorge their illegally-gained cash, and as quite senior officials ended up publicly flogged in the Forum of Trajan (as an appropriate place for the morally-upright Imperial autocrat to punish the incompetent) and sent off to remote prisons to do menial labour the Emperor was not exactly popular with the civil elite and notably did not care. As unknown outsiders from the provinces who had had good reports for their zeal and incorruptibility were brought in to senior roles in Rome and even became ministers with minimal experience there was a good deal of initial chaos as people did not know what to do and/or were conned by their juniors. Claudius' careful use of his own veteran civil service experts (mostly retired personnel) to write up 'guide-books' to correct conduct and solving problems for these men to use verbatim was only a partial solution despite his hopes that he had assembled all the answers that his new personnel would need. Ironically the only major minister from the 610s to survive the quick turnover of senior personnel after 619, the administratively expert and rather toadying 'Master of Office' Euphemius of Adramyttium (in the Troad in Asia Minor) who held office from 616 to 628, was probably as corrupt as any of the sacked ministers but he was better at hiding it. He had a loyal staff to destroy incriminating papers and he also pleased his master with plenty of new ideas for reform and tightening up regulations, and Euphemius was also close to the Empress – probably due to his using his huge network of proteges to get hold of a brilliant Syrian doctor to cure her youngest daughter's asthma, but allegedly as her lover according to spiteful nobles.

The Emperor trusted his wife and liked a woman who kept out of politics and restricted her interests to weaving, philanthropy, and harmless social activities with a circle of equally devout and respectable matrons, and if the Empress was having a secret affair (unlikely due to her religious morals) she was discreet and was unlikely to have been mixed up in Euphemius' apparent activities squirreling away a fortune under assumed names in banks well away from Rome. The Emperor's rigid social propriety and devotion to tradition also meant that although his nephew and 'Caesar' and presumed heir, Carus I's son Prince Carus (born 602), was a womanizing rake and a drunkard who lived life to the full with his fellow-officers in the 'Scholae' and soon had several illegitimate children there was no question of breaking Claudius' promise to his brother and disinheriting him. The calls by assorted 'meritocrat' Imperial allies and advisers for the Emperor to allow his successor to be elected by the Senate were ignored. Nor was there ever a chance of Claudius allowing his talented, shrewd and well-read socialite eldest daughter Princess Domitia to succeed him, or to let her capable aristocratic officer husband Marcus Lucullianus (who she married in 620) do so, as in his view the Imperial office had to descend by the male line. Carus was sent off in 622 to do military service as an assistant to the 'Count of the Rhine' and to lead local embassies to the Franks and Langobards and go on naval patrols in the North Sea to toughen him up and give him experience away from his boozy intimates who were, if military, posted off to Sogdiana or the upper Indus. Carus proved a capable officer and showed bravery in minor skirmishes and in 625–7 he was made 'dux' of Colchis, the coastal province North of Armenia, so he could go on manoeuvres and deal with raiding tribesmen in the Cauacasus followed by a year in 627–8 in the more senior role of 'dux' of Upper Mesopotamia, based at Nisibis. But though this series of testing roles reassured his uncle that he would be a competent Emperor and was worthy of the succession Carus also acquired a new series of mistresses from the provinces he served in, who accompanied him back to Rome in 628, plus tastes for more exotic drink and a collection of hangers-on from the local nobility and his Spartan lifestyle as an officer only encouraged him to hanker after luxury and acquire a mass of possessions to be piled up in his Italian villas ready for use once he was Emperor.

These years also saw a boom in drama as a protégé of the 'Maecenas'- like patron Euphemius, the Peloponnesian playwright Heliocles of Sicyon, revived the old genre of Greek tragedy in a new form of 'patriotic historical epic' featuring real people as opposed to the usual myths (possibly because as a devout Christian he did not believe in the latter or want to put 'pagan' gods on the stage). The 620s saw his series of dramas on the careers of the later Greek historical figures Demosthenes, Demetrius of Phalerum, Aratus of Sicyon, Philopoemen, Spartan reformist King Cleomenes, and C2nd AD orator and philosopher Herodes Atticus put on at the theatrical festivals in Greece and later transferred successfully to Rome, winning prizes in both places. The great playwright, taken up as a protégé of Prince Carus after the latter's return to Rome for civic responsibilities training in 628, carefully kept out of real Roman history after the third century BC to avoid potential controversy that could cost him prizes or patrons and his patriotic plays about the careers of Hannibal's defeaters Marcellus and Scipio Africanus and the virtuous ancient Roman consuls Appius Claudius (late fourth-century BC) and Cato the Elder (early-mid-second century BC) duly won Imperial approval. But in private Heliocles was a good deal more subversive about the narrow-minded, priggish hostility to Greek culture showed by certain 'heroic' Roman figures such as Cato and his real agenda was to open up Roman culture to appreciation of other cultures, those of the East included as he had travelled with his merchant father in Mesopotamia and Persia in the 590s. He probably had some influence on Carus in this as by 630 the latter was starting to encourage younger and more eclectic cultural and social 'leaders of fashion' in Rome to attack the Emperor *sotto voce* or by association for being an ignorant and Philistine military despot who only believed in rule-books and hierarchy.

Claudius was often away from Rome in the summer months in the early-mid 620s touring the Empire to receive the reports of his local commissions on the effective working of government in person, meet his local officials and assess competence in person, draw up lists of people to be sacked or promoted, and check that public works programmes and philanthropic projects were running on time and if not why not. He was known as 'the First Inspector' as opposed to the official title the Emperor had of 'First Citizen' and was grumbled about as a martinet and the caricature of a peppery ageing officer obsessed with the rule-book and neat uniforms. But his relentless inspections and checking on his officials did produce results and also enabled him to get to know many of his middle-ranking and higher bureaucrats in person (albeit superficially) and under him it was known that money had to be spent properly and every sestertius accounted for or he would be investigating and his eye for a 'coming man' selected many future successes as ministers in the mid-seventh century for their future careers in Rome. He did the same as much as was practicable in the army and knew every 'dux' and deputy 'dux' in the Empire in person together with how the military budget was run and allocated and much inefficiency was cut out of the latter in the 620s as his handpicked experts checked every item. He also encouraged the Church to supervise its expenditure on projects and the accounts of all local clergy and monasteries much more efficiently and saw to it that capable organisers as well as 'holy men' were appointed to leading bishoprics.

Arguably he 'de-fanged' the long polemic-studded rivalry between Catholics/orthodox and Monophysites in the Levant by the simple measure of seeing that officials interested in running a smooth organization not fanatical ideologues and argumentative writers were appointed to crucial sees throughout his reign, denying 'troublemakers' the possession of any of the major Patriarchates from 615 onwards. Although he was condemned by some idealistic clergy and literary men for promoting mediocrities his choices of senior clergy included one major theological figure of the era, the 'self-made' thinker and austere holy man Patriarch Sergius of Constantinople (in office 622–634) (OTL), who was chosen by him as a working-class 'success story' with formidable energy and organizational skills but who came to be known for his campaign to promote the role of the 'Theotokos', the 'Mother of God' (i.e. the Virgin Mary), as the divine patron of his city. The originally second-ranking see of Constantinople, which had lacked religious prestige or respect from the sees of Rome, Antioch, Alexandria, and Jerusalem since the fourth century as not founded by an Apostle, finally gained some religious credibility under Sergius after the Virgin was supposed to have intervened in response to her local worshippers' prayers to abate a plague in the city in the mid-620s and was apparently seen walking on the city ramparts carrying a standard. The shrine of the Virgin Mary (containing part of her alleged robe as a sacred relic) at the Church of the Virgin at the suburb of Blachernae, a village by the Golden Horn harbour best known for its imperial hunting-park, was developed from the later 620s as a major pilgrimage shrine and was visited by the Empress Marcia, who made donations from her (impressively large and valuable) wardrobe there, in summer 629.

By this point the Emperor's health had started to go downhill after a bout of pneumonia caught on a hunting-trip in the Black Forest in autumn 627 during his final inspection-tour of the upper Danube and Marcomannia. After he was finally prevailed on to sack the financially dubious Euphemius in spring 628 and a subsequent commission into the ex-minister's finances showed that he had been cheating the tax-collectors for years the shocked Claudius was persuaded not to have him flogged and executed as he intended to do as an example and most of his peculation was covered up as too embarrassing to reveal. Euphemius was formally accused of fraudulent accounting and had to hand all his publicly-discovered gains back and was then exiled to a remote Marcomannian town where he had estates to live there in disgrace minus over 80 per cent of his property, but the Emperor never dared to face up to the way that he had been conned by his closest adviser. He fell into depression and irascible outbursts of rage at his allegedly incompetent advisers for not warning him about Euphemius earlier, increasingly eccentric and from early 629 virtually a hermit in his apartments at the Marble Palace in Rome. Claudius' militarily glorious reign ended in anticlimax and the sniggers of his critics at the way he had been defrauded, and he died on 22 March 630 aged sixty-three and was succeeded by Prince Carus, now twenty-eight, who was a totally different man with a different set of priorities and had been eagerly awaiting the throne for several years but now had the politeness to pretend that his predecessor was a great man whose loss Rome would feel severely – and given his interest in the East, Carus was probably sincere in declaring that Claudius' greatest achievement was to 're-position' the Empire to face East and move into affairs in the Indian region.

Chapter 18

Carus II 630–641: The Orientophile

Carus, already somewhat of an alcoholic as well as a womanizer though publicly honouring his placid, docile, and unintellectual wife Julia Maussonia (chosen for him by his uncle in 622 as from a respectable 'self-made' Calabrian bureaucratic dynasty who now had several members at a senior level of the civil service in Rome), was met with nervousness as a potential disaster by his uncle's fiercely loyal and 'thrusting' ministers and generals. But the nobility in Rome and the senate greeted him with relief as he was more easy-going and a leading socialite and he duly turned out to be accommodating to their foibles and not too demanding about hard work and accurate accounts. The Emperor was far from a 'pushover' for his friends and flattering courtiers, as those that knew him had already found, and he was also instinctively canny and too aware of the undercurrents of disaffection with any departure from the social and political 'norms' within the elite to indulge his own fondness for the relaxed, 'Graecised' cultural world of 'Hellenism' in Rome at first. But culturally and intellectually he was close to the tradition of Hadrian whose memory he revered, holding a party for fellow-enthusiasts every year on that ruler's birthday at his Tibur villa. He was also already a major patron of the reviving drama and of the more explicit and daring types of love-poetry in the tradition of Catullus, whose Sirmium villa at Lake Como he had purchased in 626 as a 'retreat'.

The new Emperor was too cautious to sack many of Claudius' aggressive, self-made ministers at once even though they clearly did not think much of his morals or his lack of time spent on business and it was 632 before major changes were made. But when he did introduce new men to senior rank it was almost always those with an interest (or professed interest) in culture and more figures from the old nobility were promoted than under Claudius, particularly to the traditionally 'upper-class' posts of Praefects of Rome and Constantinople and to the Rome civic aedileships. Carus reversed his uncle's purges and close supervision of the Rome civic racing-factions at the Circus Maximus, which Claudius had looked on since the 602 riots as a hotbed of sedition and illegal gambling, and he recalled assorted charioteers and faction-officials who Claudius had had conscripted into the army. But his grand inaugural month of Games after his coronation in June 630 and his personal attendance thereafter at the races whenever he was in Rome plus his invitations for charioteers and racing patrons to the Marble Palace were not accompanied by any reversal of the 610s and 620s extra taxes on the world of horseracing and chariot-racing gambling. Contrary to his socialite allies' hopes he did not legalise casinos either, probably due to his need to keep the Church and moralist bishops happy. Carus was a generous patron to the Empire's universities and kept up the recent Imperial patronage of the expanding (male) schools-system and continued to build new schools across the Empire and train more teachers like his father and uncle had done. But unlike Claudius his aim in education was to produce 'civilised' citizens with knowledge of the past gems of the Arts, especially Greek and Late Republican Roman literature, not to breed patriotism and obedience and his first three ministers for education (Quintus Marullus in 630–3, Antonius Gessianus in 633–6, and Justus Caprenius in 636–9) were all poets and literary culture patrons as well as past university administrators.

Openly-pagan philosophers, especially enthusiasts for Plato and Plotinus and mostly Greek or Italian or Egyptian, were given senior posts in all the Empire's universities plus funds for their research despite Church unease and in 633 Carus opened a new university for Asia Minor at Ephesus, based on the structure and teaching models of Athens and largely staffed by former students and lecturers from the latter. But he did not rein in Christian theological teaching at universities despite the claims of friends and foes alike that he was really 'Julian II', with a similar agenda to the first Julian. He even held talks with the local Church about a new and predominantly Christian (as appropriate for a largely Christian and Catholic region) university in Lutetia or Lugdunum in Gaul though he gave this up as requiring more money and effort than the Church or local nobles were prepared to put into it. He did, however, link up to the aged and eclectically expert scholar Archbishop Isidore (d. 640) (OTL) of Augusta Sevilla in Baetica in Spain, who he had met and discussed Christian devotional writers with at a Church Council in Rome in the early 620s, to carry out the latter's long-term ambition of founding a specialist Catholic-run university at that city, to which the bibliophile archbishop duly left his huge library as the centrepiece of their new library. Though Isidore was hostile to the pagan philosophers for their inability to see that all their 'gods' were really a fumbling intellectual misunderstanding of the nature of the 'One True God and His Son' and he had doubts about the morals of assorted Hellenistic 'masters of knowledge' he had enough in common with Carus' ideals to correspond with him on the plans and then work with him on setting up the university. Funds were arranged, administrators, tutors and architects found, and a curriculum drawn up and in 634 Isidore was prevailed upon to leave his see with a deputy and come to Rome to meet the Emperor and work on the project with his educational experts. In 640 the new university duly opened and proved a major centre for high education in the Iberian peninsula and also an important centre into the study of the Church Fathers, mainly in the West and including the leading missionaries, mystics and writers of Christian Ireland beyond the Roman frontier (including St Columbcille of Iona in Dalriada). Carus' educational achievements were thus substantial and showed that though he was lazier at carrying out business than Carus I or Claudius III he was capable of directing policy in a major area and finding capable subordinates. But even with the great Isidore, a man of Mediterranean-wide prestige, on his side Carus still received Church criticism from angry moralists over his enthusiasm for 'immoral' cultural figures such as Catullus, who Church schools would not teach. He had the support of the ecclesiastical hierarchies in Rome (headed from 633 to 642 by one of Claudius' 'risen from the ranks' cautious administrators, Pope Severinus from Syria) and Constantinople. But the sees of Alexandria and Antioch were more hostile, the latter over Carus' sending a commission of scholars to collect the literary and philosophic works of assorted 'disgraced' regional 'heretic' Christian thinkers like Nestorius for teaching and study in Rome and the former over Carus' enthusiasm for extending the range of pagan Hellenistic thinkers whose works were to be taught at the university of Alexandria.

For the first time for generations an Emperor was consciously the leader of Rome's aristocratic 'high society' and a major giver of extravagant parties, but despite this and the closeness of Carus to his mostly fairly young and rich personal appointees to court offices, the allegations made by disapproving clerics and veteran officers that he was a puppet of his chamberlains and fellow-socialites were exaggerated. Their impact on politics and law was minimal apart from an easing of the harsh laws of Claudius III on immorality – extra-marital sex and homosexuality in particular. The sumptuary laws and sumptuary taxes of Rillanus against extravagant displays of wealth were also reformed, though cautiously and only in 633 after three years of effective non-enforcement. Carus sought to give the impression of a confident and tolerant ruler who respected all the sources of authority and Imperial advice in the Empire provided that he was not criticised though his attendance at military manoeuvres for the 'comitatus' lapsed after two years or so as he grew more confident of being able to handle the military and he started to 'retire' (rather early) assorted disciplinarian senior generals and strategists. His interest in foreign policy and in particular in non-Roman states was as great as Claudius' but from an entirely different viewpoint as like Hadrian or Julian he was inclined to tolerate other cultures and states and was not convinced of Rome's destiny to expand 'ad infinitum' and impose its values and political structure on the rest of the 'Oikoumene' (the civilised world, as defined by Greek thinkers). Indeed his fellow-ex-officer and close adviser Demetrius Policianus, a super-rich business dynasty heir from Smyrna near Ephesus who he soon invited to his court as an honorary official and who had travelled widely in the east as far as India in the mid-late 620s, spoke and wrote in favour of Rome tempering its Vergilian mission. It should become 'leader not the dictator' of the civilized world and in particular reach out a hand of friendship to the east, which seems to have influenced the Emperor. Vergil had stressed Rome's conquering mission; Carus preferred influence via culture.

Carus invited the new, well-educated, and highly competent – if narrowly Catholic in his ideals and world-view – Frankish king Dagobert 'the Good' (reigned 629–49) from Transrhenus and representatives of the Geatish, Swedish, Irish, Dalriadan, Langobard, and 'Scythian' Gothic kings to his first Ludi Romani in Rome in autumn 630 to watch the races and attend banquets and parties and treated them as respected junior colleagues. But his main interests were in the East, and in that capacity he summoned representatives of the main ethnic and religious communities as well as the Roman administrations in Mesopotamia, Persia, Bactria, Sogdiana, the Roman Indian provinces, the Arab ally city-states and tribes of western Arabia, and (divided and chaotic) Nubia to his capital for an official conference in winter 630–1. They were to spend three months advising him on the current situation in their regions and how Rome could govern better and win hearts and minds. This did not meet with military approval and the veteran imperial expansionists who Claudius had listened to believed in the imposition of Roman 'mores' and practices by force and the suppression of anyone who dissented. But the Emperor cannily got his 'spin-doctors' (poets, playwrights, leading socialite nobles who could spread ideas at their parties, and senators who could 'trail' ideas in their speeches) to let it be known that he was seeking allies to help a more efficient expansion of the Empire that would keep military expenditure and taxes down and enlist support not conscript it.

No actual wars followed, but the argument won over most of his critics – temporarily – and his detailed discussions with the Indian 'high caste' social elite delegates and assorted traders who had been along the 'Silk Route' as far as Taprobane or Cambodia were supposed to be intended to prepare for another Roman advance and completing Claudius' work. Carus was sincere in praising the methods of cultural assimilation and co-existence achieved in Persia by Alexander the Great. The Emperor invited a number of senior figures from the Eastern communities who were not 'tied down' to duties, business, and social life in their home provinces to move to Rome as senators and advise him and the Senate on policy, with senior social rank and tax-remission to encourage them. Other senior Eastern civil service nobles' sons were 'invited' to be his pages. Though he had to temper this later and just invite most of his choices to spend part of their time in Rome (two years out of every five would be the norm as adopted by him in his 638 law on this) he did succeed in getting around fifty new and Eastern members of high rank and/or wealth admitted to the

Senate between 632 and 641. Some exclusivist and devoutly Catholic senators complained that he was filling the body with 'pagans', including Zoroastrians, Mithraists, and a few (west -Mesopotamian) moon-worshippers plus even some Jews from Ctesiphon. In winter 632–3 the Emperor moved to Constantinople to lead the social life there and reassure the local senate that they had not been forgotten and were more than a 'rubber stamp' required to pass all legislation agreed by the Senate in Rome and not quibble. As he took to the ceremonial life of the long-neglected 'Sacred Palace' and brought in the nobility of Thrace, Macedonia, and Asia Minor to attend his court and be rewarded with gifts, sinecures, and high ranks it was rumoured that he was taking after Alexander in more than his interest in the East and adopting Persian robes and court customs would be next, even that he was a 'new Diocletian' in terms of seeing himself as an Eastern potentate. (He could not be called a 'Diocletian' in terms of religion, as he made a point of lavishing gifts on great Christian shrines and in this winter went on pilgrimage to the new shrine of the Virgin at Blachernae.) In spring 633 Carus went on to Ephesus to hold a grand theatrical and poetry festival with dozens of competitions and prizes for plays and poetry recitals by men and boys alike, establishing this as a regular annual occurrence that a special 'Imperial consul for culture' would attend every year and so boosting the revival of drama and poetry across urban Asia Minor.

After a pilgrimage to the shrine of St John at Ephesus and a parallel refurbishment for the earthquake-hit, partially collapsed 'Wonder of the World' the Temple of Artemis/ Diana nearby – now renamed the 'Shrine of the Lady Warrior' who for dubious Christians was identified with the Old Testament warrior-prophetess Deborah – he went on with his large entourage across Asia Minor by land to Syria to spend the summer at Antioch and its nearby suburban holiday resorts, rebuilding assorted neglected or earthquake-hit structures there. He also hosted huge parties for the social elite (mostly orthodox) of Syria and led the celebrations at a longer-than-usual summer racing season. The result was that he was adopted by the city's 'Hellenist' poets and orators as the 'Syrian Emperor' or 'Eastern Emperor' who cared about the region and its ex-Seleucid capital more than any ruler had done since the Severans. In practical terms the honorary and largely powerless (except in minor municipal affairs and running the city administration) 'Senate of Antioch' were given greater powers and the ability to vote on more important matters and advise the 'Praefect of Oriens', the local governor, who was required to take note of their advice and announce his decisions to them – though he was not subject to any formal veto – rather than relying on his own private council of advisers and expecting them to rubberstamp' his decisions. Although the Senate of Antioch did not yet have the powers of that at Constantinople its members were now given equal social rank and tax-remission and Carus insisted that some of their members, as with the Constantinopolitan Senate, should be admitted to senior administrative roles in the regional government and real as opposed to honorary political roles in the city government.

After an autumn expedition to the River Jordan valley to hold a grand assembly for local Arab allied tribal leaders and the representatives of the Empire's commercial allies at Mecca and Yathrib (now usually known as 'Medina' as the residence of the region's most impressive holy man and mystic, the venerated Mohammed ibn Abdallah who was Ali's cousin and related to the Ummayad oligarchs of Mecca) at a tented camp at the River Yarmuk the Emperor bathed in the Sea of Galilee. He then visited Capernaum and Nazareth to win Church approval, and spent the winter at a new palace built on a Hellenistic plan for him at Ptolemais. In 634 he went on to Mesopotamia via Edessa and Nisibis to hold another grand regional meeting of the nobility at Ctesiphon and preside at a month of Games at the early seventh-century Roman-style chariot-racing stadium there. Setting up an advisory 'Senate' at Ctesiphon, like the one at Antioch, to assist the local Praefect and to be a conduit of honours and a degree of political influence for the local nobility was more controversial than his actions in Syria as many of these nobles were of Persian and a few of Jewish origin and some of the Christians involved were Nestorians or Monophysites. But the Emperor pressed on regardless and even wore Persian-style robes at some of his ceremonies and parties at the extended Praefectural palace in Ctesiphon where he was based. He learnt some words of Persian and made it clear that the Greek-descended families of Seleucid descent on whom his predecessors had usually relied in Ctesiphon must now share its rule with the Persian nobility. After two months at Ctesiphon he went on to the old Median royal and then Sassanid regional capital of Ecbatana to reside at the ancient Achaemenid palace there, once lived in by Alexander, for two months in late summer 634 and hold outdoor tented rallies of the local nobility outside the city plus a polo-tournament and military manoeuvres. But his plans to follow up the first non-military Imperial visit to Media with one to the Oxus had to be postponed due to reports of a tribal revolt against the Avar 'Khagan' on the Ukrainian steppes leading to one of the rebel leaders attacking Azov. It was said that Carus' lack of interest in the west and the north was causing military grumbling and being exploited by dissident officers. Carus could be ruthless with dissent if it threatened him and an investigation by a disciplinary commission worthy of Claudius' military thugs followed by trials and executions under martial law followed in the garrisons of Dacia and Lower Moesia where the trouble had been reported. But he took the wise course of abandoning his eastern trip and heading quickly back to Antioch for the winter while trusted aides went on to Rome led by his capable and well-liked if somewhat colourless ex-officer brother-in-law Leo Maussonius, consul for 634, whose efficiency and moderation in sorting out assorted complaints and accusations in this role made a major impression and arguably propelled him on the road to being a credible heir to his childless sovereign.

In spring 635 Carus returned to Rome and, given his love of Eastern culture and importation of Persian noble poets and craftsmen (and apparently Persian dancing-girls and mistresses for himself) to the capital it was clear that it was caution and fear of more criticism that kept him in the West thereafter not having grown tired of the East. But he did venture by sea to Alexandria for four months in summer 636 (reforming their Senate as he had done that of Antioch and keeping a firm grip on the orthodox Church appointments there to exclude fervent anti-Monophysites). He was to go to Cyprus and Crete and Athens in his summer 637 trip, Carthage and Leptis Magna in summer 638, and Athens again and the Peloponnese in summer 639 – never being away from Rome for more than six months and not returning to Syria either. In Carus' place he sent some of his trusted courtiers and noble friends who he had made in Syria as part of a commission to Persia in 636 to investigate the current form and workings of the Roman administration there, take soundings from the local nobles and urban merchants, and suggest ways of aligning it more closely to Persian tradition. Though the fears of certain alarmed centralizing civil servants in Rome that he intended to reverse centuries of Imperial policy (by allowing a degree of autonomy and flexibility in how the Empire operated across culturally diverse areas, as had been the custom in the early Empire) was not confirmed the idea of doing this was certainly in some of his advisers' minds. There was talk of reverting to the old system of local governors allowing a degree of self-government, letting local nobles and towns run their own affairs provided they remained loyal and provided troops and taxes, and just referring those matters which were put to them by the locals to the Emperor for a decision when requested. This would have put thousands of bureaucrats and lawyers out of work and made the rigid systems of universal regulations and law in the post-Diocletianic Empire redundant – though special allowances were usually made in culturally distinct regions for their local law to continue if it was suitable for Roman use. A group of Claudius III's proteges in the finance and law ministries in Rome even launched a plot in 637 to stop this threat by murdering the Emperor and brought in a few alarmed 'career bureaucrat' senators and generals. But they were caught out due to a gossiping mistress of a participant and dealt with. The usual interrogations by torture, trials and executions followed, but Carus carried out far fewer executions than his father or youngest uncle Claudius III would have done and only a dozen or so people were actually killed though a score more were gaoled or sent to the slave mines that produced salt in southern Rhaetia. The haul of confiscated land and mansions was considerable and went to enrich assorted Levantine nobles of ancient family, especially Syrians and Phoenicians, who Carus wished to lure to Rome and enrol in the Senate.

Whether or not scared off drastic reform by the scale of the plot, Carus did not allow local law or custom to prevail or the local nobles to have more autonomy in Persia, or in the lands around the Oxus and the Hindu Kush which his commission also visited. But he did issue orders to respect ancient landholding and social customs provided they were Latinised and in keeping with Roman and Christian values. He also had assorted complaints about 'unjust' targeting of powerful provincial dynasties and the seizure of part or all of their lands by greedy Roman officials in these areas investigated in 639–40 by a special legal tribunal which returned a substantial part of those estates that were investigated. This and the reversion of assorted lands formerly belonging to those Zoroastrian 'fire-temples' that had been closed down or their 'Magian' priests (usually done on real or imagined charges of subversion since the 363–5 Roman annexations in Persia) to their original owners' descendants did a lot to build goodwill to the Empire and the Emperor in Persia. Though the extent of subversion and active revolt in the Indus valley and in the Afghan lands in recent years had been so bad that the confiscations there were approved by Carus' commission as necessary – and duly accepted by him – he did order the local and expansionist Church which Claudius had installed in power in the Indus lands to stop seizing Hindu temples' and Buddhist monasteries' lands and fabricating charges against their priests. The University of Taxila, largely Buddhist in its intellectual tone and full of learned teachers of the 'Theravada' school of Buddhism, was freed from the threat of being purged and Christianised which had hung over it since the early 620s due to interfering governors.

Carus even welcomed a Buddhist delegation to Rome in 640 as it came to thank him for his intervention, and he also used their reports of a Chinese monastic mission from the new Tang dynasty ruling at Chang-an having been in Gandhara in the 620s. They had been buying Buddhist scriptures to take back to China but also enquiring about the possibility of exporting Afghan and Sogdian cavalry horses to China to aid their Emperor's cavalry studs. Carus ordered the governor and 'dux' at Taxila to look up their spies' reports on that mission and plan an embassy of their own to the Chinese capital as a courteous reply. Some of the Roman officials and generals in Taxila, who had dismissed the Chinese monks as harmless but unimportant eccentrics from a strange foreign religion that was beneath their notice, had questions to answer about why they had not even informed the Emperor Claudius of the mission – they had not thought it important. In their haste to be useful to his disgruntled successor they argued that the embassy should be used to spy on the Chinese and see if the latter were as powerful and had as strong armies as they always boasted. If they were not, then Rome could move in via the northern steppes around Lake Balkhash to seize the Dzungarian Gates passes and annex the lands of Kashgar and Turfan west of the Gobi Desert, acquiring the riches of the fabled 'Silk Road' oases plus the manpower of the local tribes. If that was judged too risky Rome could follow the route the Chinese pilgrims had taken north-east of the Indus to annex Gilgit and then tackle the rich valleys of the Hindu rajahdom of Kashmir, making Carus truly an Eastern sovereign able to compete with the power of the great 'Maharajah' Harsha. The latter's Indian stretched from the Ganges plain East to the Bay of Bengal and south to the Deccan with an army containing thousands of elephants that even the brash Roman frontier commanders on the Khyber and Indus feared. But Carus was warned by his military 'general staff' that any commitment of troops to either project would unbalance the Empire militarily by creating a large new bloc of armies in the far East that could challenge the West in a civil war, quite apart from the difficulty of issuing orders in Rome that would take weeks to get to the new frontiers even by carrier-pigeon. If troops had to be sent they could take a year to arrive even if they were shipped from the West to Alexandria then down the Red Sea and over the Indian Ocean to the mouth of the Indus, where a new port had been built by Claudius.

The 'Eastern project' was shelved for several hundred years though the feasibility studies remained on record, and Carus concentrated his efforts on supplying seasoned troops used to desert fighting up the Nile in 640 to stop another civil war in Nubia. They were to help Rome's ally Prince Jawash of Dongola repel an attack by his tyrannical cousin Azika, the usurping ruler of Alwa (i.e. southern Nubia, upriver from Dongola), and his army of 20,000 spear-wielding black mercenaries from the Darfur tribes. Roman general Justinianus Gaetulicius and a mixed force of infantry, cavalry (mostly hired desert horses from Arabia supplied by the tribes there who were used to the heat of the equatorial deserts), Arab archers and skirmishers led by the great mercenary general Khaled from Mecca, and camel-riding nomads from 'Garamantia' (southern Libya) marched or were taken by ship up the Nile to Dongola to save the city from attack by Azika. They ended up catching his large but poorly co-ordinated army by surprise outside the city and annihilating them hours before the attackers were due to launch a final assault on it, the anti-Roman forces foolishly advancing close to the Romans on the river-bank in the hope of disrupting their landing their shipborne troops but being showered with flaming missiles and rocks by the Romans' shipboard artillery. Once holes had been torn in the Darfurians' ranks the Roman and Arab cavalry charged into them and surrounded the attackers' infantry who were then ground down and routed by the Roman infantry, and with Azika in flight by fast camel to Darfur to hide in its rocky wilderness Gaetulicius left him alone as too difficult to track down. He concentrated on shoring up Jawash as a Roman puppet-ruler by setting up a chain of Roman fortresses along the Nile from the current frontier to Dongola and more in the south of the kingdom to take over the kingdom of Alwa (or Alodia), which unlike Dongola was not run by an orthodox Christian elite but by a mixture of proto-Monophysites and animists. Rome and Alwa would keep back the disruptive but poorly-armed raiding tribes on the upper Nile South of the Alwan capital, Soba (near Khartoum). Once Alwa was overrun in spring 641 and Azika had given up his attempts to regain it and fled back to Darfur, Nubia was pacified – or at least as compared to its unstable situation in the past few decades. As with Langobardia in the 590s, a Roman ally survived as nominal ruler of the kingdom but in practice a large presence of Roman troops in Roman fortresses within his kingdom plus regular tribute and regular military assistance to Rome by a levy of conscripts made Nubia into a semi-dependant vassal-state, trade helping to bind its elite to Rome's side and 'Romanization' gradually developing over the next decades. In this case there was more annexation as the vital Nile supply-route and the main tracks East from the Nile around Khartoum to the Red Sea were needed by the Empire to protect soldiers and traders and were now garrisoned by Roman troops and a major Roman garrison was set up at Soba.

The annexation of Nubia as a vassal-state provided a much-needed boost to Carus' military reputation and was duly celebrated with a Triumph in Rome in May 641, but the Emperor's health was going downhill due to his weakness for drink and a probable sexual infection caught off one of his many prostitutes. The succession was already being mentioned before he died on 22 June of an avoidable fall in his bath-house at his current main holiday 'retreat' in the hills inland from Baiae, aged thirty-nine. Apparently he had been celebrating a visit by the winners of a drama festival in Naples which he had just presided over too enthusiastically with some of the dramatists and their actors and had tripped and fallen down some stairs. But there were stories that given his lack of commitment to expansionism in the civil-war-ravaged lands of the Avars some exasperated generals who had recently called on him to urge a major campaign there had arranged for one of his servants to 'spike' his drink or push him down the stairs. The story was never proved, but there was suspicion that the alacrity with which the Senate assembled to elect a successor with the agreement of his civilian ministers and senior generals on the 26th was not just due to a prudent fear of a civil war in the huge Empire and that some leading figures had been tipped off in advance.

Conclusion

This portrayal of how the Roman Empire might have developed if it had had a less acute and multi-faceted series of crises in the period c. 370 – 640 is of course a far rosier picture than the reality. In real life, the succession of onslaughts by outside forces on the Empire, from the Goths (in flight from the Huns) on the lower Danube in the mid-370s to the Arab invasions in the mid-late 630s, fell on the Empire as a series of hammer-blows to an already weakened, tax-burdened, and strife-ridden polity – and one where even by the 370s there was not always one leader (or two or three co-operating leaders) in the Empire who were willing and able to act together. Deploying the Empire's full resources to meet an invasion was already a problem by then, and having an adequately experienced, capable, and cautious rather than over-confident military commander in charge (usually the Emperor himself) was a big 'ask' and was often absent at this period. (It was also the case at other points in the Empire's turbulent history, but then it mattered less; the problems the state faced were worse and often more in number from the late second century onwards.) As I have explored in my 2020 online 'blog' for Sealion Books on Roman history and credible alternatives to what actually happened in the period from c. 180 to the start of this book in the 370s, better leadership and better luck might easily have altered the outcomes of events even in the multi-faceted 'Third Century Crisis'.

This mixture of bad luck and bad timing could affect matters as diverse as internal relationships within the Imperial Family, adequate rulers, less clumsy handling of the Empire's neighbours and of imported immigrant soldiers and farmers, and outbreaks of personnel-reducing plagues – and a mixture of all of these brought chaos in the mid-third century and again in the later fourth and fifth centuries. In the latter case it was fatal to the existing state structure and administrative/ military coherence of the Western Empire – though as modern historians point out, it was not as gloomy an outcome beyond the confines of 'high politics' and elite lives as has long been assumed and at a lower social level the lives of ordinary people were probably affected much less (except when they were caught up in war or invasion). The coherence of the Roman government collapsed , international trade and travel became difficult, importation of luxuries dried up at times, and society in some regions (especially further from Rome, e.g. in Britain and distant areas of Gaul, the Iberian peninsula, and the Rhine and Danube provinces) became atomised – but ordinary rural life went on, though towns did suffer sharp declines in many cases. Even the names of the current rulers and the basics of political and military events are unknown or can only be guessed-at from (often later) written sources in some cases, and the decline of literacy and the apparent extinction (or near-extinction) of the centrally-directed Christian Church are symptomatic of 'cultural impoverishment' if not of the poverty and 'barbarism' of the so-called 'Dark Ages' which used to be assumed. new languages and methods of living shown by archaeological digs, often with artefacts resembling those found in the original 'home areas' of the incoming peoples – specially Germans and in central and south-eastern Europe the Slavs – indicate some degree of 'invasions' or new settlements (invited or not) by incoming groups of wandering 'tribal' settlers. But now it seems more likely that these were numerically smaller than were assumed in the nineteenth century and much was altered by cultural 'exchange' and 'fashion' rather than by land-grabbing 'genocide' (e.g. in Anglo-Saxon Britain). In areas where there had been less disruption and at most the seizure of political power and some land by coherent groups of incomers in the fifth and sixth centuries, by contrast, the lives and culture of the old Roman or Romanised landed elite survived – as did Christianity and the Church's structure. Much of Gaul and parts of Italy and Spain are examples of this.

In the Eastern half of the Empire, indeed, the politico-military, religio-cultural, and economic structures of the Empire did survive the late-fourth century and fifth-century crises, and in the 530s the dynamic emperor Justinian launched a massive and exhausting attempt to reconquer the West and reunite the Empire – whose success in regaining both Italy and much of North Africa by c. 554, together with a slice of southern Spain, arguably shows the weakness of the new 'Germanic' states there which his armies could bring down, not least as their elites were fractured and vulnerable to being broken up with a few decisive victories. Ironically, the East Gothic/ Ostrogothic state's military elite in Italy put up a far better and more determined fight-back in the 540s than expected, possibly assisted by Justinian's own mistakes, shortage of men and money, and paranoia towards his commanders, and the resultant decade of war ruined the peninsula – it was Justinian's wars not the Germanic takeover that economically ruined town and countryside alike and brought an end to the Senate in Rome itself, a city now reduced to a shell of its former self.) The impressive-seeming reconquest by Justinian hid economic and social exhaustion and a growing difficulty for the overburdened army and taxpayers to keep the state running, which the grand plans of the palace elite isolated in the capital tended to ignore.

The bitter controversies which the obsessively anti-'pagan' Christian enthusiast Justinian caused then and in retrospect about his over-grand planning and his obsessive micro-management (of thought and culture as well as politics) do however ignore the bad luck that his campaigns coincided with another major plague in the mid- 540s, the worst since that of the similarly multiple crises of the 250s, which made matters a lot worse by killing off large numbers of soldiers and taxpayers and undermining the exhausted state's ability to fight on. In the 250s the Empire split up amidst multiple coups, rebellions, and invasions; in the 540s Justinian carried on doggedly though some sources say that up to half the population of the capital died and the disaster was probably the worst loss of life across the Mediterranean world until the Black Death in 1348.

The Empire, larger than before but now with extra burdens from defending its war-ruined new Western provinces, soon faced the new threat of the Lombards moving into Italy from 568, with all of Justinian's reconquests in the north and centre eventually lost, and the emperor's own homeland of the central Balkans overrun piecemeal by bands of incoming Slavic farmers and in a more coherent series of attacks by the horse-borne Asiatic 'Avar' nomads (successors to the Huns) moving in from what is now the Ukraine. A mixture of Avar ravaging and internal revolt and civil war in the Empire from 602 brought disaster in south-eastern Europe, and to add to this the Empire's militarily strong and administratively impressive Eastern neighbours and long-time enemies, the Sassanian Persians under Chosroes/ Khusrau II, took advantage of an illegal, brutal, and much-disliked new military regime in Constantinople from 602 to invade and overrun Syria, Palestine, and Egypt. The shrunken Empire faced disaster on two fronts and the armies of both Avars and Persians heading for the capital in 626, but under the remarkable Emperor Heraclius it fought them off and evaded seemingly inevitable obliteration, pushing the Avars back and with Caucasian and steppe Khazar help in invading and breaking up the Persian empire. The Empire was technically restored again, a tribute to its resilience and resources under a capable and charismatic leader with a reliable army – only to face the invasion of its (crucially, already war-weakened and exhausted) Levantine provinces from the desert by flexible armies of tribal Arab nomads united under Islam by the Prophet, commencing in 634. Before the Empire had recovered from one massive crisis it faced another – and this time the provinces east of Anatolia could not be reconquered so easily and the Empire was drastically shrunk in both size and resources.

It is at this point in its real story that I halt this study of what might had happened had luck and circumstances (small as well as large events) been different and the Empire had different leadership and less of a strain on its resources – which includes avoiding both a number of its worst and most inconveniently-timed civil wars and the crucial 'Plague of Justinian'. My main changes to reality begin with the third century (as showed in my blog articles), where I propose a less extensive series of crises that are resolved sooner and with less damage to the Empire's unity, infrastructure, and self-confidence – preserving a society better able to afford the costs of the tax-heavy, bureaucratic 'Late Empire' (from c. 284 onwards) and its huge armies. In the period from 375 to 641 covered by this book, we see a succession of capable rulers lasting longer and less civil wars – meaning that in turn the Empire's enemies are less emboldened than in reality to 'take a chance' and become major actors within and later to dismember the Empire. The strong if controversial Emperor Julian, the 'last pagan', survives for longer instead of being killed at the age of thirty-one and deals a crucial blow to the power of the Sassanians in Iran/Persia, preventing them from aiding in the fall of the Empire and adding extra resources of manpower and income to the Roman state. His most successful if religiously antipathetic 'heir, the militantly orthodox and persecutory emperor Theodosius 'the Great', last ruler of a united Empire in reality, lives longer instead of dying aged forty-seven and is able to diminish the scale and impact of the Gothic incursions into the Empire under his sons. The Empire is divided under them as in reality, but in the West a succession of strong military leaders – Stilicho, Constantius III, Aetius, and Majorian – have longer and more successful careers and manage to integrate, not alienate the Germans into the Roman power-structure as they all face the threat of Attila's Huns. Indeed, it is the mixed Romano-Germanic military machine – never achieved in reality – which makes my Western Empire, not the real Eastern Empire, the stronger of the two halves of the Empire after Attila's death. An imaginary new dynasty of emperors in the West, with the skills and charisma needed for such a task, reunites the Empire in the early sixth century – in this scenario Justinian is a minor 'player', not the man who reunited the Empire (shakily), and there is no place in a relatively tolerant Roman world for his real-life aggressive Christian monotheism and purges of 'pagan' thought and personnel. This is a world where more of the physical and cultural structure of the Classical world survives, not least the Olympic Games and a vibrant 'pagan' Platonist philosophy, and the early seventh century sees the reunited Empire finally swallow up Sassanian Persia – and remain too strong for the Arab tribes to tackle. But, as will be seen in future volumes, the surviving -and united – Roman Empire which I deal with is far from that of the early Caesars, with much of 'actual' European history and its personnel in it. Also, as with the real-life Eastern Roman ('Byzantine') Empire, it will be relying as much on cultural 'outreach' and inter-ethnic co-operation in a 'civilizational' project as on military force against often numerically superior rivals.

Glossary

A libellis: Imperial palace bureaucracy junior official.

Aediles: Rome city magistrates supervising buildings and city markets; ditto for other major cities.

Agentes in rebus: imperial couriers and central administration inspectors, sent out to deliver orders to and compile reports on provincial officials.

Annona: the state's grain supplies to Rome and Constantinople, as run by a government office of that name headed by a Praefect.

Aureus: gold coin.

Aurum oblaticium: official tax on property of senators.

Auxiliae: name for the regiments of 'auxiliaries', i.e. soldiers from Rome-allied states and other non-regular sources serving with the Roman army but not listed as part of it. Usually under their own commanders or a trusted Roman 'Count', responsible to the relevant frontier's senior commander.

Auxilia Palatina (or Palatina): the regiments based at the Imperial Court and accompanying the Emperor or his close relatives on state occasions (like UK's Household regiments).

Basileus: the Greek term for 'King' or by extension any sovereign, and so used of 'Emperor' too; it was used of the Roman Emperor in the Greek-speaking East and in OTL was to be used of the sovereign in the Greek-speaking Eastern Roman/ 'Byzantine' Empire from the seventh century onwards. In my version it is less used than in OTL as the capital of the reunified Empire from the early sixth century is at Rome, in a Latinspeaking region, but it is still his formal title in Greek documentation. The Romans had a traditional fear of the use of the term 'king', i.e. 'Rex' in Latin, as used in Roman Republican myth as the title of the deposed Early Roman tyrannical 'kings' who the nobility had driven out when establishing the Republic in ?509 BC. Calling a senior or the sole senior political leader in Rome 'Rex' was seen as a term of political abuse, showing pretensions to tyranny – and in OTL and in my Roman Empire it was avoided. Augustus made sure that he was referred to under his titles as a 'normal' and legal magistrate within the Republican constitution, or under the honorary title of 'Princeps'.

Beneficarii: a rank given to state officials in each provincial administration who had reached a certain grade in the hierarchy.

Bucellarii: military bodyguards, usually to a senior commander in the army (either the central army in Italy, the 'Comitatus', or a provincial frontier commander or 'dux'/ 'count').

Cancellarii: a rank given to senior officials in the Imperial bureaucracy based in Rome, usually at or near the main Imperial residence (hence our 'Chancellor'); they would have the rank of 'cancellarius' in a named department.

Canonici (aka canons): clergy of an episcopal church, i.e. the official seat of a bishop (usually in large town) or his senior, an archbishop.

Capita: units of population, as registered for paying tax in an area within a province.

Capitatio(n): tax on units of population in an area within a province.

Cardinales (hence our 'cardinals'): rank given to senior clergy of an episcopal church, as above: either for a bishop or an archbishop's assistants. Existed for all bishops and archbishops, but in text usually refers to the most senior staff of the most senior cleric in the Empire, the Pope in Rome, or of his fellow-Patriarchs.

Castrensis: official term referring to senior ranks of domestic servants in the Emperor's household, often eunuchs in the priod in question (especially in the Eastern Empire).

Castrum: fortress or a fortified town which usually had soldiers or a locally-raised volunteer town guard there.

Cathedral: the official seat of a bishop or archbishop, in a usually large or prestigious town; usually the largest and most ornate church in that town. The term comes from the 'cathedra' or official chair of the said cleric, placed there for use during services.

Censor: official state evaluator of resources, usually of numbers of residents in a city / town/ province or of other figures for a tax. The most senior were originally the senior senators chosen by the senate to conduct a population 'census' for taxation under the Republic, and later to check on the numbers and suitability for office of the current senate membership – and to sack unworthy or inadequately resourced members.

Centenarius: official grade of a rank of senators, and of a rank of NCOs in the Roman army.

Centuria: a unit of land measurement.

Centurion: an army officer, originally so named from commanding a unit of 100 men (more likely to be around 80 in practice).

Chartularii: middle-ranking legal official under the provincial head legal administrator, the 'praefect' or 'prefect' (not to be confused with the 'Praefects' of major cities); junior to the 'adiutor'/ adjutor,

Chrysargyron (Greek term) or Collatio Lustratis (Latin term): a new five-yearly tax on registered traders, including small as well as large ones, introduced by Constantine the Great; much resented.

Clarissimus: a senior rank of senator, a grade awarded for long service or after being given distinguished and important/senior duties (or sometimes merely for belonging to an important family and having done important govt work before being put in the senate).

Coenobia: monasteries, i.e. official and formal groupings of professed monks belonging to a recognised religious Order headed by an abbot as opposed to more 'irregular' and selfgoverning hermits in a hermitage.

Cohort: an army infantry regiment.
Cohortales: the officials attendant on and carrying out the orders of a provincial governor, or in the army the clerks assisting a senior commander of a province or garrison in his office.
Collatio(n): a government tax; several different sub-species of these existed, eg levies on coins or on traders or provincial and state border customs.
Collegia: guilds of skilled workers professing a particular trade or craft; admission was granted by vote of the relevant body in a town or city after a period of training as an apprentice to a serving member of the guild.
Coloni: official tenants, either of state of private land; either for life or for a term of years. In the case of the lower ranks of this category, permission of the owner had to be sought for a tenant to cancel the lease and/or leave the property for a new home/ job.
Counts/ 'Comes', plural 'Comites': senior military or in some cases civil commanders/ officials, eg:
C. Africae: military commander of the province of 'North Africa' i.e. modern Tunisia.
C. Civitatis: commander of the garrison of a city.
C. Consistorianus ('Count of the Consistory'): rank of a member of the Emperor's Council of State.
C. Domesticorum ('Count of the Domestics'): commander of the Emperor's corps of Imperial Household military cadets, in attendance at the Palace. In effect one of the most senior army commanders, close to the Emperor and in his Council, and a valued military adviser and chooser of his cadets for future promotion in the army.
C. Domorum ('Count of the Domus'): the most senior administrator in the Imperial Palace/ Household offices (the 'Domus', i.e. 'Home').
C. Excubitorum ('Count of the Excubitors'): commander of the most senior regiment of the Imperial Guards at the Court, the 'excubitors' – usually mostly young aristocrats, as a sort of 'Household Cavalry'.
C. Foederatorum ('Count of the Foederatii'): commander of the non-Roman troop regiments at the Imperial Court, the 'Foederatii'/ 'Federates'.
C. Largitionum: 'Count of the Largesses', the most senior financial administrator in the government, usually on the Council: later the 'Count of Sacred Largesses'.
C. Metallorum: 'Count of the Mines', later minister for ditto; Council official heading the office running the Imperial mines.
C. Orientis: 'Count of the East': over-governor of the 'Diocese'(i.e. group of provinces) of 'Oriens'/'the East', namely Syria and upper Mesopotamia and eastern Asia Minor – before the conquest of Persia, the crucial eastern borderlands. Its regional controller and thus given a rank denied to most 'diocesan over-governors'; senior to the governors of each of the provinces under him and to the Praefect of Antioch, the regional capital. C. Patrimonii: Count of the 'patrimonia' i.e. the Emperor's extensive estates in Italy, centring on his palaces and holiday residences around Rome.
C. Portus: the Count in charge of the port of Rome, i.e. Ostia, and so of food-supplies and other goods coming into the huge capital.

'C. Res Privatae': 'Count of the Privy Purse', i.e. of the private lands and other income of the Emperor (as opposed to his annual official budget as head of state from state income/ taxes/ senatorial grants).

C. Stabuli: 'Count of the Stable' i.e. the Imperial horses, studs, and Guards regiments' cavalry horses and studs. (Hence our 'Constable'). The Imperial corps of attendant Court military officers in the third and fourth centuries AD included a number of senior figures given the title 'Comes'/ 'Count', coming from the Latin for 'companion' (i.e. companion of the Emperor), entrusted with various civilian and military duties and commands – especially in the then frequent crises. This probably led to the multiplication of use of the word 'Counts' for men in official authority in civilian as well as military life. The choosing of the word for 'companion' for trusted Imperial aided may have come from Alexander the Great using his 'Companions', from the corps of Macedonian elite 'Companion Cavalry', for senior duties. The commands of a 'Comes' or 'Count' also existed in the army for various special commands on the frontier, sometimes within a province and junior to its overall commander ('dux') and at other times controlling the frontier troops across a region within several provinces in a mobile striking-force. Some naval commanders also had the rank of 'Count' for a special command, and various posts within the Imperial Guards regiments in Rome and Italy were given to a 'Count' – either as a rank that went with the job or as a personal favour from the Emperor for a valued general.

Comitatenses: soldiers of the 'Comitatus', i.e. the large Imperial 'field army' stationed in Italy, mostly at Rome and (nearer the Northern frontiers) Mediolanum/ Milan.

'Concilium Principis' or 'Consistorium'/ 'Consistory': the Imperial Council, attendant on the Emperor. Some but not all of the members were heads of particular government departments, others were individual nominees of the Emperor e.g. his relatives., senior senators, and military commanders (often with Household roles or retired) living in Italy.

Consuls: two each year, appointed by the Emperor and formally by the Senate; the official year took its official title from their names.

'Consularis': rank given to civilian governors of each province, as the governors were equivalent in rank to honorary consuls (and had originally all been ex-consuls appointed after their year of office by the Senate). Originally only given to the governors of particular, larger or more important provinces; in that era, the provinces not ruled by 'consulares' were governed by men with the lower rank of 'praeses' (plural 'praesides'). Constantine the Great extended this rank to most governorships.

'Correctores'/ 'Corrector': alternative name for a governor.

Cubiculariae: the Empress' official ladies-in-waiting.

Cubicularii: the senior Household (male) domestic servants, attendant on the Emperor in his apartments. Originally in this era mostly eunuchs in the Eastern Empire – so chosen as they would not have offspring to intrigue on behalf of.

Cura Palatii: the senior official in charge of and running the Imperial palaces; later the rank, as 'Curopalatus', was more widely used as an honorary one and was given to Imperial relatives, favourite friends, and a few distinguished foreign royals/ noble ambassadors but they did not actually do this work.

Curator: manager of either a group of Imperial estates or of the finances in a city.

Curia: the council governing a city, by extension also the council of senior officials attendant on a City Praefect or an archbishop/ Patriarch or Pope.

Curiales; honorary rank given to city councillors and their families, bringing legal honours and entitlements but also special taxes on occasion. The possessors were also relied on to pay for annual civic Games and if necessary to 'top up' city taxes' funding for new public buildings – and some richer ones paid for new buildings voluntarily to show off and win electoral support.

Cursus: the public post, with a special and higher-ranked 'Cursus Imperialus' i.e. Imperial Post to carry Imperial and government letters/ orders.

Decurions: members of town councils.

Defensores: legal and political officers working for the government's local provincial administration offices and for Church diocesan (i.e. bishopric) offices. In effect, the civil authorities' officials of this rank often amounted to being the 'police', but they were not the only people who could bring legal cases – private citizens and officials working as individuals could do so, prompted or financially assisted by the state as needed.

(One of these ranks: 'defensor civitatis', i.e. 'defender of the city'. Term used for an additional rank of provincial judge created by Constantine the Great to provide quicker and speedier justice than that available in the limited number of, overburdened, official courts. Operated in a whole province or in a specific city or group of cities within it.)

Delatores: official term for government informers, working on or off the payroll of local state 'police' offices.

Denarius: coin, small size and value. Silver; under the coinage system as updated by emperor Aurelian in the 270s there were five denarii to the new coin which he introduced, the 'nummus'. Constantine the Great then introduced another new and larger coin, the 'solidus', qv, gold, in the 320s. There were supposed by the early C4th to be 96 denarii to a pound in weight of silver, and the solidus to be 72 of this to the pound in gold.

'Domus fiscales': the 'Domus' or '(Imperial) House/ Property' belonging to the 'Fisc' or Imperial Treasury; a category of Imperial property administered by its own subministry within the latter.

Donative: a one-off bounty of money given to the army at the accession of a new emperor, and thereafter at five-yearly intervals at the anniversary of his accession.

'Dux', plural 'duces': military commander, officially one for each province and in charge of its soldiery – origin of our 'Duke'. Extra duces were appointed on the frontier for various special commands, and many provinces away from the frontier were later stripped of their 'duces' and their troops except for special local regiments, often of nonarmy volunteers.

'Duovir': the (usually two) chief magistrates of a city, serving as leaders of its council and representing it to the government.

Deportatio: legal sentence of exile from either one part of the Empire to another, or from the entire Empire.

Dignitates: word for the collective offices of state, whose holders had special legal and honorary ranks.

Dioceses: originally two types: (i) the groups of 'over-provinces', i.e. a group of secular provinces collected into a regional authority under the 'Vicar' (origin of our word) who was in effect an 'over-governor', above the provincial governors in the chain of authority and under the Emperor, ministers, and Senate. These groups were: the provinces of Britain; northern Gaul; the Five or Seven Provinces, i.e. southern Gaul; the Spains; (northern) Italy, i.e. everywhere between the Apennines and the Alps; Suburbicana, i.e. central and southern Italy, centred on Rome, plus Sicily, Sardinia and Corsica; North Africa (except Egypt and Cyrenaica); Pannonia (western Balkans and upper Danube), Moesia (north-east Balkans), and Thrace in one Balkan overprovince; Greece and Macedonia, plus Crete (as split off from the rest of the Balkans by Constantine the Great in the 320s); Asia Minor and the south coast of the Black Sea; Oriens ('East') i.e. Syria, Mesopotamia, Phoenicia/ Lebanon, and Palestine); and Egypt. To this was added 'the Germanies', beyond the Rhine, after the 450s. The vicars of the Gauls and the Balkans ('Illyricum') were later removed and full authority given to their immediate superiors who were the emperors' representatives in these areas, the 'Praetorian Praefects' – whose command covered the same regions. The command of 'Italy', plus the province of Pannonia on the upper Danube, was given to the 'Praetorian Praefect of Italy', the Emperor's representative in this region and th vicar's immediate superior, resident at the regional Imperial court and palace at Mediolanum/ Milan. The dioceses were later removed as an unnecessary extra level of bureaucracy and source of cost, but after the period covered by this book. (ii) the religious version, i.e. the area of authority of a bishop – usually centred on a city where he had his residence, offices, and cathedral. The term was also used interchangeably for an 'archdiocese', i.e. the area of authority above this, of an archbishop or 'metropolitan' – usually of a province and corresponding in area with the latter, except where there were several major cities with equally important bishops and cathedrals in one province.

'Ementissimus': rank given to members of the 'equestrian' order of wealth-holders if they also were serving in particular State or local government jobs, or as a personal grant from the Emperor.

'Equestrian ' order (single 'Eques', multiple 'Equites': the rank, as determined by the amount of taxable and non-taxable property listed in the possession of, given to citizens who were next down the 'pecking order' in wealth from the senatorial order. Originally determined in the early republic, as per the meaning of the word ('Horseman'), as someone able to afford and owning a horse, and hence able to serve in the Roman army as a cavalryman.

'Epistulae', also known as 'Scriniae': 'Writing (Department)', a sub-section of the Imperial administration at central and provincial level concerned with sending out, receiving, and documenting letters and orders – and by extension maintaining archives of all such material. Headed by the minister ('Magister') 'Ad Epistulorum', i.e. 'For Letters', who sat on the Imperial Council. There was also a parallel 'Scriniae Libellorum' office, headed by a 'Magister ad Libellorum' on the Council, who prepared legal cases for the Imperial law-courts and documented them in an archive; 'libellorum' in the Latin legal wording means 'little books'. The Eastern Empire until reunification had separate offices for Latin (M ad Epist. and M. ad Libell.) and Greek speaking (M. as Epist. Graecarum and M. ad Libell. Graecarum) letters and documents/ legal cases; after reunification this extended to the central government of the entire Empire.

Exarch: term of rank for a senior general, usually when commanding a civilian province as governor and military chief combined in OTL this was the usual title of the Eastern Empire's resident governors of reconquered Italy and of reconquered North Africa from the 530s, but in my version of events this region is always Roman and Rome is the capital so an 'Exarch' is usually found on a crucial frontier in a crisis.

Excubitors: senior regiment of Imperial Guards based at Court.

Fabricae: state arms factories and depots.

Fasti: the official state list of annual consuls, two appointed each year.

Foederatii ('federates'): term given to official or unofficial regiments, and of these when settled on a frontier, in the Imperial army – sometimes granted a frontier territory to settle in as Roman allies, subject to the Empire but in practice autonomous under their own leaders.

Follis: monetary unit, originally set at a bag containing 1000 'nummi' coins (single: 'nummus') , worth 12,500 denarii as ordered by Diocletian c. 300; later altered in value due to fluctuating inflation. Also a term given to a (small) tax on senators introduced by Constantine the Great, with three classes of payment valued at 8, 4, and 2 'folles' (coins) according to registered wealth. This amounted to 40, 20, and 10 'solidi' (coins) per family and was minimal considering their wealth.

Fundus: estate or farm.

Gloriosi (hence our 'Glorious'); honorary grade given to a rank of senior senators, in the fifth century, superseding the earlier term 'illustres' (hence our 'illustrious'); included senior ministers, Praefects of cities, Praetorian Praefects etc.

Homoiousios: 'of like substance'; theological term used by groups of opponents of the term below, to distinguish their view of the nature of Christ and His divine Father from that of orthodox Catholicism as defined by the AD 325 Church Council of Nicaea.

Homoosious: 'of the same substance': theological term used by the orthodox Catholic theologians of the Church who won Imperial acceptance and legal backing from Constantine 'the Great' at the Council of Nicaea in AD 325, to define the relationship between Christ and His divine Father. In terminology very close to the above, but seen as vastly different in its interpretation of the relationship within the Holy Trinity and remained a point of conflict between rival Christian sects for centuries to come, especially in the C4th to C6th – and this 'trivial' terminological dispute's bitterness was duly ridiculed by the critics of the Church, led by emperor Julian and the Neoplatonists.

Honestiores: legal definition, giving various privileges, for upper-class and middle-class citizens of the Empire. The lower-class equivalent was 'humiliores'. Rank was accorded by a mixture of descent, possession of property, and employment and could be changed by a legal grant or rank by the Emperor. Senators, members (reckoned by ratable wealth) of the equestrian class which came next down the 'table' of class, decurions i.e. members of town councils, and members of the professions were reckoned as entitled to this rank.

Honores: term for the offices of state, hence our 'honours'; a grant of the latter brought with it added legal status and rank, with legal privileges and social esteem. Holders of these offices were known as 'honores, i.e. 'the honourable…'.

Hospitalitas: 'hospitality', in the legal Roman sense of an order to station or billet someone, usually soldiers, in a town or rural region – including grants of estates to groups of Rome-allied 'barbarian', non-citizen, soldiers within the Empire. The resident owners would either be evicted or would have to provide accommodation and food to the incomers at their own expense, so it saved the state money – and in OTL this term was used in the C4th and C5th when stationing a large body of incoming allied Germanic troops in a region as its defenders if the army could not defend it or the Germans had to be 'bought off' with land. The OTL grants included large parts of provinces, eg Moesia for the Goths in 381-2 under Theodosius I, the eastern Balkans and later Epirus (Albania) and Illyricum (Serbia etc) to Alarics Goths in the 390s, and Aquitaine to Wallia's and Theodoric I's Goths in the 410s – in practice as autonomous allied states. In my version the Romans do less of this and keep greater control (and more of the tax-revenues of the granted land), which symbolises less of a 'loss of control' than in OTL.

Illustres: senior grade of senatorial order, as of the C4th; partly superseded by the term 'gloriosi' in the C5th, but less in my version than in OTL. The term initially covered only the highest rank of senators, going with having held one or more of a number of important posts, but was later extended in the fifth century to all senators; it carried with it certain rights, eg that to be tried by the Praefect of the capital not by an ordinary magistrate and of immunity from paying special tax-levies.

Indiction: the annual Imperial budget. By extension, a term for the financial year covered by this budget. The term meant 'requisitions' and originated in irregular special requisitions of property and money from citizens, as listed for wealth in the records, when needed by the state, usually in emergencies – and then stabilised and made regular as a bureaucratic system with fixed rates of payment at fixed times under Diocletian.

Insulae: a block of flats in a city.

Iudices/ Judices (Romans did not use 'J'): judges.

Iugatio: tax on or assessment for tax purposes of land.

Iugerum: unit of land measurement. 20 iugera were five-eighths of a modern acre.

Iuridicus: term for a judge. Usually for the senor lawyers who assisted or substituted for those governors of provinces who also had legal rights to try cases.

Laeti term for non-Roman, 'barbarian, settlers within the Empire either as individuals or 'en bloc.'

Largitionales (i.e. 'largesses – men'): term for the officials of the Imperial finance department, which was headed by the Count of Largesses (later Count of Sacred Largesses).

Largitiones ('Largesses'): the Imperial finance ministry.

Laura (in Greek 'Lavra'): a large group of hermits settled in a specific location, either a group of buildings or of caves, as a formal entity recognised by a Church charter; more organised than an individual hermit and his disciples, but less organised than a monastery and usually with no specific 'abbot' in charge and no membership and rules of a specific monastic Order. The 'Great Lavra' was to be, in the ninth and tenth centuries, the term given to the original settlement of hermits on the 'Holy Mountain' of Mt. Athos in Greece (and still exists). More common in the East than in the West.

Libellenses: clerks of the Imperial ministry of the 'Scrinium Libellorum', i.e. the 'Writings of Little Books', which documented and handled legal cases and maintained an official archive of them.

Limitaneii: term for regiments of Imperial frontier troops, often divided up by their specific geographical location (eg at and around a fortress) and granted land to farm on when not on duty, eg on Hadrian's Wall in Britain.

Magister ('Master'): term for senior ministers or military commanders with a specific function and body of assistants. Eg:

M. Epistolarum: secretary of state for correspondence.

M. Equitum: 'Master of Horses', i.e. commander in chief of the Imperial cavalry.

M. Libellorum: secretary of state for handling judicial papers and keeping record and track of all legal cases, including giving the Council judicial advice.

M. Militum: commander in chief of the Imperial infantry; sometimes the term was used of the infantry commander on a specific frontier and/or in a particular region, including the commander of the infantry working with a co-emperor who was governing one part of not all of the Empire. Usually the 'M Militum' of the (united) Empire or of one, divided part of the Empire was joint commander in chief with the 'M. Equitum'. There was occasionally an overall 'M Militum Praesentales' or 'M. Utriusque Militae', the commander in chief of all the forces, who commanded both cavalry and infantry and had a 'M Equitum' and a 'M Peditum' under him – the most notable examples of this were Stilicho and Aetius in the West and Aspar in the East in the fifth century (Both in OTL and in my version). From the time of Constantine the Great's sons, in the 340s and 350s, regional commands for 'Magistri Militum' to add to the existing MM for Infantry and Cavalry were created – usually one each for the Gauls (i.e. the Rhine frontier), 'Illyricum' (i.e. the upper and middle Danube frontier), Thrace (the lower Danube), and the East (the Persian frontier). This reflected the need for a 'man on the spot' in each threatened frontier zone, and as such I have this practice diminishing after the Empire secures various frontiers better in the mid-late fifth and sixth centuries.

M. Officiorum: the 'Master of Offices', a new post created by Constantine to supervise the Imperial secretariat (the 'scriniae', i.e. Epistolarum, Libellorum, and Memoriae departments) and the body of Imperial couriers, plus later the administration and discipline of the 'Scholae regiments. Later became the most important civil service ministry and sometimes its holder amounted to a 'chief minister' with the Praetorian Praefect. (In my version, the MO in effect replaces the PP by the seventh century.)

M Peditum: commander in chief of the Imperial infantry.

M Rei Privatae: minister in charge of all the lands personally owned by the Emperor and administered by his 'Privy Purse' (the 'Res Privatae'). Aka also the 'Count RP'. M Scrinii: chief Imperial secretary, i.e. head of the entire secretariat.

Mansiones: Imperial post stations along the main roads, providing relays of horses and when needed messengers for the Imperial posts and for sending official orders/ letters/ reports to and from Rome.

Memoriae, aka 'Scrinia Memoraie': the part of the Imperial secretariat that drafted and sent official replies and orders in response to private citizens' letters or requests to the Emperor and the Council. Headed by its own 'Magister', a Councillor.

Militia: official term for government service/ employment.

Milliarensis: small coin created by Constantine, rated at 96 to each pound of silver and at 24 to one pound of gold. From then on, also the 'semissus', plural 'semisses' (worth one half of a 'solidus'), and the 'tremissus', plural 'tremisses', worth one third of a 'solidus'. In my version, the old coin age value of 'sestercius' from the Classical period is brought back for the 'semissus' in the early C6th.

Mittendarii: Imperial messengers.

Modius: measurement of corn.

Navicularii: state shippers of goods.

Nobilissimus: high honorary term, originally mostly granted within the Imperial Family to male heirs or close kin of the Emperor and later extended to high-ranking officials as a personal favour by the ruler (including princes of allied states).

Notarius /Notary: official term given to Imperial bureaucrats working in the capital for the Imperial civil service, especially in the ministries centred at Court. Originally just regarded and ran ked as ordinary secretaries, but during the fourth century the higher ranked among them rose to become ministers and/ or close Imperial advisers; some became effective senior ministers and/or courtiers and the increased power of the role attracted more upper-class men to take this duty on. As a result the higher grades of the official corps of notaries came to rank with senor ministers and governors in the rank of 'spectabiles', and middle-ranking ones as 'clarissimi'.

Notitia, aka 'Notitia Dignitatum': the official state register of military ranks and offices and their responsibilities. The 'ND' for c.400 (OTL) survives in part and is a major source of information for the era, including the size and location of the then army – but was it idealised and did it reflect the actual situation or not?

Novel: a new law.

Numerarius: a state financial official.

Numerus: term for regiment.

Nummus: a new coin created by Constantine, as above.

Officium: a term for a state ministry, hence our 'offices'.
Officium Admissionum: the ministry regulating and timetabling Imperial audiences.
Pagus: the rural district legally dependant on a particular city and subject to its council and its legal authorities.
Palatini ('palatines'): (i) the soldiers of the central army, attendant on the Court and the Emperor and stationed in and near his capital. (ii) term for the civilian officials of the state ministries, based in the capital. (iii) officials of the state finance ministry and the private Imperial property department (Res Privatae).
Parochiae: parishes, i.e. the sub-divisions of a bishopric under the authority of lower-ran ked clergymen.
Patrician: senior title of honour, given to favoured individuals of high civilian or military rank and sometimes (but not always) given to men of wide authority such as Praetorian Praefects, ex-consuls, magistri militum / commanders in chief, or marital connections at Court of the Imperial Family. Sparingly bestowed by the (Republican Roman) term's reviver Constantine as a personal favour to close aides; more widespread later. The original term was a legal distinction and honour given, hereditarily, to a more or less fixed body of ancient, mostly rich landed families high in EarlyRepublican politics who monopolised the consulship and senior offices, and so it had social status throughout the Republican and Imperial periods and was used as a general term for old and respected (or disliked as snobbish) landed nobility families.
Perfectissimus: an honorary rank given to holders of upper-middle-ranking civilian offices with a degree of public responsibility such as most provincial governorships under the Diocletianic system. Constantine then upgraded most of these to the next rank up the 'ladder', i.e. 'consularis'.
Phylarch: term / rank given to Rome-allied forces' cavalry commander in the East, especially a commander of allied tribal Arab forces in Syria/Palestine.
Plebeii: legal term given to the lower classes, as a legal distinction (eg in rights to hold particular jobs and in taxation) from the upper classes. A Republican Roman term, originally covering all citizens (including quite rich or ancient families) who were not listed as 'patricians'.
Praefectus Annonae/ Praefect of the Annona: the minister in charge of Rome's grain supplies.
Praefectus Vigilum/ Praefect of the Vigiles: the official in charge of the latter, the Rome fire brigade who also served as effective or ineffective police and 'riot control' officers. (Also Praefecti/ Praefects of the two main Imperial capitals, Rome and Constantinople, and later of the major city of Antioch which post was combined with the overgovernorship/ Vicarate of 'Oriens'.
The 'Augustal Praefecture' title in Egypt was given to a man who had the joint role of Praefect of the city of Alexandria, formerly the Ptolemaic capital, and governor of the adjacent province of Lower Egypt. In my version, after Emperor Julian conquers Mesopotamia from the Sassanians he creates a Praefecture for their ex-capital, Ctesiphon on the River Tigris.)

Praepositus Sacri Cubiculi: the court official in charge of the Imperial domestic staff, in effect 'Master of the Imperial Household'/ chief chamberlain. Usually a eunuch.

Praeses: overall term for the civilian governors of provinces, who had been split off from having any command of the province's troops (as in the early Empire) in the later third century.

Praetorian Praefect: the chief imperial minister in the third to sixth centuries, evolving into a man with civilian (including judicial) supervisory roles from its original role in the early Empire as the – miltary in ranking – commander of the Imperial/ Praetorian Guard. The latter had often had an unofficial civilian role too as the closest and most crucial advisor to the Emperor and the commander of the only large armed force in the capital, so able to stage a coup or run a regency if required; this evolved into a largely civilian role by the third century and by the fourth there were separate military supremos, the Magistri Peditum and Equitum. The Praetorian Praefect was, however, the official military 'Chief of Staff' in modern terms, organising strategy and administration for the army and advising the Emperor on this. He also had to assess the annual budget needs of the government in the lands which he administered |(in terms of coinage, food, timber, and labour on public works) for the next year once a year and draw up and issue the taxation / public service manpower levies from the taxpayers to fulfil this. The annual requirement would be issued once a year to each district of each province which he administered (via the regional chief city/town's officials) and met in three instalments. Also the chief 'judge of appeal' in the Imperial legal system from the time of lawyer PPs in the second century onwards, acting as the head of the Emperor's palace legal court. Often a civil servant or a lawyer by this period (major second and third century legal writers and experts had been PPs, e.g. Papinian and Ulpian), and also sitting as a very senior magistrate as directed by his sovereign. There was one PP per Emperor when the Empire was divided, so this led to several PPs being in office within the Empire simultaneously. When a former division of the Empire was ended, the PP for that region often retained his role within that region – e.g. the PP for Italy and Africa, who then eclipsed the local Vicars of the relevant 'Dioceses' (qv) so to avoid duplication the two roles were merged.

Praetors: senior city magistrates in the two main Imperial capitals of this period, Rome and Constantinople. Originally the city magistrates of Republican Rome.

Primicerius: legal rank for senior clerks or administrators in the civil service, especially in the capital(s). The chief of the men who held this rank, and of all the 'notaries' (qv), was the 'Primicerius Notarium', a senior minister on the Council.

Princeps (aka our 'Prince'). Rank given originally to the Emperor, under Augustus who used this as his main civilian title in emulation of the earlier Princeps Senatus', the honorarily senior member of the Senate. Later also used of the most senior clerk in a state ministry.

Proconsul: the term used of the governors of particular, senior/important provinces, as originally the governors were appointed from the ranks of ex-consuls (usually just after their year of office in Rome expired) and so retained their legal powers as consuls over their new province.

Procurator: Imperial financial official, and also the agent/ manager in charge of a private estate (especially its finances).

Protector, plural Protectores: term used for officer-cadets in the Imperial household regiments based at the Imperial Court and capital.

Provinces: note that the number of these had been increased by Diocletian in the late third century, by sub-dividing almost all Early Empire provinces into smaller ones (usually two or three new ones in each old province). This was probably done to diminish the resources and ability to revolt of governors, who were also stripped of their troops. The recent emperors in the 260s and 270s had also apparently banned, or at least severely reduced, the appointment of senators to be governors and relied on the (less likely to have the pretensions to revolt) next rank of citizens in wealth, the 'equestrians', and exofficers. From Diocletian's time on the only senators appointed as governors were in the Italian, Sicily, and Greek provinces plus the 'proconsular' governors (i.e. ex-consuls) of (North) Africa, based at Carthage, and 'Asia' (i.e. western Anatolia) based at Ephesus/ Sardes.

Quaestor: the title given to a city magistracy in the Imperial capitals of Rome and Constantinople. This involved some supervision of the cities' finances, and originally the 'quaestor' had been the annual city magistracy in Republican Rome that dealt with that city's finances.

Quaestor Sacri Palatii: 'Q. of the Sacred Palace'. In the fourth century, the magistrate/ accountant/ state lawyer who supervised the private finances and legal affairs of the Imperial household and its property in the capital. Later his financial role was superseded by assorted senior officials of the state (Largitiones) and private Imperial (Res Privatae) finance departments and his 'brief' moved over to running Imperial legal affairs.

Rationalis, plural rationales: Imperial financial officers. Headed by the 'Rationalis Rei Summae'/ Rationalis Summarum', the original title under the reorganised Diocletianic empire of the Imperial financial minister. Eclipsed by other ministers in the 'Largitiones' office, especially their 'Count', in the later fourth and early fifth century.

Rector Provinciae: the title used for certain civilian governors of provinces in the West in the fifth century, mostly in Gaul. Also at times 'Praefect' could be used for this office's holder too, but as an individual honorary title for a distinguished holder not always going with the office. (More common in 'devolved', fragmenting OTL fifth-century Gaul than in my version where strong central control continues and so does the traditional usage of titles.)

Rectores/ Rectors: in the Church, the officials who ran the estates of major clergy, mainly the Papacy, in the localities as their representatives and managers. (Later became used as 'rectors' of parishes too, i.e. clerics of junior and local rank, in the modern sense.)

Regiones: sub-divisions, in a geographical manner, of the Imperial estates, each with their own managers. Later became used in the sense of modern 'regions', as part of a province.

Res Privatae: the state ministry of the private lands owned by the Emperor as an individual, headed by a Count as minister.

Rescripts; Imperial replies to petitions.

Sacellarius: the keeper of the Emperor's private finances and dispenser of money for his personal needs, i.e. in modern terms 'Keeper of the Privy Purse'. Usually a eunuch, at least in the Eastern Empire, in this period. Later superseded the old 'Count of Sacred Largesses' as the main finance minister in the Eastern/ Byzantine Empire in OTL; in my version this does not happen to such an extent and both offices survive, with separate spheres of influence, and as the sole capital is Rome there are fewer eunuch holders of this post.

Scrinia (officially 'Sacra Scrinia'): the Imperial civil service secretariats at the Court: the 'epistulae', 'libelli', and 'memoria' departments, qqv).

Senate: The old governing body of the Empire when it was a Republic, neutered by Augustus into a body that still had the duty to initiate, debate, and approve legislation but was in effect controlled by the Emperor – who made all appointments and added new members to the Senate by giving them senatorial rank or various official posts that brought senatorial rank with it. The old 'patrician' noble families, some of very ancient birth and senatorial membership and others added on over the Republic's history, were constantly added to by 'new men', often civil servants and army officers, given these offices and senatorial rank by successive Emperors. There were around 600 senators in the early fourth century and many more as the decades progressed, but old families died out or were purged in Roman politics and new divisions arose of seniority within the senatorial order based on the rank given to men according to their current or past office within the administration. The sons of senators could enter the body by holding the (largely honorary) quaestorships (qv), which they were entitled to do by their birth, but this still depended on them being chosen by the Emperor; all others entered via their jobs in the administration (often only 'sinecures') or the armed forces, by nomination by the ruler. The foundation of Constantinople also led to the creation of a new and separate Senate based in that city as an Imperial capital – but this was even more of a strictly advisory body than the Senate in Rome, honoured and given formal 'powers' and prominence in social life but with little if no political 'clout'.

Spatharius: commander of the Emperor's personal 'crack squad' of Household bodyguards who attended on him on private as well as state/ public duties, in the East (and in OTL Byantium) eunuchs and commanded by a eunuch .

Satraps: the Iranian word for governors of provinces, surviving from the Achaemenid empire in the sixth-fourth centuries BC.

Scholae: collective term for the regiments of the Imperial Guards, headed by their own commander or 'Comes Domesticorum'/ Count of the Domestics. The latter also had duties as a military adviser to the Emperor at times, or this post was given to a trusted senior military aide of his.

Scrinium: term for the department of a ministry within the Imperial civil service.

Senator: member of the Imperial Senate; one senate for Rome, one for Constantinople after the latter city was created as a second capital by Constantine the Great. Also a term given to a rank of NCOs in the army.

Senatus Consultum: a decree of the Senate as voted for by them, having the full force of law.

Senatus Consultum Ultimum: the 'Ultimate Decree', only issued in emergency circumstances in the Late Republic (and in my version occasionally later used in the Empire too). It meant that 'The Senate will take steps ...' i.e. authorise its representatives to restore order if there was a major riot or a feared coup, and the forces of law and order were immune from prosecution for any actions (usually killings) carried out in the process.

Solidus: new gold coin created by Constantine the Great as he stabilised the currency. Reckoned at seventy-two of these to a pound weight of gold. Silver was rated by him at 4 solidi coins to the pound weight.

Spectabilis, plural spectabiles: a grade of the senatorial order, given to holders of senior offices.

Stipendium: official term for State pay, in both the civil service and the armed forces.

Tabularii: state treasury financial officials. The original 'tabularium' after which they were called was the Republican Roman treasury building on the Capitol Hill in Rome, overlooking the Forum Romanum.

Tituli Largitiones: term for the taxes issued on behalf of and collected for the 'Largitiones' state finance ministry.

Tremissus: a new coin created by Constantine, set at value of three-eighths of a solidus.

Tribunes: (i) military rank given to the commanders of regiments, both in the regular army and in the palace/ Household regiments in the Imperial capital. The latter rank was often an honorary sinecure for retired officers or even for men who were courtiers and other 'favourites' but not serving soldiers. (ii) city officials in Rome, surviving from the Republic when they had originated in a class of official chosen in the Early Republic in the 490s BC to represent and serve the non-patrician classes in their dealings with the often arrogant and autocratic Senate. As such they had then, and continued under the Empire, presided over the public Assemblies of Roma citizens and created their own or carried out the wishes of the voters in framing legislation there; they had immunity from arrest and a 'sacred' inviolability like priests to protect them from upper-class prosecution and violence. This 'tribunician immunity' and tribunician powers were then taken over by Augustus as one of the powers of the Emperor, who dated his reign by his length of time holding the tribunician power (and at first sometimes shared it with his chosen deputy or heir). By the fourth century AD the 'Tribune Plebis', 'Tribune of the People', this civilian title/ office, was that of a rank of magistrate with specific duties and powers in Rome and Constantinople.

Tributum Capitis: the poll tax, paid by all citizens (i.e. all adult males) in some provinces and by those of a certain age in others; in some provinces (eg Syria) adult females paid too.

Tributum Soli: the 'Land Tax', paid by land as rated by an official and regularly updated assessment in the Imperial registers. Was rated in Syria, for which we possess some records, as one per cent of the value of land held; possibly this was the same across the Empire. Apparently other forms of property, eg houses and ships, were also included in the rating .

Vexillatio: a cavalry regiment.

Vicar: the governor of a diocese (qv) i.e. a group of provinces.

Vigiles: the corps of night-watchmen and firemen in Rome, with some 'police' duties eg keeping public order.

Vindex, plural Vindices: the director of public taxation in a city. An office created by Eastern Emperor Anastasius c. AD 500 to supervise the annual tax-collection at a local level, i.e. more intensely than the previous system of a provincial oversight by the governor and city councils; each of them was given the sum which he was required to hand over and was responsible for raising this, but in practice often raised extra to compensate himself and add to his salary. This was duly resented and led to riots and helped to cause revolt later; in my version when the Western Empire takes over the East this is cancelled by the new, unifying Roman government as a popularity measure and is made up for by confiscations of the property of opponents of the new regime.

PLACE NAMES: Latin ones first as used in this book, then the modern locations of these places.

Adrianople Edirne, W Turkey ('Hadrian's City')
Aquileia City in NE Italy near site of Venice
Alexandria in Arachosia, Kandahar, Afghanistan E Iran
Ancyra Ankara, capital of Turkey
Antioch (capital of Syria) Antakya, SE frontier of Turkey with Syria
Aquae Sextiae Aix-en-Provence, France
Aquae Sulis Bath
Arausio Orange, on the R. Rhone, S France
Arelate Arles, S France
Arpinum Arpinum, E of Rome (home town of Cicero)
Attaleia Antalya, S coast of Turkey
Augusta, in Rhaetia Augsburg (Bavaria)
Augusta Prahavorum Prague, Czech Republic (MY INVENTION)
Augusta Taurinorum Turin, N Italy
Augusta Treverorum Trier, NW Germany (an Imperial capital in sub-division of Empire in fourth century).
Basilia Basle, Switzerland
Beneventum Benevento, Italy
Beyrutus Beirut, Lebanon
Bononia Bologna, Italy
Burdigala Bordeaux

Caerluel/ Carlisle Luguvallium
Caesarea Philippi, City near Golan Heights, Israel/ Syria Palestine
Carthage City near Tunis, Tunisia
Clausentum Bitterne, Southampton, Hants.
Clusium Chiusi, NW of Rome
Colonia Agrippinensis Cologne, Germany
Constantinople Istanbul, Turkey
Corduba Codoba/ Cordova, Spain
Corinium Cirencester, Glos.
Ctesiphon (formerly City near Baghdad, Iraq Sassanian Persian capital)
Deva Chester
Dubris Dover
Durnovaria Dorchester, Dorset
Dyracchium Durazzo, Albania
Eburacum York
Ecbatana Hamadan, Iran
Edessa Harran, E Turkey
Florentia Florence, Italy
Gades Cadiz, Spain
Gariannonum Burgh Castle, near Great Yarmouth
Gesoriacum Boulogne
Glevum Gloucester
Halicarnassus Bodrum, SW Turkey
Iconium Konya, SE Turkey
Isca Dumnoniorum Exeter
Leptis Magna City near Tripoli, Libya
Lindum Lincoln
Londinium London
Lugdunum Lyons
Lutetia Paris
Massilia Marseilles
Mediolanum Milan
Moguntiacum Mainz, Germany
Naissus Nis, Serbia
Nemausus Nimes, S France
Nicaea Iznik, NW Turkey (in Bithynia)
Nicaea Nice, S France (in S Gaul)
Panormus Palermo, Sicily
Patavium Padua, N Italy
Persepolis Former capital of Achaemenid Iran, near Istakr
Perusia Perugia, N of Rome
Philadelphia Ammonitis Amman, Jordan
Pons Aelius Newcastle, Northumberland (i.e. 'Bridge of Hadrian')
Ptolemais Acre, Israel

Ragae/ Rayy City near Tehran, Iran
Reggium Reggio, S Italy
Rutupiae Richborough, Kent
Sirmium, on R. City W of Belgrade Danube
Smyrna Izmir, W Turkey
Sorviodunum Old Sarum hillfort, near Salisbury
Susa City near Ahwaz, Iran
Tarentum Tarento, S Italy
Tarraco Tarragona, E Spain
Thessalonica Salonica/ Thessaloniki, N Greece
Tibur Tivoli, E of Rome
Tingis Tangier
Trapezus Trebizond/ Trabzon, NE Turkey
Venta Belgarum Winchester
Venta Icenorum Caistor-by-Norwich, Norfolk
Verulamium St. Albans
Vindobona Vienna
Viroconium Wroxeter, Shropshire

Bibliography

AD 361–492: JULIAN TO TIBERIUS ANTHEMIUS AND ZENO

Primary Sources
Ammianus Marcellinus, *The Later Roman Empire (AD 353–378)*, tr. Walter Hamilton, Penguin 1986.
Aurelius Victor, *De Caesaribus*, tr. H W Bird, Liverpool UP, 1984.
Eutropius, *Breviarum ab Urbe Condita*, tr. H W Biord, Liverpool 1993.
Lactantius, *Liber de Mortibus Persecutorum*, tr. J L Creed, Oxford 1989.
Orosius, *Historiarum adversos Paganos Libri VII*, tr. L Deferrati, Washington DC 1964.
Socrates Scholasticus, *Ecclesiastical History*, trans Paul Schiff.
Sozomen, *Historia Ecclesiastica*, tr. E Walford, London 1855.
Theodoret, *Historia Ecclesiastica*, tr. Rev. B Jackson, New York 1892, rper. Grand Rapids 1969.
Zosimus, *Historia Nova*, tr. H Ridley, Melbourne 1982.

Secondary Sources
Norman Baynes, *Constantine the Great and the Christian Church*, New York ed. 1975.
Robert Browning, *The Emperor Julian*, London 1975.
T S Burns, 'The Battle of Adrianople: a Reconsideration' in *Historia*, vol 22, 1973, pp. 336–45.
Alan Cameron, 'Theodosius the Great and the Regency of Stilicho' in *Harvard Studies in Classical Philology*, vol 73 (1968) pp. 247–80.
Claudian: Poetry and Propaganda at the Court of Honorius, Oxford UP 1970.
B Croke, 'Argobast and the death of Valentinian II' in *Historia*, vol 25, 1976, pp. 235–44.
John Eadie, *The Conversion of Constantine*, New York 1971.
A Ehrhardt, 'The first two years of the reign of Theodosius' in *Journal of Ecclesiastical History*, vol xv (1964), pp. 1–17.
Edward Gibbon, *The Decline and Fall of the Roman Empire*, 6 vols, Dent 1966.
Michael Grant, *The Climax of Rome*, New York 1968.
——, *The Fall of the Roman Empire: A Reappraisal*, London 1976.
Patrick Guthrie, 'The Execution of Crispus' in *Phoenix*, vol 20, 1966, p. 325–31.
A H M Jones, *The Later Roman Empire AD 284–602*, 2 vols, Norman, Oklahoma 1964.
Peter Jones, *The World of Late Antiquity*, London 1971.
Robin Lane Fox, *Pagans and Christians*, New York, 1987.
Jack Lindsay, *Arthur and his Times*, Frederick Muller, 1966.

John Matthews, *Western Aristocracies and Imperial Court, AD 364–425*, Clarendon Pres, Oxford 1998.
J Morris, *Prosopography of the Later Roman Empire*, Cambridge UP 1992.
Charles Odahl, *Constantine and the Christian Empire*, Routledge 2004.
Stephen Williams and Gerard Friell, *Theodosius: the Empire at Bay*, B T Batsford, London 1994.

AD 492–590: SOURCES USED FOR SPECULATION ON THE SIXTH CENTURY.

Primary Sources
Agathias, *Historiarum Libri Quinque*, ed. R Keydell, Berlin 1976.
The Mabinogion, tr. Jeffrey Gantz, Penguin 1976.
John Malalas, *Chronographia*, tr. Elizabeth and Michael Jeffreys and Roger Scott, Melbourne 1986.
Procopius, *Anecdota/ Secret History*, ed. and tr. H B Dewing, London 1935.
The Wars, ed. and tr. H B Dewing, 5 vols, London 1914–28.

Secondary Sources
John Barker, *Justinian and the Later Roman Empire*, Madison, Wisconsin, 1966.
P. Bartholomew, 'Fifth Century Facts' in *Britannia*, vol 13, 1982, pp. 261–70.
Anthony Bridge, *Theodora: Portrait in a Byzantine Landscape*, London 1978.
Robert Browning, *Justinian and Theodora*, London 1987.
J. B. Bury, *The History of the Later Roman Empire from the death of Theododius to the death of Justinian*, 2 vols, London 1923.
—— 'The Nika Riot' in *Journal of Hellenic Studies*, vol 17, 1897, pp. 92–119.
Alan Cameron, *Porphyrius the Charioteer*, Oxford UP 1973.
Averil Cameron, *Change and Continuity in Sixth Century Byzantium*, London 1981.
—— *Procopius and the Sixth Century*, Berkeley UP, California 1985.
—— *The Mediterranean World in Late Antiquity*, London 1993.
Glanville Downey, *A History of Antioch in Syria*, Princeton UP 1961.
J. A.S. Evans, *Procopius*, New York 1972.
The Age of Justinian: the Circumstance of Imperial Power, Routledge 1996.
Edward Gibbon, op. cit.
Judith Herrin, *The Formation of Christendom*, Oxford UP 1987.
Joan Hussey, *The Orthodox Church in the Byzantine Empire*, Oxford UP 1986.
A. H. M. Jones, op. cit.
Peter Jones, op. cit.
Cyril Mango, *Byzantium, the Empire of New Rome*, London 1980.
J Moorehead, *Justinian*, London 1994.
John Morris, *The Age of Arthur*, Oxford UP 1973.
James O'Donnell, *Cassiodorus*, Berkeley UP, 1979.
Miciej Salmon, ed, *Paganism in the Late Roman Empire and Byzantium*, Cracow 1991.
A. A. Vasiliev, *Justin the First*, Dumbarton Oaks, 1950.